Lost Legend of the Thryberg Hawk

Lost Legend

of the
Thryberg Hawk

*The Mystery Crossbow Boy Who Saved the
Fortunes of York at the Battle of Towton*

Jack Holroyd

PEN & SWORD
FICTION

First published in Great Britain in 2010 by
FACTIONpress
Published in Great Britain in this edition in 2014 by
Pen & Sword Fiction
An imprint of
Pen & Sword Books Ltd
47 Church Street
Barnsley
South Yorkshire
S70 2AS

Copyright © Jack Holroyd, 2010, 2014

ISBN 978 1 78383 181 4

Printed and bound in Malta
by Gutenberg Press Ltd.

Pen & Sword Books Ltd incorporates the Imprints of
Pen & Sword Aviation, Pen & Sword Family History, Pen & Sword Maritime, Pen & Sword Military, Pen & Sword Discovery, Pen & Sword Politics, Pen & Sword Atlas, Pen & Sword Archaeology, Wharncliffe Local History, Wharncliffe True Crime, Wharncliffe Transport, Pen & Sword Select, Pen & Sword Military Classics, Leo Cooper, The Praetorian Press, Claymore Press, Remember When, Seaforth Publishing and Frontline Publishing.

For a complete list of Pen & Sword titles please contact
PEN & SWORD BOOKS LIMITED
47 Church Street, Barnsley, South Yorkshire, S70 2AS, England
E-mail: enquiries@pen-and-sword.co.uk
Website: www.pen-and-sword.co.uk

Contents

Introduction

FOLLOWING THE BATTLE OF BOSWORTH in 1485 and the defeat of Richard III by Henry Tudor of Lancaster, suppression of events of the previous twenty-five years and re-writing of history inevitably took place. The Yorkist reign of Plantagenet Edward IV, along with that king's victories over supporters of the rival party, received scant and unsympathetic recording by chroniclers of Tudor times. As a consequence, many events which occurred during what would later become known as the Wars of the Roses are hazy and tantalisingly lacking in detail. For example, it is from local folklore that the story of the Yorkist boy archer slaying Lord Dacre from the vantage point of a burr elder tree is gleaned. 'The Lord of Dacres was slain in North Acres', ran oral tradition. The legend first appears in print in 1585. To have achieved such a well-aimed shot during a snow storm is astounding. Again, the despatching of another Lancastrian lord (Sir John, Lord Clifford) the previous day in a similar way – an arrow in the throat as the victim removed his neck protection in order to take a drink – is an intriguing coincidence. From other sources we learn that Edward IV was offering a bounty of one hundred pounds on the heads of certain leading lights opposed to him. Unfortunately, all the fascinating detail is absent from the records, we have only the briefest information.

The likely weapon used in the instances mentioned would have been the crossbow with its flat trajectory and pin-point accuracy, rather than the longbow. For maximum efficiency, crossbow boys worked in pairs, one loading and the other shooting. My thanks to Jack Sheldon, former British Military Attaché in Berlin, for detailed information concerning the organisation of a continental mediaeval crossbow unit. Both sides in the Wars of the Roses employed foreign mercenary formations within their armies.

This work began as an attempt to offer a plausible explanation for some 'missing' history, an attempt at unravelling some of the mysteries surrounding a crucial period in the late fifteenth century when, for a period of twenty-six days, England had rival kings. The situation was settled on Towton Field with the bloodiest engagement ever to take place in this country. At the close of that Palm Sunday, 1461, the heralds counted 28,000 corpses hacked and stabbed to death. About the same number of Englishmen killed on the first day of the Somme by artillery- and machine-gun fire.

Surprisingly, very little about this period is part of public awareness.

What have doubtlessly worked against the period ever becoming popular are the misconceptions and irritating put-offs. For instance, the Wars of the Roses were not battles between the counties of Lancashire and Yorkshire (a concept aggravated by the borrowing of the term in connection with the present-day cricket competition). Geographically, it was, in the main, *Lancaster* in the north of England and *York* in the South, but that is an over-simplification. Further complication is the fact that the base for *Lancaster* was at one period at the city of York, whereas the House of *York* could be said to have a London base, although Middleham, Sandal and Conisbrough were Yorkist manors. Allegiances differed widely, even within the areas which we would have expected to have been staunch supporters of a particular side. Take the case of Barnsley, which came under the holdings of the honor of Pontefract and the Duchy of Lancaster, yet it favoured the Duke of York and arrested two agents of Lancaster and had them imprisoned in Sandal castle. Following the death of the duke at the Battle of Wakefield in December, 1460, the agents, Thomas Philip and Thomas Tipton, took their revenge on the Barnsley community.

Translation of documents from Latin to has confirmed the warring and denouncing between neighbours during that period of civil unrest. Mediaevalist Celia Parker opened up fresh insight with her translation of Conisbrough Leet Court rolls, for the first time, enabling a glimpse of the effect the Lancastrian host's march through South Yorkshire had on the people. Also the settling of accounts following the Yorkist victory at Towton.

The mediaeval period lay heavy under religious superstition; events and stories contained in the Bible were applied to everyday life, given the required 'spin' and mixed with fanciful tales, then dispensed by the Church to a largely compliant laity. Voices of dissidence were often quelled by fire. In order to achieve a true flavour and sense of time and place in the late fifteenth century an understanding of how superstitiously-charged religion influenced the masses was essential. Numerous references to holy writ and Church history were resorted to in compiling this work.

It is to hoped that this book will awaken an interest in a most fascinating time in the history of this country, when rival kings vied for the throne, during a period which became known as the Wars of the Roses.

Four riders entering Conisbrough Castle, Thursday evening, 21st June, 1509. Three days before the coronation in London of Henry VIII.

Prologue:

Ere Comes the Dawn on St Ethelreda's Day

MANACLES SECURING the prisoner's wrists clattered to the cobbles, unlocked by the tired serjeant-at-mace once the four riders had passed under the portcullis and into the narrow outer barbican at Conisbrough Castle.

'Stand fast – I gave no leave for his release!' yelled the accompanying priest, outraged by the officer's act.

'No longer a need for shackles,' grunted the burly serjeant, swinging down from his chestnut palfrey and assisting the aged and bedraggled prisoner to dismount. The old man's legs were in no condition to carry weight and the two guards moved swiftly to prevent him from falling to the cobbles.

'Bring the horses, Father,' called the serjeant over his shoulder, adding under his breath, 'Do something useful, you fat pig.' He was wearying both of the job of guarding the old man and the the young cleric's arrogance.

The journey from Lincoln had taken the best part of a day and church bells were announcing Vespers as the four riders entered the royal property in the West Riding of Yorkshire. It was the 21st day of June, 1509, at the outset of the reign of a new monarch, Henry VIII. Walls and towers were bedecked with flags and banners in honour of a special occasion – the crowning at Westminster of Henry and his queen, Catherine of Aragon, on Sunday, the 24th. By then the prisoner would be dead, for John Hawksworth was sentenced to undergo death by burning on St Ethelreda's Day, Saturday the 23rd.

It had been an agonising journey from Lincoln to Conisbrough. John's tormentors, officials at both Lincoln Castle and the Bishop's Palace, had taken pleasure in ensuring that his securing was devised in such a fiendish fashion as to cause him the greatest discomfort. Each time the ancient parrot-faced caballus stumbled on the rutted highway John's flesh and bone screamed in agony. However, he had noted that the manner of the two accompanying guards towards his plight had become kinder with every furlong that distanced them from the ecclesiastical court.

Along to represent the bishop and to take careful heed should any wavering lead to the doomed man's abjuration was the bloated-faced, well-rounded Father Rollo, who continued to remain aloof, disapproving and hostile. The priest's protests had been ignored when, upon arriving at Worksop, the guards had removed the throat collar and chain, a devilish contrivance which had been causing John especial distress. Their final destination was Doncaster, where he was to be committed to the flames at the instigation of the Right Reverend Bishop Smith of Lincoln. A terrible example to others who would dare dissent. It was of utmost concern to Mother Church that Lollardy had made inroads into that part of Yorkshire and north Lincolnshire. It must be ruthlessly stamped out as would a smouldering rag.

John was resigned to his awful fate. Betrayed, arrested, examined, tried and condemned, he was about to suffer martyrdom. He would follow in the footsteps of Christ, his apostles and all the saints and prophets who had perished aforetime.

As they had been about to leave Lincoln Castle a mysterious and urgent letter had been delivered to the constable. It directed that the Lollard was to be taken to Doncaster by way of Conisbrough, rather than the more direct route through Tickhill. Consequently, Conisbrough Castle dungeon, rather than the one at Tickhill Castle, was to serve as his final place of confinement. The letter had arrived from the Bishop's Palace and without question carried the unbroken seal of the Bishop of Lincoln. Oddly, execution of sentence had already been deferred by three weeks. He should have been committed to the fire on the feast day of St Boniface, but some matter, of which no one had bothered to inform him, had brought about a welcome stay of his martyrdom. So by chance and the grace of God, he was to spend one night, his final day and night, at the very place he had frequented as a boy.

For John to spend his final hours at this place, albeit in the guardhouse dungeon, was a blessing for which he silently gave thanks to the Almighty. Just three miles to the south, towards the township of Rotherham, he had spent his childhood in servitude to the Reresby family at their manor in the village of Thryberg. He and his brother Edmund had on many occasions driven swine from the Reresby herd for slaughtering at the castle kitchens for food and tallow.

Grateful for the support of his guards, John raised his aching head and looked about him: it was from here that his younger brother had shot seven incredibly accurate crossbow bolts which had shaken the Yorkist lords, nobles, knights, heralds and the thousands of men-at-arms who, on that day in 1461, crowded these very castle walls and packed the surrounding grounds. By so doing, Edmund had won a silver bolt and was catapulted to the attention of King Edward IV. It was at Conisbrough Castle that his brother took his first faltering steps in society, rising above his degree to become a figure of legend. Dubbed 'The Thryberg Hawk' by locals, tales had arisen that had in their frequent recounting, come to be preferred – at least until the reign of Tudor King Henry VII – to the rousing capers of Robin of Loxley. There had been royal discouragement of relating the young Yorkist hero's escapades following the Lancastrian victory over Richard III at Bosworth. Would stories of the Plantagenet boy hero now become lost forever?

And what exciting stories! Men still debate as to whether or not a mere boy, who in a matter of days soared from being a herder of pigs to command a mercenary band of crossbow boys, really did hold the Yorkist left flank at Towton Field and in so doing prevented its collapse. But then, John could vouch for the truth of it – it was no fable – for he had fought and laboured alongside Edmund as his *Ladenshütze*. As indeed had a foremost Yorkist noble, Sir William, Lord Fauconberg, the two of them toiling shoulder to shoulder, spanning bows for his brother. Many tales had grown up around the doings of The Hawk and persisted despite official disapproval.

Upwards of sixty men, women and children fixed the arrivals with curious stares. They packed the barbican walls, gatehouse towers and every stairway. Heads bobbed hither and thither as each sought to catch a glimpse of the condemned man who had arrived among them trussed like a goose. John Hawksworth searched the faces gathered at every possible vantage point at the castle entrance, looking for someone, anyone, he might know. The silence was broken by the barking and snapping of four tethered Irish wolf hounds as the group of four entered the inner bailey. No command came from the castle guards to quieten the animals as the dogs strained at their chains in efforts to sink yellowing fangs into the visitors. The racket contrasted with the silence of the crowd as the prisoner swayed along. Was it indicative of sympathy or did it bespeak loathing for his straying from Mother Church? John had long since come to realise that his chosen way aroused extreme passions in the hearts of some men and prompted diabolical cruelties, hard to imagine, in others. Perhaps with this crowd the silence was due to curiosity; it had been some time since the County of Yorkshire had burnt a heretic.

That unnerving quiet was suddenly rent by a solitary voice yelling from among the crowd.

'*Cui bono!*'

Prisoner and escort had been about to enter the gatehouse. John stopped and straightened. With aching eyes narrowed, he peered at the crowd which was beginning to gather around, trying to identify the owner of the voice.

'There is no advantage!'

Came the cry from the same throat.

An elderly man stepped from the crowd and began limping towards the group. Then John was looking directly into the old worn face of a castle tanner judging by his clothing, apron and aroma. His teeth were worn down at one side and he had not a single hair on his hide-brown wrinkled head.

'There is no gain,'

John gasped in response from a throat so parched that those few words brought further pain.

'*Cui bono.*' The tanner now repeated the Latin phrase softly with a catch in his voice and slight quivering of his bottom lip. Another figure detached itself from the crowd and hobbled forward to join them.

'Are thar John Hawksworth?' the second man called in a heavy local accent.

From his working attire, John gathered that the man was the castle smithy, unbent and still blessed with a working man's physique though in his sixties. A piercing gaze stabbed into his own; a good mop of dark blond hair topped his head, defying the few grey strands of age.

John answered with a nod. There was little point in denying who he was. He hoped that his guards would intervene should the two set upon him – for he suspected the reason why each dragged a leg. A wave of excited chattering spread through the crowd. The hubbub grew to a crescendo as the news flashed among them that the brother of The Hawk was indeed standing before them.

John gasped and staggered backwards dragged by the priest towards the guardroom door. 'He talks to no man, on orders of the bishop!'

The restraining hand of the furious serjeant-at-mace clamped down the cleric's arm. 'Damn you, pestilent dog!' he snarled through clenched teeth. 'The prisoner is in our hands, not yours.'

'You will answer for it if he has intercourse with anyone,' Father Rollo threatened, red-faced from his unaccustomed exertion and fear of being struck a blow by the serjeant.

The serjeant-at-mace was curious at the manner of their prisoner's reception. Again the two aged men were standing side by side before the prisoner. John presented a pitiful sight, clad in heavily stained rags unchanged in weeks and wick with lice; dirty bindings covered wounds occasioned by his inquisition and flesh rubbed raw by securing irons. Two weeks' growth of beard decorated his face and his hair, stiff with dirt, clung to his head like a matted cap.

'Sir Edmund, your brother, The Hawk, what of him? Is he still alive? How does he fare?' The tanner asked in tones gentle but with some eagerness.

'I have had no sight nor news of Edmund these past five years.' His voice sounded strangely distant to his ears 'He was at Rouen in France...but...then...' He slurred, for his mouth seemed to be distancing itself from his brain. It was so hot. Waves of nausea washed over him; there was a weakness overcoming his legs. Behind the men's heads the castle keep was swaying dangerously. The men were growing into giants before him and the cobbles beneath his feet began to spin and move upwards to meet his face, accompanied by the buzzing of a thousand bees arguing in his ears. There were arms about him, then nothing more.

It must be his blood, John decided, as a warm fluid was rubbed over his face, body and limbs. In a vague detached way he wondered what new satanic mischief his so-called Christian tormentors had devised. Unconsciousness was much to be preferred and his mind readily complied. When again he open his eyes he felt oddly comfortable. He was lying on a low pallet covered with an eiderdown mattress and wearing a fresh, clean shirt. His wounds had been treated with oil and wrapped in clean linen. His fingers explored his chin and found it shaved.

Shadowy figures busied themselves about the cell, for cell it certainly was. The smell of fresh rushes mingled with that of herbs discharged a harmony of aromas most agreeable – predominantly lavender. Two candle stands were being set up. A small bench stool was being manoeuvred through the heavy trap-door and down the wooden step-ladder.

'Saints preserve us, he's awake!'

All eyes turned to peer at him as he raised himself on one elbow and squinted about the room at the half-dozen attendants.

'Thar must be famished. Take a swig o' this.' He was proffered a flagon of ale by the blacksmith, who turned out to be a man called Thomas Tipton, or 'Tiptoe'.

His drinking was deep, long and noisy, and was accompanied by the sound of a blazing row going on overhead in the castle guardroom. The tanner, who made his name known as Tom Philip, dubbed 'Old Tommy' by all, indicated the fracas above with his thumb.

'Thy friend, the plump priest, wants thee back in irons or, he says, we will all be damned for eternity in Hellfire.' He shook his head. 'Thas been likened to a ferret in a hen coop, with thi devilish teachings, which thas been spreading abroad among the people hereabouts.' He was blowing and tutting in mock disapproval.

'Tharra dangerous man,' added Tiptoe. 'Truly the brother of The Hawk and of that there can be no mistake.' He nodded solemnly. 'And nar, would tha like a bowl of pottage, some fresh-caught trout, and maybe some of Mam Pell's rabbit pie?'

A feeling of relief flooded over John. He was environed by kindness – fellows who would do him no hurt, cause him no pain. Shoes, doublet and hose were proffered and in no time at all he stood fully dressed. His attempts to offer words of thanks to his benefactors, who had begun disappearing up the steps to the guardroom above, were greeted by the odd, embarrassed grunt that only Yorkshire folks can emit when being thanked. The trap door was left open and the sound of arguing seemed to be concerned with that very fact.

He took in his surroundings and recognised that he had been here before. This cell was the sinister place which had held such fascination for him as a boy. On one of his many visits to the castle the men-at-arms had regaled him and his brother with tales of torture and entombment of prisoners whilst still alive. Victims who were never to be seen again; tales connected with the hole under the guardroom floor. Curious, egged on and provided with a lit candle John had been encouraged to step down the ladder. The trap was allowed to drop. Terrified, he had banged frantically on the trap-door screaming to be let out. The incident had provided great amusement for the castle retainers. He was released on conditions, along with dire warnings of his permanent confinement there should he fail their orders. He was to obtain a keg of the best fresh ale from the kitchens, preferably laced with honey.

The cell proved to be much smaller than he remembered – three-and-a-half cloth yards by five-and-a-half. In the right-hand corner of the dungeon was a latrine that had no outside egress and would require emptying by shovel and bucket. However, all smelled sweetly at present.

The castle chaplain appeared; he was small and thin, with thick iron-grey hair sweeping in all directions from a lopsided tonsure. He was nervous and busily fingered a large wooden crucifix which was secured to his belt by a rosary. The chaplain avoided looking at the prisoner directly, but fixed his gaze on some point on the wall behind John's head. He sat himself on the edge of the small stool. Next to appear was the guardian priest, Rollo, who positioned himself on one of the lower treads of the wooden steps. He glared at John as if seeing him for the first time. Indeed, it was the first time that he had seen the prisoner in such a presentable condition.

The chaplain began to speak in a tone unnaturally high and self-consciously dropped an octave to begin again... 'Will you, John Hawksworth, undertake and swear before Almighty God not to attempt to escape?'

'This man has been found guilty of heresy under canon law, and condemned to death and yet you seek his parole not to escape?' said Father Rollo. 'On whose authority do you interfere?'

'What have you to say, John Hawksworth, your word?' The castle chaplain asked, continuing to peer in the flickering light at some spot on the wall.

'You have my word if...' John paused long enough to ensure that he had their attention, 'if you allow me my English Bible.'

'You will have your Bible the day after tomorrow at the stake, when it is hung about your worthless neck, along with your satanic writings,' said the priest. Wearily, the chaplain turned to his fellow cleric 'What harm can it do brother?' His resigned tone reflected his mood 'Surely a small price for our peace of mind, for, as you can see,' he indicated the cleaned-up cell, 'there are many at this place who would prefer it if he didn't burn.'

Frustrated, Rollo said, 'His Grace, The Bishop will have to be informed about all that has taken place this day.' In a sudden pique of temper, he stood up from his seat on the step and smacked his head on the cell roof. 'Bloody Mary, Mother of God!' he howled as he rubbed his head and turned to climb out of the cell.

For the first time since he had entered the dungeon the chaplain looked directly at John, eyes a-twinkle. 'Something for our brother's confession time?' Glancing up the ladder to make sure that they were alone, the chaplain leaned forward and lowered his voice.

'Tell me, is it true what was recounted to me by a travelling friar that, following the Battle of Tewkesbury, the whereabouts of the Holy Grail was disclosed by divine revelation to your brother, thus confirming his purity of heart?'

John smiled and, shaking his head, disabused him 'Edmund would be the least likely person to be granted such favour, for he never has had time for what he regards as superstition.'

Disappointment was evident on the cleric's face. John hurried to continue 'He has always considered that images, relics and the like provide no advantage to mortal man. In giving such things attention there is no benefit in his eyes.'

'I don't suppose... he slew the Sudbury Worm?' the cleric asked in such a way as to indicate that the question sounded foolish in his own ears.

'I don't suppose he did.' John answered in what he hoped was a kindly way 'Whatever type of creature that was.'

Not giving up, the chaplain tried to authenticate other tales credited to the prisoner's brother.

'They say about him that he can turn himself into vapour. Whenever there's a fog or marsh mist he can become a part of it. They say he bewitches living creatures, exercising dominion over beasts of the field and birds of the heavens, and even eels and all manner of fishes give themselves willingly for his table.'

'There is some truth in some of what you say, however...'

Before John could clarify what he meant, he was interrupted. The chaplain had taken his response as confirmation of Edmund's ability to render himself invisible and to bewitch animals. Thus encouraged, he proceeded with further questioning.

'Minstrels have long sung songs concerning the much-vaunted *Wespen*, the crossbow boys, and how they took on and slew the Flower of Craven. Yet others argue that The Hawk met them all, in turn, in mortal combat and vanquished all five hundred – single-handedly.'

Before John could reply, the chaplain hurried on,

'And what of the Black-Hearted Clifford, the scourge of the House of York? They say that The Hawk fought him hand to hand and decapitated him with a single swipe of a dagger.'

The chaplain's face was alight with enthusiasm as he warmed to his quest for confirmation. 'What of the saving of the three hundred men of Lancaster? Did that really take place, when The Hawk hoisted his surcoat on Towton Field as a signal for salvation? There are those at this very place who insist that it happened and never cease telling of it on every possible occasion.'

Suddenly, the chaplain's questions were interrupted as a Bible hit the cell floor. Brother Rollo followed down the steps carrying an essay written by John and other papers. *De Trinitatis erroribus* had been specifically written by John in a fruitless attempt to persuade members of the clergy of the falseness of what he had come to be convinced was a God-defaming doctrine. Also a paper written by John Wycliffe on the illusion of transubstantiation. Writings that had been submitted in evidence against him at the ecclesiastical court. Rollo flung the books on the table with an exaggerated display of revulsion. 'Fuel for the flames that will help transport you to Hell!' he said.

The chaplain picked up the damaged Bible, carefully rearranging loosened pages and removing fragments of dirt. He placed it gently on the table. He was seething with anger and struggled to contain himself. Turning to John, he spoke in a friendly tone with measured voice 'And now, John Hawksworth, your parole, please, to whit that whilst at this place you will refrain from all escape attempts despite any here who would encourage your flight.'

'Whilst at this place,' John declared, 'I do hereby give my troth and thank you both for allowing me this comfort from God's Word.'

'Take comfort from confession and a refuting of your heretical ways' said Brother Rollo.

'Enough! In the name of God Brother, enough!' the chaplain cried.

'Your questioning about the so-called Thryberg Hawk, the Plantagenet sorcerer, will be reported.'

'Are yaw two still at it?' It was Tiptoe who interrupted with the promised meal. Entering the dungeon with great care, he set the bowl and wooden platter on the cot, along with a horn spoon and knife. Immediately, Rollo lunged forward, grabbing at the knife as he did so.

'He is not to have a knife!'

Both the chaplain and Tiptoe groaned in unison.

'What the blood in Hell is he supposed to have done to deserve all this?' said a fuming Tiptoe.

Glad of an opportunity to re-assert what he considered to be his threatened authority, the priest Rollo reached into his belt purse and produced a folded parchment 'So that all are clear as to the offences committed by this man, you may now pay heed to this commission and see what authority you are flouting.' Unfolding it and holding the document in both hands, he tilted it towards the light from a candle and proceeded to read aloud the indite. Included in the itemised list of offences were denials of the effectiveness of acts of confession, pilgrimages, use of images and even included condemnation of Pope Julius II himself. Hardly charges that would invoke leniency from Mother Church.

Convinced that his authority was re-established by his reading aloud of the commission of excommunication and permission to carry out the sentence of death, Father Rollo took a very deliberate look at each of them in turn. He did this with such an air of self-satisfaction and arrogance that when Tiptoe, feigning interest in the document, moved closer and passed a candle under the velum causing it to ignite, there was a burst of laughter from the chaplain and John.

Squealing like a stuck pig, the priest extinguished the flames by dropping the warrant and stamping on it.

'You did that deliberately,' he whimpered, crouching and tenderly holding the smouldering parchment.

'Thar wants to take better care o' yond thing,' called Tiptoe as he limped up the steps to the guardroom above.

'May the Black Death visit that man! I'll report him to the castle constable. He'll pay for this!' Without giving the chaplain or John a second glance and breathing further curses, he scampered up the ladder.

The chaplain, introduced himself as Jack Naulty, and seated himself on the cell steps. 'Enjoy your repast, my friend, and permit me to tarry, for I have much to ask.'

Never, as far back as he could remember, had he enjoyed such a meal. After weeks of stale bread and watery gruel he was in danger of gorging himself. Jack Naulty, looked on with a smile. Minutes later, when John was coming to the end of the meal, the chaplain asked not about things concerning his brother, but other matters which troubled him. Matters of doctrine. 'Confession to a priest...why do you find fault with this?'

Taking the battered Bible, which consisted of four Gospels, Acts of the Apostles, most of the epistle of St Paul, St Peter, St James and St John, he turned the pages to St Paul's second epistle to Timothy and read aloud '"For all Scripture, inspired of God, is profitable to teach, to reprove, to chastise, to learn in rightwiseness, that the man of God be learned in all good works."'

The chaplain, his forehead creased in a frown, reached over and peered at the text. 'I've only ever heard the Bible read in Latin. And I have read it to the congregated without understanding very much of what it meant for many years.'

Beginning with that text, John began to explain matters from the scriptures concerning the error of confessing to men.

'Maybe, but I would need to see more on this matter and consult learned teachers,' he said cautiously. Naulty appeared uncomfortable and made as if to leave. Quickly, John changed the subject. He was enjoying friendly company for the first time in months. The doings of The Hawk were evidently uppermost in the chaplain's mind. John closed the Bible and placed it away from him. 'For a number of years I have considered writing the account of my brother's life.'

'Splendid! It must be written down – it must. They talk of little else around here but of the boy knight, who once herded pigs at Thryberg, towards the town of Rotherham. And of how St Leonard appeared to him in a vision...'

'I'm afraid not' John interrupted, stifling a sigh 'St Leonard did no such thing. The truth about what happened in these parts fifty years ago should be recorded. However, I fear that it has been left too late, for they have done for my writing.' He indicated the damage that had been caused to the knuckles on his right hand. 'There is little enough time left for me, this night and the morrow only. I would prefer that my last night be set aside for preparation, devotions – a vigil of prayer.'

'It could still be done, for the castle secretary is a friend of mine and much taken by the stories of The Hawk.' The chaplain turned to climb the steps. Then he paused, his face transfixed in thought. 'The Lady Fitzwilliam often tells the story of how The Hawk raised from the dead a beautiful young widow. Can that possibly be true?'

'The Lady Isabel? Yes, in a way I suppose he did bring her back from the dead, but that event requires some clarification, as indeed do so many other reported acts of his.'

'Ink, pen, parchment and competent scribe will be with you within the hour.' Thus saying, the excited castle chaplain girded his loins by pulling his habit up through his legs and tucking it into his belt. With his legs free for running, Jack Naulty vaulted up the ladder and out of the dungeon, at the same time calling down at the top of his voice 'The truths about The Thryberg Hawk must be chronicled ere comes the dawn on St Ethelreda's Day.'

*   *   *   *

In the absence of the good chaplain John began to arrange his thoughts for the relating of the true account of the life of his brother, Sir Edmund Hawksworth. At last, myth and error would be dispelled with a written record. No longer suppressed, the Yorkist hero would have his story told. The account would serve as a tribute to the truest knight and most noble soul in the whole of Christendom.

Where was he to begin? He lacked the time to tell the complete story of the part his brother played in the thirty years' struggle between the houses of York and Lancaster. Sufficient time surely, to record the amazing three months in 1461 where it all began. A miracle whereby in a matter of days a boy – a lowly *porcarius* – soared above his degree to become a knight.

Surely, it all began with Edmund's dramatic public declaration in the church of St Leonard's, Thryberg, just three miles from Conisbrough, on Epiphany Sunday, some forty-eight years ago.

Chapter One

Anointing of The Avenger

THE CHURCH DOOR swung back with an almighty bang, doubtless encouraged by a bitter north-easterly which swept into the nave, extinguishing candles and causing the heavy tapestries adorning the walls to flutter like banners. The congregation of around thirty souls, comprising family and servants of Reresby Manor, along with crofters of the villages of Thryberg and Dalton, spun as one to discern the cause for that fierce interruption of Holy Mass.

As if an integral part of the icy wind, in swept the Abbot of Roche, Father John Wakefield, followed by two attendant monks, who scurried after him, slamming the north door with much haste, shutting out the freezing weather on that feast of Epiphany, Sunday morning, 6th January, 1461.

The priest, William Reresby, had been standing before the altar and had reached the high point of the Mass. He was in the process of elevating the Host when the sacrilegious entry of the Abbot halted him in mid chant. The old squire-priest, flushed with annoyance, tottered out from behind the screen into the nave to confront the Abbot, who was striding down the side aisle towards him. A heated exchange in hushed tones ensued between the two men of God. The words 'danger' and 'immediately' were audible to many in the congregation. The Abbot was becoming increasingly insistent on being allowed his way on a pressing matter.

From their elevated positions seated on coffin stools at the rear of the nave, the two Hawksworth brothers were able to witness the welcome distraction to advantage. Alongside them in her usual place was Eleanor the Bastard. She was an unfortunate little runt some eight years of age and seemingly stunted in her natural growth, possessing the frame of a child may be three years younger. She had attached herself to the boys, or rather to Edmund, ever since the incident of the broken eggs last St Wilfred's Day. As was her usual practice, she sat as close as she could get to Edmund, having adopted him as her family. Not only did she hang on to every word he uttered, but she aped each movement and mannerism. That served to irritate the elder boy, John, but apparently left Edmund unaffected.

The three youngsters were not permitted to assume places on the newly-installed bench pews, since those were reserved for Reresby family members, household servants and villagers. All three were regarded as orphans and as such in receipt of charity from both church and manor – and were made to know their place. Although, in truth, both the fathers were very much alive. In the case of the boys they had simply been abandoned; so, too, Eleanor, but with additional awkward circumstances. Her father, Arnold, was the youngest of the three Reresby brothers and was retained by the Clifford household of Skipton, serving as a mounted archer. His fathering of the illegitimate child, Eleanor, by a servant girl of the Reresby household was barely acknowledged by the family. Although the child was housed and employed within the manor-house kitchens, her existence remained a source of embarrassment. Not one of the family would pay her the slightest heed, never addressing a kind word to her or even casting the merest glance in her direction as the mite went about her chores. It was suspected by the boys that the family would have preferred, and indeed viewed it convenient, if Eleanor had perished along with her mother at her birth.

The aroma of fresh-planed wood permeated St Leonard's as William Reresby, in his position as the eldest son, had continued to beautify the family church. He had even financed a fine pointed spire to decorate the tower and introduced more bells to sound out a respectable peal to announce the hours and devotions throughout the manor. The outside stonework he had had covered in plaster and kept whitewashed. Inside was likewise plastered and whitened, and the squire-priest had commissioned wall paintings depicting the lives and invariably the deaths of favourite saints.

On the rear wall was a painting of Adam and Eve and the serpent in the Garden of Eden – which depiction fascinated John as both figures were completely naked. The vulgar painting was, he suspected, the artist's way of repaying the fussy priest for his constant interference and meddling occasioned during the period the work was carried out. William Reresby was determined to make the family church a glittering jewel in the crown of the West Riding of Yorkshire. To further that end, he sought to acquire some holy relic that would, he hoped, result in his precious St Leonard's becoming a shrine and a destination for pilgrims. Until he could acquire a sacred bone of a saint, or some wood, earthenware, or piece of cloth with holy provenance that thousands would travel to do obeisance before, he would continue to add to the fabric of the building. This included some stained glass, executed and installed at great expense.

The fine oak pews, positioned as they were with one end up against the north wall of the nave, had been introduced in recent months. An aisle about a yard wide ran the length of the south side of the nave, in which aisle was being acted out the drama between the two clerics.

Father John Wakefield, having succeeded in convincing the squire-parson of the need for him to address the congregation, mounted the pulpit and surveyed the seated throng. He was not unknown to the people for he had visited St Leonard's on previous occasions in the church calendar to carry out some religious duty or other, unusual for a monk of the strict, inward-looking Cistercian Order. He swung back a rain-soaked cloak to reveal a white habit with a black cowl trimmed with rabbit fur. A white enamelled and bejewelled pectoral cross suspended from a gold chain swung in front of him; again, unusual grandeur for an order associated with austerity.

Pushing back his hood, he revealed a head resembling the shape of a pear, with eyes sloping upwards at the corners. Thick grey eyebrows hung off a pallid face from which dark eyes peered at them from either side of a viciously sharp-bridged nose. Should a demon ever manifest itself before men, then it would likely resemble the peacockish Father John Wakefield, Abbot of Roche.

Little Eleanor was terrified and sought to hide herself within the folds of Edmund's oversized hand-me-down coat.

The Abbot began to speak in a low, husky voice.

'By now most of you will have heard of the terrible blood-letting at Sandal castle which violated Holy Week of the Christ Mass.' His voice was low, but with a resonance that carried his words through to the rear of the nave. He paused, doubtless noting the few nodding heads.

'It is likely that there are those among you who will have acquaintance with some of the good men and true from the Wapentake of Tickhill who took part in the fighting.' His voice rose in volume 'A battle in which our noble lord, Richard, Duke of York, foremost prince of the realm and judged by law to be the rightful heir to the throne of England, was slain.' He paused before continuing 'As you will recall, it was the twentieth day of December when he arrived in these parts.'

With increased intensity, he added, 'Nine days later, at a time of truce when the Good Lord has decreed peace to men of good will, Richard of York and his small band were betrayed! They were tricked and defeated by a superior horde of knights and men-at-arms issuing forth from Pomfret Castle.'

His voice continued to rise as he warmed to his account of what had occurred at Sandal Castle on the 30th December, 1460 just past.

'As I speak to you now, the head of the duke is impaled on the end of a pike and his enemies have placed it over the Micklegate Bar, York.'

There were gasps of horror from among the congregation. Satisfied that his audience was with him, he continued, dropping his voice in affected solemnity, 'And, I have to inform you, that the head of the Earl of Rutland is alongside that of his father, Duke Richard.'

This last piece of news prompted cries of disbelief from many of the people.

'Yes,' he carried on in a measured tone, 'and great mockery and game was made of those gruesome trophies by the perpetrators of the evil.'

'It is reliably reported that Lord Clifford, captain of the much-vaunted Flower of Craven, personally did for the boy on Wakefield Chantry Bridge,' his voice rang out, 'after the lad had surrendered himself to the mercy of Lancaster!'

At the mention of the Flower of Craven John felt his brother stiffen and, glancing at him, was shocked by hatred flashing forth from his eyes.

The Abbot, carried away by his own rhetoric, barked out, 'What merciless monster would slit the throat – as a butcher would a pig – of a helpless sixteen-year-old?' There was a long pause as he allowed the picture he was painting to sink in. 'Laws of chivalry and knightly practice of Christian warriors are to hold captives of noble rank for ransom, but those fiends chose neither mercy, nor pity, nor charity, but rather they indulged in satanic blood lust. In that way also perished the Earl of Salisbury, he meeting his end at Pomfret Castle at the hands of a mob.'

With his listeners in the palm of his hand the Abbot cried out, 'Who among you, if it were within his power to do so, would not seek to dispense justice for these bloody crimes?' It was as though he was appealing for some act of retribution against Lancaster, and in particular against Lord Clifford. 'There will be a reckoning!' he cried. 'From this realm an Avenger of Righteous Blood will arise!'

Suddenly, before John could prevent him, his brother leapt to his feet and yelled out.

'I vow to be the Avenger of Blood!'

Spontaneous laughter rang out from the congregation. As one the people turned to glimpse the one who had called out from the back of the church. Even the dour Abbot smiled. Looking directly at Edmund, who stood with his right arm half-raised and with a look of determination on his face.

The Abbot continued hurriedly, 'Truly, as I have said, there will be a reckoning for the innocent blood spilt. Doubtless there will be a rightful 'avenger of blood' but a personage of renown, mayhap in the family bloodline, such as the Earl of Warwick, or the Earl of March. Divine justice will hardly be left in the hands of a commoner, a mere boy.' Then he added in a kinder tone of voice, 'However, your enthusiasm is well noted and we commend you, child, whoever you are.'

Then, with second thoughts, the Abbot frowned and called out with some solemnity, 'Boy, by what name are you called?'

John was surprised that Edmund had managed to utter words so loudly, for his brother had been afflicted by an awful stutter from the night their mother died down to that day. He was capable of coherent speech only if he resorted to whispering, which meant that John often acted as his brother's interpreter and mouthpiece, much in the same fashion as Aaron on Moses's behalf when before the Pharaoh of Egypt.

'Edmund Hawksworth, Father Abbot!' John called out for his brother, 'Swineherd to this manor.'

Unlike the congregation that morning at St Leonard's, John did not for a second have any doubt in his mind as to the genuineness of Edmund's avowed intent. Nor did he doubt his brother's ability to carry out an act of recompense on the House of Lancaster, especially on the longbow men of Skipton, the fearsome warriors of Craven. Edmund would never have called out unless he meant it. John's concern centred on the ways and means: just how was his brother going to set about achieving a meaningful act of vengeance? He felt sick at heart for what lay ahead.

Meanwhile, some members of the congregation continued to have their heads turned to look at Edmund, their faces alive with smiles. It seemed appropriate that John stand longside him. Eleanor was already at Edmund's side, her right hand raised in imitation, a look of determination on her elfin face.

At that time it was inconceivable to John that in less than three months Edmund would deliver such a series of staggering blows to the House of Lancaster that it would rock the kingdom. His incredible feats at arms and accomplishments on the field of battle would turn the now good-natured laughter of the people of Thryberg into plaudits of acclaim. They would tell stories about him to their children and attribute to him incredible feats of glory and valour. They would, every one of them, within a matter of weeks, boast of knowing him. The legend of The Hawk was about to begin.

The reason for Edmund's heart-involvement in the warring described by the Abbot was the mention of the private army, retainers of Lord Clifford, the five hundred mounted bowmen known as the Flower of Craven. Further to this, both had had some dealings with the seventeen-year-old Earl of Rutland when, during Advent, the Duke of York's small army had arrived at Conisbrough Castle from London. The boys had been delivering a fatted sow to the castle slaughterhouse and the Earl had addressed some words to them whilst he and a party of knights were crossing the inner bailey. He had inquired concerning the possibility of some fresh pork to go with the barrels of salted meat his attendants were gathering as provisions for their depleted baggage train. That evening, after appropriate permissions, they had selected five pigs from the Reresby herd and driven them the three miles to the castle. The young Earl of Rutland was well pleased, rewarding them with what at first they had taken to be two groats, over and above full payment for the swine. They were surprised to discover that one of the coins was a golden half nobel – surely a mistake? Edmund had insisted on informing the castle constable and, sure enough, the young Earl, also called Edmund, had indeed made a mistake with his gratuity. It was his father, Richard, Duke of York, who had rewarded their honesty by graciously permitting them the high value coin.

Now their severed heads, father and son together, were over a town gateway at York, a feast for the birds. Edmund, distressed and guilt-ridden at what he considered to be failure on his part to prevent the death of his mother, sought to assuage his inner torment by identifying an evil upon which to concentrate. It was vented on the father who had abandoned them to serve 'Black-Faced' Clifford.

There was indeed a further reason – a pressing incentive for the younger brother setting out on that bold errand. A disturbing event had occurred just three months earlier around Michaelmastide. It had been the annual hog drive and the brothers had experienced first hand the ruthlessness of the northerners who were supporting the cause of King Henry VI and the House of Lancaster. The boys had barely escaped death at the end of a rope.

The Abbot regained the attention of the gathering through the device of much throat-clearing.

'King Henry is at this time safely ensconced in London and protected against those who would control him and seek great things for themselves.' The Abbot paused, 'But Henry does not wear the crown easily for, as is well-known, he is of gentle disposition and holy persuasion. His attendant counsellors rule the kingdom and his French Queen would hold the reigns of power, as Jezebel, consort of Israelite King Ahab. Queen Margaret is gathering her party at York, intent upon marching south, determined to seize the King and thereby all England.'

William Reresby nodded in agreement at the likening of Jezebel to Margaret. There were, however, those present who were shocked and discomfited to hear Henry VI's queen, Margaret of Anjou, compared with the wicked Queen Jezebel of the Bible.

'As we are gathered here and speak, the French woman, Margaret, and those lords of the House of Lancaster allied to her persuasion, are leaving the City of York in mighty battle array. She has found a champion in Clifford and has knighted him for his murderous work. Now they are marching on London to wrest the King from the care of those who would best serve the kingdom.'

The Abbot began stabbing the air directly in front of him with his forefinger.

'Now, give heed for your very lives. By tomorrow's noon a large force of armed men, the vanward of the Queen's army, and among them mercenaries drawn from among bloodthirsty Scots, will be passing through Doncaster on the Great North Road. Foreprickers will, there is no doubt, cross Thryberg Manor, and that of Conisbrough, on their way south. Your animals, provisions, valuables and goods are in danger, if not your very souls.'

A great deal of muttering began as families and friends began to confer concerning the imminent danger until a great hubbub filled the church.

Holding up his arms for silence, the Abbot announced, 'The constable, Edmund Fitzwilliam, has wisely decided to close Conisbrough Castle gates against the Northern hordes. Those who would seek refuge there must arrive at first light. Take what provisions you can carry – enough victuals for each person for seven days.'

Some got up to leave and then the Abbot announced that should any wish to find sanctuary at Roche Abbey, they were to make their way there before Vespers that very Sunday.

'*In nomine Patris, et Filii, et Spiritus Sancti...*' Both the Abbot and priest began to deliver the benediction together in discordant unison as the faithful began to file out.

The order of leaving was as usual: first, Agnes Reresby clutching her precious *Hararium*, accompanied by her husband, Ralph – younger brother to William, the squire-priest. Then followed the two attendant ladies-in-waiting clasping the hand of the Reresby boy, also called Ralph. The rest of the Manor household filed towards the door in order of precedence: Ann Thicket, who served as steward (with greater proficiency since the departure of her husband). The three 'orphans' remained until all had filed past.

Many a one laid a hand on Edmund's head, time and again his hair was tousled in a good-natured way. 'Do for 'em good, young Hawky,' and, 'You cut that lot down to size, lad'.

The cook, John Clay, said nothing as he passed the three youngsters. He paused, looking long and hard at Edmund as if deeply troubled. Ever since last St Wilfred's Day and the incident of the broken eggs, he had acted towards the lad as if he didn't quite know how he should address him. Embarrassed, he nodded in Edmund's direction and made haste out of the church, only to return again to stand inside the door.

Bringing up the rear was Father John Wakefield with his two monks. They also made as if to pass, but then, the Abbot paused and turned to peer long and hard at Edmund. It was as if the boy's forthright public declaration unsettled him. Edmund met his gaze and held it, not dropping his eyes nor showing discomfort at the cleric's scrutiny.

Then it happened, suddenly a shaft of light from the morning sun, low in the wintry sky, pierced the east window, passing through the stained glass and, travelling the length of both the chancel and nave, bathed Edmund's face in a multi-coloured rainbow of light.

The Abbot jerked as if shot through. Rapidly, making the sign of the cross, he pulled up his hood and scurried through the north door as if pursued by demons. The Abbot's accompanying monks reached the door where one turned to look back at Edmund and uttered, quite awe-struck, 'Tis an anointing!' So saying, the troubled cleric crossed himself and fled after his master.

Edmund smiled at his brother. Then, leaning forward, he whispered, 'It's an anointing John,' at the same time holding up his hand as if to capture the beam of light, within which danced myriad minute dust particles. He shook his head in obvious disbelief. If his brother remained unimpressed by the phenomenon, John was much taken by it.

Little Eleanor had been clinging in fear to Edmund's leg, overwhelmed by the events of that morning and still terrified of the Abbot. Edmund swept up the mite, whereupon she flung her arms around him and buried her face in his neck. They left through the north porch together, passing through the small graveyard on that side of the church, and followed the household in procession the few yards to the Manor House south door. That part of the burial ground was for use by the lesser ones and their mother's bones rested there. Since the incident of the broken eggs last September, one or other of the boys always carried Eleanor the short distance between the church and house.

She seemed to weigh next to nothing. Even a month-old piglet appeared to have more substance than Eleanor.

Each Saturday evening the boys were directed to attend at the Manor House. There they were to bathe and pass the night. In the morning they donned clothes kept especially for divine services on Sunday. They joined the household attending St Leonard's and partook of meals at the house throughout that day, albeit inter-spaced by chores. Following Compline on Sunday evening, they would resume their working clothes and return across the fields to the ancient stone quarry where their croft was situated and the herd of swine was penned. During holy festivals they were expected to remain a number of days at the Manor. Thus it was that William Reresby fulfilled his Christian obligation as outlined in Scriptures, to '...care for fatherless and motherless children in their tribulation...' . The friendly, smiling countenance of the squire-parson promised much, but delivered little.

Their mother had died in the prolonged winter of 1456 when Edmund was nine-and-a-half years old. Both Edmund and John laid blame for her death firmly at the door of their father, John, who had absented himself, giving no support, but had brought disaster when he did appear. He was retained by the Cliffords and, along with Arnold Reresby, rode with the Flower of Craven, a popular member of that armed band. Their father fought in border skirmishes and sought his fortune by ransom and plunder; he would most certainly have been at the Battle of Wakefield and might have witnessed the terrible deeds perpetrated against the House of York. On his livery he wore with pride the charge of the Red Wyvern, the livery of the bitterest enemy of York – Lord Clifford.

Their mother had washed clothes and bedding for the Reresby servants. The impoverished family's rude dwelling was situated on a wide ledge of the quarry face and positioned well above the pig pens. The croft had been substantially built by the previous herder. Edmund had vastly improved upon that man's labour and he had even channelled a small stream from the land above, bringing it through the rear of the croft so their mother, in that respect at least, was well convenienced.

When their father did appear at the quarry in late summer of 1455, it was so that their mother could nurse him. He had sustained a deep and vicious wound to the left side of his face caused by a broadsword. Lord Clifford's surgeon had worked well upon the wound, but their father needed care in order that healing and full recovery could take place. Their mother had entertained hopes that he had come home for good, and would settle down for the benefit of the three of them. However, after healing, following his wife's tender care, their father upped and left just as the bite of winter was taking a hold on the land. Not a farthing did he leave behind, but he had depleted their store of winter resources and meagre preserves. Heart-broken and smitten with melancholy, their mother had sickened and taken to her cot. She was unable to provide for them or carry out any sort of work. Messages were sent to their father informing him of their plight, but brought no response.

During that terrible winter Edmund had worked with a near frenzied determination to sustain them. With a home-made crossbow he had provided meat of some kind each and every day, knowing that if he should miss his prey then his mother would go to sleep hungry. Even when sparrows were the only food available, they were felled in a relentless manner with an ever improving marksmanship born out of sheer desperation. Fifteen to twenty sparrows made a passable meal. Hot broth was always to be had, apart from one occasion when Edmund failed to bring home meat, his failure due to his being racked with a fever and weakened. He just stood at the threshold of the croft, unable to bring himself to enter and sobbed as if his heart would break. His mother had fetched him inside where she rocked him, singing a lullaby, until he fell asleep in her arms. As she grew ever weaker, Edmund had continued to provide the food whilst John prepared it and fed her. They took turns in keeping vigil throughout those long nights of her dying.

On the days that the warrener 'looked the other way', they had rabbit. During that desperate fight to survive John

begged bread
crofters of Th
Edmund wa
crossbow, he
and coal from
exposed. Thai
pigs to care
season's supp

On what m
mother, Cecili
succumbed dy
bitterness was
ability to utter

Words of co
which explaine

follower of John Wycliffe. On t
father, that would only be a
destined to occur on Palm

As it turned out, th
about to befall th
the Abbot, war
before the a
of the W

attendants in heaven and their mother had received a heavenly appointment to serve, brought only bitter anger. Certainly, Edmund was not comforted and asked, through John as his spokesman, why it was that their mother had been killed off, leaving her two boys orphaned so that God's mother could have extra help. Did she not have thousands of angels at her beck and call? William Reresby had been disturbed by Edmund's bitter objections. It was at that time that John first heard those words of his brother's that would become so familiar, and that would become his rule for living. He had glowered at the clergyman and whispered to his brother, 'There is no advantage in this, John. There is no gain.' So it was that Edmund became alienated from the Almighty, viewing Him as capricious and callous. Edmund was sceptical of miracles and questioned the existence of any divine purpose in life. Hence his lack of enthusiasm concerning the phenomenon that had taken place with the shaft of light. His rancour would only begin to disappear at a time in the future when he was in a position to present his questionings concerning the mysterious doings of God to a

...e matter of his hatred of their ...ppeased by an act of vengeance ... Sunday eve, 1461.

...e urgent message of imminent calamity ...community, delivered with such feeling by ...premature. It would be a further twelve days ...mies of Queen Margaret passed through that part ...st Riding and Reresby Manor.

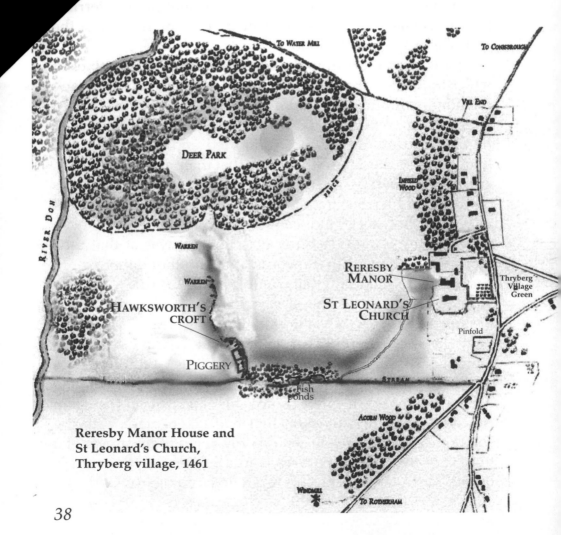

**Reresby Manor House and
St Leonard's Church,
Thryberg village, 1461**

Chapter Two

Hog-Drive at Michaelmastide and Broken Eggs

WITH THE ONSET OF NIGHT, Rollo the malevolent priest, greatly subdued and sporting a bruised mouth and swollen nose, departed the mighty stronghold on horseback. At the same time it was noted that Tiptoe appeared nursing bruised knuckles. Great was the worry of that conscientious emissary of the Bishop of Lincoln that the brother of the so-called Hawk would somehow escape the burning he so richly deserved. Representatives of Mother Church at Doncaster would be informed of the blatant flouting of canon decree taking place at Conisbrough Castle. Clearly, in the mind of the priest, enforcement of the ecclesiastical warrant for the heretic's execution might become necessary by force of arms.

The evening was drawing in and the tiny cell at Conisbrough Castle was filling to overflowing with an audience hanging on to John's every word. The air was fetid and the scribe was falling behind in his attempts to record the story in an abbreviated Latin rather than English preferred by the storyteller. Besides which, he was woefully slow. Castle chaplain, Father Jack Naulty, called a halt and moved prisoner and scribe into the guardroom above. Another recorder was sent for from Reresby Manor to assist the castle cleric.

Whilst awaiting the Reresby scribe John managed to rest, even sleeping amidst all the clamour of the crowd that was growing by the hour. Like something akin to the plague, word was spreading throughout the West Riding and North Lincolnshire: the brother of The Hawk was a captive at Conisbrough Castle.

Cock-crow signalled the arrival of morning and the order was given to raise the castle drawbridge. In an ever-increasing queue, like ants besieging a cracked honey pot, the curious thronged the approach road to the gate. There they were being assessed as those meriting admittance and assisted by the colour of their coinage. Minstrels and troubadours were being granted priority by the castle deputy-steward, since it was deemed necessary that they should hear at first hand the true account of the doings of the Plantagenet hero. It would be their skills that would be concerned with spreading the tale through ballad and song throughout England, despite supression and discouragement by the ruling House of Tudor.

Shortly after breaking of the fast, two scribes made known their craft and gained admittance. The dowager Lady Lucy Fitzwilliam took a hand in matters, directing that the storyteller and his two guards, along with the four assembled scribes, be removed to the bedchamber in the castle keep, where control of the pressing throng might be more easily managed.

In that splendid fortress tower, well-fed and at his ease, surrounded by upwards of thirty people, and with an unknown number crowding the staircase to the chamber below, John seated himself. His words would be relayed by word of mouth to those gathered in the bailey.

All eyes in the room were fixed upon him, awaiting his opening words. The focus of attention only served to unnerve him and swept clean away all thought. Nervously, he glanced at the two clerks seated at a *tabula plicata*, poised quills in hand, and behind them within the solar window two monks, ready to replace them at the desk. Silence cloaked the room – all were awaiting his opening words.

After what seemed an age, he spoke 'Ah, where to begin?' was all that he could find to utter.

Lady Lucy, along with three attendant ladies and a number of children, was seated close to him and one member of that party, a young girl of twelve or so her face alight with eagerness, called across, 'Eleanor and the broken eggs. Tell us of The Hawk and the little girl.' She turned for support to her young companions. 'And the animals,' called another child, 'Tell us of his enchanting of the animals.' A loud 'yes' was chorused.

Groans came from some of the men who awaited the account of what had happened when Margaret's Lancastrians flooded through the district. Most had forebears who had been caught up in the bitter side-taking and acts of revenge following the Towton victory. Others were desirous of learning how The Hawk had begun to go about settling accounts on behalf of the House of York. How a commoner, a child, could become a knight, nagged the minds of still others. Chattering grew and swamped the room.

Suddenly, a lute intervened and a minstrel, well-arrayed in the velvet of knighthood and with a voice as rich as that of any nightingale sang out:

Yellow and black, yellow and black,
with stings as deadly as Hell,
Yellow and black, and twenty fine lads
were eclipsed on that day
When The Hawk proved cock of the pack.

The minstrel's song immediately prompted appeals for the account of the crossbow competition shot at that very castle in March, 1461, when young Edmund had first come to the notice of newly-acclaimed sovereign, Edward IV, his lords and captains of York.

'Yes, yes, *die Wespen*! Tell us about the Wasps! We would hear about the mercenary's *kinderschrots*,' called out one.

'*Boltzen aus Silber*!' called another 'Tell us of the winning of the Silver Bolt, when your brother hit ten target shields of the House of Lancaster.' That was greeted by cries of agreement from those men packed into the bedchamber.

'My brother, to the best of my knowledge, never hit a single shield in his entire life! Ah, and there were but seven shields, not ten.'

The room fell silent at that apparent denial. The storyteller's authoritative explanations were all the more awaited.

A tug at his sleeve brought his attention to the face of a very determined-looking little seven-year-old. A blue-eyed girl with fair hair glared at him with eyebrows furrowed and mouth flattened in obvious annoyance. 'Eleanor and the broken eggs,' she persisted. She would not to be denied.

The account of the events of St Wilfred's Day, 1460, would certainly reveal a side of The Hawk that should be told: the boy knight was thought by many to be a cold-hearted killer, but his older brother would now reveal another facet of Edmund Hawksworth.

So there it was. The children commanded the events of that dawn of John's last temporal day, for tomorrow's light would herald St Ethelreda's Day and, following the period of None, his journey to Doncaster and martyrdom. So the storytelling began.

*   *   *   *

The star of good fortune, hovering on the horizon for the House of York, seemed to take on an ascendancy in the summer of 1460. The worthies of the City of London had sided with related family members the Lords Salisbury, Warwick, Fauconberg and the Earl of March. Duke Richard abandoned all pretence and publicly laid claim to the throne of England.

To accommodate the Duke of York's challenge to the throne yet still leave Henry VI as sovereign, a compromise was arrived at by Parliament – they called it the Act of Accord. Henry would retain the throne until his death. Thereafter, Richard of York and his descendants would inherit the crown. Until that day, Richard would have to be content with the position of Protector.

That compromise disinherited Henry's son and the succession of the House of Lancaster; enmity was thus guaranteed and would seethe in a cauldron of hate for years to come – Queen Margaret would see to that. Her child Edward would not lose his birthright. The House of Lancaster would continue to rule the kingdom while ever she could rouse support. Thereby the Wars of the Cousins was assured.

On Michaelmas Eve 1460, a sumptuous banquet was held in the Guild Hall by the Lord Mayor of London. It was attended by a thousand guests and lasted for four hours. An uneasy peace existed between the supporters of Lancaster and York.

On that very same night in the West Riding of Yorkshire lesser mortals, who were soon to be caught up in the threatening maelstrom, were intent upon other pressing matters. The demands of the season required that a hog-drive be undertaken. This was in readiness for 'blood month' when the slaughter of animals for winter supplies took place – meat for salting at both Yorkist properties at Sandal and Conisbrough. Both castles and their manors belonged to Duke Richard.

Sir Thomas Harrington of Brierley, on behalf of Richard of York, had purchased a herd of swine from a breeder near Aberford. The two brothers, John and Edmund, were loaned to Conisbrough Manor to assist in the drive. It had become common knowledge that the boy, Edmund Hawksworth, could ensure a successful and speedy drive. The brothers' services had been sought ever since news of the amazing control Edmund could exercise over a herd of pigs had spread throughout the Riding.

'How many days, O wise enchanter?' The reeve called out to Edmund, impatient to get the drive started.

The brothers had arrived at the large piggery south of the town of Tadcaster riding on one horse and accompanied by a herder from Conisbrough manor, 'Smudger' Smythe, on another. The two palfreys were in part payment for the herd. Five other men from Sandal Manor made up the team of drovers.

Edmund whispered to his brother and John called back, 'Less than three days if the weather stays fine.'

'They'll be a bounty in it if we make it in two,' shouted the reeve.

The reeve, William Scargill, was a short, tough-looking veteran of the annual hog-drive, a bullying Yorkshireman who treated his drovers little better than the swine, bringing down his staff on the back of man and animal alike. Standing on an up-ended food trough, he addressed the ragged herders like a captain at Agincourt.

'We're avoiding Pontefract. It's rumoured that men in array are gathering at that place in support of Lancaster and are intent on mischief.'

He proceeded to assign each man his position and duties, after which he added, 'Some o' yond,' he indicated the pens, 'have not been ringed and will be wanting to root, so keep them as is not ringed int' middle of t' herd.' Pointing his staff at Edmund 'Ah thar ready, young Hawksworth?' Edmund nodded and began to move off towards the pig pens. Scargill called after him, 'We're crossing the Aire at Castleford.'

Without turning his head, Edmund acknowledged that by holding aloft his staff.

John found much amusement in watching and listening to the drovers as they peered eagerly after his brother. For those simple men were about to witness what they considered to be a miracle take place before their very eyes. They would never know his brother's secret. Edmund moved from pen to pen as if searching for a particular animal. Eventually, he settled upon a gigantic sow, the matriarch of the herd, and began talking to it. Suddenly, the huge animal sat on its haunches and looked up at him, its head tilted to one side. Edmund held out the palms of his hands in front of the pig's snout. The sow immediately nuzzled his hands and snorted as if understanding every word. Suddenly she began to jerk her head up and down, for all the world as if she was nodding.

'He's bloody-well talking to it!' gasped one of the drovers, a novice in herding.

'Arr, he is, an what's more that old sow is talking back to 'im!' replied Smudger shaking his head. 'Yond lad is bewitched.'

Another man, the drover's cook, added, 'That's reight, nar that he's told yond snorter what he wants her to do, we'll be moving off.' The cook, a bandy-legged character named John Brigge from Crofton, winked and nodded his head 'I've seen him do it afore.'

Edmund turned to where his brother was standing beside the other drovers and held up his staff.

'Open the pens!' John yelled as he moved off to join Edmund.

The men scurried to take up the positions allocated to them by the reeve, and the annual hog-drive for 1460 got under way. A small two-wheeled handcart loaded with a cooking-pot, kindling, food and other items, including Edmund's crossbow, was pulled along by two of the men. Edmund walked off towards the old Roman road heading south to

Castleford and the sow trotted along behind him like a lap dog, snorting and grunting. The sow's daughters, granddaughters and geldings dutifully joined in the procession and, in no time at all, the entire herd was on the move south.

After about an hour, Edmund called a halt and the herd, following the example of its grand matriarch, stopped. At once the hogs began investigating the scrubland at either side of the ancient causeway. Some of the herders anticipated difficulty in getting the pigs moving once more in the right direction after the rest period. And sure enough the majority of the animals, not having been ringed, were ripping up the ground. However, when Edmund decided it was time to move on, the pigs obediently stopped rooting and trotted off behind the grandmother sow and other leading sisters. Turnip dumps had been left at strategic points along the way to ensure the animals did not lose too much weight during the drive. So far the journey progressed smoothly and uneventfully. The weather remained mild and the weak sun of autumn smiled upon them.

'Listen! What, by all the saints, is that?' gasped Scargill to Smudger.

The two of them were taking their turn in the most unpopular position of any hog-drive – bringing up the rear. The tail-end of the herd had just cleared some woodland where autumn-dressed trees crowded in tight on either side, obscuring from view the road behind. Growing ever louder was the unmistakable thundering of horses' hoofs slamming on compacted earth.

'Look out!' Scargill yelled, pushing Smudger aside.

Forty mounted bowmen at full gallop and wielding eight-foot lances forced a way through the herd, scattering the terrified squealing pigs and their minders in all directions. Yelling at the tops of their voices the riders stabbed at panicked targets, before thundering on without change of gait, disappearing from view down a dip in the road. Howls of laughter were heard over the drumming hooves.

It took all Edmund's skills to settle the animals down once they had been re-gathered and to re-organise them so that the journey could continue.

'The Dacre household,' growled Scargill, having identified them from the distinctive badge worn by the riders 'Lord Dacre of Gilisland. I'll be glad when this drive is over.'

'Just high spirits and they're gone – what harm can they do us?' asked Smudger 'We're working for the great Duke of York himself Who would dare interfere with us?'

'Too many armed bands on the road for my liking,' complained Scargill. 'Ever since t' French wars ended highways are dangerous places,' he said. 'Why are armed men gathering at Pomfret Castle? For what purpose? Tell me that. Why are Dacre's men this far south? Pontefract-bound, that's where they're headed.' Scargill was sweating profusely and his brash, bullying tone had all but disappeared.

'Hawksworth!' Scargill shouted. 'Can thar ger us to Castleford afore nightfall?' Concern was carved on his pock-marked face and the edge to his voice unmistakable. 'And can we continue moving during darkness?'

Edmund whispered his answer and John spoke up. 'We will be at the Aire by dusk, but shall have to stop and wait for first light on the morrow. They will not move at night.'

'Can't you tell the damned swine to do as they're told?' snapped the reeve.

Edmund merely shrugged his shoulders and trotted back to his place at the front of the herd. Then they were moving again, but not for long, for light was fading fast.

Things were not right at the Aire. From their vantage point the drovers could see carts were blocking the bridge. Scargill grabbed Edmund by the arm. 'Come on, you two!' he rasped, and headed towards the bridge where a group of townsmen were waiting.

'You can't bring your pigs through here!' called out one of the group. He was an officious-looking fellow, proudly wearing a chain of office. Obviously a newly-elected constable of Castleford. 'You're not to cross here,' he repeated.

'And why not?' said Scargill, defiantly standing before the seven citizens of Castleford. 'We've crossed here afore and paid pontage with some o' t' beasts,' he said. 'What's so different now?'

'Bridge is in repair and unsafe,' answered another, with some haste.

'Then we'll pass them over a dozen at a time,' replied Scargill indicating that he had allayed their fears for the safety of the bridge.

'You're not to cross here, and that's an end to the matter,' said the constable.

In a voice resigned yet relieved and with a shake of his head, Scargill persisted. 'How many pigs do you want? Ten is as many as I'm prepared t' part with at this crossing.'

Ignoring the generous bribe, one wearing the badge of town bailiff stepped forward and shoved his face inches away from the reeve.

'You can use Ferrybridge crossing, three miles down river, but you're not passing over here, and that's the final.'

Scargill stepped backwards, cursed, and turned on his heel. He strode towards the herd, which was on the north side of a rise in the ground and hidden from the men at the bridge.

Somewhere a church bell sounded Compline. It was quite dark and the herders were soon crouched around a camp fire with a pot of stew heating up over spluttering and crackling logs. There was an uneasy quiet among them.

Once all had eaten from the pot, the suggestions as to what should be done began. Some, less endowed with wit, were for rolling the carts into the Aire and forcing a crossing at first light. Still others, for crossing at Ferrybridge. Scargill continued, 'Why deny us the bridge? There has to be a reason' he said, shaking his head. 'I don't like it. Something is wrong.'

'What could be wrong?' offered Smudger 'Who is owner of this herd?' Then answering his own question, 'Sir Thomas Harrington of Brierley is our master and his master is Duke Richard, cousin and Protector of the King of England, Henry VI. We're on King's business!' His tone was bright and reassuring.

The reeve swivelled on his haunches to look at Smudger. 'And what's the state of affairs between Henry's Queen and Duke Richard?' asked Scargill. 'They loathe each other! This herd is to provision both Yorkist properties at Wakefield and Conisbrough. These hogs could as well fill the bellies of Margaret's supporters.' He returned to his main gripe 'For what reason are we being denied?'

Bandy-legged Brigge from Crofton interrupted 'Smudger is reight. Them as belong to Lancaster might not look kindly on ar' labours, but we're well favoured.' The man looked around for support and some nodded and muttered in agreement.

Suddenly, the reeve turned to Edmund 'Well, enchanter of beasts, what think you?'

'Yond could make 'em fly just like crows reight over t' river!' called out one flapping his arms in the air and snorting.

'It's a good thing that t' Almighty didn't give hogs wings – just think of their droppings!' added Brigge, as he pretended to duck and dodge things falling from above.

The mood of the group brightened.

'Yer,' laughed Smudger, 'lad could get 'em to fly over Castleford and empty their insides on them as denied us the crossing.'

This brought howls of laughter and each one began contributing his own particular piece to the flying pig wit.

Edmund smiled at their banter and whispered to John at some length. When what passed for humour among them subsided, John addressed the reeve. 'Edmund considers your unease likely well-founded.'

There was silence as John proceeded to convey his brother's estimation of the situation.

'Lancers of Dacre would have had a hand in rousing the citizens of Castleford against our passage. Crossing the Aire at Ferrybridge will take us too close to the walls of Pomfret Castle. There is no advantage for us in this. Should the knights of Lancaster be considering mischief against York, then our charges will be considered fair game. We should avoid Pontefract at all costs. We should send a runner to Sir John Savile at Sandal Castle informing him,' said John.

It wasn't what the majority wished to hear, although Scargill appeared relieved and nodded at Edmund.

'My brother suggests that we head towards the west and the crossing at Ledes and the swinegate bridge. Should an opportunity arise along the way to ferry the Aire, then we can take it. Two men could take the handcart back to the last dump and load up with turnips.'

'What tomfoolery is this?' cried Smudger. 'Driving at Ledes, collecting turnips!'

This was greeted by hoots of agreement from the others.

'And how long would all this take?' asked Smudger. 'And what about when we drive across a lord's manor and woodland,' – it suddenly occurred to him – 'without pannage?' He looked around the group for approval.

Scargill spun on him. 'Then we'll tell 'em we're on the Duke o' York's business and that Sir Thomas Harrington of Brierley will take up the matter!' Having used Smudger's own reasonings to support his point the reeve was well pleased. 'As for the matter of pannage, when t' beasts feed in any woods belonging to a lord, then the masters can sort it out between 'em.'

'And how many extra days will this trip to Ledes take?' asked Smudger, his voice edged with annoyance. All eyes turned to Edmund, who had been honing his knife. He held up three fingers. This was greeted with howls of derision from the drovers.

'Three more days? I say that we take our chances crossing at Ferrybridge!' said Brigge.

The reeve asked for a show of hands should they favour that route, reminding them that it would take them past Pontefract and the strongest Lancastrian stronghold in the country should they choose it. The six drovers were not prepared to spend any more time on the drive than necessary; they would take their chances crossing at Ferrybridge.

Next day, after a repast of rabbit stew and bread, the drive got under way. In less than an hour they had reached the Great North Road and were over the Aire at Ferrybridge. Never had the drovers worked so hard.

Because of the pace the herd was strung out for upwards of half-a-mile. Edmund, with the lead elements, had brought them beyond Pontefract and within a mile of the village of Ackworth when they were overtaken by riders.

Edmund, at the point of a spear, was prodded back to join the rest of the drovers. They were the same spearmen who had scattered the herd the previous day.

The leader, capless and with premature grey hair, sat tall and proud on his snorting black destrier. He was likely in his fortieth year, with tanned skin, his chin scarred and his lower jaw out of line with his face. His hair was cut in the style of a knight on campaign. His surcoat, unlike the red ones worn by his men, was black. The scallop badge on his left shoulder was larger than the badges worn by the other riders and had been embroidered with gold thread. Here was a valued retainer in the House of Dacre of the North.

Each herder, with the point of a spear at his back, was thrust forward. In silence, the riders remained mounted, awaiting the commands of their black-clad captain. When he spoke, his speech was strained and awkward.

'Who is in charge?' he croaked.

The drovers all turned to look at Scargill. Thus identified by the others, the reeve was prodded forward. Scargill's face was as white as swan down and he was trembling. Again the strange tortured voice of the captain spoke out.

'For where are your hogs intended?'

Scargill sank to his knees and began to mutter a reply of sorts, which was barely audible.

Edmund suddenly crossed to where John was standing. Yells of 'Stand fast!' from the mounted rider guarding him were ignored. He began whispering with some urgency. Not for the first time was John impressed by his brother's quick wit. He would have to convey Edmund's words and stepped forward with his arm around his brother's shoulders. Bowing low, he addressed the fearsome knight. 'We are swineherders from the manor of Thryberg, my liege. Our master is William Reresby, a respected man of God and parson at St Leonard's.'

The scarred warrior had obviously never heard of the Reresby family. Telling the truth and successfully misleading this Lancastrian captain suddenly seemed a real possibility and Edmund whispered again. John called out, 'Could I ask if you have news of our father my lord?' then hurried on 'His name is John Hawksworth – he and our master Arnold Reresby ride with the Flower of Craven.'

At the mention of the Clifford family's retainers brought a chorus of good-natured howls and hoots from the riders. There was more laughter as one called out, 'They ride side-saddle with the pretty flowers, the "Primroses" – the Craven, do they?'

Edmund squeezed his brother's arm. Immediately John understood and, half-turning to the semi-circle of riders, he smiled and loudly offered the information that one day he and his brother hoped to ride with the Flower of Craven. That was greeted with more good-natured cat-calls.

Their captain might have been smiling, but it was difficult to tell. He placed his lance in the saddle frog, which was a signal for the others to put up their weapons.

'You would be best advised to ride with the House of Dacre rather than with our good friends from Skipton,' he muttered with difficulty as he kicked his mount on, jerking the fiery beast's head round, and began heading back towards Pontefract.

The riders wheeled about and began to move off. The boys helped the reeve to his feet. He looked at them both with such an expression of relief and gratitude that it caused John to feel a pleasing glow. Then it happened. As the spearmen turned, one of them asked Smudger where Thryberg was. When he told them that it was near Doncaster they at once halted their mounts.

'This is not the road to Doncaster. You are moving away from the Great North Road,' one of the riders pointed out.

'Why were you seeking to cross the Aire at Castleford?' asked another.

A couple of the riders dismounted and took Smudger a short distance away where a deep conversation ensued. The mood of Dacre's riders underwent a dramatic change.

Crack! John's ears rang as he was struck on the back, sending him spinning into Scargill, who in turn yelled out in pain from a stunning blow across his head. John called a warning to Edmund, but it was too late for his brother to parry the swipe from a mace which knocked him off his feet. The three of them were pressed face-down into the dank earth by boots on the backs of their necks.

Ropes were produced from saddle satchels and all three were hauled to their feet. Arms were secured behind them and a noose passed over each of their heads. A group of crack willows close by was indicated and they were prodded towards them. The fearsome Dacre captain, in painful voice, addressed them and the other drovers.

'Your deceit is manifest! You are driving these hogs to Wakefield and Conisbrough, where they will grace the tables of that foul traitor, Richard of York. He who doth seek the throne.'

He croaked on 'You are guilty of giving succour to those engaged in treasonous acts and shall die. You two whelps are ones who maketh a lie and as such will be cast out of God's kingdom, along with witches, whoremongers and idolaters.'

'*Suspendatur!* Now rot in Hell!' he yelled.

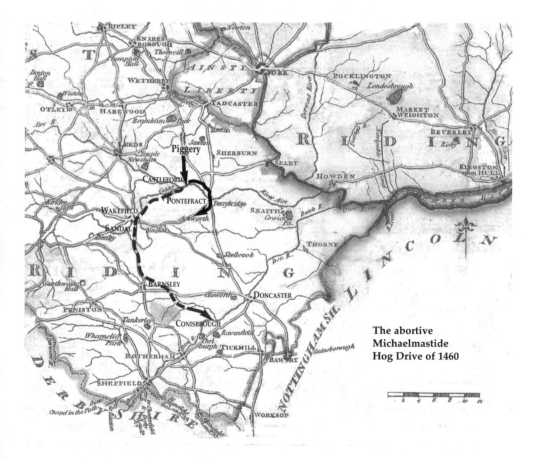

The abortive
Michaelmastide
Hog Drive of 1460

As he was speaking, three ropes were thrown over a branch. With a new-found bravery, born of the inevitability of his death, Scargill cried, 'They were not lying! You will be guilty of innocent blood if you harm them. Every word they spoke was true. The foolish children were duped; they knew nothing.'

The reeve was doing all he could to save the brothers as he was being prepared for hanging. 'They were hired because of their skills at handling swine. Their father does ride with Lord Clifford!'

The black-clad examiner and tormentor looked over to where Smudger and the others were. The herders were being made to watch the proceedings as a lesson. The herder from Warmsworth, nodded his head.

John could only wonder: William Smythe, Smudger, had surely not worked very hard to save the reeve. Nor, for that matter, the herd, from falling into the hands of the rival party of his masters. Where did his sympathies lie, with Lancaster or York? Maybe he was concerned with the saving of his own skin. These were times when treachery abounded and a man's hand raised up against father and brother.

'Loose them. They can help drive this herd to Pontefract. Hang the traitor!' called out the captain, who proudly strutted under a well-earned nick-name given him by his men – 'The Snuffer'.

They headed back the way they had come, herding the pigs towards the township of Pontefract and a thousand Lancastrian bellies. Behind, a single figure hung suspended by the neck. But for him, there would have been three drovers choking slowly side by side. John prayed that the Lord would accept the reeve straight into Paradise, having earned remission for his sins by saving their lives. Edmund, however, was busy memorising the appearance of each of those riders of Dacre, especially the one called, The Snuffer. He would seek a way of making him pay for murdering the reeve, if he could.

*   *   *   *

That terrible hog-drive of Michaelmas 1460 was over and the drovers had lost the herd. It was the evening of St Wilfred's Day, 12th October, when at last John and Edmund arrived back at Thryberg Manor in the middle of a hue-and-cry. Eleanor, the bastard, had disappeared. She had last been seen shortly after dawn that day, when she had fallen foul, yet again, of the housekeeper, Ann Thicket.

Eleanor had many chores to perform in and around the Reresby house. One of her tasks was to search out and gather hens' eggs from all the secret places that domestic fowl find to deposit their treasures. The under-sized seven-year old had collected above a dozen in a wicker basket. As she had entered the Great Hall one of the dogs, with a great deal of puppy-play still in him, bounded up and sent her tumbling. When Ann Thicket came hurrying out of the kitchen in response to the youngster's scream, she beheld Eleanor covered in egg yolk and broken shells from head to toe. The sight of the wasted precious food served to infuriate the housekeeper, who immediately set about the child with a wooden ladle.

A lashing, both physical and verbal, was the little girl's lot in life and she had come to expect nothing better. She observed kindness being shown to others, even to domestic animals, but she was far too wicked for that. Her mother's name had not to be mentioned in the household, because, of course, she too had been very very wicked. She knew that her mother had been called Mary and that she was fifteen-years-old when she had given birth to her, but she knew precious little else. God had punished her mother by sending her to the grave to await Judgement Day. Eleanor was very much alone in the world; her only friends were the household dogs and farm animals. Now she seemed to have vanished from the face of the earth.

The master, Parson William Reresby, had ordered an all-out search after Eleanor had failed to appear at mid-day. The cleric was conscientiously carrying out his duty to 'look after widows and orphans in their tribulation,' according to the holy scriptures, at least, in his own mind. In reality, he held to the hope that she would never appear again at the Manor House. The sin of his youngest brother, Arnold, would then fade from the minds of his congregation. He had sought to punish his brother for taking advantage of the fifteen-year-old orphan girl, Mary Wrend; a number of pilgrimages had been prescribed to help purge the young man of his sin. Arnold had set out on the first of many holy journeys which his brother had decreed that he should make. To Canterbury he dutifully travelled to pay homage at the shrine of Thomas-à-Becket. However, as far as the household servants could see, that was enough – no more penitent sinner guise for him. He had confessed to the warrener, whilst worse for drink and full of chatter, that in his travelling he had come to the conclusion that he was not sorry at all for what he had done. He further boasted, was not every other young blood seeking to bed a wench – and as often as circumstances and good fortune would allow? Thus firmly convinced, he had taken off to seek his fortune among the retainers of the Clifford household at Skipton.

As for William Reresby, he secretly considered that while ever the tiresome little brat existed she served as a thorn in the flesh to each one of the Reresby family. But now she was missing and the Christian thing to do was to attempt to find her, preferably before darkness fell.

The Manor House and all the adjacent buildings had been thoroughly searched. The hunt had been widened to the woods and deer-park. Every croft, cowshed and sty in the village of Thryberg had been explored. Possibilities were being bandied about by the searchers as to what may have happened to the girl. Even kidnapping by gypsies or outlawed Jews was discussed, along with the likelihood of her having fallen into the River Don.

Ann Thicket was explaining for the hundredth time to some from nearby Dalton, who had just arrived to join in the search, how she had justly chastised the child for clumsiness. John approached the house steward in trepidation, for she had a cutting tongue and little time for those whom she considered her inferiors. She was very thin, with skin resembling parchment, and had very few front teeth, and those she had protruded in various directions. The epitome of efficiency and good housekeeping, Ann Thicket had taken over the role of steward upon the disappearance of her husband. He had, all assumed, operated with great proficiency and skill for a number of years. However, it had become apparent to the Reresby family who really had been organising the smooth running of their domestic affairs. They were pleased to allow her to continue.

'Mistress Thicket,' John ventured, 'please pardon my interruption, but we wondered what was said to the child?' He nodded in the direction of Edmund.

'Oh indeed; do you wonder?'

With a great show of impatience, she placed her hands on her hips and repeated her account of the events. Edmund shook his head and whispered again to his brother.

'Edmund would like to know the exact words used,' said John. 'He says to take your time and to think hard.'

'Oh, does he indeed?' She was clearly furious at being questioned by mere boys. 'I've better things to do than tittle-tattling with the likes of you.'

'Why not tell the boys what they want to know?' volunteered the cook, John Clay, who had just come in from searching lanes leading to the next village, Hooton Roberts. 'They know every corner of this manor better than most.' There was a logic in that statement. Thicket, practical-minded as she was, could not deny it. With a deep sigh, she made an effort to recall her very words.

'I told her the truth of the matter!' She began slowly and then paused, for she was about to try and justify her harsh words to the child. 'I told her...' She was beginning to feel uncomfortable and biting her bottom lip hastened, 'As everyone knows, that child is thoroughly wicked and will come to no good, just like her mother. She needed to be told.'

John nodded in encouragement as the house steward continued. 'I said "If she didn't mend her ways she would end up with her mother!"' At that point she jabbed a finger in the direction of the adjacent graveyard. 'Heaven knows, and God is my judge, we have all tried to make something of that brat – but to no avail. I told her that she'd be better off with her wicked mother!'

Edmund moved quickly. Running to the fireplace on the north wall of the Great Hall, where bedding was drying before a roaring coal and log fire, he grabbed an eiderdown cover and ran to the south door. As was the way, the door was bolted. It was the door that was used only on Sundays and feast days for the household's procession to the adjacent church. It was the tradition of the Reresby that family members so journeyed, to and fro, until such a time as they would pass eventually through the south door of the house, enter the north door of St Leonard's Church and finally through the south door to their eternal rest in that part of the graveyard. Carved pious recumbent figures of the ancestors of the family adorned the tomb chests on the south side: Radulph de Normanville, Adam, Radulph and Thomas de Reresby, with their hands clasped in prayer. All usual entry to the church was by way of its north door via the path through the commoners' burial ground.

Slamming back the bolts and swinging the bar, Edmund flung open the south door of the Great Hall and dashed out into the night. In a matter of minutes he returned, carrying a bundle wrapped in the eiderdown.

Hurrying to the fireplace, he gently lowered himself with his burden. All gathered around, members of the family, servants and those who had been involved in the search. Edmund was cradling little Eleanor, who was caked in mud and clay. Her large brown eyes darted fearfully from one face to another. She sensed that she had done something terribly wrong and was preparing herself for some awful punishment, as befits the 'very wicked'.

Calling in a hoarse whisper for a bowl of hot water and taking a cloth proffered by one of the servant women, Edmund began to wipe the girl's face in a tender and gentle manner, all the while rocking her as if she were a baby. Everybody looked on as if mesmerised, no one uttering a word. Then there was a gasp as Edmund stopped his rocking and gently lifted up one of her hands. It was bloodied, the nails torn and broken. Eleanor, never for a moment, winced as he worked on each of her tiny fingers, cleaning first one hand and then the other, dressing them in silken cloth. There had been no protest when Edmund had reached for an under-garment drying by the fire and tore it into strips.

A change came over Eleanor; the expression of fear had begun to leave her eyes. She gazed unblinking at Edmund's face, as if drinking in his every feature.

'Are you 'Love'? she asked quietly.

He smiled and nodded, brushing back strands of hair from her face. Then leaning close so that his cheek brushed hers he whispered 'Eleanor, would you like something to eat?'

At that point the mite's bottom lip began to quiver, in the manner of a tiny baby. A heart-rending cry ripped from her, the like of which John had never heard afore. Crying, as far as Eleanor was concerned, was always to be avoided; she had learned a long time ago that her tears always brought further distress and, more often than not, punishment. But, in the loving arms of this boy swineherd, she was safe and perhaps no one could harm her ever again, now that she was in the arms of 'Love'. Her tears flowed as she sobbed uncontrollably.

Like the rest, John could only look on fascinated; it was as though his brother was a stranger. Nor was he prepared for what Edmund did next. Gently drying her eyes, with no hint of a stutter, he began singing to Eleanor in a most engaging voice, the like of which John never suspected he had:

Rocking, rocking, rock-a-bye,
The birds have gone to ground.
The stars are climbing in the sky,
The saints are gathered round.
Hush, hush, hush-a-bye,
The cattle they're asleeping.
The moon is smiling from on high,
My baby's in safe keeping.

It was the song their mother used to sing. The last time John had heard it was on the one and only occasion Edmund failed to bring home meat for the pot. She had cradled and sung him to sleep.

There was embarrassment, for his brother was shaming them all. Certainly, the womenfolk of the household should have shown the child more care but instead, for years, they had made her the butt of their ill-humour. An attempt by Ann Thicket to take over from Edmund was stopped by a single word. Glancing up at her, his grey eyes flashing for a second in anger, he rasped out: 'Scold!'

In tears, she fled the Great Hall. She stood accused for the oppression of Eleanor. As such she could receive trial and punishment through the leet court.

From that day forward Eleanor's life underwent change. Although the Reresby family continued to distance themselves from her, the hard attitude of the household servants mellowed. The undersized runt was never truly happy unless Edmund was around. Each Saturday, as the brothers made their way to the Manor House from their croft in the quarry, Eleanor would race across the fields to greet them. She would squeal with delight as Edmund caught her up and swung her around. 'Make me a bell!' she would call. The two brothers would swing her back and forth between them as they walked along. Edmund's every move was copied by her and she even took to whispering. On Sunday eve she would escort them part-way back and wave until they had gone from sight beyond the fishponds. The women servants allowed her time to play and no longer banned her from mixing with other children.

It was around that time that John noticed some in the Reresby household seemed unnerved at the very presence of his brother. Despite he and Edmund carrying out the lowliest jobs at the manor, the servants appeared to be at a loss as how his brother should be addressed and would speak via him whenever they wished to talk to Edmund.

Immediately following St Wilfred's, Ann Thicket did all she could to avoid Edmund. However, the following week he sought out the house steward and respectfully asked her permission to allow Eleanor to accompany them to Rotherham on an errand. That request brought about a favourable change in Ann Thicket. Edmund was giving back her authority, dignity and along with it her self-respect. She was much relieved that she no longer need fear a presentment to the bi-annual Court Leet to suffer judgement as a common scold. When asked why he had done that to the 'Shrivelled Shrew', as some were wont to call her behind her back, Edmund shrugged and whispered aloud, 'There is no advantage in having her resentful, John, in that there is no gain.' John could only shake his head bewildered.

As for Parson William Reresby, he had a huge stone placed over the partially excavated grave of Mary Wrend.

*　　　*　　　*　　　*

SILENCE REMAINED on the gathered throng in the upper room of the castle keep, as John completed that part of his account of the doings of The Hawk. The scribes were writing furiously and kept having to ask those who were acting as prompters for the details missed.

The auburn-haired little girl who had insisted on the story of Eleanor and the broken eggs tugged at John's sleeve 'How could Edmund Love know where Eleanor was? Did the dogs tell him?'

'My brother could no more talk to animals than you or I.'

'But... but... the pigs...? What about the great mother sow?' Her protests were heart-felt.

'Edmund had a trick for moving pigs about. He used a truffle with which he enticed the grandmother of the herd. Sows love the smell of the truffle and will follow it anywhere.

'When he wanted the herd to stop and rest for a while he would hide the truffle, which he kept in a muslin purse, among a small bag of onions. Pigs dislike the smell of onions. With the scent thus masked and lost, the sows would stop and begin rooting. When he wanted to renew the drive, he would pull out the truffle and the sows would follow once more.'

Clearly, the child was disappointed and yet another myth surrounding his brother had been explained away.

John concluded that part of the tale by mentioning that it had been news of the stolen herd conveyed to the Duke of York in London, which prompted the Duke to travel north with a small army. Hence his arrival at Sandal Castle, Wakefield, and the battle in which he was slain on the 30th December, 1460.

Lady Lucy Fitzwilliam, in a quiet voice as though remembering, said, 'I am familiar with what occurred next,' she said. 'The Abbot of Roche travelled the manors telling of what had befallen the nobles of the House of York, and warning of northerners who would soon descend upon us.'

Turning to John, she said, 'That is when your brother, The Hawk, declared himself to be the Avenger of Righteous Blood and was accepted as such by God.'

Turning to the scribes John saw at a glance their readiness to continue. Each was making hurried adjustments to his scrolls; fresh quills were prepared and tested.

John decided to continue his brother's story with the account of what happened next; the arrival at Reresby Manor House of the mysterious, miserable-faced stranger, a Benedictine from Monk Bretton Priory, near the settlement of Barnsley. A spy most certainly, but was he for Lancaster or York?

Chapter Three

A Swan Argent Ducaly Gorged and Chained

SHOULDER OF MUTTON, cold, was served to the stranger at Reresby Manor House three days after he had arrived. Ann Thicket, acting on behalf of her master's interests, took it upon herself to encourage the man to move on. True, his task was over, for he had delivered a letter containing questioning over church doctrine and the master, William Reresby, had penned his observations by way of reply. However, the courier seemed in no hurry to leave, claiming that the foul weather was making passage along the roads difficult. The man was likely in his sixth decade, but appeared fit enough to make the short return journey of a dozen miles on foot to Monk Bretton Priory.

The old squire-parson was considered an authority on Canon Law, especially that part known as the Decretal, the decrees and decisions of early popes on disputed points. Apparently Richard de Ledes, Prior of St Mary Magdalene, Barnsley, had a pressing matter to settle involving some aspects of the doctrine of transubstantiation and required an authoritative ruling.

If serving of cold shoulder of mutton to the stranger at Saturday evening supper was meant to make it clear that he had outstayed his welcome, then it failed. Some of the household considered the monk thick-skinned, but, as later transpired, he had motives which delayed his departure.

Indeed, the ecclesiastical messenger, Brother Wilkin, had another agenda. It was Edmund who alerted his brother 'This monk is no mere bearer of letters. All should guard their tongues.'

Following supper the serving household gathered around the grand fireplace before a roaring coal and log fire. Their masters, Parson William, his younger brother Ralph and wife Agnes, her two lady attendants and young son, also called Ralph, had withdrawn to the chambers behind the high table. There they would gather around their own fires and play board games, the ladies to embroider, sew garments and discuss betrothals, hair styling, the latest price of Arras tapestries, menus for the next feast day festivities and similar. As for the two brothers, William and Ralph, they would continue their arguments concerning the present crisis that threatened to rip apart the fabric of all their lives. It was no secret that the parson favoured the claims and aims of the House of York. He was greatly perturbed over the recent fighting at Wakefield, the slaying of the Duke of York and his lords and the sacking of Sandal Castle. On the other hand, Ralph favoured the ruling Lancastrian party. He had not forgiven his elder brother for allowing the Abbot of Roche to deliver that blistering sermon of condemnation on Epiphany Sunday.

In the harsh months of 1461 the threat of an ever-expanding conflict hung heavy, much like winter storm-clouds over every household. In villages and town throughout the Riding tensions were beginning to crystallise into clearly-marked divisions. Time when words alone signalled men's loyalties was at an end. Actions, which necessitated the taking up of arms at the direction of some lord, became the pressing requirement of the hour. Commissioners of Array were hard at work and armies were growing. Blacksmiths were kept busy at their anvils beating plowshares and sickles into bills and glaives.

At the time the Reresby family members took their leave of the high table and withdrew for evening pastimes, those of lesser degree in the house began to assemble.

Encamped around the huge fireplace in the Grand Hall were all the servants, apart from two maids of the chambers who were seeing to the needs of the Reresbys. In a semi-circle around the hearth, clothes-horses covered in drapes formed a perimeter wall to keep out the wintry draughts. Ann Thicket, as steward, had the one and only chair and the rest were on benches and stools. Truly a favourite time for all fifteen or so incumbent members of the household – the Saturday winter's evening gathering. Those were the treasured occasions when the week's events, village gossip and tales of daring-do were exchanged. It usually followed a pattern: first one and then another would regale all with an anecdote, or an account of a current happening. Eventually, a number of conversations would develop and be carried on simultaneously. The general chatter would be brought to an end when someone produced a pipe, bagpipes or shawm. Songs and ballads were sung by the few with gifted voices, the *hay downe, ho downe, derrie derrie downes*, being chorused by the rest. Ample supplies of bread were toasted and spread with blackberry preserve and cheese. Fresh ale was drunk and, on special occasions, Ann Thicket would permit all to imbibe from an extra-large goblet of wine.

On the eve of the feast of the Conversion of St Paul, Saturday, 24th January, 1461, Edmund and John completed their duties later than usual. Whenever at the manor they worked as scullions; one of their jobs was to clear all left-overs from the kitchen. They would fill three or four large buckets and take them to an out-building. From there they would cart the pig food to the quarry on Monday mornings. During winter months they had but four pigs to care for, so the work was not excessive. However, on this night pork shreds had been accidentally tipped into the waste barrel and they had spent more time than usual sorting it out. The master had decreed that pigs were not to be fed their own flesh.

As always Eleanor ran to greet the boys, and taking Edmund's hand, led them to a position close by the fire. There were no objections, for Edmund was beginning to be viewed as somehow 'different'. He was attracting respect though no one quite understood why. Invariably, words intended for him were addressed to John. However, on the occasions when Edmund was spoken to directly his brother detected a change in the person's voice. The household was both intrigued by him and discomforted at the same time. Even John was becoming increasingly mystified by his brother's odd behaviour.

Wilkin, a medium-girthed individual with doleful eyes and matching mournful countenance, had paused in his diatribe, interrupted by the arrival of the Hawksworth boys. He barely concealed his irritation. The mood of those gathered was not the usual one for a wintry Saturday evening, and it was evident that the subject under discussion was a sombre one.

The warrener, Hugh Grene, took the disruption as an opportunity to interject a comment 'That's all well and good, but will it make one 'apeth of difference to the likes of us who rules England?' His question was directed at Wilkin, who was buttering himself a slab of toasted bread.

The guest, who was overstaying his welcome at Thryberg manor with some gusto, sucked his thumb clean of butter and countered, 'The fact is unavoidable: Henry is our sovereign king, and as such is entitled to our fealty.' Thus saying, he bit a large piece out of the bread and carried on with his mouth amply loaded. 'And, his son, Prince Edward, by divine right of succession, should... well, when the time comes, should succeed him.'

'And what matter then of King Henry's competence to rule?' asked the bailiff and sergeant-at-arms, William Whelpdale, as he placed a log on the fire. 'He has not the wit to choose an able counseller at his court, nor a skilled commander for his army.'

'That's true,' agreed the warrener 'All that his father, Henry V, gained by a sword's edge and point, this man has lost to England,' he said with a tone of resignation.

A voice spoke up in defence of King Henry.

'He is a holy man and better suited to deliberations of a spiritual nature, rather than vulgar conflict,' said the manor clerk, Brother Bellard. 'His kingship is from God. Those who would take a stand against him, take a stand against God himself. Look at what occurred at Sandal, Wakefield just four weeks past at Christmastide; the claimant to the throne was defeated in battle and now his head decorates York Castle. Verily, I consider that the Almighty has spoken on this matter.'

'The king was in London. It was the earls of Northumberland, Wiltshire, along with Lords Roos and Dacre, John Lord Neville and the man they are now calling "The Butcher" John, Lord Clifford.' said John Clay 'The matter was in the hands of those pillars of Lancaster who have been plundering the property of the Duke of York.' The cook's voice had begun to rise. 'King Henry has done nothing to control the excesses of his supporters.'

The parker put in, 'And when Henry is united once more with his wife then a woman rules England. Is that what you call divine will?' The question was directed at no one in particular.

'By St George! A warrior king is what England needs on the throne, not a saintly man of God.' said Whelpdale. 'After years of conflict and much spilling of English blood – what value now the victory at Agincourt?' He stood and addressed the gathering, 'What French lands are we left with?'

More than one voice chorused a single word, 'Calais'.

'Calais, by the saints; a toehold in France and how long before that French queen sells us out to her countrymen, and the once mighty boot of England is kicked off into the Channel?' Whelpdale challenged loudly.

It was no usual Saturday evening gathering. Ann Thicket was visibly perturbed by the subject, the passions it was arousing and the divisions that seemed to be occurring. She tried to interrupt but was ignored by the men who were determined to air pressing matters close to their hearts. There occurred a lull, then the stranger offered a further argument that caused Edmund to squeeze John's arm.

'What then of loyalty to your masters? Does this house favour the red rose of Lancaster, or the falcon and fetterlock of York?' Whelpdale made as if to answer and was stopped by Ann Thicket tipping ale into his lap. She fixed him with a withering look which said, 'you are going too far'. However, the warrener, oblivious to the impropriety of the question, offered in answer, 'And there if you like is a pretty pot for us all to drink, as our priest favours York and his brother, Lancaster.'

'Aye, and the youngest Reresby, Arnold, rides with Butcher Clifford's finest, The Flower of Craven,' volunteered another.

Suddenly, Ann Thicket was on her feet and sweeping through the draught barriers and heading towards the withdrawing chambers. The wild gossiping had to stop.

'Now you've done it,' said Whelpdale, shaking his head. 'You've gone too far. She'll have you all thrown out.' By his words he sought to distance himself from those comments concerning the masters. He, as bailiff, would be the one called upon to take any action demanded by the Reresby brothers.

The steward's dramatic departure had caused silence to descend on the gathering. All eyes turned towards the withdrawing chamber door as it opened to admit, not Ann Thicket, but a servant of the chambers.

'What, in the name of all the saints, is going on?' asked Charon the chambermaid upon reaching the gathering.

'They are entertaining opinions and expressing comments they have no right nor business to,' said Whelpdale.

That brought a chorus of objections from the gathered men who began pointing out the bailiff's own part in the debating. Charon seated herself by Edmund and, taking a hair brush, began busying herself on Eleanor's hair. 'What is it that you have been saying? Mistress Thicket is demanding to see the parson and she ordered me to stop my duties and leave.'

Brother Bellard offered an explanation, 'We were merely saying how difficult it is for us all to decide the rights and wrongs of the conflict between the Houses of Lancaster and York, for both are clearly traced from Edward III.' His voice carried the tone of bewildered innocence. 'After all, it is of no little consequence to us as we may be called upon to bear arms...' He trailed off.

'Lives, fortunes and expectations are being determined throughout the land,' added John Clay, nodding his head.

'Well, here's a tale of warning for you all,' said Wilkin 'It was the leading lights of Barnsley who chose the wrong side at Advent time. It cost them dear. They were foolish enough to arrest two agents of Lord Percy of Northumberland. The provisioners turned up at Barnsley before Christmastide just past and, would you believe, hands were laid upon them and they were hauled off to Sandal Castle. They languished in the dungeon until freed following the defeat and death of the Duke of York.'

He wagged his finger as if in warning. 'Upon their release they rode on Barnsley attended by mounted archers. The town narrowly averted sacking by paying a ransom. St Mary's church was stripped in order to pay the Lancastrian fine of forty marks.'

Then he took a metal badge from the folds of his garment and held it aloft. It was the size of the palm of his hand. 'Do any of you recognise this device?' He hurried on, 'A swan argent ducaly gorged and chained... the badge chosen by the queen for her seven-year-old son, Edward Prince of Wales.'

All craned their necks to view the white enamel swan with a golden crown around its neck secured by a golden chain. The whole badge dangled from a chain of silver.

'The queen grants these favours on knights, lords and nobles who would support her cause: the freeing of King Henry and the succession of her son as the future king.'

'You are indeed for Lancaster,' observed the parker.

'Did I say that it was at the hand of Queen Margaret that I came into possession of this pretty trinket?' He swept the faces with a knowing look and a wink.

'Then you support the House of York and subscribe to the Act of Accord,' snapped the warrener.

'I don't recall saying that either,' replied Wilkin.

'You make jest with us, on matters demanding sobriety,' grumbled Brother Bellard.

Wilkin turned to the monk and addressed him with all seriousness. 'Brother, what do the holy scriptures say on this matter?'

Bellard was taken off guard and shrugged his shoulders. Plainly with the advantage, Wilkin continued, 'Saint Peter in his second epistle wrote, "Honour ye all men. Dread ye God. Servants, be ye subjects in all dread to lords, not only to the good and mild, but also to tyrants. Honour ye the King!"'

The gathering fell silent, for this authoritative quote seemed to scribe a line under the debating. Neither Ann Thicket, nor any of the masters, had as yet made an appearance.

It was the parker who lamely offered a comment, repeating what had already been said 'But when the king is weak in the head and competing lords battle for control of the kingdom, what are we to think?' His voice trailed off.

Suddenly, John Clay called across to where Edmund and John were seated.

'What has Edmund to say on this matter?'

The words were addressed to John, for all the world as if his brother was a mute or simpleton.

Wilkin glared at Edmund. Was the opinion of the boy swineherd, a kitchen scullion, really being sought by this gathering? He noted that all present were taking the inquiry seriously. Yes they were, one and all, leaning forward waiting as Edmund whispered at some length in his brother's ear.

Of late, with every passing day and increasing frequency, there occurred instances where Edmund surprised him. Here was yet another such occasion. Concerned, John asked for clarification. With great patience, Edmund repeated his whispered words. John's obvious reluctance and hesitation came to an abrupt end when Eleanor suddenly jumped from Charon's knee and stood before John, hands on hips 'John, tell them Edmund Love's words, or it will fall to this maiden so to do!' The good-natured laughter this roused helped the occasion.

Clearing his throat, John began nervously '"Do men gather grapes from thorns, or figs from the briar?"' John paused as Edmund had instructed him to allow these words to sink in. Clearing his throat he continued, '"With the onset of summer season every healthy tree produces good fruits, but a sick tree produces pitiful fruitage. Therefore, by their fruits ye shall know them."'

The effect on the cook was marked. With mouth slightly open he gently shook his head, eyes narrowed and firmly fixed upon Edmund.

John continued, 'These are the words, not of Saint Peter, but those of our Lord Jesus Christ.' Bellard and Wilkin hastily crossed themselves. John carried on with growing confidence.

'As to the excesses of Lancaster, they heed not from where they draw support. As we speak thousands of armed men, invaders from Scotland, from Wales and the west country, even men from Normandy, are massing to march on London. Englishmen's homes, flocks and lives have already suffered for the ambitious queen's determination. Let all mark well, then, the fruitage of Lancaster.'

Those gathered nodded in agreement. John said, 'Edmund asks you to inquire from the swineherders, for they have suffered firsthand the merciless conduct of the northerners.'

John added his own account 'Last Michaelmastide riders of the House of Lord Dacre hanged our reeve. They beat us and stole the herd. Are thieves and murderers worthy of our allegiance? Edmund reminds us of what it says in holy writ: By their fruits then, shall they be known. And their fruitage is rotten, for it is merciless and cruel.'

The debating was brought to an end. Calls of 'Well spoken young Hawksworth' were directed at Edmund. Sensing that her hero had, somehow, won the day and, brimming with pride, Eleanor marched up to where Wilkin was sitting. Pointing at Edmund, the mite announced loudly, 'Edmund Love is the vendor of frightened blood!'

When the Reresby brothers entered the Grand Hall, accompanied by Ann Thicket, they were greeted by the sound of loud, good-natured laughter and the clapping of hands. A possible crisis apparently averted, they turned and scurried back to their own quarters. Ann Thicket headed for the buttery and her room above it with a face as black as a three-legged cauldron.

The warrener volunteered to the stranger, 'It is said that young Hawksworth underwent an anointing at St Leonard's church. They say . . . that is, some are saying, he has been selected by God to punish Lancaster.'

'As the Holy Mother is my witness, I saw the finger of God touch the boy on the forehead,' affirmed John Clay. 'And it occurred at the exact time of the lad's declaration before the altar, that he would champion the right of vengeance against the manslayers.'

Wilkin shook his head and smiled at their enthusiasm 'Come now, my good friends, abandon these stories of elves and fairies. What can a herder of pigs accomplish against lords high and mighty?'

'Who can say? David slew Goliath didn't he? All I know is he's the keenest crossbow shooter in the Riding.' The warrener looked about him for confirmation and got it. All present had a tale to tell of Edmund's prowess with the crossbow.

Suddenly, Wilkin jumped up. Turning, he addressed the gathering, 'If your pig-minder is such a fine marksman, let him show his skill this very night.'

'There is no benefit in this,' Edmund stuttered aloud.

'Benefit, is it? The boy seeks benefit,' called out Wilkin in an assumed jolly voice. 'Must we then resort to temptation to have him confirm his reputation?' So saying, he held high the silver swan badge of the Prince of Wales, along with a drinking vessel. 'If Master Hawksworth can cleave this cup, then the trinket – worth a year's wages – will be his. Let the distance be from the high table to the buttery screen. What say you to that? Or perhaps your skills are no more than fable and fancy tales for the telling by gullible folks on a winter's eve?'

'It's too dark. It would be no test of skill,' said John Clay.

Some hurried away to the kitchen for the extra-large candle stands and candles. A trestle table-top was propped up against the wooden screen and Wilkin stuck his knife into it, about five feet from the floor. He then passed the handle of the small horn mug over the knife handle. Two feet above the target mug he draped the badge chain.

'Strike the mug with a single shot and the badge is yours,' challenged the stranger.

Nervous glances were cast in the direction of the door and stairs leading to Ann Thicket's chamber. Many eyes scoured the deep shadows of the minstrel gallery above for signs of the house steward. There were urgently whispered appeals for Wilkin to keep his voice down. Ann Thicket would never have approved such liberties within the Manor House.

It was the parker who produced a crossbow and quiver of bolts. There was to be no gainsaying the gathering, for all were eager to see the shot. Never had there been a Saturday evening like it.

Edmund shrugged his shoulders, selected a quarrel and, taking up the crossbow, walked to the high table where John joined him. John squinted at the target the small horn cup hardly showed up against the table top. However, the swan badge, hanging two feet above the target, glittered and sparkled in the candlelight.

'Time has come for our visitor to take his leave,' Edmund took a step forward with his left leg and leaning slightly, raised the charged bow, aiming and stroking the trigger in one continuous movement. The strike was perfect and the swan badge was skewered to the table.

A chorused gasp went up from the watchers and all eyes turned to the stranger. Wilkin tutted once and walked slowly to the upturned table. Barely containing his anger, he attempted to remove the impaled badge. Even in the flickering candlelight his red flushed neck could be discerned. Turning to face the gathering he announced, 'The pig boy is, as you all claim, a marksman. Whether, by his shot he seeks to better me or insult the royal House of Lancaster, is not clear.' With further effort he freed the broken badge and thrust it into his robe, tossing the quarrel across the hall where it clattered against the south wall.

'Mayhap it was a missed shot,' he said.

'He does not miss his aiming point!' called the parker.

'Amen, and so be it!' The stranger strode to where his staff and bundle were by the fireplace. 'Then, good people of Thryberg Manor, I must take my leave. Sands of my welcome here have just run out.'

Charon hurried to him and, placing a hand upon his arm, urged him to wait until morning. There were sounds of agreement from the others, for most felt uncomfortable at the dramatic turn of events. The entire gathering crowded in a semi-circle around the stranger.

Taking no heed of the appeals to stay, Brother Wilkin placed his hand on the latch of the north door, whereupon he turned and his eyes roved about until he caught sight of Edmund in front of the high table. Peering through the gloom, Wilkin looked long and hard at him. He wagged a finger in Edmund's direction, clearly indicating that he intended that they would meet again. Then it was that John noticed that his brother acknowledged the stranger's gestures with a barely perceivable nod. It was as though some secret understanding passed between them. Brother Wilkin made the sign of the cross and loudly addressed them with his blessing,

'In nomine Patris, et Filii, et Spiritus Sancti.' He turned abruptly, and was swallowed up in the rain-lashed night.

*   *   *   *

THE PAUSE John introduced in recounting his brother's story gave opportunity for some in the audience to seek clarification.

'Do you suppose... that Wilkin favoured the red rose
... or mayhap 'twas York that was dear to his heart...?
Pray do tell to us all... he with queen's favour so small
and thereby that monk's secret impart.'

So trolled the richly-clad minstrel, strumming chords to match his full tenor-toned words.

'Your eagerness, good minstrel, pray hold...
For in due course all will surely unfold.'

John sang in mimicry, although with much less ability. The audience applauded with delight.

The scribe at the *tabula plicata* asked for another to take his place, whilst he caught up and expanded his own brand of abbreviated script. Exactly what manner of the written story of The Hawk would finally be produced, John could only guess. But shortly it would be no concern to him, for by the same time tomorrow he would be dead.

'How did your brother know enough of holy writ to better the learned monk?' asked one of the ladies. 'For, as you say, he had little time for the Almighty.'

'Our mother read the Bible to us every day. Despite holding a grudge against God for taking her from us, Edmund was fascinated by Bible stories. Sermons by our squire-parson were paid more heed to by Edmund than I ever realised.'

Tiptoe called out to John from the bedchamber doorway 'Thar knows who them two were who got thessens chucked in Sandal Castle dungeon? 'It wor Old Tommy and me,' he said. 'As young uns we joined with Lancaster and were sent to find provender from t' vills rarned Barnsley.'

Suddenly realising he had taken centre of attention, he stuttered on 'When we were let out of Sandal dungeon we went back to Barnsley wi' a team of Clifford's Craven and threatened ta burn 'em out if they didn't pay us a hundred silver marks. They could only raise forty, and that was stripped from St Mary's chantry.'

'And your limps?' John asked him 'Both at Towton Field?'

'We were,' he replied. 'And we were facing Fauconberg's *Wespen*. By God, them lads could shoot, but it was t' Hawk who stopped ar breakthrough.'

The old blacksmith's voice became strained as he remembered that awful day forty-eight years ago. With his lower jaw shaking, he muttered, 'The young beggar saved ar lives... he did.' His trembling voice fell to a whisper. 'There was to be no quarter, and there was butchery after Lancaster broke, but not with The Hawk, God bless, not with the Hawk.'

Tiptoe shook his head as tears filled his eyes and spilled onto his cheeks. Overcome he stared at the floor. 'Bless him.'

'That was the time my brother truly found his voice,' With all eyes upon him, John explained. 'Seeing captives were being poleaxed, Edmund tore off his surcoat, stuck it on a lance and, holding it aloft, yelled above all that hideous din, "Quarter! Quarter! Salvation with the *Wespen!*"' Applause greeted his words. John had just confirmed the oft-told tale of the Plantagent boy hero and endorsed the previously suppressed account with his seal of truth.

On Sunday morn at cock-crow, following departure the previous night of *agent provocateur*, Wilkin, two fugitives sought shelter at Thryberg Manor. Unlike the Benedictine the couple were no strangers to the family.

The King to all to whom etc, greetings. Know that our faithful lieges the community of the town of Barnesley at the time when the most noble prince our father, whom God save, started his journey northwards captured Thomas Philip and Thomas Tipton, our enemies and the enemies of our said father, and took them to our castle of Sandhill [Sandall], in which they were imprisoned as we have understood; by occasion of which imprisonment our said lieges were, after the death of our same father so threatened and vexed by the deeds and accusations of the same Thomas and Thomas that of urgent necessity, for the saving of their lives, goods and chattles, they were compelled to agree with the aforesaid Thomas and Thomas for the sum of forty marks, which they paid them out of the goods and chattels of the church of Barnesley, originally acquired for sustaining and ornamenting the church and sustaining divine service there. Now therefore in consideration and respect of the aforementioned, and future goodwill and affection of our same lieges for ourselves and our said father and in recompense and satisfaction of the goods of the said church taken away as aforesaid, of our special grace, we have granted to the same community ten marks to be received annually for the term of four years to discharge the said sum of forty marks, from the revenue of the farms, profits and reversions of our wapentake of Stayn Crosse within our honour of Pontefract, by the hand of the Bailiffs, Farmers or other occupiers of the same wapentake for The Community of Barnesley have 40 marks to be paid within four years as below: Time being, at the feasts of Easter and Michaelmas by equal portions. In of which etc, given etc, at Westminster 16th December in the first year etc by letter under signet

King Edward IV's grant of an annuity (in Latin) to Barnsley in gratitude for the town's actions in support of the Duke of York in 1460. The Lancastrian agents, Thomas Tipton and Thomas Philip are named in the document.

Chapter Four

Blooding of the Avenger and A Bride's Forfeit

RICHARD DEL WARDROP and his bride of two weeks had successfully evaded many groups of mounted archers on the Rotherham–Doncaster road. The young couple sought to reach Conisbrough Castle where the faithful Yorkist steward, Edmund Fitzwilliam, had raised the drawbridge and closed the gates against hordes of London-bound Lancastrians who were swilling through the district. The short journey from Aldwark Manor – separated from Reresby Manor by the River Don – to Conisbrough was fraught with danger. They had narrowly missed riding in among mounted bowmen at the nearby village of Hooton Roberts. That close encounter had caused the pair to veer off across muddy fields to the small settlement of Ravenfield. More shadowy figures, uttering curses in a strange dialect, were sacking the crofts. Wheeling about, they doubled back across open scrubland and, with dawn breaking, rode down from the rain-lashed hills into the Manor House courtyard. The couple were admitted to the Great Hall and temporary sanctuary as dawn's grey light began to give substance to the whitened walls of St Leonard's Church, the clustered crofts and leafless sycamores, ash and oak which dotted the village of Thryberg.

The couple's reception at the manor was mixed. Servants had aroused the masters. The old squire immediately had them ushered into the withdrawing-chamber. However, when Ralph Reresby appeared, roused from his bed and in ill temper, he did little to hide his disapproval of the young couple's presence at the house.

Wardrop was a renowned supporter of York and, as such, bound to be sought after by adherents to the red rose. He it was who had been entrusted with the transference of cannon, cannonballs and powder from Sheffield Castle following the death of the incumbent Lancastrian steward Talbot, the Earl of Shrewsbury, at the Battle of Northampton. That Yorkist victory had occurred the previous summer, prior to the Duke of York preparing for his doomed campaign in the north. The Yorkist claimant to the throne had sought to protect his properties in the West Riding and had entrusted young del Wardrop to carry out the transfer of heavy ordnance for use by the duke's faithful steward, Edmund Fitzwilliam, at Conisbrough Castle. Should the pair of young Yorkist supporters be discovered and taken at Thryberg Manor, then the Reresbys would doubtless suffer dire consequences.

Ralph had instructed his wife to remain in the bedchamber. Her pleas to be allowed to welcome the young bride and oversee her needs were abruptly silenced. She was to stay, secure the door and to concentrate on her breviary. She obeyed without demur, thankful and relieved that, for a while at least, her husband had a fresh focus for his seemingly perpetual ill-humour.

In the withdrawing room and after stirring red-hot embers in the fire grate into flickering life, Ralph added logs, then stomped to a corner of the room where, to all intents and purposes, he became engrossed in sorting through letters and bills of manor business. However, he was paying close attention to every word.

The young bride, Isabel, white and shaking from her flight and near-capture, sat close to the fire sipping a cup of hot mead, brought from the kitchen by the bleary-eyed, unshaven, John Clay. She was strikingly beautiful with long, fair hair, which she had been vigorously drying with a harding cloth; it now flowed in tousled folds around her shoulders. Her eyes were azure blue and encircled by a narrow band of the deepest woad-like hue, ensuring the immediate attention of any man coming into her presence. Bow-shaped lips, likewise, guaranteed the rapt attention of the beholder. As her body warmed, the deathly pallor occasioned by the cold, wet February dawn disappeared and her youthful, complexion glowed smooth and flushed, adding the perfect base to her breathtaking beauty.

William Reresby, despite his advanced years and his celibate calling, found his gaze constantly returning to the vision as he listened to her husband's description of their near-capture and harrowing ride. Richard del Wardrop paced backwards and forwards by the fireplace, his eyes darting frequently in the direction of the younger brother. Ralph's barely concealed hostility served to ensure that an oppressive atmosphere settled on the room.

'Every lane, every meadow is swarming with riders,' Wardrop explained. 'We escaped challenge for the reason that in the darkness they took us to be of their band.'

He was in his early thirties, fair-haired and handsome, with an aptitude for organisation and a flair for invention and improvisation. He had proved himself, time and again, to be a valuable servant to Edmund Fitzwilliam and in gratitude the couple had, on their recent marriage, been granted stewardship of Aldwark Manor.

Five months earlier he had helped turn the castle at Conisbrough into a formidable fortress bristling with cannon.

As the chambermaid entered with a warm robe to wrap around Lady Isabel, her husband was describing the violent passage through the West Riding of the northern host.

'Either side of the Great North Road, for a distance of five miles, bunched in straggling crowds, according to their affinities, identifiable by their livery. Lords, knights... captains ride ahead of billmen and archers. Like ants to a jam-pot, they're everywhere.'

'What is that to us?' Ralph Reresby banged a ledger on the table as he spoke.

'All manors along the way cannot help but be affected. A baggage train stretching back ten miles and more, filling up the Great North Road. Every cart track which appears to lead south swarms with marching men, hundreds of women – wives and camp-followers,' said del Wardrop, as if hoping to break through the hostile atmosphere in the room.

'Scourers, foreprickers, scouting out the way ahead and probing outward like fingers for miles either side of the main host. The vanward of the army is commanded by the Earl of Northumberland – must be 15,000 men and boys under arms. Middleward, led by the Duke of Somerset, numbers upwards of 8,000 footmen, so it is said.'

'You're well informed,' said Ralph.

Richard del Wardrop ignored the sarcasm. 'The driving force behind them is Queen Margaret. She'll have the head of every Yorkist lord on the end of a lance ere this matter be ended.'

'That's what happens to traitors,' said Ralph. 'Hanging drawing and quartering – not a pretty sight.'

'Then there's the rearward. Pray it passes through without harm to this manor.'

'And why should we be concerned?'

'There are many foreigners, including border and highland Scots, under the command of the Duke of Exeter. They're barely controlled. No one is safe.'

'The house of Reresby will take its chances,' said Ralph.

'There are reports of outrage, cruelty and theft throughout the countryside,' Wardrop said. 'The Clerk family at Hartshill were held at sword point and eight of their oxen stolen.'

Old William Reresby shook his head and tutted. 'How will all of this ever be put to rights?'

'Every man's hand is being turned against his neighbour,' said Wardrop. 'It was a freeman who had once been in service to the Clerk family, John Gawsell. He led men-of-foot to the farm to steal the oxen.'

'How do you know the beasts were not fairly bought?' Ralph's tone was sharp.

'It is as though England were invaded by a foreign army,' said del Wardrop, continuing to pace the floor. 'The French could have done no more to ravage England than these supposed supporters of King Henry.'

'You could hide here until they've passed through the Riding,' proffered the squire-parson, glancing towards his brother as he spoke.

'Stupidity! They will be at our door before noon!' Ralph spat out at his older brother. 'If you think Arnold would forego an opportunity to pay us a visit along with his carousing friends, then you are growing dull-witted in your old age,' seemingly oblivious to the impropriety of his words.

'I'm sure that Arnold would...' began the parson in protest at the insulting attack.

'You can be sure of nothing, save that our precious brother Arnold will turn up with his friends to drain the buttery of wine and ale and empty our stores!' interrupted Ralph. 'You're a fool if you think that because he rides with Lancaster it will save this property.' The younger Reresby launched to his feet, pointing at the couple 'If they are found here, be prepared to have your neck stretched. It will not be my neck!'

'I regret the trouble we ...' del Wardrop began.

Ralph stormed past him, heading for the door 'You're not involving me in this folly,' he said as he slammed out.

'We had best take our leave,' said del Wardrop, making steps towards his wife. 'Our horses will be rested.'

The old parson shrugged his shoulders in resignation. In the light of his brother's opposition, what more could he do? Perplexed, he considered the couple's possibilities. They would have to take their chances in the fields and lanes. Maybe they could hide in the deer-park until the danger had passed.

'Perhaps I could help,' said John Clay, fixing his master with a meaningful look.

'What more could be done?' asked the old parson lamely, 'Ralph is right in what he says; Arnold rides with the Flower of Craven and he's bound to turn up with some of them at any time.'

Richard del Wardrop stood with his arms about his young wife, trying to reassure her that everything would be all right. She began to weep; their situation seemed hopeless.

'We shall never reach the castle alive,' she sobbed.

'The Hawksworth boys!' John Clay interjected. 'I beg your pardon, Master, but I know they could guide the steward and his wife through the countryside to Conisbrough Castle in safety. If anyone could escort them safely through, they could.'

'Ar yes, our scullions!' The parson beamed, 'Why, of course, the strange boy.' He wagged a finger at the young couple. 'Now there's an odd thing...' Excited, he began to relate what he considered to be the supernatural occurrence he had witnessed,

'On Epiphany Sunday a miracle occurred in St Leonard's.' The urgency of the situation dissolved in the mind of the old man as he told about the strange beam of light which had pierced the length of his beloved church and shone on the young swineherd.

'It happened before the very eyes of the Abbot of Roche. And I can vouch for it myself. I saw it, truly I did, and there were others, too.' Already, the incident was becoming embellished in the telling and retelling. 'The child's face became as an angel's face, and, I'll swear that I heard a heavenly *Kyrie eleison.*'

'Master!' interrupted Charon 'we must hurry. It is already light.'

'Yes, of course. Summon the boys. The one who whispers will know what to do,' decided the parson, nodding. 'Verily, 'tis strange,' he muttered, 'but he always seems to know. He found the kitchen waif when all others failed.' The old man turned to the fugitives and with great solemnity repeated, 'It was the finger of God, you know. The Abbot saw it, a miracle in St Leonard's.'

John Clay found Edmund and John in the kitchen scrubbing chopping-blocks and asked if they could lead the couple by some circuitous route to Conisbrough, so avoiding the roving armed bands.

Edmund walked to the door which opened over the vegetable garden and peered out at the winter's dawn. 'We must make haste, John. 'There will be a fog over the Don valley for most of the morning. We will take them by that way.'

Edmund slung his crossbow over his shoulder and gathered up a quiver of bolts. The three hurried across the Great Hall and into the withdrawing chamber. They entered as Richard del Wardrop was attempting to persuade his wife that it would be for the best if they parted. She was to go with the cook and two boys. A small group on foot might well go unnoticed. On the other hand, he would stand a much better chance as a lone horseman on the road, riding hard for the castle. Isabel, desolate at the thought of separation, pleaded, 'We should stay together, my love, my dearest, and should anything untoward befall us, then we would stand before the Judgement Seat hand in hand.'

His young wife's clinging naiveté exasperated del Wardrop and, holding her at arms' length, he addressed her sternly 'Do your vows, so recently taken, have no consequence?'

'Richard!' she gasped, taken aback by his abrupt manner.

'Before the altar and in the sight of the Holy Trinity and the Blessed Virgin and all the saints, thou didst swear to obey me.'

Unable to maintain his strict tone any longer, he pulled her to him and, embracing her, pleaded, 'Please, please do as I bid, my love. There is a far greater chance of success if we part. My fearful concern for you would only lessen my chances of getting through.'

Resignedly, she conceded, 'You must promise to take no unnecessary risks, my love!' Her voice was racked with intermittent sobs. Then she added haltingly, 'Should any harm befall you my life would be at an end!'

Even though her face was streaked with tears, and she was clasped in the arms of another, John was instantly besotted by her. Never had he beheld such beauty in the whole of God's creation. He secretly pledged that, should the need arise, he would gladly fight an army and sacrifice his life that she might remain unharmed. Edmund, seemed unmoved by the pathetic scene of parting lovers. He was impatient: there was no advantage to be gained in the heart-wrenching exchange.

Richard del Wardrop sought to allay his wife's fears by introducing a playful note. Taking an expensive looking blue silken scarf from inside his tunic, he first wiped her tears, then proceeded to appeal to the child in her 'A sport we shall make of it – indeed, a race!' He laughed. 'The last one of us to sit at Uncle Edmund's table in the castle keep shall a forfeit pay. What sayeth thou, O wayward wench?'

'And what pray shall the forfeit be?' she asked, pushing him playfully.

Her husband pretended to ponder, then, giving her a knowing wink, leaned down and whispered in her ear. She gasped aloud in embarrassment at his words and, blushing deeply, turned away, biting her bottom lip. At that moment, John hated Richard del Wardop.

'I entrust to you her safety!' Those words were directed to John Clay. 'Whatever happens, you are to deliver my wife without harm to her uncle, the castle constable. I care not how long the journey takes you.'

John Clay nodded 'On my life, I swear it,' he replied.

Wardrop took a purse of coins from his belt and pressed it into the cook's hand. He then looked long and hard at the three of them. 'You have a most precious charge *Deus vobiscum:* may God go with you.' Turning to his wife, he took her face in his hands and kissed her tenderly. Straightening up, he solemnly charged her, 'I shall await thy arrival at your uncle's table, for thou shalt find me seated there. I shall surely win this wager.' He proceeded to pat her playfully on the nose with his forefinger. 'And the forfeit you shall surely pay – in full.'

He and the old parson escorted them to the kitchen and through the door leading to the vegetable garden. They watched as the four set off across the fields and into the mist in the direction of the ancient quarries, Edmund, John and John Clay carrying pig-swill buckets. The Lady Isabel tended to dawdle and continually looked back. Eventually, John dared to call to her, 'Please, my lady, remember the wife of Lot!' The thought of becoming a pillar of salt had effect and she ran to catch up; then they were at the fish-ponds and the house was swallowed up in the mist.

Richard del Wardrop climbed into the saddle and, thanking the old squire profusely, rode off at a gallop in the direction of Hooton Roberts, on the Doncaster road.

At the abandoned quarry, Edmund led the way to the croft perched on a rock ledge. It was tucked behind a rocky projection which sheltered the simple home from the prevailing westerly winds. Edmund had diverted a small rivulet that ran off the demesne land above the quarry, thus bringing running water into the rear of the dwelling. A cleverly-sited fireplace and metal cauldron – another ingenious device of Edmund's – ensured a supply of heated water. A short covered walkway at the rear led to a small cave with a narrow, seemingly bottomless, crevasse which served as a privy and midden. The croft was situated at sufficient height and distance from the pig-fold so that the smell from their charges seldom gave offence.

John offered his hand to the fair Isabel to assist her up the rough-hewn steps to the ledge. She took it readily enough and, at her touch, a thrill ran through him, the like of which he had never before experienced.

Once inside, John Clay and Isabel seated themselves at the simple trestle table. Edmund, in his usual undertone, explained to his brother in some detail the plan for the journey and the route to be taken. As he relayed the information to the others, Edmund began adjusting the draw-weight on his crossbow, increasing the tension so that *point blanc* moved up from thirty yards to fifty. Spanning the crossbow would require that he use a goat's-foot lever and, consequently, loading would take a few seconds longer, but it meant that a heavier bolt could be shot with increased accuracy over a greater distance. Edmund was preparing the weapon for possible use against human prey – an undertaking he had never countenanced before this day. But it was a course to which he was committed through a public vow. Once he had completed his work on the crossbow, he busied himself with a grey blanket, cutting slots into it. John didn't ask why.

They were about to depart, having fed the four breeder pigs, when the Lady Isabel suddenly let out a gasp of dismay.

'Richard is without his talisman!'

In her hand she was holding the embroidered silken kerchief used by her husband to dry her tears. It was her personal wedding gift to her lover. She had lovingly worked it with needle, crafting with finest silk and golden thread, so that her dearest would be kept safe from his enemies. It bore the motto *Jesus vado per suus medius*. This referred to the occasion mentioned in the gospels when Jesus passed through the midst of those seeking to hurl him from a cliff. It had become fashionable to work the phrase into clothing, and even on to armour, to serve as a protective charm to the wearer. Now her husband was far more liable to be taken and harmed. John Clay tried to reassure her, but she had lapsed into inconsolable gloom.

As Edmund had predicted, the dank mist persisted and clung to the Don River valley, chilling them to the bone as they set off in the direction of the river. John was in the lead, followed by Lady Isabel, with John Clay bringing up the rear. Edmund, according to his plan, was following unseen at some distance. John was to head for the deer-park and from there on to Reresby's water mill. They were to cross the Don at the mill race and make their way to the deserted plague village at Birdswell Flat. From there they were to head north, avoiding the manor settlements of Swineton and Mexburg, and turn due east. They were to cross the Dearne River and enter Cadeby woods. There they were to wait until Edmund joined them. He would scout out and decide the safest way to make an approach to the castle, re-crossing the Don by way of the King's Ferry at Conisbrough. Edmund's instructions were precise and he would be expecting John to follow them exactly. Throughout the journey Edmund would be stalking them as if they were prey.

Warmed by their exertions, they entered the deer-park pale by way of the southern deer-leap. Once across the Don they would be less likely to encounter riders of the red rose. Apart from startling a group of yearling hinds, they saw nothing untoward in Reresby Park. As they left through the northern deer-leap, the mist closed in, but John knew well the way to the river corn mill. There was no mistaking the direction, for the sound of the turning mill-wheel could be clearly heard.

As they approached the outbuildings John thought he heard the sound of a horse snorting. They halted and listened for what seemed an age. Where was Edmund? John looked back, but could see nothing through the swirling grey clag. No sound could be discerned above that of the running water of a nearby stream emptying into the Don and the noise of the revolving mill-wheel. Half-crouched, John went ahead and began approaching the mill. The squeaking, clanking and grinding sound of the turning water wheel grew louder, drowning out all other noises. But why was it turning at all? Was the miller and his lad working? John waved to the others to join him and as they came up a voice cut through the mist.

'Oi, Kep!'

An enormous bulk of a man loomed up out of the fog. A babbel in a tongue which they took to be Gaelic flowed from him. He was wearing a rust-coloured kilt made of thick woven material that hung in a ragged untidy hemline. A broad belt of leather secured by an ornate buckle encircled his fat belly and another narrower belt was slung from his right shoulder and crossed to his left. This finished in a tartan-bound scabbard. On his head was a leather cap upon which were sewn metal plates. Red hair, plaited into numerous ropes, hung to his shoulders. A bushy red beard completed the awesome apparition. He had drawn his sword, a weapon which appeared somewhat longer than the usual blades and, stepping up, placed the point at John Clay's throat. They were to go ahead of him into the mill yard. There, two others appeared from the corn store and outbuildings. Judging from their appearance, they must have spent the night at the mill and were busy rifling the flour store and loading sacks onto a cart. Three horses had been saddled and awaited their riders.

At the sight of the captives being thrust into the yard, the men walked over and a hurried conversation ensued. They were a scruffy-looking pair, both wearing thick, coarse kilts of grey and arrayed for fighting in the fashion of their leader. The tallest was clean-shaven and had a skull-like face with deep-set blue eyes. Black, lank hair protruded from under a large dish-like cap. Around his waist were five old-type francisca throwing axes, each in a leather holster. Strapped to his leg was a broad-blade dirk. The youngest was thickset with fair hair and matching small beard and seemed to be referred to by the other two as Tihge. The big man was addressed as Amish. Scots mercenaries, there could be no doubt. Their wages consisted of 'legitimate' plunder of English property, under the license of a desperate Queen Margaret of England.

Finally a decision was reached as to what should be done and they began nodding their heads. The youngest, Tihge, was directed by the other two to speak. In an accent so thick he could barely be understood, he asked where they were journeying. John Clay explained that the village of Mexburg across the river was their destination and was relieved when it became clear, through words accompanied by gestures, that they were being told to be about their business.

They nodded and made to move off, when the huge red-headed Scot called Amish grabbed Lady Isabel's arm.

'*Caileag fan!*' he grunted.

'The girl stays,' translated Tihge, with a leer.

Lady Isabel gasped and turned to her companions, eyes wide with silent pleading.

John Clay suddenly burst into action. Grabbing Lady Isabel's other arm he wrenched her away from the mountainous Scot and, hoisting the child off her feet, ran with his precious burden under his arm, heading for the river. It would be better that she take her chances in the cold waters of the Don.

With a bound, the lank Highlander set off after them at speed, followed by the fair-haired Scot. Yards from the river bank, John Clay was brought tumbling to the ground. He and the Lady Isabel were roughly handled back to face the leader, Amish, a knife at the throat of the Reresby cook. The loathsome Amish yanked Lady Isabel to him and spun her around. He threw his head back, uttering a raucous laugh, he thrust his huge hand down the front of her bodice. Hoisting her off her feet, and with her kicking, screaming and calling her husband's name, he loped off towards the corn store, yelling back over his shoulder, '*Beum amas braghad!*'

At that command, John Clay was forced to his knees and the lanky one drew an axe from his belt, raising his hand to strike.

There was a sudden swish, followed by a sickening thud and a crossbow bolt smashed into the greasy Scot's forehead, penetrating his skull as far as the fletching. The Scot jerked backwards, his legs crumpled and, like a sack of old clothes, he flopped into a sitting position. With eyes rolled back and mouth gaping wide, he slowly slid sideways.

Tihge froze, then quickly dropped to his knees, crouching for cover behind John Clay. His head swivelled about, trying to pierce the fog for the hidden shooter.

Then they heard the unmistakable 'clunk-clack' of a goat's foot lever being worked against the wooden tiller of a crossbow. John estimated that Edmund would be loosing his second bolt in about four seconds.

The beast carrying Lady Isabel had stopped at the warning call of his fellow mercenary. Holding her as a shield, he began swinging about, unsure as to where to place her thin body for his protection. There was a horrible-sounding smack as a bolt tore into the man's face, smashing his cheek bone and ripping through his palate. Screaming in agony, the huge Scot dropped his protection and, clawing at the transfixed bolt protruding from his mouth, staggered about the mill yard in a spray of blood.

Clunk-clack; again the ominous sound of a crossbow being spanned. The Scot had but seconds to live. The next bolt, when it came tearing out of the mist, finished the job, thudding into the Scot's neck and severing the spinal cord. Like a huge rotten tree felled in a windstorm, the mountainous man crashed to the ground – dead as mutton. Edmund afterwards said it was a quarrel of mercy.

Clunk-clack!

This time the man, Tihge, also heard the goat's foot being operated and knew he was next. He glanced up at John from his position crouching beside John Clay. Their eyes met – there was a fleeting look of desperation. Strangely, John felt pity, for he knew that he was seeing a fellow human-being with seconds left to live. The fair-haired Scot leapt forward in a dash for the horses at the very instant that a bolt, from the depths of the swirling mist, tore through his kilt and thudded into the mill door behind him.

Then John Clay made his move. Snatching the dirk from the leg scabbard of the slain man, he tore after the Scot. He must not be allowed to alert others. Yards from the tethered horses, Tihge was brought tumbling to the ground. In his work at the manor kitchens John Clay had on so many occasions performed butchery. With speed and efficiency, he had humanely killed sheep and pigs for the manor tables. Now, for the first time in his life, he used his butchery skills on a human victim. As in the case of the animals, the kilted warrior died quickly and quietly.

Edmund appeared wraith-like out of the mist and into the mill yard from a direction John least expected. He was covered in the grey blanket and a similar grey cloth draped from his head. The result was that he so successfully merged into the fog that no clear outline could be perceived. He took the Lady Isabel gently by the arm and brought her over to where John was standing as if rooted to the spot. Throughout all the action John had never lifted a finger. For all his brave intentions and fine thoughts entertained concerning the protecting of their fair charge, when the need arose, he had failed mightily. Yet none of the others seemed to notice his lack of participation in the awful events. Or if they did, it was of no consequence to any of them. Lady Isabel was shaking, holding tight together her torn clothing and uttering noises of disgust over and over again. John was curious as to how the taking of human life for the first time, the blooding of Edmund, would affect him. John Clay seemed to be a bundle of nerves following his first human kill, but then he was covered in his victim's gore, whereas Edmund had killed at a distance. As John might have guessed, his brother appeared unmoved. Of course he would see no gain in his being perturbed; where would the advantage be? John wondered then, what would the final end of Edmund be – a now blooded ruthless killer?

'These men must disappear from the surface of the earth, as if they had never existed,' Edmund whispered. 'Tie them on the horses. They can disappear in the plague vill of Birdswell Flat.'

Even the Lady Isabel helped as sacks were tied over the heads of the three corpses. As they were carrying out the gruesome task of binding the three slain, John Clay muttered under his breath to John, 'God help Lancaster'. It was as he had suspected all along, the young swineherd's declaration in St Leonard's on Epiphany Sunday had been no empty, rash, childish outburst of bravado. Not only did Edmund Hawksworth mean every word, but he had the skill, determination and resourcefulness to carry out his vow.

The bodies were dragged to the river and the three horses led under the banking where they were more easily loaded with the slain Scots. Dirt was brushed over pools of blood in the mill yard before the party set out once more on the circuitous route to Conisbrough Castle.

For the next mile their fair charge was unable to stop shaking. Her bottom lip quivered uncontrollably and she made shuddering noises as if contemplating some loathsome object. This eased once the dead Highlanders had been tipped into a well at Birdswell Flat. The weapons belonging to the three Scotsmen Edmund hid among the overgrown ruins of the crofts. Metal was a precious commodity and could bring a good price when recovered from this place at some future time.

Within the village only the fireplaces and hearths of the houses seemed to have survived over the years; the wooden posts, rafters and wattle had all but rotted and perished away. Local people avoided the place, believing it to be cursed. They were also greatly afeared that anyone walking there might stir

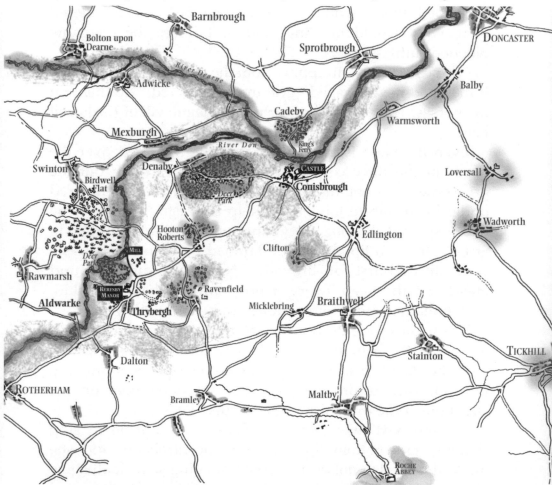

Part of the West Riding of Yorkshire in 1461, showing the River Don valley between Rotherham and Doncaster and Reresby Manor House at Thryberg.

up the vapours of the Black Death that had once spiralled into the crofts like the tenth plague in Egypt, wiping out the inhabitants over a century ago.

Over the next two miles, one after another the three horses were set free in the woods. It was during that stretch of their journey that they thought they heard the sound of thunder. By evening they reached Cadeby vill. From a vantage point high on the hillside, and in the failing light, they could see across the valley to Conisbrough. The Don valley had cleared of mist. However, a far more ominous haze had taken its place – a pall of smoke hung over Conisbrough dwellings. It was difficult at that distance to see whether or not the castle itself was burning, or which flag flew from the keep. Had the castle been taken by Lancaster? John Clay and Edmund would guard their precious charge and John would go ahead to see if it was safe to make an attempt to reach the Yorkist stronghold.

The ferry across the Don had not been destroyed. There was no sign of the ferryman or his wife. Working the ferry chain capstan to haul the boat across was hard work for a boy yet, after about ten minutes, John was across to the island. The bridge from the island to the south bank had been broken but, locating planks, he placed them across the gap.

A small cluster of homes on the road leading from the river had been deliberately fired. As John passed between the houses the heat was still intense and acrid smoke stung his eyes; sparks showered down as roofs collapsed. Smashed items of furniture and clothing were scattered everywhere; broken pottery crunched under foot. The din of the holocaust was deafening. Would Hell be like this, he wondered. Clear of the burning houses, he came upon the body of an elderly man with no obvious injuries that might have caused his death. Shock at the sacking would likely have done for him.

The inner bailey was crowded with townspeople, their goods and some domestic animals. Many of them were on the walls, guessing which particular dwellings had been fired. It transpired that all those who had sought refuge in the castle were deemed traitors by the Lancastrian mounted archers and their abandoned homes plundered and put to the torch. A smell of burnt black powder in the air meant that the castle cannon had been in action. The thunder earlier in the day must have been the castle's battery of guns which ringed the curtain walls on all sides.

After explaining to the weary, smoke-begrimed captain of the retainers what his business was – that he was with a party charged to deliver safely to her husband the Lady Isabel del Wardrop – John was led without a word to the castle chapel by the gate.

Inside, before the altar, was laid out the body of Richard del Wardrop. By his head was seated Edmund Fitzwilliam, lost in grief over the death of his faithful servant and friend. Women of the constable's household knelt in prayer beside the castle chaplain.

'Blackfaced Clifford arrived with his Craven,' the aged warrior whispered to John. 'They demanded we yield and presented Master del Wardrop for us to see bound with a rope about his neck.'

'They caught him then?' John realised how foolish that must have sounded.

The artillery captain ignored the question and continued, 'They demanded that we open "In the name of King Henry", saying we were rebels.'

The captain was near exhaustion from the fighting and drew John outside, where he slumped on an upturned empty saltpeter barrel. 'We were given one hour to surrender the castle or they would hang Master Richard.' The captain looked about him 'Fetch me a drink, lad, that's a fine squire!'

With his thirst slaked, he went on 'Our constable wasn't about to give in and was working on a plan to sally forth and bring about a rescue, when,' the captain shrugged, 'that heartless swine Clifford just upped and hanged him before our eyes.'

He swilled some of the water around in his mouth and spat it out. 'They must be short on time and they were in no mood to carry out a proper investment of this place. So they hanged him by the neck from the back of a tipped-up cart. And they worked on him to make sure that he died. Then, they just rode off.'

Further sadness, it was John's duty to inform the grieving constable that his friend's wife was at the ferry awaiting news of her husband. Clearly, Fitzwilliam blamed himself for the death of his friend and, as if in a trance, ordered a party of mounted archers to bring in the Lady Isabel.

To John's amazement, Isabel del Wardrop accepted the news of her husband's death in a most matter-of-fact way. The terrible experience she had gone through that morning had drained her of all emotion, so she was in a daze. In her mind, the fact that her lover had forgotten to carry and wear his talisman sealed his fate. So, of course he was dead; what other outcome could there possibly be? Had her husband not promised that he would be seated at Edmund Fitzwilliam's table in the castle keep, awaiting her arrival? He had entered Conisbrough Castle before her, of that there could be no gainsaying. Therefore, she was committed to honour her vow. She had pledged her troth that should he be there first, she would pay a forfeit. Therefore, she would enter the castle and she would expect to find her husband seated at the lord's table. Then her forfeit she would pay. So the distracted mind of the child-bride reasoned.

News of Isabel del Wardrop's expectations regarding the meeting-up with her husband were conveyed to the constable. She would consider no protests nor demurring on the part of anyone. They waited for about an half-an-hour whilst preparations were made for a macabre reuniting of the newly-weds. There was silence as the party entered the inner bailey. There was a parting of the masses of people, forming a roadway leading to the keep. Lady Isabel dismounted, whereupon a number of ladies-in-waiting hurried forward to escort her into that impressive white stone tower.

After a short while John, Edmund and John Clay were summoned to attend the Lady Isabel in the Lord's Chamber.

Upon entering, they were greeted by a sight of apparent normalcy: Richard del Wardrop had been seated at the head of the table in the master's high-backed chair, his head tilted slightly forward, with both arms resting on the table. A retainer stood either side of the body, preventing it from toppling over. His wife was seated beside her dead husband, his hands clasped in hers. Edmund Fitzwilliam, some clergy, ladies-in-waiting and others were standing behind and either side of the chair. Upon their entry into the room, the Lady Isabel arose and declared loudly, 'Behold, The Hawk! The boy they all wonder about. They whisper in corners, asking, "Is he really... could he possibly be the anointed Avenger of Righteous Blood, for is he not a mere boy?"'

She began to walk towards them, a strange faraway look upon her beautiful face. She suddenly spun to face those gathered about the master's chair and pointed at Edmund, 'Away with your wondering, for before you stands the one destined to pay back eye for eye, blow for blow, blood for blood, for I have seen with my own eyes. Verily, I have observed the work of this Angel of Death!'

John heard his brother emit a low groan.

Thus prompted, John hissed through flattened lips, 'Please, my lady, not another word!' It would be better that no one would ever come to know of the slaying of the three Scotsmen.

Like one well soused in drink, she twirled about removing the love-token kerchief from around her neck. Turning before Edmund, she dropped to one knee and begged, 'My lord, the Avenger, grant this my boon?'

The sobbing of the ladies-in-waiting grew louder. It called for Edmund to make some reply himself without John acting as intermediary. He stuttered and stammered his acknowledgement of her request and asked her to make known her desire. Loud and clear she called out,

'Blood on behalf of blood...'

Then she whimpered, 'It is only fair, please, my Lord Avenger, please will you slay Sir John, Lord Clifford for me?' She hurried on as if some justification was needed for her awful request, 'He took the life of my love, so it is only right "Life shall go for life, eye for eye, tooth for tooth, hand for hand, foot for foot."'

Her eyes then blazed in anger and she screamed out, '"And thine eye shall not pity, sayeth the Lord God Jehova."'

'Amen.' Edmund nodded by way of agreeing to her request. He had fully intended to seek an opportunity for a clear shot at 'Butcher' Clifford of Skipton, anyway, this being just payment for the lives of the Duke of York and his young son, the Earl of Rutland. Still, this performance before the gathering in the Lord's chamber was not to his liking. The Lady Isabel del Wardrop was as one who was struck by the moon.

The pathetic scene of this beautiful girl of breeding doing obeisance before a boy swineherd was not lost on those assembled in the Lord's chamber of Conisbrough Castle. Clearly, the terrible events of the day had affected Lady Isabel's mind. All feared she had gone completely mad.

Stepping close up before Edmund so that she was looking into his eyes, she took the silken scarf talisman love-token and put it around his neck 'Wear this, my Lord Avenger, for protection and upon the death of Clifford, and your safe return, this bride's forfeit I will pay in full, for I have little else left to offer but myself.'

John looked hard at his brother and wondered, did Edmund understand the import of her pledge? She was offering him some sexual favour: the price for the death of a man, a lord and captain of Lancaster. John was irritated, even annoyed – perhaps, yes, even jealous. The Lady Isabel suddenly let out an anguished cry, calling on the Virgin Mary and her beloved Richard, then she returned to take her place once more beside the corpse of her husband.

Conisbrough Castle in 1461.

Chapter Five

Flower of Craven and A Blow to the Hawk

L IGHT STREAMING THROUGH the solar window indicated that it was mid-afternoon on this, the last complete day of John's life on earth. A halt had been called to his storytelling so that refreshment might be distributed among those assembled in the Lord's Chamber. Men stretched their limbs and shuffled about, standing so as to walk around and leave for a visit to one of the two garderobes located within the tower keep or inner bailey. Ladies absented themselves briefly in order to address similar functions and other necessary tasks. And one or two who had been listening from the stairs slid into the room, hoping that no one would question their presence.

The interruption was welcome, for John needed to be alone with his thoughts. Sadly, he had entertained hopes that his final evening would be spent in prayer and meditation, that he might be strengthened for his ordeal – the dreadful spectacle appointed to take place in Doncaster fish market. The Church would consider the burning a dire warning to any who might also be considering dissension. John would view his blazing departure as a martyr's death, causing others to ponder and make inquiry concerning the magnitude of his supposed offence.

A hand on his shoulder startled him. Jack Naulty, castle chaplain, his face racked with concern, sought to implore him,

'Look about you, John Hawksworth. See, this castle is filled with those who wish you well. All around are ones seeking to hear stories of The Hawk.'

He sat down in the window seat and indicated that John join him. 'Word of you being here is spreading and folks throughout the West Riding are travelling to hear stories concerning your brother that have been supressed these many years.' The chaplain pleaded, 'See for yourself, John! The roads hereabouts are thronged with those eager to catch a glimpse of you, brother of the Thryberg Hawk.'

He placed a hand on John's arm and gave it a gentle squeeze. His voice was reassuring and kind,'I'll wager, not a single soul, ne'er a single one of them, desires your death.'

Abruptly, he stood up and formally addressed the captive.

'John Hawksworth, I do hereby release you from your sworn oath and free thee from thy parole.'

John smiled and gently shook his head 'Good friend, do you recall the reply of our Lord when Saint Peter, with good intent, suggested that he be merciful unto himself, that he need not journey to Jerusalem there to suffer death?' The chaplain nodded and looked away. John continued 'There can be no question as to Peter's good intent. However, verily his words served to discourage Jesus at a time when every ounce of courage was needed to undergo the awful fate before him. Likewise, your words make it more difficult for me to face that stake. For face it I must.'

Though he had to admit to himself that since arriving at Conisbrough he was feeling less inclined to meet his fate. Torment suffered at Lincoln Castle had served to temper him in the way a smith's fire did the cutting edge of an arming sword. On the other hand, being treated like a lord was dulling the edge of his resolve.

Jack Naulty nodded and, with tears glistening in his eyes, he picked up the quote '"Get thee behind me, Satan, for thou savours the thoughts of men, not of God."' Then, despite what he had just quoted from scripture, he added, 'Pray, what good will your death accomplish?'

'Would you have me become an outlaw dwelling in the forests? Should I live as a hunted animal, a fugitive with a price on my head, awaiting some poor beggar to betray me for the price of a day's wage? Would you have me spend the rest of my life sleeping with one eye open?'

He patted Jack Nulty's arm 'We all must die some time, good friend, and I have lived three score years and some. It matters little whether I die at the stake or abed. Surely, it is better that I die on the morrow for what I believe to be true, rather than face a lingering demise upon some couch a few years hence. Should my death cause good men to think on matters that will affect their eternal salvation, then I will have achieved something in the service of the Kingdom of God.'

Finally, convinced that the prisoner would not be seeking his help to escape, Jack Naulty shrugged in resignation. From within his garment he produced a covert roasted chicken leg, forbidden by Canon Law on a Friday. 'In that case, John Hawksworth, you had best take repast, and hurry, for your audience is gathering once more. Abstaining from flesh on a Friday will have no meaning for one such as yourself, holding as you do your novel beliefs.'

John's answer was to take a bite from that succulent morsel.

When he stepped from within the solar window recess and into the bedchamber John was greeted by a sea of eager faces. The people had taken their places once more and were settling down. The packed room fell silent. So it was that John determined upon a dramatic introduction to the next part of his narrative:

'Good friends, it was on the 8th day of April, 1434, in this very chamber, mayhap in yonder very bed,' he indicated the four-poster opposite him upon which many were seated, 'a child was born to Thomas, Lord Clifford and Lady Margaret

Bromflet. Following the purification of Lady Margaret, the baby boy was christened John, probably in the chapel annex yonder.' He paused to allow the significance of the coincidence to register. 'Fortune decreed that this one, like his father before him, should grow to become the hated enemy of the Duke of York. Yes, my friends, Black-faced Clifford, the butcher, first drew breath in this very room!'

'In the icy winter month of February, 1461 my brother and I were about to meet that murderous fiend face to face.'

*   *   *   *

AFTER CHANGING his bloodstained clothing at the castle, John Clay accompanied the boys as far as the deer-park. There he left them, making for Reresby Manor House, waving as he set off at a steady trot. When next they set eyes upon their friend the cook, he would be liveried for Lancaster.

As they drew closer to their home in the ancient sandstone quarry, they caught sight of a figure, barely discernible in the failing light. It appeared standing atop the quarry edge, apparently watching out. Of course, it was little Eleanor. The mite had a roaring fire awaiting them in the croft and the makings of a meal all ready to be cooked. That is what the child liked best of all, to care for her Edmund Love. John too, should he happen to be with him.

'There's lots of horses and soldiers at the house and they bear the red wyvern,' Eleanor suddenly blurted out.

'Craven!' said Edmund, stabbing his knife into the table.

'Mistress Thicket wants your help at the house,' she said. Then in a most serious tone she added, 'And you are to say nothing of where you and cook have been.'

'The Master Ralph must be aware of our helping Richard del Wardrop's wife, the Lady Isabel,' said Edmund thoughtfully.

'Mistress Thicket said that the Master Ralph would be keeping his counsel on that matter,' volunteered Eleanor, obviously proud to be the bearer of such information.

'And pray, why would he do that?' John asked incredulously.

'Because,' interjected Edmund in a loud whisper, 'he well knows that some things are better left unsaid. It would bring down trouble on the Reresby household.' Edmund got up and prepared to leave. 'The Master Ralph prefers to be the one in charge of redress and punishments. This night there are far greater lords and more powerful masters at the manor than he.' On saying that, Edmund took up his bow and bolts.

John felt sick with fear. Edmund had vowed to exact vengeance on the lords of Lancaster and Sir John Lord Clifford was at the house. His brother's resolve had been reinforced that very day by the pleading of the Lady Isabel, begging for Clifford's blood. By all the saints – the terrible event had every likelihood of occurring that very night! How could Edmund slay the man, surrounded as he was by his armed retainers?

'This is foolishness, Edmund,' he said. 'Are you not satiated with the blood of the Scotsmen barely cold, that you seek to shed more afore the day ends?'

'John!' whispered his brother 'John, John, you need not come along, for you have pledged, nothing.' His voice was reassuring, but his brother was having none of it. So saying Edmund walked into the night with that awesome instrument of death over his shoulder.

'What Scotsmen?' clamoured young Eleanor, skipping after him. 'Why are the Scotsmen cold, Edmund Love?'

John hurried to the door and called out as the icy February night closed around the two of them, 'What of your escape? Do you no longer care what becomes of us? You're selfish and full of blood-lust. You are worse than the butchers of Lancaster. You'll rot in Hell! You see if you don't!'

Edmund gave no answer as he helped Eleanor down the rocky steps into the quarry bottom.

'I hate you! May the Devil take you!' John's despairing cry rang out into the cold, empty night.

Inside, he slumped at the table, feeling more alone than he could ever remember. No matter how hard he tried, he was unable to grasp what was happening. He ran events through his mind: it had been a mere two weeks and one day since Epiphany Sunday when Edmund had declared that he would assume the role of the Avenger. How they laughed, but what would happen to that laughter if they had seen Edmund slay two fully-armed warriors? Here was the reality and Edmund meant deadly business. Here also was the opportunity: a leading Lancastrian lord less than a mile distant from the croft. Two men that day had fallen to his crossbow; their slaying served to blood his brother. Edmund now knew that he could kill a man with the same cold-blooded efficiency as one might kill a rabbit or bring down a sparrow in flight. He had shown not the slightest hint of remorse. John could scarce believe the speed of it all. Edmund would surely die in his determination to fulfil this vow. If only their mother was alive. What was to become of them? Tears of frustration and fear welled up. He sat and wept like a baby.

He caught up with Edmund and Eleanor by the manor fish-ponds.

'John! It's not fair, Edmund Love won't tell me about the Scotsmen!' She slipped her hand into John's. 'Ding dong, make me a bell,' cried the tot.

Between the two of them they swung her off her feet, backwards and to-and-fro as they strode towards the Manor House, the lights of which twinkled in the cold night. The three had often walked together that way since last Michaelmastide. Would this prove to be the last time? John glanced toward his brother in the moonlight to see if he could discern any hint of reproach for his outburst and harsh words.

Edmund smiled at him and winked. Immediately John felt reassured and encouraged. Edmund would not hold a grudge nor be angry at his brief disaffection, for where would the advantage be in that? John shrugged as he thought about it. Maybe the shaft of light that had lit his brother's face in St Leonard's was in truth a sign of divine approval after all. Odd that his brother refused to accept it as such.

Upon their entry into the Manor House from the vegetable garden, the steady roar of many voices could be heard. There was much hustle and bustle as servants tended to the needs of the 'guests' packed into the Great Hall. Edmund had wrapped some sacking around his bow and sought out a long length of rope from the gardener's shed. Calls from the household for them to help in some chore were acknowledged, and then ignored. John directed Eleanor to find Charon and told her to remain with the chambermaid.

Hurrying up the creaking stairs which led to the minstrel gallery, they were relieved to find none of the visitors there. The vantage point afforded by the gallery was near perfect, albeit the scene was dimly illuminated by light from flickering candles and flames from the crackling fire in the Great Hall hearth. It was smokey and dark enough to hide their presence from the 150 or so men packed beneath and seated around the trestle tables.

Immediately the smell of leather, damp clothing and unwashed bodies assailed John, for these were men on campaign. Around the great fireplace were gathered the vintenars, having secured the prime places, and there right among them was John Hawksworth, their father, the ever-popular leader of men. How his brother felt at the sight and sound of him he knew not, but John felt an instant loathing. There was the man who had left them to fend for themselves and, because of his wanton desertion, their beautiful, kind, loving mother had declined before their eyes. She had finally succumbed to a consumption, weakened as she was by a broken heart. The boys had fought so hard to keep her alive and, despite all efforts, had failed. John was ashamed to admit it, but he hoped and prayed that Edmund would reserve a bolt for their father and that he would see him drop in the very same way the Scotsmen had. The heavy scar which cleft the left side of their father's face served to render him fearsome to behold. Such a sliced jaw – like a badge – declared his experience in combat, adding weight to his command over men.

They were able to count eight vintenars, each having command of nineteen mounted archers; that gave them a good guide as to the numbers packed into the Great Hall. Against the south wall some of the men had settled down to sleep, using their padded jacks as pillows. Items of clothing, armour, belts, swords and bows were stacked everywhere. Others played games of backgammon or dice. The result was a deafening clamour as numerous excited players vied for plaudits from their fellows or argued on some point of rule. There had not been enough platters upon which to serve food and slices of dry bread had been utilised. As a consequence the table-tops resembled ragged tapestries of food remains, mainly of venison, salted pork and herrings. There would scarce be anything left to eat or drink at Reresby Manor once the 'guests' had departed. Ale had all been consumed hours ago, leaving un-matured brewings of transforming wort along with plain water to slake the thirsts of Clifford's élite. At the top table were three captains deep in conversation, but no sign of any of the Reresbys or Sir John, Lord Clifford.

Edmund moved quickly and quietly to the small minstrels' chamber at the southern end of the gallery where, with seemingly little difficulty, he removed the single narrow window along with its frame. Next he secured the rope to a rafter with a knot that could be released by a thin cord with a sharp tug from the ground below.

'Should we become separated, John...'

Interrupting him was a mighty roar from over a one hundred and fifty throats: 'A-Clifford, A-Clifford, A-Clifford!' That salute was followed by the sound of clashing metal as the Craven in unison beat out a tattoo. The chant changed to '*Desormais, Desormais, Desormais*', interspaced by a rhythmic thumping of fists on tables.

Hurrying back to the gallery, they looked down on the object of that acclaim – Sir John, Lord Clifford. He had emerged from the withdrawing chambers accompanied by one of his captains, none other than Arnold Reresby, and following behind them was the Master, Ralph. Clifford, recently knighted by Queen Margaret following the victory over the House of York at the Battle of Wakefield, stood proudly before his men, his right arm raised high in acknowledgment at their salute. Clifford's loathing for the House of York stemmed from the death of his own father at the Battle of St Albans in 1455. He was a bitter, twenty-seven-year old out for revenge. His reputation was earned by the merciless slaying of the surrendered earl of seventeen summers and the removal of his head, along with his father's, Duke Richard. 'Butcher', 'Bloody' and 'Black-faced' were becoming popular prefixes for Clifford.

With the target clearly identified, there seemed little purpose in delaying. Edmund whispered his instructions to John. Following their fleeing from the house, they were to part and cross the Don. They would meet up at the plague village of Birdswell Flat. At the earliest opportunity they would seek to reach Barnsley, a place sympathetic to the House of York.

A mighty hue and cry would follow the death of Clifford, but they knew the countryside better than most and once over the Don they should, with luck, evade any pursuers. John felt calm and unafraid; after all, Edmund seemed to know exactly what had to be done.

Uncovering the bow, Edmund spanned it with a goatsfoot lever and selected a bolt, placing it on the tiller. John looked on fascinated, for Black-faced Clifford was but seconds away from a place in Hell.

As Edmund began to raise the crossbow a restraining hand was placed upon his arm. They had both been so intent on the terrible matter at hand that they had failed to see Charon's approach from the darkness of the stairway.

'What are you about?' she said above the din coming from the gathering below. Without waiting for an answer, she continued, 'Mistress Thicket wishes your attendance on her at once.'

Led by the chambermaid and leaving the crossbow hidden away in the shadows, they hurried to the stewardess' chamber. This was reached by a few steps from the minstrel gallery. The steward's room was small and contained a four-poster bed, a number of chests, a high-backed, crudely carved chair and a wooden bench. The brick fireplace which had been added in recent years, less than effective in removing smoke, took up a corner. Seated in the high chair by the hearth was the squire-parson, William Reresby. He was obviously ill-at-ease. Mistress Ann Thicket was standing at the other side of the chimney-breast, arms folded.

At their entrance the stewardess and the Master proceeded to speak at once. Immediately, Ann Thicket tightened her mouth and looked at the Master for him to continue. She would have been annoyed at not being allowed to question the boys, but true to her character, she knew well her place and deferred to her better.

'What news?' Is it true that del Wardrop was caught and hanged?' asked the Master, his face drawn by concern. 'And what of the Lady Isabel, is she safe?'

'John Clay, the cook? Has he not returned?' John counter-questioned. Surely they should have been informed of these matters upon his arrival at the Manor House two hours ago?

'On his return he was ordered away by my brother Ralph, who intends to join the Lancastrian march on London,' answered the aged Master, shaking his head in disapproval. His household was being mustered to arms under the banner of Lancaster and it was not to his liking.

'What have you to report?' snapped Ann Thicket, clearly annoyed that John should seek to question his betters.

'Indeed, Richard del Wardrop was hanged in front of Conisbrough Castle drawbridge. However, Lady Isabel is safely delivered to the constable,' he replied.

'Oh dear, oh dear, if only young del Wardrop had gone with the whispering boy.' The old parson groaned aloud. Then, looking across to Ann Thicket and nodding towards Edmund, he continued, 'He would still be alive, for the boy was anointed in St Leonard's by the Holy Virgin herself.'

The steward smiled briefly and politely at the Master before turning to the boys, her lined face hard and her eyes narrowed,

'Why were you on the gallery armed with a crossbow? What were you intending?' she said. They both remained silent. She always seemed to know everything that occurred in the house.

'I know what you were about. You must forget it here and now.' She had the reins and the old parson was content to allow it. 'Whatever it is that you feel has to be done must not take place under this roof. Or indeed, anywhere upon Reresby Manor property. There would be bloody retribution following an assault on a lord. Innocents would suffer. These northerners are callous and would show no mercy.'

The boys shuffled uneasily, for they could see the wisdom in her words. Edmund nodded and whispered loud enough for her to hear, 'What I was about to do would have brought evil down on this house. Please forgive me.' So saying he dropped on one knee before the house steward and the Master.

Ann Thicket was taken aback, as indeed was John. She had not ceased to wonder as to what sort of person he was since the incident of the broken eggs. On that occasion Edmund had humiliated her before the entire household. He had then sought the first opportunity to restore her dignity before everyone. She felt indebted to him for that kindness, but was uneasy in his presence. It was as if somehow the scullion was her equal, or perhaps even, her better. Hurriedly she dismissed the very thought. Here was a boy with an old head on his shoulders, she decided, and there was nothing more.

'Have you both eaten?' she asked in a voice remarkably gentle for one with such a shrew-like disposition. 'Best keep away from that party in the hall,' she advised. 'I will need help in the morning to clean up when they have left. Most of the men of the Manor are under arms and will be leaving with Master Ralph. I shall need all the help I can get.'

That night they slept on the floor in the minstrels' chamber. The loud snoring of men at arms packed into the Great Hall shook the old walls.

If they were not to despatch Lord Clifford at the present when it was so easy, what did his brother intend to do? Edmund explained that on the morrow they would take a horse from the Reresby stable and ride to get ahead of the scourers of Craven. Because of the vast force travelling south, their pace of march would not be too fast as it would be governed to some degree by the support wagons. Then they could seek an opportunity whilst distant from the Manor.

The warriors were roused by their vintenars at cock-crow, many suffering with thick heads and rumbling insides as the wort which they had so foolishly drunk the night before began its inevitable work on their innards. Many there were of them who sought the kitchen garden with urgency. Eventually, in that cold February dawn, they rode off to meet up with the remainder of the Flower of Craven at Worksop. However, Sir John Lord Clifford and Arnold Reresby dallied in order to inspect the muster of men-at-foot from the Reresby household.

Some thirteen souls were assembled in a hotchpotch of protective mail and plate. Various styles of helmets were in evidence. Some were quaint and ancient and others dated from the more recent French Wars. There was much rust in evidence. The men had just celebrated Mass in St Leonard's and now, back in the Great Hall, bills were doled out to each

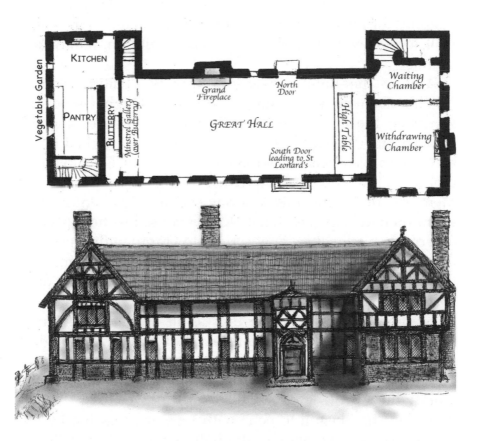

South-facing side of Reresby Manor House and floor plan in 1461.
See Chapters One, Three and Five.

man, along with a mix of daggers and short falchions. There were a few padded jacks to be seen, but most had only heavy woollen coats for protection against arrows and slashing blades. There were insufficient tabards in the Reresby livery for all, so some had to make do with a simple badge consisting of a black cross patonce on a white background attached to a length of red material draped over the left shoulder. Each had a leather or canvas bag bulging with supplies for the long march to London. Gathered in the Great Hall to bid their farewells were wives, children, family and friends.

Among the Reresby warriors was the bailiff, William Whelpdale, who was acting as decenar; Hugh Grene, the warrener; the parker; the woodkeeper; the hostler and the clerk, Brother Bellard. The monk had a mace attached to his belt, for it was deemed wrong for a man of God to draw blood. He would seek to crack skulls in any fighting. Memories of the previous Saturday evening's gathering when Edmund had helped each man to crystallise his thoughts and determine his loyalties now served to cramp enthusiasm for the task at hand. News that for the duration of the campaign they would be paid five pence a day had done little to lift their spirits.

Leading that dreary little unit as its captain was Ralph Reresby. At least he had on a full suit of armour, although it was of earlier times, having been made for his father, Sir Thomas Reresby. Recent attempts to remove rust had not been wholly successful.

Since it had begun to pour with rain, the blessing by the parson would take place in the hall. Sir John, Lord Clifford and Arnold Reresby looked on with barely concealed amusement as the men formed themselves into a ragged line, prodded and shoved by an irritated Ralph. How the second son would conduct his command of men in the heat of battle was a mystery. He had some difficulty conveying information and instructions in the everyday running of the Manor. How would he fare when arrows were flying? In sharp contrast to Ralph was the younger brother Arnold, a loyal retainer of the Cliffords and veteran of campaigns. He wore armour and bore weapons with the flair of a fighting commander who had shed blood in earnest.

Edmund, apparently engaged in his chores, had moved closer to where Sir John, Lord Clifford and Arnold Reresby were standing in order to observe the muster. As the men began to move to the north door in single file, the cook, when drawing level with the boys, dropped on one knee before Edmund and mumbled awkwardly: 'Please forgive this act.' Involuntarily, Edmund reached out and placed his hand on the man's shoulder whispering, 'Let it be this time, good John Clay, for the loyalties of your heart are known.'

Arnold Reresby observed this and blurted out, 'Holy Mother of God! What is this, when a swincherd and kitchen scullion receives the honour due only to his betters?' He shook his head in disbelief. 'Truly, matters have got out of hand since I absented this Manor.' Turning, Arnold addressed his two older brothers 'Is there no longer observance of degree within this household?'

The words between John Clay and Edmund had gone unheard by those around, but their actions were unmistakable. The acceptance of homage by that instinctive placing of the hand on John Clay's shoulder outraged social order.

'A whelp should be taught its place, lest it harbour thoughts of grandeur.'

So saying, Sir John, Lord Clifford stepped forward and brought the back of his mailed hand across Edmund's face with such force that he was sent crashing to the ground. It was then that Lord Clifford noticed the blue silk scarf about Edmund's neck. Wrenching it from him, he held up for all to see.

'Finest damask about the neck of a pig-herder? There has likely been thievery!' Turning to the parson, he promptly thrust the valuable item into his sallet, and bellowed as he led the party from the hall, 'Best look into this matter, Reresby. A day in the stocks will serve to remind yond dog of its God-decreed place!'

Edmund, barely conscious, remained on the floor until the armed party had departed the courtyard. Eleanor was cradling his head and sobbing quietly as she tenderly wiped away the blood from around his mouth. With her help, Edmund arose unsteadily to his feet. His eyes betrayed nothing.

As expected, Parson William Reresby made some half-hearted attempt to carry out the direction to remove Edmund to the stocks on Thryberg village green. With the bailiff, warrener and other men gone, John was directed to take his brother and secure him in the stocks. John made as if to lead him away, only to be repeatedly pushed back by Eleanor, who was verging on hysteria and with every exertion of her little body she screamed repeatedly, 'No! No! Not Love!'

With eyes full of pleading, John looked at the parson 'Master, with the men now gone, another day for the stocks?'

Ann Thicket hurriedly pointed out that there was much work to be done and that both Edmund and John would be needed. 'Would the Master please grant his permission for the boys to move to live in the house? At least until such time as the men return from the fighting in the south?'

Thus cleverly, and quite deliberately, the steward presented the parson with another immediate decision to consider and so had deflected his attention. The old squire nodded and muttered about what the outcome of all this would be as he headed for the withdrawing chambers.

The old man's allegiance was firmly bound up with the House of York, despite the rest of the family's support for Lancaster. He turned events over and over as he tottered along. There was the disturbing matter of the young scullion. The very finger of God had touched the boy on Epiphany Sunday. That miracle had immediately followed the boy's vow. Could it be that the Almighty would use this boy to wreak vengeance on Lancaster? How could it possibly be? Yet, had not the 'Butcher', Lord Clifford, just come face to face with the anointed Avenger? Enmity had flashed up betwixt the two. No! The old squire-parson suddenly decided, he wanted no part in punishing the boy, either that day or any other. In fact, as God had seen fit to choose the boy and bestow favour on him, then he would not act against him. What did fate have in store for his brothers, Ralph and Arnold who, through the very act of bearing arms, were committed to the cause of Queen Margaret and Henry VI? He was greatly perplexed, for henceforth, until the matter be settled, his prayers would be divided and complicated.

It took the best part of three days for Edmund to recover from that cruel blow to his face. To judge from the amount of swelling it appeared that the jaw had been cracked. During that time, he was cared for at the Manor by Charon and Eleanor. Even Ann Thicket tended him and had special food prepared.

As he worked at the seemingly never ending chores from dawn until dusk, John puzzled over where destiny was leading them. There would be no slaying of Lancaster lords for the foreseeable future. So how could it all come about?

Chapter Six

Lancaster Victorious and A *Bacele* of Hard Riders

ON THE SECOND DAY OF LENT, on the eve of St Hilary's, William Smith – Smudger – a known rascal from the vill of Warmsworth, arrived at Reresby Manor astride a fine courser gelding and leading another courser. Slouched upon the latter was the wounded cook, John Clay. The two brought tidings of the Lancastrian clash with Yorkist forces north of London. It was William Smith, who had been on that disastrous hog-drive last Michaelmastide. It was from him riders of the House of Dacre gleaned information concerning the true owners of the herd. Some of the blame for the murder of the reeve could be laid at Smudger's door. At least, that is what the other drovers had discussed at the time.

Smudger, along with upwards of five hundred others from the surrounding manors of Doncaster and Rotherham, had joined the march south under the banner of the Lancastrian Prince of Wales. The wily Smudger had secured for himself an early return from the ranks of the host under the guise of an act of kindness – escorting the wounded cook home. There had been a tongue-lashing from Ralph Reresby, who accused Smudger of evading his duties. The crafty ex-drover from Warmsworth had shrugged at the news that his daily wage would cease upon absenting himself from the host. Already the campaign to free King Henry VI had proved lucrative enough and he was well satisfied. He had successfully relieved a number of households of their valuables, both on the march south and again following the battle at St Albans, when the northern hordes had run out of control in an orgy of looting, sacking houses and shops in that town.

He wore with ill-concealed pride a bandage about his head which covered a wound he had sustained in a dispute, not with a Yorkist billman, but with a French mercenary over possession of a pair of calf-length grey leather boots. Naturally, his wife would remain ignorant of the true value of his lucrative looting campaign. He would even leave the wounded Reresby cook with the courser upon which he had been carried home. 'What a fine fellow, leaving John Clay the horse,' they would say. Being thus convinced of his enhanced reputation, Smudger rode off to hide his loot and return as the mighty conqueror to his weary, long-suffering wife.

News of John Clay's return spread quickly and the crowd gathered around the fireplace in the Great Hall at Reresby Manor that Saturday eve numbered upwards of thirty. Wives, family members and friends were eager for news of their loved ones.

As far as John Clay knew, not one of the men from the Manor had suffered ill during the battle to recapture the king. He was the only one from Reresby Manor to suffer injury. They were insistent and eager that he recount everything. At first the cook was reluctant to speak of what he had witnessed and been a part of, as if recalling the events caused him distress. Finally, when he was at last persuaded, he addressed the gathering in a voice bitter with feeling:

'Never again will I bear arms under the banner of the House of Lancaster! Even if it should mean my life.'

Chatter among the gathering ceased and a hush settled upon them.

'As God is my judge, I swear it will be the choke-at-York rather than I take livery again for Lancaster.'

The cook gingerly moved his wounded leg into a more comfortable position, wincing as he did so. 'The Earl of Warwick blocked our path to London at St Albans. 'Warwick had fearsome weapons to use against us, but the commanders of Lancaster were better than he.'

He shook his head from side to side. 'On Shrove Tuesday, before dawn, we slammed into the Yorkist lines from a direction they did not expect. Soon we were in the centre of town and would have brought the matter to a conclusion, but Yorkist archers held us back with a hail of arrows. We approached from Dunstable along the old Roman road, Watling Street. Then we charged up towards the heart of town, but the Yorkist archers barred the way. They were ranked as a solid wall at the Eleanor Cross in the market square.'

He winced again, moving to ease his discomfort. 'Flight after flight thudded into us and so it was that an arrow found its place in me. It availed them Yorkies little, for by midday it was over.'

Once again questions rained down on John Clay as to the welfare of each person's loved ones. He repeated that he had seen little of their kith and kin after he was wounded, but as far as he was aware they had come to no harm.

'King Henry had been taken by Warwick from the Tower to the battle lines. The Earl sought to buttress his cause, but the king's presence served their cause not one jot. When York finally fled the field, the king was left as spoil to the victors.'

'So they have the king and hold London?' said Charon.

'No. London town closed its gates to Queen Margaret and against us northerners,' replied John Clay.

'Our weak-minded king is reunited with his queen and young son, Edward Prince of Wales. Rewards have been granted for those who fought for Lancaster and captured Yorkist lords executed. I fear that this is not over and more English blood will flow afore there is a settling.'

122

Following failure of the victorious Lancastrian royal party to persuade the mayor and magistrates of London to open the gates, the Queen ordered a general withdrawal north. News that the Duke of York's son, Edward Earl of March, had won a great victory in the Welsh Marches at Mortimer's Cross and was moving on the capital with 40,000 Welshmen no doubt hastened the withdrawal.

Once more towns and villages were revisited and trampled over, although further looting amounted to a gleaning work. Indeed, bands of deserters from the Lancastrian army, Scotsmen for the most part, had been filtering back, laden with booty even before the Battle of St Albans took place on that Tuesday, 17th February, 1461. The freeing of the English sovereign had been far from their minds. Heading north, fifteen miles either side of the Great North Road, as far as the River Trent, every town and vill had been plundered.

Still, it was felt that the Reresby cook had not recounted all the tale of the fighting at St Albans. What had he seen that had caused him such distress? Edmund brought a pitcher and refilled John Clay's cup with ale 'You have more to tell us, good friend?' he whispered.

Turning to Edmund, he echoed the lad's words 'By their fruitage thou shalt know them.' Slowly nodding his head, he recalled, 'That's what you told us, here in this very place. And I've seen enough of the fruits of Lancaster, not just at the flour mill...' he paused and bit his lip, realising that, perhaps, he had let slip the killing of the three Scots mercenaries. He hurried on, for only Edmund and John knew to what he alluded. 'Not only at Conisbrough, for I've seen rotten fruitage at Grantham town where Margaret's mercenaries took their wages in plunder.'

'Are our men plundering?' interrupted an elderly skinner from Ravenfield.

John Clay shook his head 'Not that I saw. It's the Scots and the Frenchies. They've sacked every manor house, croft, church and monastery south of the Trent.' He paused to take a drink and to draw breath. 'Stamford, sacked! he continued, his voice bitter and growing louder 'As was Peterborough, Huntingdon... Royston, Dunstable, and after their victory, I say 'theirs' for it was not mine, came the turn of St Albans. Appeals to the king and queen to bring a halt to the wanton sacking of towns fell on deaf ears.'

'What else did you see that caused you such distress?' asked Edmund.

The cook looked long and hard at Edmund, his eyes narrowing. Suddenly he nodded his head 'As you say, there was something else. For I have witnessed the "justice" of Lancaster.'

There was deathly quiet as the gathering suspected that some disclosure was about to be made.

'Those injured in the fighting were taken to St Albans Abbey, to the chapter-house to have their wounds dressed. I was tended in some haste by a Cistercian monk and, when the place was suddenly cleared, I was left behind. I was lying unnoticed on a bench in the Abbey library. From that vantage point I was able to observe the royal court in session.'

The Master, William Reresby, had been hovering on the edge of that Saturday evening gathering around the great fireplace. Upon hearing his cook about to relate what he had seen at the court of King Henry, he pressed in closer. When Ann Thicket caught sight of him she halted the story-telling and, giving up her chair, indicated that the Master should join them.

With one eye on the Master, John Clay began the account of what he had seen at the victors' court. 'King Henry was found by his rescuers sitting beneath an oak tree away from the field of battle. Having the king's assurance that there would be no dire consequences for their chivalrous act, two Yorkist knights had agreed to stay with him so that he might come to no harm. But, more of this in a while.'

The cook described the honouring of the victorious Lancastrians which took place in the richly decorated chapter-house. The abbot's chair at the eastern end of the vaulted chamber served as a throne for King Henry VI. A further chair, covered by an ermine-trimmed cape, made a throne for Queen Margaret and on a stool placed between them was the seven-year-old, Edward Prince of Wales. Packing the chapter-house were military leaders of the cause, lords, knights and squires. The king was beaming and the atmosphere was euphoric. There was an air of gaiety and good spirits and laughter came easily to the victorious warriors.

It was the Queen who began the proceedings her speaking punctuated with heavily accented English. Occasionally she would resort to a Latin word or phrase when English failed her. She spoke of the God-given victory gained over her hated enemy, that would-be king, Richard, Duke of York during the holy week of Christmas just past. She reminded all how his severed head overlooked the city of York and now his much-vaunted supporter, the Earl of Warwick, captor of the king, had been soundly defeated that very day. He, too, would be caught and executed in due time. She then thanked them all for their support of her son, the Prince of Wales, and for their loyalty to their divinely anointed king. Those words of the maid from Anjou were greeted with an almighty cheer it seemed would raise the very roof.

Sir Henry Beaufort, Duke of Somerset, answered on behalf of their subjects gathered, reaffirming fealty to King Henry VI and to his issue 'To Hell and damnation with York and the Act of Accord! Long live Edward Lancaster, Prince of Wales!'

The response was a rousing cheer. The young prince, dressed in the purple brigandine of a warrior, stood in acknowledgement of the acclaim. Whereupon his father, the king, swept along by the occasion, arose and called for a sword. Taking the proffered blade from Somerset and amid tremendous applause, he dubbed the youngster a knight of the realm, 'Arise Sir Edward, Prince of Wales!' His father's mild and timid voice mustered a measure of authority for the occasion.

'Sir Edward, our loyal subjects must be rewarded this night,' called out Queen Margaret to her son.

The king reversed the blade, proffering the hilt to his son. Upon receipt of it, he turned to his mother for direction. A herald passed a scroll to the Duke of Somerset, who in turn passed the hastily written list of thirty names to the Queen. She lowered her voice to a whisper, indicating a name at the very top of the list.

Silence descended for the prince, who mustered up all the dignity he could 'We have found pleasure in the service of one, Andrew Trollope.' The youngster's piping voice took on an assumed dignity that would have been amusing, even embarrassing, on any other occasion and announced, 'Brave captain of Lancaster, approach the throne of thy sovereign!'

The young captain of Calais detached himself from the press and limped forward, palms open in mock supplication 'My lord I am not deserving of this honour, for I have been unable to perform my duty fully this day.' He had gauged the mood of the gathering well. Turning, he made pretence of an appeal to his comrades 'For I slew no more than fifteen men!'

This was met by a loud roar of laughter. He carried on his travesty of affected humility, looking first at one then another. 'I was skewered to the spot by a foul caltrap. For the whole time I stood still in one place.'

His timing in the telling of the tale was faultless. He shook his head as if puzzled and continued loudly, as if to himself, 'They came to me...' And then, as if the truth had dawned, 'but still, they stayed with me.' Trollope permitted himself a weak smile.

The applause was deafening and this skilful Lancastrian tactician fell to his knees before the boy and received the accolade. The knighting of the others followed and then there was a hush. By now the entire assembly of warriors sat, either on benches or on the floor of the chapter-house.

Five captured Yorkists, Lords Bonville, Neville, Berners, Charlton and Sir Thomas Kyriell, arms bound behind them, were forced through to the front and pushed to their knees before the thrones. One of them, John Neville Lord Montagu, was the brother of the vanquished Earl of Warwick. Lord Bonville and Sir Thomas Kyriell were those who had stayed behind to protect the king when other Yorkists made their escape.

'Traitors, tormentors of the royal personage,' began Queen Margaret, 'the Lord God has given us the battle and delivered you treasonous men into our hands.'

Lord Bonville managed to regain his feet and, turning to the king reproachingly gasped out, 'You gave us your word!'

King Henry was fast losing interest in the proceedings. The Abbey church bell was tolling, calling the faithful and he felt that his place was with them. Many of the people of St Albans had been in the Abbey since Vespers and could not be persuaded to leave. They had suffered the plundering of their homes and were packed into the Abbey church for protection. Who knew how far the northern invaders were prepared to go in their violations?

The monks would be making their way to the church for Compline and King Henry wished to join them for the final devotions of the day.

Bonville could see that he did not have the attention of the king and became urgent in his reminders, 'My liege, your word! We stayed by your side when we could have made good our escape. We did our duty so that no harm might befall you.'

'Your insolent words should be addressed to the one whom you sought to disposess, Sir Edward, Prince of Wales. Mayhap, he will show you mercy.' Obviously Margaret had little time for the promises of her weak-minded husband.

Henry sat gazing distractedly at the huge crucifix hanging from the rib-vaulted ceiling.

Bonville, ignoring the youngster before him, addressed his words to Margaret 'Whether we rode with the House of York, or of Lancaster, it matters not in this case. Our foremost duty was the safeguarding of the personage of the king, which duty has brought us to this pretty pass.'

'We shall ask the Prince of Wales what is to be done with you,' replied the Queen.

'Madam!' snapped Bonville, exasperated 'Wouldst better ask the king, who granted us his royal protection, than a boy?'

'Ah! *Completorium*,' said the king pressing his hands together in an attitude of prayer. Then he began to sing softly the hymn, *'Te lucis ante terminum'*.

At this Bonville, in desperation, called out, 'Your word, sire! God damn you, your word!'

He was knocked back to his knees by a guard as the king carried on singing quietly to himself.

'Enough! What is your judgement, Sir Edward? What do you say should be done with these traitors?' said the boy's mother.

The youngster, feeling the importance of the occasion, and his first opportunity as a seven-year-old to issue command in an assembly of grown-ups, declared pompously 'They shall have their heads struck off.'

This was greeted with silence from the men gathered there. They had no particular love for Lord Bonville, or the other Yorkists, but it did not sit comfortably with them that a king's word counted for nothing, and that in England a mere child held the power of life and death. After all, what stood for one lord and knight now, might well go for any one of them later.

Resigned to his fate, Bonville looked at the prince for the first time 'May God destroy those who taught you such manner of speech.'

The next day a suitable butcher's block was located and placed in St Alban's market place. Lord Bonville, Sir Thomas Kyriell and others followed in their turn to be beheaded. The gathered crowd was strangely silent throughout the executions. Lord Montagu escaped that fate, for he was held as a captive, the intent being to bargain with him for the Duke of Somerset's brother held captive by the Yorkists in Calais.

John Clay finished his account to a subdued audience in Reresby Manor Great Hall that Saturday eve. 'Some said that Bonville talked himself and his friends to the block. From what I saw nothing would have saved them apart, mayhap, a single word from the king himself. But then, he is moonstruck. '"By their fruits shalt thou know them",' he concluded.

*   *   *   *

Joining the many thousands of Lancastrian men under arms streaming back northwards was a mounted *bacele* consisting of three knights and two squires. The five were mounted on fine animals and led three coursers, used as pack-horses, laden with baggage. They kept themselves separate from other knights and mounted archers and each night they camped some distance from other groups. Never more than a mile from the royal party, they discouraged friendly approaches from individuals of similarly armed bands.

The five riders wore the livery of the Duke of Exeter. However, when a royal herald approached and made inquiries of them concerning their affinity, they uttered non-committal remarks, then melted like phantoms into the night. When they appeared again, a few miles ahead of the royalist vanguard, they were badged as retainers in the livery of the Earl of Shrewsbury. A day later they were seen by an observant millenar, a retainer of the Duke of Buckingham, sporting livery of that affinity. The fact that they were so well mounted and even their pack-horses were of quality, aroused his suspicions. The man made the mistake of seeking them out at dusk in the croft that served as a billet. The mysterious riders left the shelter of the croft and rode off into the teeth of a howling gale. The millenar was discovered next morning at the foot of a ladder – his neck broken. The five men were riding hard once again, this time in the guise of retainers of the Earl of Northumberland.

Once across the Trent at Newark, one of their number detached himself and rode hard westward, heading for the Cistercian Abbey of Dieulacres, adjacent to Leek in Staffordshire. A rendezvous took place there with three travelling friars with surprisingly fine steeds for men of piety and in holy orders. After committing intelligence from the knight to memory, one of the friars rode south through the night, making for Watling Street. He arrived at Dunstable at dawn the next day where he delivered his information to an officer attending on the Earl of March, recently pronounced Duke of York. At the same time that the friar rode towards London, another of the party of mysterious knights rode at a fast gallop heading north-east, crossing the wild Pennine moors in a blizzard, heading for Sheffield Castle.

Upon arriving at the fortress the hard rider, Sir Matthew Lovatt, regaled the steward with harrowing stories of bloody atrocities, pillage and outrage done under the royal banner of King Henry VI by the forces of Lancaster. Much of his recounted information was guesswork and greatly exaggerated. His flair for embroidering on gossip and his aptitude for storytelling reached a climax and so accomplished its aim. He concluded with the news that the royal party and its supporting killer bands, who had sold their souls to the Devil, were heading back to their lair at York. The thoroughly alarmed castellan needed no persuasion, for he had heard similar rumours from other sources. With much haste, he ordered that further provisions be acquired for the castle.

As Sir Matthew rode off at great speed towards Rotherham, he noted with some satisfaction that plans were being laid to deny Sheffield Castle to Lancaster.

Meanwhile, an identical result was being achieved by another member of the band of mysterious hard riders at Tickhill Castle. Sir Nicholas Gilliott, with much repetition, loudly regaled the constable with accounts of such horror that the poor man ordered the shutting up of the castle immediately. The constable had been a staunch supporter of the king, but the mayhem carried out under command of his French Queen surely nullified all his vows of fealty. He, too, had heard first-hand of the foul acts perpetrated by roaming bands of wild Scotsmen. Sir Nicholas drove home his point by acquainting the constable with the disheartening news that the Lancastrian vanguard was but one day's march away, 'I do not wish to cause you unnecessary alarm, but Tickhill is in direct line with the Lancastrian route of march.' Having achieved the desired result, the hard rider set off at a gallop for a prearranged secret rendezvous.

Another of the mysterious hard riders, Squire David, had been sent to contact the loyal and faithful supporter of the House of York, Sir Edmund Fitzwilliam. The youngster was to confirm that at Conisbrough all was well and was still for York, and that the stronghold could be used as an assemblage point for the forthcoming Yorkist campaign in the north.

The leader of the hard riders had reserved the most difficult job for himself – that of bringing about the denying of the stronghold of Pomfret Castle to Lancaster. He had a caretaker steward to contend with. His task was to try and convince the man that he should forbid King Henry, along with his Queen, the Prince of Wales and entourage, protection of the stronghold. Just over two months previously the castle had been firmly committed to Lancaster. It had been the rallying point and base when Lancaster had proceeded against Sandal Castle. No constable had been appointed for the duchy of Lancaster stronghold since the death of Lancastrian Lord Egremont at the battle of Northampton the previous July.

The caretaker castellan was a nervous individual who perspired easily. Experience had taught him to keep to hand a list of reasons and excuses for possible defence against the results of his poor judgements and decisions.

The leader of the hard riders, Sir Geoffrey Goddard, accompanied by his squire, Gareth Jack, gained admittance to the castle under the guise of loyal Lancastrians. On their left shoulders they wore the white crescent badge which was set against a field of black and red, indicating their retention to service of the Earl of Northumberland. They were shown hospitality in the steward's lodge and enjoyed simple repast.

In a voice barely audible, the tall, imposing and balding Sir Geoffrey, sporting an unfashionable beard, began his tale of woe. The caretaker steward, a portly, well-dressed man of about forty years, more acquainted with figures and quill than sword and mace, leaned forward in his chair so as to hear every word.

'Even London denied us entry. Not even the royal party gained admittance,' Sir Geoffrey began. 'The Lord granted us victory at St Albans, as He did at Wakefield during the week of the Nativity of Our Lord, just past. But many of us fear that divine favour is fast evaporating because of the sacking of monasteries and churches. You must show discernment as to whom you grant admittance to this place. The immediate royal party of course, but you should deny any Scotsman entry. Rue the day, should you permit them to enter the barbican,' said Sir Geoffrey.

The steward nodded his agreement, for he had heard many complaints from travellers. The Scots were behaving as foreign invaders rather than supporters of the king and queen of England.

'Nor shall a Frenchman pass through these gates,' declared the steward with determination in his voice. 'My father died fighting them at Agincourt.'

Having virtually secured the closing of Pomfret Castle to Lancaster, Sir Geoffrey offered his services to the constable. As he turned and crossed the bailey to his room in the Constable Tower he reflected on the dark history of Pomfret Castle. Just three months earlier, following the battle of Wakefield, the captured Yorkist leader, Richard Neville, titled the Earl of Salisbury, had been dragged out of his cell at the instigation of the 'Bastard of Exeter', William Holland, and handed over to a mob for beheading. Some sixty years earlier, the deposed King of England, Richard II, had died here under mysterious circumstances. Some say that he was starved to death in the dungeons beneath the castle keep. Sir Geoffrey shrugged off his dismal thoughts and looked forward to his first good night's sleep in weeks.

* * * *

With most of the able men absent, tasks at the Manor House seemed interminable for the Hawksworth boys. From dawn until late at night they were kept busy gathering wood and coal, cleaning and clearing away in the kitchen, seeking fodder from nearby Manors for the depleted stores, as well as cleaning the stables. Now that Edmund's facial injury had healed, he was working hard alongside his brother. John Clay helped where he could as his leg began to heal.

In the early morning of St Patrick's Day, Tuesday, 17th March, Ann Thicket called the boys to attend to the horses of four riders who had arrived at cockcrow. Two knights and their squires were admitted to the hall and were in the withdrawing rooms with the Master. It came as a surprise when Charon sought the boys out and instructed them to repair to the Master at once.

As they entered the room they passed between the two squires standing either side of the door. Master William was seated at the table with one of the knights, Sir Matthew Lovatt. The other knight, Sir Nicholas Gilliott, stood by the fireplace. All four were in harness, the finest German plate armour. All four were armed to the teeth.

'The whispering boy you seek is before you,' said the master, indicating Edmund. 'He was anointed by God in St Leonard's.' The old squire parson was not going to miss this opportunity to tell of the 'miracle' he had witnessed.

'Was he?' said Sir Nicholas, motioning to Edmund to step forward. Clearly, he was not impressed by tales of miracles and he had much to do that day. He was a slim man in his fiftieth year, handsome and with metal-grey hair, who kept himself in good health. In more peaceful times he enjoyed a measure of success in the joust and had a following, especially among the ladies, who shamelessly offered their favour and vied for his attention.

He held out a small leather purse and beckoned Edmund to take it.

'It would seem that we have a friend in common,' said Sir Nicholas, whose disarming smile flashed up readily, 'Best open it and all will be revealed.'

Edmund had no need to loosen the thongs for he already knew what he would find. However, John had no inkling and let out a gasp when his brother withdrew the metal swan badge, which was bent and ruined by a bolt hole.

'Brother Wilkin wishes you and your brother to join him at Roche Abbey three days hence at mid-day.'

The boys turned to look at the Master. He shrugged, looked dismayed, then pointed out that they were needed at the Manor, since there were none to do the work.

Sir Matthew then spoke for the first time. He was a white-faced hulk of a man, a veteran of the French Wars. 'They are needed to do service for the king,' he drawled.

Like a blow from a maul, the remark struck all three together, Reresby, Edmund and John. Were the boys being called to serve Lancaster?

'Not Lancaster! There is a new King of England!' announced Sir Nicholas, 'One worthy of the name: Edward IV, the Rose of Rouen. Mighty in battle, fresh from his victory at Mortimer's Cross, and recently acclaimed king by the lords and commons of London.'

'This England has had enough by far of being ruled by a weak fool and his French wife. They have fielded foreigners and behaved towards their subjects like enemies,' growled Sir Matthew. 'The wind of change is blowing through the land. We now have a sovereign, fair-faced and a mighty warrior who will lead us in battle.'

'There is work to be done ere peace settles on this realm. There is a pretender to dispose of and his supporters to tame,' said Sir Nicholas.

'Boys skilled in the art of the crossbow are mustered and marching north under the charge of Bavarian mercenary, Jason Dietz, for a certain special task.'

'Yes.' Suddenly William Rerseby was all bright-eyed and eager, 'and this boy is The Avenger of Righteous Blood! Of course it all makes sense now. They will be at Roche in three day's time. At noon, you say?'

Within the hour the four hard riders were once again in the saddle and heading north. Their task? To locate the whereabouts of the Lancastrian host and make report. They were on secret assignment for the newly acclaimed, rival King of England, nineteen-year-old King Edward IV.

Chapter Seven

Arrival of the Wasps and 'Snort' and 'Grunt'

THEY TOOK A SPOT in the centre of the sparsely furnished room above Roche Abbey gatehouse, caps clasped in hand and eyes lowered. From behind a small trestle table Brother Wilkin sat glaring at them, long and hard. He was arrayed, not in the habit of the Benedictine order as on the last occasion the boys had seen him, but in clothing usually worn along with the harness of war. The hour was around mid-day, it being the period of Sext and celebration of High Mass. The sound of melodic plainchant floated in odd waves across the intervening Abbey grounds. It served to provide background accompaniment to Brother Wilkin's guttural, broad Yorkshire accent when he finally addressed the boys. *Obbligato* was provided by the occasional rattle of sleet mixed with rain which crackled against the small leaded panes of the gatehouse porch. In the distance, away to the west, the rumble of unseasonable thunder provided an intermittent bass. The sky had changed from dark grey to a black velvet, burdened as it was with a late winter storm lumbering across the West Riding. They had reached the shelter of Roche barely in time.

'I can see Black-faced Clifford has left his mark upon thi, young Hawksworth,' taunted Wilkin, referring to Edmund's swollen and bruised face. Was the Yorkist agent still smarting from the showing-up he had suffered at Edmund's hand on the eve of the Feast of the Conversion of St Paul?

The mysterious man of holy orders leaned forward, placing his arms on the table as he did so and, in a voice which conveyed his annoyance at having to bandy words with mere boys, snapped out, 'I'll come t' point.' He shuffled for a moment in discomfort and then he leaned back and folded his arms.

'On the fourth day of this month of March a true claimant to the crown was proclaimed by the good people of London.' Leaning forward again, he asked, 'You have heard of Edward, Earl of March, eldest son of York?' They both nodded. '"The Rose of Rouen" as some call him. Well, 'e has been declared rightful sovereign of England, and titled Edward IV. Attainders have been issued on supporters of Lancaster and commissions of array are being served. The mightiest army ever raised is marching on Yorkshire.'

He followed that dramatic announcement with an indication that they were to be seated on the floor. John could not help but risk a question.

'But, bro...' He stumbled in an attempt to find a suitable form of address for that doleful-faced spy and agent of York. Was he truly a monk, knight or a mingel? 'What is this matter to do with us? Why have we been summoned to this place?'

'It would seem that t' good Abbot of Roche believes thi whispering brother to be one ordained by the Almighty.' He shook his head as if he considered the idea to be absurd. 'To wreak vengeance, no less, on t' lords of Lancaster.' His voice was heavy with sarcasm.

There was the sound of feet on the stairs hurrying from the gate chamber below. The door was flung open and into the room swept John Wakefield, Abbot of Roche. His usual dramatic manner of entry into a room. Edmund and John sprang to their feet and Wilkin arose slowly from his chair behind the table.

Throwing back his cowl, the Abbot glared at the boys like a kestrel eyeing its prey before swooping. 'Ah yes, the whispering boy from Thryberg, the one many refer to as The Hawk.' He seated himself at the trestle table and indicated that Wilkin resume his seat and the boys step closer. The Abbot addressed Edmund.

'Are you prepared to serve your rightful king and take your place as an Avenger? For an opportunity, by the grace of God and Holy providence, is about to present itself.'

Wilkin interrupted, pointing out that they were nothing more than pig keepers, scullions and mere children at that. The Abbot ignored him, 'News of your blooding is spreading throughout the Riding, and that is why I had you summoned here.'

'Blooding! What blooding?' exclaimed Wilkin in annoyance. His eyes darted from one to another. The Abbot paid him not the slightest heed.

'You sought to cover up your deeds, but Edmund Fitzwilliam told me what happened at the flour mill. Have you sought absolution?' The Abbot turned to John and waited for him to speak for his brother.

Edmund whispered his reply and John cleared his throat 'Edmund says that there can be no benefit from seeking absolution at this time.'

'And why not?' snapped the Abbot, taken aback.

Again Edmund whispered his reply 'My Lord Abbot, the killing has just begun. There can be little advantage in seeking forgiveness until this matter is at an end.'

Wilkin joined in 'Every Christian knight, squire and yeoman makes his peace with God before battle and seeks pardon and divine protection. Are you greater than all of us?' He turned to the Abbot and, with ill-concealed irritation, persisted with questions concerning the 'blooding' of Edmund.

The Abbot leaned back in his chair, chewed the corner of his mouth and sighed; he began in a resigned, flat voice, 'The boys were charged with escorting the Lady Isabel del

Wardrop from Thryberg to the safety of Conisbrough Castle. Three Scots mercenaries attempted the violation of Lady Isabel.' He pointed a long talon-like finger at Edmund, nodding his head in his direction as he did so. 'They say that The Hawk promptly rendered himself invisible and slew all three. A bolt in the neck, and all dead before they hit the ground. The neatest executions ever witnessed.'

'Holy Mother of God! What nonsense!' blasphemed Wilkin, unable to contain his anger. 'The stories they tell abart this brat are daft. We are wasting precious time, there are far more...'

The Abbot struck the table with his fist. 'The story has been confirmed.' He was wearying of Wilkin's scathing manner. 'The Lady Isabel directed Fitzwilliam's men to a deserted plague village by the river Don...'

'Yes, yes, Birdswell Flat... I know of the cursed place,' interrupted Wilkin.

'...there the bodies of the slain Scotsmen were found concealed in an abandoned well.'

Wilkin jumped to his feet and, moving quickly from behind the table, took John by the arm, and with some force dragged him away from his brother.

'Nar speak for thisen, scullion! Answer me, did you, in all truth, and before God, slay the Scotsmen found at Birdswell?'

Edmund did not attempt to speak aloud, for he would have been racked with stuttering if he had tried. Instead he whispered loudly and was heard clearly to say, 'Thou sayest.'

Puzzled at this, Wilkin said, 'Plainly I say, or tha'll feel the back of my hand! Now what does tha mean, pigkeeper – did you kill those men?'

Unruffled, Edmund persisted, 'Thou sayest, you yourself are saying it. '

The old Abbot suddenly cried out with delight, '"Thou sayest": why of course, of course, our Lord before Pilate, when asked directly if he was a king.' The sharp-nosed Abbot was grinning from ear to ear and explained excitedly, 'The Beloved of God neither denied nor confirmed it, but answered the Roman governor in that manner.' He chuckled from sheer pleasure as he repeated over and over again Edmund's reply.

'Thou sayest, you yourself are saying it, the lad will give you no further answer, I'll be bound.' Looking heavenwards, the old cleric clapped his hands 'Bless my soul, the boy is scripturally literate.' He turned to John 'By all the saints – I swear I have never before heard the like! Parson William Reresby taught you boys well!'

Infuriated and frustrated at apparently being bested once more by Edmund's use of scripture, Wilkin pointed with outstretched arm and yelled at Edmund, 'I warn you, scullion, answer me in plain words: do you believe yourself to be anointed by God to be an Avenger of Blood?'

The centre of the storm, scudding across the West Riding, arrived over Roche Abbey at that very moment. On cue and sounding as if it might be the very voice of the Almighty, a flash of lightning flooded the room – promptly followed by a mighty thunderclap which rattled windows and door and near extinguished the candles.

Three of them in that room above the gatehouse were suitably impressed. However, Edmund stood there calmly, legs slightly apart, hands clasped in front of him. He had a gentle smile on his face, amused by the fortunate coincidental timing of the peal of thunder which, much in the manner of a Christmastide mystery play, had seemingly intervened on his behalf and given answer.

'*Dirige, domine, Deus meus, in conspectu tuo viam meam.*' The Abbot was on his knees rocking backwards and forwards, hands clasped in prayer, eyes fixed on the floor. Believing his chastisement to the point of death to be imminent, he sought to petition the Almighty with some urgency.

Wilkin had backed away from Edmund. His legs appeared to give way, causing him to sit heavily in the Abbot's chair.

His face was white and his bottom lip quivered uncontrollably.

Stepping before him, John asked quietly what was required of them and where they were to go.

At first Wilkin appeared to have some difficulty collecting his thoughts; it was as if the thunderclap had completely wiped his mind. Then another, a less dramatic peal, as the storm rolled on towards Doncaster, acted as a prompt and stirred the cleric's senses. Without raising his gaze from the table top, he informed them they were to make their way to the vill of Harthill, in the Manor of Conisborough, and there await the arrival of the crossbow boys. These were led by a Bavarian mercenary who went by the name of Jason Dietz.

That unit, known as the Wasps, was retained by Sir William, Lord Fauconberg and attached to his mounted archers. The *Wespen*, as they were called, could be recognised by their distinctive yellow and black surcoats, along with an oak leaf badge on the left shoulder. On arrival in Yorkshire, the crossbow *Fähnlein* would camp in the churchyard on the south side of All Hallows Church, Harthill.

Further questions fell on deaf ears as Wilkin withdrew within himself. As they left the room, John Wakefield was still on his knees, petitioning the Almighty for absolution as he unburdened himself of guilty secrets and nefarious past deeds. Wilkin continued to stare unblinking at the table.

Edmund was greatly amused by the whole incident, as indeed he had been by the beam of light in St Leonard's, and failed to see any hint of divine intervention. John, for his part, was not so sure; should Edmund complete his avowed task then that would indicate quite clearly whether or not God favoured him. One way or another, time would tell. John considered himself to be nothing more than an onlooker who could no more alter the fated outcome of events than a flea on the back of a hog could prevent its rooting.

*   *   *   *

It was eight miles to Harthill, the southernmost vill of Conisbrough Manor. The crofts they passed along the way were deserted and many had been looted. There was an absence of livestock; not a single goose, hen or chicken remained. By contrast, the vill of Dininngton had not been pillaged at all and the few people they did see uttered not a word as they passed through. Later it would become clear why that treacherous place had escaped the ravages of Margaret's army.

They arrived at Harthill as darkness fell. Not a single living soul could be discerned; it was as if the plague had descended and swept them all into the depths of Hades. The boys sought shelter inside the church of All Hallows. The incumbent priest, Sir Richard Banester, was absent, no doubt bearing arms under a banner of the House of Lancaster. The church and surrounding crofts had, apart from a few barking, hungry dogs, all been abandoned.

John could only look on as Edmund, in his usual manner, got to work at once. After having first constructed a makeshift shelter from altar cloths in one of the chantries, he sought out a chest containing candles. Not showing the slightest compunction, he used the objects dedicated to holy worship as a source of warmth and light. At John's objections he shrugged and asked, 'Did King David of Israel hesitate at consuming the tabernacle showbread when he and his men were hungry? What, then, are a few sticks of tallow?'

Once again John was taken aback by his brother's grasp of holy writ and his seeming wisdom in applying it to their situations. Had he taken into memory every Bible story told them by their mother? And every sermon their squire-parson had ever uttered in St Leonard's? Yet, despite all his understanding of scripture, Edmund's anger at God for taking their mother was relentless and day by day grew

142

increasingly bitter. In passing before the altar John would make an act of genuflexion, whereas Edmund turned his back and looked away.

As a consequence of Edmund's bold irreverence and disrespect for all things holy, the brothers spent a freezing night in complete comfort, wrapped snugly all around. Creaks, thumps, rustlings and other disturbing sounds persisted throughout that night as the wind scurried through and inside the old church, playing cruel games with John's imagination. The crypt beneath them contained the mortal remains of their betters. Suppose they were guilty of sacrilege, invading the rest of these high-born persons? Cockcrow heralded John's relief as the grey light of day bathed the interior of their makeshift tent.

Edmund had slept the night through, having no concerns for the likely proximity of spirits of dead men. If Heaven existed and the chants and prayers of the living could ensure safe arrival there, why would their ghosts bother hanging around burial places scaring the living? There was no sense in that.

It was during the period of Prime that, from a vantage point in the church tower, they first spotted riders on the southern approaches. Emerging from the dank mist and steady rain which began to fall, was a group of horsemen, about twenty in number. The riders split into pairs and began combing the village. From the blue and white livery, along with what appeared to be the fish hook badge, they knew that those mounted scourers were retained by the House of Fauconberg, uncle of the newly-acclaimed Yorkist king. The mounted archers regrouped in the churchyard beneath the tower, seemingly satisfied that no enemy lurked among the crofts and outbuildings waiting to ambush the scourers. After a brief look around inside the church and its vaults, the party despatched two of its number to report, whilst the remainder lit a fire on one of the chest-tomb graves close by the church door. The boys remained for a while in the tower, wondering whether to make themselves known to those nervous bowmen or wait for the boys known as the Wasps.

Then it was that they heard it – a faint, incessant drumming carried to their ears in waves of sound by the grey vaporous blanket of that March morning mist. It was the beat of naker sticks on tabors and the boom of a larger drum.

As the pulsating beat grew louder, they began to discern rhythmic patterns, complicated and insistent. The hair on the back of John's neck stood on end as he began to discern two distinct sets of drumming. It was as if one set of players was talking to another as the complicated beating was picked up and repeated with variations. As one set of tabor players ended the sequence the other team picked up the rhythm and proceeded to elaborate on it, exploring, innovating and complicating the beat before handing it back as if to say, 'Better that, if you can!' Suddenly, there was the squeal of pipes and of shawms picking out a tune and then a counterpoint. Those pipes joined the competition, for that's what it seemed to be. Never had the brothers heard music played in such an intense manner before. That vibrant beat was to accompany marching feet and it was – yes – by all the saints – it was exhilarating. It was the music of war.

They came into sight, led by a mounted knight, two columns of boys aged between twelve and seventeen years ranked in pairs – eighteen boys in total. They were the ones providing the marching music, grim-faced, intense and fully occupied in their competitive playing. Behind them was a cart pulled by two horses in tandem and behind it, masses of marching men emerging from the mist with banners flying. With a minimum of shouted orders and calls on horns, the host began to split up into well-ordered companies, households and fraternities.

Churches were used as rallying and regrouping places during campaign marches, and the captains knew which aspect of the church building served as their particular gathering ground and camp site. Just as the twelve tribes of Israel were allotted tented positions around the tabernacle in the wilderness, likewise each company making up the host on the march knew its place. The arrangement contributed to good order. Should an enemy suddenly make a stand and draw up battlelines, then the vanward of an army could be brought into a defensive position speedily.

Their sudden appearance at the church door caused consternation among the scourers who, as scouts, should have discerned their presence in the church but had failed to do so. As a consequence, they were unnerved and angry. Upon John saying, 'We're for the *Wespen!*' they were roughly handled and pushed to where the boys had wheeled round and halted at the southern aspect of the church and within the churchyard boundary.

The host had been marching since first light and every man and boy was tired and hungry. Eighteen pairs of eyes glared at the Hawksworth boys, some with ill-concealed curiosity and even hostility. Then the spell was instantly broken when a woman dressed in man's attire, and who had been driving the cart, banged on a pewter plate. Like well-trained performing dogs, the boys quickly formed two orderly lines; there was neither pushing nor shoving and no talking. Soon they were dipping lumps of bread into a steaming hotchpotch which had miraculously been produced in a cauldron by the slightly-sized woman.

It was John and Edmund's first sight of *Die Mater* or 'Mother', some said a 'wise woman'. For most of the boys Mater was the only mother they had ever known. She it was who nursed them through illnesses, bound up their wounds and set their broken bones. Their clothes and shoes were repaired by her and their disputes she judged in firmness. Her favour was sought by each one as they vied for her attention and affection.

Mater beckoned the brothers over and inquired if they were for the Wasps. She smiled kindly from soft brown eyes which at once put them at their ease. It was difficult to judge her age, for she lacked wrinkles, yet streaks of grey in her coal-black hair suggested perhaps a fourth decade and five years. Her frame was slight and her manner mild; she should have been occupied in a more peaceable livelihood than that of campaigner in sanguinary wars. She called over a small boy aged about twelve whom she addressed as Wee Willie. He was clad in cast-offs, his surcoat over-sized for him and the black-coloured material faded to a pale grey. He was to take them to *Hauptmann* Jason Dietz, the mercenary commander of the *Fähnlein*.

'Once you have made yourselves known to the master over there,' she indicated a group gathered around the village Saxon cross, 'you may wish to break your fast with us.'

As they passed the line of busily feeding boys they were once more given a critical looking-over, but never a word was spoken at them.

Jason Dietz, the *Hauptmann*, was being shaved by one of the boys and they took their place before him, waiting until the job was completed. It was likely that he was once handsome but a leather patch now covered an empty left eye-socket and, what could only be described as a healed-over hole, a round indentation measuring half-an-inch across, decorated his right cheek where a crossbow bolt had once penetrated and pierced the bone through.

'*Der armbrustschütze?*' he rapped out, glancing first at one and then the other with violent moves of his head. 'Which ist shooter?' he attempted again in broken tongue.

They did not understand a word he said through his heavy Bavarian-Swiss accent and they could only shuffle and utter sounds indicating lack of comprehension. Then the boy who had been shaving the scarred warrior intervened.

146

'Which one of you does the shooting?' This youngster, a gangling sixteen-year-old who was known throughout the host as Didi Wattle, offered helpfully, 'One of you loads the bow and one of you does the shooting – which is which?'

'My brother never misses and I load for him.'

'What? Never?' Didi Wattle's voice raised incredulously. 'You're not going to be popular around here. Have you met Fleshy, our *Rottmeister*? He, too, claims that he never misses. And guess what? I don't believe him either!'

There was a good-natured ripple of laughter from some archers standing close by and John discerned that they were smiling at the pallid-faced youth in anticipation. It was as if they were expecting him to say something else to amuse. That was John and Edmund's introduction to one of the *Wespen* jesters. Two of the boys went by the names Wattle and Daub, and played the fool for the entertainment of nobles and their retainers. It was the ever-optimistic Wattle who explained the organisation of the crossbow *Fähnlein*. *Hauptmann* Dietz had other matters to attend to and limped off in the direction of a group of knights gathering by the church door.

Jason Dietz, the one-eyed, fearsome-looking Swiss-Bavarian, had organised his eighteen-strong crossbow *Fähnlein* on the lines of a continental mercenary *Abteilung*. The boys were paired up, each having a crossbow but only one of them – the better shot – the *Armbrustschütze*, took care of the shooting. During battle the loader or *Ladenschütze* passed his spanned weapon to his partner and then loaded for him. With practice, a well-matched pair could loose off twelve aimed bolts a minute, causing bloody devastation among the leaders of the opposing ranks. Rivalry among them was fierce as each pair sought to outshoot the others. In their march from London they had all been talking about and looking forward to a competition shoot for a silver bolt. That competition was to take place once the final mustering point for the Yorkist campaign in the north was reached. Young King Edward was to present the prize to the winning pair.

The *Fähnlein* was split into two divisions, *Rotte Schwarz* (Black) and *Rotte Gelb* (Yellow). The leader of *Rotte Schwarz* also served as the *Rottmeister* for the whole *Abteilung*. His name was Alvar Fleischer, an eighteen-year-old who had served with the *Hauptmann* for three years, mainly on the continent as a mercenary selling his skill at arms to feuding lords in Burgundy. He considered himself the best shot in the *Fähnlein*.

'Did you hear us playing as we marched into the vill?' asked Didi Wattle, full of enthusiasm and with some pride. 'What did you think? You have never heard the like of it, have you?'

Each of the boys was expected to learn to play either the tabor or a wind instrument. Whenever a town or village was encountered along the march, Dietz would give the order to play the *Fähnlein* through the streets. Again, there was keen rivalry among them as to their playing skills. The boys equipped with tabors sought to out-drum each other. Competition was especially fierce between the *Rotten*.

Didi Wattle led the brothers to where the Wasps were seated finishing off their breakfasts. Warning them about the leader, *Rottmeister* Fleischer, he hurriedly whispered, 'He doesn't like to be called 'Fleshy'. So be careful. Even if any of the others tell you to call him that, don't. They seem to think it a great jest. And don't play dice with him. He'll have all your coins and the shirt off your back.'

The *Rottmeister* beckoned them over to where he and a couple of his young aides lounged on a stone tomb-chest. Immediately, the brothers were on their guard. He was of average height, full grown, with a dark complexion and campaign hair cut. His black hair was extra long on the left side so as to hide where his ear had been clipped some time in the past for theft. His dark brown eyes were set wide apart and glowered from a fully rounded face. His mouth was small, bordered by thin, bright red lips and when he spoke it was with a faint lisp, as if his tongue was too large for his mouth.

'What are you called? And where are you from?'

He brightened up considerably when he discovered that the newcomers were swineherds. He stood up, stepped forward and, in an act of mock solemnity, 'baptised' them both, pouring the contents of his leather tankard over their heads:

'*In nomine Patris, et Filii, et Spiritus Sancti,* thou shalt be called "Snort".' Then, nodding at Edmund he said, 'and I name thee "Grunt"!'

There followed a discordant chorus of "amen" from the men and boys gathered there and then a clapping of hands. The farce over and greatly satisfied by his performance, Fleischer got down to the business in hand.

'You will join to *Rotte Schwarz* – that is, Section Black. You will be given a Wasp surcoat and badge when I deem you've earned the wearing and not before. This will be after the Silver Bolt shoot at Doncaster when we see what you're made of. Harness and jack you will scavenge for yourselves where you can. We have crossbows taken at our victory at Mortimer's Cross. These you will find in Mater's wagon. Go feed your faces before Mater gives the left-overs to the outriders.'

John and Edmund headed for the wagon to a chorus of grunts and snorts. John considered that their joining the *Wespen* was off to a miserable start and was heavy of heart at the thought of the ridicule that would be heaped upon them in the days to come. However, it seemed not to bother Edward, who merely smiled at his brother, winked and gave a few grunts. John felt much better and pondered once more how a younger brother could lift the spirits and even make his elder feel reassured.

In less than one hour the signal to prepare to march was given by the blowing of a horn. Vintenars began yelling commands, rousing men to their feet, and identifying banners were placed at paced-out intervals along the road for rallying adherents to that particular company.

Foreriders and outriders made hasty adjustments to horses' harnesses before swinging up into their saddles and trotting off northwards to make contact with scouts. The Wasps formed up where they were; they would march through to the front of the entire vanguard, drumming as they went. John's heart sank as he saw Fleischer, the bullying *Rottmeister*, bearing down on them swinging a mace, a weapon which both served to denote his rank and to knock and prod his charges into orderly ranks.

'You two march at the rear!' Thus saying, he cracked John across the upper arm and thrust them both into line. 'We'll decide what melodic gifts you possess another time.'

Just then one of the boys, a stocky Welsh lad called 'Mealy' Madoc, hobbled up, protesting that a sprained ankle he was suffering from was worse and could he ride with Mater? To make his point, he held high his boot which he'd removed and pointed to his swollen limb. It was a horrible dark blue to near-black in colour. Fleischer had denied Mealy his request for a ride for the past twenty miles; however, there was no ignoring the injury now. With obvious ill-humour, the *Rottmeister* nodded and then yelled for Wee Willie to take Mealy's place in the ranks.

As the boys began lining up, the steady beat of a drum signalled the step and within no time the two companies were formed. A strange rocking motion was produced along the length of both *Rotte Gelb* and *Rotte Schwarz* as the boys marched on the spot. The *Rottmeister* ran from one group to the other correcting the step of first one boy here and another there, all the time enforcing barked insults with prods and blows from his mace. Once satisfied that all were stamping in perfect rhythm, he ran part-way to the churchyard where *Hauptmann* Dietz waited, mounted on a magnificent black courser stallion. A raised gauntlet suddenly dropped and at that signal Fleischer spun around and blew on a small horn. Every second boy carried a tabor and they all began drumming in unison. The two boys directly in front of John and Edmund suddenly marched away, leaving them flat-footed. Before they could gather their wits and catch up, the *Rottmeister* was there flailing about him with his mace. At that moment the pain from the beating detracted from the sheer magic of the sound produced by the *Fähnlein* on the march. *Rotte Gelb*, consisting of ten boys ranked in pairs, was leading, and from among them a complicated drumming sequence was struck up. The boy in front of John, a willowy youth with long fair hair called Snowwhite, immediately picked up the beat on twin tabors attached to his belt. Both his hands appeared to dissolve into a blur. *Rotte Schwarz* had by far the best drummer in its ranks.

The *Wespen* had barely reached the bottom of the road leading north away from Harthill when two riders caught up and they were halted. The *Fähnlein* fell silent. There was a brief exchange with Fleischer who then strode back along the ranks towards the Hawksworths. 'What now?' John mouthed to his brother.

'You're wanted!' Fleischer lisped. His eyes were filled with what may have been anger mixed with contempt. 'The lords demand your presence!' Pointing his mace at them he snarled. 'Give mind to your degree, else lose your heads!'

They were hoisted up behind the two riders and arrived back at All Hallows church, where a number of captains were gathered around a herald, who was obviously discomfited as he juggled a compass, lodestone and quadrant. Muttering to himself, he peered at first one and then another of his instruments before consulting a parchment upon which was scrawled a crude strip map. Periodically he held the astrolobe quadrant to his eye before glancing back at the map and shaking his head. The captains were becoming impatient. It was then that a lord of obvious distinction rode up and dismounted by the group. They stood back to allow the new arrival through.

'What holds back this march?' he roared at the quivering herald.

Sir William Neville, Lord Fauconberg was short in stature and short in patience. His face was tanned to the hue of saddle leather, with the nose flattened, evidence of a blow once taken full in the face by a French mace. He was bald on top where the constant wearing of the sallet during lengthy campaigns had taken its toll. About his chin a small, grey-streaked beard added to the old warrior's fearsome appearance. The sixty-year old veteran of marcher skirmishes and the French wars now commanded the van of Edward IV's mighty host and was greatly irritated at the continuing delay.

Hauptmann Dietz drew the group's attention to the boys' arrival and they were lowered to the ground and nudged forward. Removing their caps, they dropped the knee before Lord Fauconberg and waited.

'To your feet, boys, to your feet!' Not unkindly spoken. 'We were expecting a guide to take us the quickest way through Conisbrough Manor property and to the castle. He has failed to grace us with his presence and our herald here seems to know not one wit as to where to take this host. Now you could earn a groat apiece should you know the answer to three questions. How far is it to Conisbrough? What road is best suited to wagons? And are you fit to lead us?'

Edmund whispered his preferred route to his brother and, nodding, John addressed the gathering with his gaze firmly fixed on Lord Fauconberg's belt buckle 'My lords, 'tis twelve miles and the tracks are poor. It will be nightfall, after Vespers, ere the castle. We can lead you.'

Turning to the captain of the foreriders, Sir Walter Blount, the veteran warrior nodded with satisfaction, then cursed loudly, as only old campaigners can, and snapped out his orders 'Keep alert. Remember what happened at Advent just past when the Duke of York, God rest his soul, his foreriders and outriders were environed at Worksop and came off the worst. This Riding is wick with supporters of Lancaster.'

John raised his hand to be allowed to speak and was given a curt nod. 'My lord must know that the next places along your way, the vills of Anston and Dinnington, have not been pillaged by the northern hordes. Livestock and store barns are untouched.'

'And these places, can they be skirted? We want no hostile exchequers counting off our numbers for the enlightenment of Somerset and his satanic brood!'

John glanced at his brother, who nodded.

'We will return and take care of these nests of vermin once we have settled the matter with Henry and his French she-wolf,' the grizzled veteran assured his captains. 'The foreriders must not permit too great a distance betwixt them and the outriders – three-bow shots, and no more.'

So saying, Lord Fauconberg settled his sallet firmly on his head and pushed up the visor. Fifty plus knights immediately followed this action by their commander. John noticed that captains lacking visors still brought up their right hands to touch their foreheads. It was a novel fashion, a form of salute to a commander. From places scattered all around the church, squires brought forward the rested, fed and watered destriers, coursers and palfreys, helping their masters to mount. It all seemed confusion, yet horns sounded and order sprang from chaos as centenars, vintenars and decenars ordered the companies in columns on the main road through Harthill.

Two bowmen foreriders held down their hands and the two boys swung up behind them. John's rider was Sir Robin Carle, a surprisingly gentle man for a warrior, and he was pleased to be with him. Edmund's rider was Sir Alan Mortimer from Kent.

Mist was clearing as the period of Sext was just past and a watery sun made gallant efforts to struggle through the gray overcast. From his vantage position on the back of the magnificent war horse John could see clearly the colourful array of massed billmen and archers gathered behind the banners of their fraternities, interspaced with horse-drawn carts, and pack animals stretching back as far as the eye could see. Then they were off at a gallop and John hung on lest he be unseated. Waiting for the guide to arrive had delayed the vanward battle far too long and the captains were relieved to be moving again.

Within half-an-hour they were a mile or more from the recently deserted village of Brampton, crossing gorse scrubland locals called Laughton Common, when suddenly Edmund, whose horse and rider were half a bowshot ahead, began waving his arm and pointing to a ditch running through a clump of evergreen bushes. As they caught up, Edmund indicated a flock of carrion birds gathering excitedly around an object concealed from sight in a hollow. Both mounted bowmen looked at each other and shrugged before nudging their steeds in the direction of the excited ravens.

There had been a hurried attempt to cover over the body of an elderly man. Edmund slipped from the back of the horse and crouched over the partially stripped corpse in the ditch. Though the victim's face was contorted and frozen in its death agony, there was no mistaking who it was. The dour face of the dead man was easily recognisable.

'It's Brother Wilkin, he's been strangled,' Edmund stuttered aloud.

'You know him then? Who is he?' asked Sir Robin.

'We know him to be a Benedictine monk favouring the House of York. He it was who directed us to Harthill to await the arrival of the *Wespen*,' said John. Then it was that the horror of the discovery swept over him.

'How can this be? The last time we saw him was yesterday, alive, at Roche Abbey.'

John was beginning to tremble and it wasn't the bitter nip in the air. The sight of violently slain men was still novel to his experience. Unlike the strangers, the Scotsmen cut down at the water mill, John had shared this man's company at Thryberg Manor and again at the Abbey only the previous day.

'If, as you say, he is from Roche then he is surely the guide Lord Fauconberg was awaiting,' Robin Carle suggested. 'He must have been set upon and robbed.'

The outriders trotted up, followed by a number of knights and finally Fauconberg himself. Growing ever louder in the distance was the unmistakable thump of the large drum of the *Wespen*.

'This man was carrying much coinage and silver bars from Roche Abbey as a contribution to his liege lord, King Edward,' muttered Fauconberg. 'He was to have been our guide to Conisbrough. By mischance he must have fallen foul of thieves. Since the ending of the French wars the north is infested with desperate men, outlaws seeking a crooked livelihood. Could have been a deserter from the hordes of that witch Margaret who did it. The work of the Devil!'

Edmond began speaking to his brother with urgency.

'Speak up, boy, or you'll feel my hand,' growled Fauconberg, fuming that money to help pay the host had been taken by robbers.

'The agent for York was not killed by common robbers that chanced upon him, nor did he die at this spot.' John paused to let that sink in. 'He was brought to this place from that direction,' John nodded towards the east, before adding, 'about the time of Prime, slung over the back of a packhorse.'

'How could you know that?' demanded Jason Dietz.

'There were two men. One rode a well-shod destrier, therefore at least one was of high degree.' Lowering his voice,

John said, 'My brother believes this to be the hand of a lord of Lancaster.'

'Witchcraft! How else could the boy know this detail?' gasped one among the crowd of knights and squires gathered round to peer at the corpse.

'It is not difficult, my lords. The upper part of this man's face and head is discoloured, as also are the feet, where blood within the body settled after death. He was brought here with his head hung down, as if transported draped over the back of a horse. The soil and grass beneath him is wet; by Terce this morning the rain had ceased, so he must have been dropped to the ground after that period.'

There was a low whistle of acknowledgement from one of the knights. A surge of self-importance swept over John, but of course the field-craft and wisdom were not his. The good feeling was immediately replaced by one of guilt. John pointed across the track to where three distinct sets of hoof-prints churned the soft ground. 'My brother also notes that three horses came to this place this morning, one horse went back lighter.'

A dozen heads turned and peered off in the direction indicated 'What place lies over yonder?' was the next question called out.

'The vills of Dinnington and Anston,' John muttered, staring off in the same direction.

'For Wilkin to journey from Roche Abbey to Harthill to meet the host of York he would have had to pass through Dinnington and Anston. My brother feels that it is in those places that answers are to be found.'

The faces of the gathered men bore that same look that John had begun to observe in so many others where his brother was concerned. It was as if they did not know who he was; as if they were looking at him for the very first time and trying to figure him out – a cautious reserve, maybe in the case of some, an inconceivable grudging respect, even awe.

Fauconberg had a decision to make and it made him irritable. He could detach some knights to try and find the culprits and retrieve the money, or press on and leave the matter until after the defeat of Henry and Margaret's northern hordes. 'We press on to Conisbrough.' he decided, 'This matter will have to wait.'

'The trail will have grown cold ere this matter with Lancaster be settled,' offered one of the nobles, John, Lord Fitzwalter. 'Should we pursue this matter now, likely we will retrieve the money and bring to rights the murderers.'

Then another called out, 'Ask the whispering boy who it was who committed this crime and save us all time.' This was greeted by a great deal of good-natured laughter, which Fauconberg silenced with a glare. A faithful agent of York lay throttled at his feet and monies meant for the campaign against the detested enemy had been stolen. This was not the time nor place for levity.

Suddenly, the inept guide, the herald, who was still clutching compass, quadrant and rolled maps in one hand and restraining a restive palfrey with the other, called out, 'Ask the boy who it was who killed this man, for there are rumours that a boy from these parts has been touched by the Almighty. Mayhap 'tis this one?'

'We burnt the French maid, Joan of Arc, for witchcraft. We shall make no use of such enchantment here,' roared Fauconberg, impatient to restart the march north. Then he asked, 'Could your brother possibly know?'

Once again John conveyed Edmund's words to the lord but in low, guarded tones. Thankfully, Fauconberg drew the two boys a short distance away where John was able to explain. His words would amount to an accusation against their betters. 'When we passed through Dinnington yesterday the two dozen villagers and crofters were all there. That would surely indicate that their master was about. He would be well-mounted – the only man of that vill owning a well-shod war horse.'

'And who heads that community?' Fauconberg asked, his voice slow and deliberate as he peered across the common with narrowed eyes.

'The living, as rector, is held by Sir Richard Nowell,' John answered, knowing that if Edmund was mistaken then they both could find themselves at the end of a rope. But there was every indication that someone from Dinnington was involved. Wilkin's route from Roche Abbey to meet up with the Yorkist army massing at Harthill would have taken him through Dinnington shortly after cock-crow that morning. After the murder Wilkin's body had been brought out two miles onto the heath from that direction. The only man in the vill owning and riding a destrier was the rector, Sir Richard. There had been no time before the body was found for it to have been anyone else. If the rector was not the killer, it was likely that he was implicated. Had it not been for the sharp eyes of Edmund noting the ravens and all the signs on the victim, along with the indications in the soft ground, it would have looked as though the Barnsley monk had fallen prey to robbers. Having recently transported the three corpses of the Scotsmen over the backs of horses, the brothers were familiar with the discolouring to the bodies this brought about.

Fauconberg made his decision; he now had a name, the culprits could be sought out after the matter at hand had been settled. On to Conisbrough Castle was his order.

As the host continued on its way towards the vill of Wickersley, a densely-packed column stretching back over five miles, word of the whispering boy with the gift of divination who consults the flying creatures of the heavens spread like a heath fire. Edmund, of course, when asked directly concerning his miraculous powers, continued to deny any supernatural gifts.

Shortly before Compline, as daylight began to fail on Monday 23rd March, 1461, the feast day of St Gwinear, foreriders of the vanward battle of the host of Edward IV rode into the cobbled square of Conisbrough. They were greeted with cheering, followed by merrymaking, as a greatly relieved populace made known its pleasure. Ten miles behind the rearprickers of the vanward were the foreriders of the middleward. This middleward battle flew the Royal Banner of the Sovereign of England, Edward IV. Marching north via Coventry was the Earl of Warwick, who was aiming to join up with the vanward and the middleward of Edward's army at Conisbrough. The Duke of Norfolk, gathering another strong contingent, the rearward, was a further day-and-a-half behind the rest and would miss the rendezvous.

*   *   *   *

FORTY-EIGHT YEARS ON, Friday 22nd June, 1509, also, coincidently as the bells summoned to Compline, others rode into Conisbrough town square, before wheeling their mounts around and clattering through the narrow crowded streets down to the castle. On this occasion the crowd lining the route was not cheering the riders; rather, it was menacingly silent. The serjeant-at-arms of Doncaster and six men-at-arms who accompanied Brother Rollo, emissary of the Bishop of Lincoln, were grim-faced and determined that the law would be carried out. Their intent and purpose was to lay hands upon the storyteller, John Hawksworth, and convey him to Doncaster where, on the morrow, he was to be burned to death in the town's fish market as a condemned heretic – a despised Lollard.

Chapter Eight

The Final Muster and The 'Againrising'

SOMEONE HAD RAISED THE ALARM and news of the arrival of armed men at the castle gate rippled through the crowd crammed into Conisbrough Castle inner bailey. Up the outer staircase the news flowed from mouth to ear, up the turning stairway of the keep itself. Light was fading, candles were being lit in the Lord's Chamber as the story telling came to an abrupt halt. Those assembled turned to the door. Silence descended as all awaited the appearance of the intruders. Shortly, the clumping of feet was heard on the steps. The progress of the serjeant-at-arms and his men was impeded by the crowds on the stairs. After what seemed an age, the burly, red-faced and pox-scarred officer was framed in the door.

'By what authority do you impose yourself on this gathering?' demanded Lady Lucy Fitzwilliam.

'There is at this place a condemned heretic who must be handed over to us,' was the shouted reply. The man's eyes searched among the packed faces turned toward him. 'There is a warrant for a John Hawksworth and we are instructed to take him in chains to Doncaster.'

No one moved to allow the serjeant-at-arms into the room. Indeed, they were deliberately forming a solid human wall and the furious officer of the town authority made as if to draw his sword. There was a struggling on the steps as the serjeant's men were jostled and impeded in every way by the hostile crowd. The spilling of blood seemed but seconds away.

What would Edmund do if he were here? John asked himself. The situation held potential for a series of nasty incidents. For a start there were the two guards who had escorted him in chains from Lincoln Castle. They had 'misplaced' their weapons and, it could be argued, had allowed the present situation to develop. From the beginning, the two escorting guards had joined the audience of those seeking to hear the legend of The Hawk. They stood together by the fireplace with ashen faces, their eyes darting about nervously as if looking for a means of escape. They would be called to face a garrison court at Lincoln Castle for dereliction of duty and, without doubt, they would be punished.

Moving across the crowded chamber, John positioned himself between his former guards. 'I am the one you seek! I am John Hawksworth.'

There was further uproar as people protested. The richly-clad minstrel called out that the story of the Thryberg Hawk was not yet told, that the record being penned by the scribes was incomplete.

John called over the heads of the people, 'It is flattering that you have been sent to escort me, but my guards have never left my side and will deliver me at noon tomorrow.'

In a hesitant gesture, the serjeant-at-mace, Robert Williams, placed his hand gently upon John's arm and the other guard followed his example. Then the crowd parted to allow the serjeant-at-arms into the room. He stood before the three of them, sweating profusely, out of breath and glowering in fury.

'What?' he began.

'We're to convey the prisoner to Doncaster on the festival day of St Ethelreda, which is on the morrow, and hand him over to the town bailiffs for the proscribed execution of the warrant,' said Williams. The Lincoln serjeant-at-mace, having found his confidence, spoke with quiet authority. 'May we inquire on whose say-so you seek to lay hands on the prisoner in our charge? Has there been a change of our orders?'

The Doncaster serjeant-at-arms spun around looking for Brother Rollo. The hapless cleric did indeed successfully reach the lord's chamber but, on arriving, was hoisted off his feet and passed kicking and yelling over the heads of the crowd all the way down the staircase again. He stood unsteadily outside the keep, breathing excommunication, damnation and visitation of the Black Death on every man, woman and child in Conisbrough. The contents of a bucket of water aimed by the mischievous Tiptoe served to cool the monk down. The crowd, pressed together in great numbers in the inner bailey, applauded in approval.

'The Lady Fitzwilliam has requested that the prisoner tell the story of his brother, the Thryberg Hawk.' John's keeper bowed his head in deference towards Lady Lucy. 'We saw no dismay in granting her ladyship's request.'

'They have acted correctly in all matters,' said Lady Lucy, 'We are greatly pleased with the consideration and kindness of these men. I shall be writing to the Bishop of Lincoln to thank him for their offices whilst sojourning here.'

Raising her head, she looked down her nose, her manner hardening 'As for you, had Sir Henry Wyatt, our bailiff and constable, not been attending the coronation of our sovereign, King Henry VIII and his Queen, Catherine of Aragon, at Westminster, he would have by force of arms barred you from entering this place.'

The tables were turned and it was the officer of the court's turn to wriggle in discomfort.

'We were given to understand that the prisoner had been set free, your ladyship, and was bound to escape.'

'Please remove your helmet!' Lady Lucy was not requesting, she was ordering.

The startled serjeant-at-arms stuttered his apologies, doffed his helmet and clumsily dropped to one knee.

'When and where does sentence have to be carried out?' demanded Lady Lucy.

'Tomorrow, my lady, some time after the period of None but before Vespers, in Doncaster fish market.'

'When the prisoner was brought to this castle, who was charged with the responsibility for his keeping?' she demanded.

'The castellan of this place, my lady.'

'You have answered correctly, and as the castle constable delegated his oversight to me and the duty is still being done, and the guards appointed by the Bishop of Lincoln are still carrying out their duties, I fail to understand the purpose of your intrusion. Why are you here at all?'

'My lady, we crave your forgiveness. We are the victims of foul intelligence.'

'You may rise.' Her voice had taken on a more gentle tone. 'Should you still feel the need to provide reinforcement, for fear of the crowd, to escort the prisoner to Doncaster on the morrow, that is for you to decide. In the meantime you and your men may retire to the outer bailey until such time as the prisoner leaves with his assigned escort, about the period of Sext. Do I make myself clear?'

'Yes, of course, my lady.'

'Please take your men and leave at once.'

Red-faced, no longer from exertion, but from acute embarrassment, the serjeant-at-arms made his way down through the throng on the stairs and out into the inner bailey where a dripping Rollo met him, demanding to know the whereabouts of the prisoner. A blow from the serjeant's clenched fist sent the monk reeling backwards into the castle pigsty. Again, to loud applause from the delighted crowd.

With the interruption at an end, Lady Lucy turned and with the kindliest of voices asked, 'Do you think you could conclude your story of The Hawk by noon tomorrow?'

John bowed graciously and the crowd clapped.

The ginger-headed child turned to her companions. 'You see, I told you, Edmund questioned not the birds at all, he just knew how they behaved.' She looked over to John for confirmation and called out, 'Isn't that so, Storyteller?' John nodded and returned to his place by the solar window.

The richly-clad minstrel added his observations 'So, concerning the matter of the murdered Benedictine, The Hawk was not possessed of miraculous knowledge so as to deduce the true place of his death, but rather, he observed by the state of the corpse that it had been moved post mortem.'

'As I explained,' John said, 'we had previously moved three dead men by horseback and as a consequence knew that blood settled in and coloured the extremities. Edmund merely recognised the discolouring signs on the body of the Benedictine.'

Fresh quills and parchment were produced and those scribing indicated that they were ready. John, it appeared, was expected to continue recounting the tale into the night. There would be little time for him to make his peace with the Almighty. On the journey to the stake perhaps he would find opportunity to make preparation in prayer. Suddenly he felt the desolate grip of fear; his time was drawing ever closer. The story-telling would serve as a welcome distraction.

Before picking up the threads once more, he took time to gaze out of the solar window at the village of Conisbrough and at the Norman tower of St Peter's Church and at once recalled the pain of that previous time – both physical and also to his adolescent emotions. Across the valley he could see the road leading eastward from Conisbrough, slicing across the green hillside, upon which a lone cart presently laboured the incline, the carrier perhaps on his way to Warmsworth or Doncaster. Once, oh so long ago, that same road had been packed with marching men which had presented such a heartening sight to those of the Yorkist vanward already camped about the castle. It had been a solid wall of writhing, clanking metal. Like a huge serpent from Hell, it had weaved its way down towards the settlement by the Don. Halberds, bills, pole axes, war hammers, sallets and body armour had glittered in the watery sun of that morning in March, 1461. The whole heaving mass had been interspersed with standards unfurled for the occasion. Banners and colourful surcoats had indicated the various household affinities and representative soldiers of numerous townships. What a stirring display of might it had been.

Heaving a heavy sigh, John smiled at his companion, Brother Naulty, then turned to address the crowded room. Once more he began his task of telling the incredible story of Edmund Hawksworth. An account of a living legend no longer supressed – at least for a while.

It was so different forty-eight years ago when John had arrived at Conisbrough village, for then he was feeling quite proud of himself and yearned to impress the girl widow who had captured his heart. He felt no embarrassment in making known his youthful secrets and feelings to the strangers gathered about him, for they wished only fair fortune, of that he was convinced. In a matter of hours he would be dead anyway. Oh, how he hoped he would die bravely in the manner of the Lord Jesus, for he was able to say to those who would follow him, 'In the world ye shall have tribulation, but trust ye, I have overcome the world.' So comforted with this scripture from St John's gospel, John took a swig from a tankard of mature mead and began once more.

*　　*　　*　　*

THE SIGHT OF THE MIGHTY white-stoned fortress of Conisbrough, which guarded the strategic King's Ferry crossing of the Don, caused his heart to race. Would the Lady Isabel del Wardrop be there to see him arrive in dignified splendour seated behind the fine mounted archer? John could think of nothing else but that beautiful vision, the child bride so cruelly widowed by the evil Black-faced Master of Craven. John had left the manor of Thryberg as a mere scullion and now he was returning guiding a mighty army. Edmund's part in this was, of course, relegated to the back of his mind. Also lurking there, suitably suppressed, was the young maiden's granting to his brother the intimate promise of her favour. Edmund, he felt sure, would never prevail upon her to pay him that avowed forfeit, whatever it was. John had become convinced of that. Would it transfer to himself he wondered?

For his services to the new king, Edward IV, mayhap he would have good fortune to become a squire, and then, who knows? His mind danced tantalisingly over possible destinies, all including the beautiful girl Isabel and that possible sexual favour. Realistically, he knew enough to realise that for the time being his fortunes were tied to his brother. One who with each passing day, by skill, cunning and ability, was coming to the attention of the Yorkist lords, knights and captains of horse and of foot.

It had been the feast day of the Conversion of St Paul, Sunday 25th January, 1461, when they delivered the beautiful wife of Richard del Wardrop to this very castle, only to find that her handsome young bridegroom had been done to death before the castle bar in a failed attempt to persuade the garrison to capitulate. How had the young widow fared in the intervening two months?

Their task as guides was over and they waved a cheery farewell to their riders when they were dropped off at the southern aspect of Conisbrough village church, where they were to await the arrival of the *Wespen*.

And there it was – mingling with the peal of St Peter's bells sounding the final call to Compline, the unmistakable rattle of tabors of the *Fähnlein* on the march. That incredible sound which made the blood race and caused a tingling sensation at the nape of John's neck. Involuntarily, he stiffened and gained a further half-inch. Doncaster was to be the rallying point of the Yorkist host marching north, the final muster, and the crossbow boys would leave their mark on the place with a most impressive display, the like of which had never been seen.

Conisbrough Castle and its manor had become a royal property upon its owner becoming, in quick succession, the Duke of York and, within weeks, the King of England. The mighty fortress, which had so loyally held against Lancaster, would become the secure and firm base for the new King's operations in the north, as it had for his father three months earlier at Christmastide. Edward IV was resolute, it was time to rid the nation of his half-cousin, the overly gentle, ineffective Henry VI, who surrounded himself with self-seeking and incompetent advisors. The French woman, Henry's Jezebel Queen, Margaret of Anjou, would be packed off back to France from whence she came.

Lord Fauconberg's vanward was streaming into the village and castle environs behind the tabors and pipes of the crossbow boys. As was their usual practice, the harbingers were seeking for the retainers of the lords' fellowships the very best lodgings from the good people of Conisbrough. Unlike the Lancastrian hordes' with their plunder and robbery, the Yorkists were paying for victuals and shelter. Willing locals acted as guides, pointing out the water sources and winter grazing grounds. From hidden places flour stores were opened and the smell of baking bread and frying bacon soon began to lay siege on the nostrils of hungry men.

As the steady stream of carts arrived at Conisbrough, tented camps began springing up on the commons and scrubland. Barrels of ale concealed from the Lancastrians began to appear and men from Kent, Essex, London and the Welsh Marches gathered around a hundred crackling camp fires which caused a red glow against the wintry sky. The men were in high spirits, for they would be receiving their pay on the morrow. The ale was fresh and everywhere the smell of hot bacon contended with that of newly baked bread. Games of dice and cards were breaking out like the spread of the plague.

Converging on Doncaster was a large contingent under the command of the new King, Edward IV, and the Earl of Warwick; these would begin arriving some time after cock-crow and comprised the middleward of the Yorkist host.

Meanwhile, the heralds were busy at their counting of the vanward and had arrived at a figure of over 10,000 men mustered already, with Fauconberg's mounted archers, the retained of Lord Fitzwalter, of Lord Grey of Ruthin, of Lord Abergavenny, of Lord Scrope of Bolton, of Sir John Wenlock, of the Earl of Suffolk. Then the men raised by the Kentish captains of foot: Horne, Fogge, Scott and Hopton. And then there were the London men. What the final tally would be was a matter of conjecture and speculation (not to mention some discreet wagers). By the shoot for the Silver Bolt at around Sext on the morrow, Wednesday 25th March, the Feast Day of the Annunciation of Mary, Edward IV would know for a certainty how large an army he commanded for the approaching bloody finalé.

Following the wanton devastation caused earlier by the Lancastrians south of the Trent, men and boys, all along the route of their pillaging, flocked to the banner of the new King, including the communities of the towns of Grantham and Peterborough. Further, the townships of Cambridge, Coventry and Nottingham had representation in armed men. Many were eager to come to grips with the northerners who had ravaged their homes, stolen their treasures and violated family members. If not able to retrieve specific valuables taken by the liveried and therefore identifiable thieves, they would seek compensation and revenge after the defeat of Lancaster on the field. They openly discussed the possibility that their liege lord, King Edward, might reintroduce the cry 'havoc', as was rumoured he was considering. The young King felt justified in calling for no mercy after the callous murder of his younger brother on Wakefield bridge, followed by the mutilation of his and their father's bodies.

One large contingent of the Yorkist host, under the Duke of Norfolk, comprising the rearward battle, would fail to arrive in time for that final muster at the fortress on the banks of the Don.

'Snort and Grunt! Wood gathering and water carrying!' This was yelled at John and Edmund by an irate Fleischer. The bullying *Rottmeister* had every intention of making the new boys pay for riding from Harthill to Conisbrough mounted behind foreriders.

The square swarmed with activity as it continued to fill up with men, carts and horses. By the light from torches and braziers, men and horses seemed to be milling about in noisy disorder. The clattering of baggage carts for twenty or more contingents were jostling for position. Wagons, wheel-hub to wheel-hub, were being shunted and manhandled into some semblance of order under the direction of sweating and cursing decenars. All was not helped by the constant yapping of village dogs which snapped at men and horses alike. Further carts were lined up along the road, waiting to move into the centre of Conisbrough. Soon areas east and west were filling up and more camp fires added to the glow already lighting up the night as group after group of retainers and levies became settled.

Where the brothers were to find wood and coal against that overwhelming clamour for fuel presented them with a problem and Edmund set off to scrounge. Taking two leather buckets from Mater's wagon, John joined a lengthening queue at one of the wells. But before long Wee Willie was tugging at his sleeve 'To your betters, all haste, John Hawksworth, to St Peter's church.'

Fleischer's face was a picture of twisted fury as he blocked John's way at the church door. The boys of the *Wespen* who had been busy erecting portable shelters in the churchyard halted in their labours to watch as the *Rottmeister* prodded him in the chest with his mace.

'Where do you think you're going, Snorty?' he spat out. 'Water, water, water, that's what you're about, idiot. The Mater wants water. Now, get back to the well or down to the river, you lazy swine keeper. Or if it's a beating you're seeking, I'm the one to give it!'

Yet at that very moment a Cistercian monk appeared framed in the church doorway, demanding to know where the Hawksworth boys were. Greatly relieved, John held up his hand and, looking past his tormentor, identified himself to the monk.

'Hurry boy, the Lord Abbot wishes to speak with you!'

Speechless with frustration, Fleischer glared first at the monk and back at John. How could swineherds be in such demand by their betters? He satisfied himself by bringing his mace down hard across John's shoulders.

'Both of you lazy *schlacke* will pay for ducking your chores. I'll see to it.'

Inside St Peter's church thirty or more centenars were making themselves comfortable for the night after attending Compline. Locals were filing out to return to their homes to help in the settling-in of their welcome visitors. In a chantry on the north side was laid out the body of Brother Wilkin, covered in a black altar cloth. Benedictine brothers at Monk Bretton Priory had been informed of the murder of a member of their order. They would be arriving shortly to take the body of the warrior monk back to Barnsley for burial.

By the light from flickering candles John could make out two female figures kneeling by the altar, however, his attention was diverted by the sound of raised voices coming from the vestry.

'The boy has been selected by Our Lord!' The voice was unmistakably that of the Abbot of Roche.

'How can you be so sure? The claim is a serious one and not to be believed lightly.' This was the calming voice of Father William Wynstanley, incumbent priest at St Peter's.

'The claim is not his, by all that is holy, it is my claim, my claim! Do you understand? I am the one who maintains that he has been anointed by God. The boy roundly denies it. Or more truthfully, he refuses to confirm it.'

'My Lord Abbot, it would not be my place to question your judgement, but upon what evidence do you arrive at this?'

'Three counts! That is my witness! Three counts! Judge for yourself, Reverend Brother.' John Wakefield was becoming more agitated by the minute in his efforts to convince the priest of St Peter's.

There followed a brief silence and John moved closer to the vestry door in an effort to catch every word. For he, too, wanted answers to questions that were troubling his mind concerning Edmund.

Oft times and increasingly so, his brother was becoming a stranger, behaving in a manner which took him by surprise. How could someone who openly declared that he hated God have been selected by that One for a special work – if such were true? Yet Edmund hotly denied any divine favour in his case. But he was capable of saintly qualities, such tenderness. For instance, his kindness to the unfortunate mite, Eleanor the bastard, demonstrated before all the Reresby household, around Michaelmastide. Who could ever forget, who saw it, the way he cleaned and bound the little girl's broken nails and bleeding fingers after she had tried to disinter her mother's remains? Or the way he carefully spoon-fed the child? Or the lullaby he sang to quieten her fears as he cradled her in his arms. Yet the same one, weeks later, could despatch two fearsome Scotsmen with such callousness as chilled the blood, an act which seemed to be of no consequence to him, either at the time nor since. Then there was the matter of his dealings with the steward, Ann Thicket, first denouncing her hardheartedness and then treating her with respect, giving back her dignity when he could have had her dragged before the Leet court to be punished as a scold. Why, even Good John Clay involuntarily dropped the knee before him, rendering obeisance in the presence of others. Edmund was not yet fourteen years old. Maybe somehow his brother's present manner and demeanour stemmed from his failure to keep their mother alive. He wore himself to a near frenzy, driving himself on to provide meat for the table. Edmund blamed himself for her death and blamed God for taking her.

John concluded that, because of that, Edmund suffered from a persistent distemper, an imbalance of the humours, which caused a malady of the brain.

The Abbot began his tale.

'If you recall, during the Feast of Epiphany last, I was calling through the manor churches hereabouts bearing news of the battle at Wakefield. At St Leonard's, whilst preaching a blood revenge against Lancaster for the killing of Duke Richard, the Earl of Rutland and Lord Salisbury, I called for an Avenger of Righteous Blood, meaning that some family member would surely become the avenger.' The Abbot paused and John heard the scraping of a bench on the stone floor. He imagined that the fiery John Wakefield had risen to his feet and was leaning across a table towards the priest.

'That boy who whispers, that boy who stutters, cried out before all the congregation that he would accept the role and that he would take on the responsibility of being the Avenger of Righteous Blood.'

Father William interrupted with a chuckle. 'Bravado! A boy's bravado, my Lord Abbot! To be commended I would hasten, but hardly a matter to...'

That was as far as he got, for the Abbot must have banged the table with his fist.

'Hear me out!'

There was a stuttered apology, then the Abbot continued, 'Within minutes there was a response, I declare this to you – as God is my judge! A shaft of light beamed from the altar, penetrating the chancel screen. From thence it travelled the length of the nave and lighted up the boy's face. Many saw this miracle.'

'And you take that to be a response from Our Lord and not a trick of light?'

'It was confirmed less than two days ago. Our Benedictine brother lying dead out there demanded of the boy the truth of the matter. The boy gave an answer from holy writ using the same words as our Lord before Pilate. Then confirmation... affirmation from the very heavens out of a thunder cloud, just as on that very first Palm Sunday when Our Lord called to the Father saying, "Father clarify Thy name," and a voice came from heaven and said, "I have clarified and hence I shall clarify it".'

'Of course, the Gospel of St John when the crowds thought that it had thundered. My Lord Abbot, you have heard the very voice of the Almighty?' The priest of St Peter's, doing his level best to keep an incredulous tone from his voice, was becoming impressed despite himself.

'As the Blessed Virgin and all the saints are my witnesses, yes, I have.'

'You said that there were three counts.'

'The child single-handedly despatched three pillaging Scots who were set to violate Lady Isabel del Wardrop. Clean shots to the neck. Dead as mutton, all three. Verified, I tell you, my brother, verified.'

In the constant retelling, the deaths of all three Scotsmen were being attributed to Edmund, when it was John Clay who had killed the third. But how were they to know the detail of that awful day?

Then Father William spoke in deliberate tones as if weighing up all he had heard 'I do know of the slaying of the Scotsmen, my Lord Abbot. There are many tales being told of this. Even that the boy had transformed himself into a wraith, merging with the mist from whence he executed his prey like the Angel of Death.'

The abbot's tone became calmer. He had seemingly realised that his fellow clergyman was perhaps accepting his emotionally presented argument. 'Furthermore, the boy is scripturally literate. He knows and understands the sacred scriptures. How could that be if he were not gifted with miraculous knowledge from God, as took place with the Blessed Church at that first Pentecost?' The abbot began pressing his point. 'Brother Reresby teaches well, we know, but the boy has understanding which is unusual in one of low degree. And the odd lesson once a week is hardly likely to have educated the lad to the extent he clearly manifests. He can hold discussion with learned men as did Our Lord when a boy at the temple at twelve years of age.'

There was the sound of sudden realisation from the priest 'Of course... of course, it is no great mystery that the boy and his brother have education above their station – their mother...'

John moved with his ear up against the door so as not to miss a single word.

'Their mother married *enubo psi*, beneath her degree. She was the daughter of a prominent northern lord. The name of the family escapes me for the moment. She had been promised in marriage to a son in a branch of the Percy family. It would have brought her parents land and wealth. She refused to comply with her parents' aspirations and instead married at the dictates of her heart. She was declared *exsul extorris profugus*, made an outcast, disowned and disinherited. It was said she departed her family home with what she wore and could carry in her arms.'

174

'Ah, yes! So their mother must have taught her two boys to read, write and perhaps even calculate figures.' It was the Abbot's turn to come to a realisation. 'That does explain their manner of speech, which is unlike all others of their living and degree.'

Hardly daring to breathe, John moved quickly away from the vestry door and positioned himself by the body of the murdered monk, Wilkin, where he lowered his head in an attitude of prayer. At the same time he noted that the two hooded figures kneeling at the altar turned briefly to look in his direction before returning to their devotions.

Before the two men of God could make an appearance, Edmund trotted through the nave to join his brother. Unable to contain himself, John grabbed him by the shoulders.

'She was a lady, Edmund! I knew it!' John whispered, his voice charged with emotion.

Edmund stared at his brother, a frown creasing his forehead.

'Don't you understand? Our mother was a fine lady who was cast out by her family!' John cried aloud, shaking Edmund in his excitement.

Having drawn the attention of the other occupants of the church, John quickly explained in a whisper what he had just overheard. Edmund's reaction to the news was typical of him. He asked over and over again without a hint of emotion, 'What is our mother's family name. Who are we?'

John could begin to detect a quiet anger growing within his brother.

'To which family in the north are we blood-related? It likely supports Lancaster.'

John was unable to supply that information. But he knew he had just given Edmund further targets for his crossbow. There was, of course, their father, the ne'er-do-well, John Hawksworth, who had abandoned them to abject poverty. He would have to pay the supreme penalty, life for a life. Once

Edmund had the opportunity, he would avenge their mother's death. Also their maternal grandparents, whoever they turned out to be, those who had condemned their daughter and issue to a life of miserable impoverishment.

'When the present affair is at an end, there are others I will need to visit.'

John knew that Edmund would, somehow, discover those who had disowned their mother. There were no doubts in his mind after what his brother had done to the Scotsmen, that their grandparents would pay. They, too, would answer to the merciless Avenger of Righteous Blood.

What John had overheard helped to explain so much, as the three of them had eked out an existence in the ancient stone quarry at Thryberg. Their mother had books, which she often read to them at early light. She was able to speak and read Latin and French. Little wonder she always seemed sad, having been cast away by her family and deserted by her husband. Many was the time she had sought a quiet place and wept. On those occasions Edmund would find her and then labour frantically to try and make her smile. On the times when he failed, he would curl up on her lap and shed tears with her, or persuade her to read the Bible to him. Their hearts bonded as one and such a oneness grew between them that John knew that a part of Edmund died with her. Perhaps his childhood went to the grave. A cold-hearted killer had been born that night.

Suddenly the vestry door was flung open and out strode John Wakefield, Abbot of Roche, followed by Father William Wynstanley, priest of St Peter's.

The Abbot was concerned over the murder and theft of the enormous amount of over a thousand marks, an intended contribution to the payment of the Yorkist host. When John explained the conclusions Edmund had arrived at, through his investigation, as to the possible perpetrator of the crime,

St Leonard's, Thryberg, once the manor church of the Reresby family and here viewed from above the surviving fish ponds, looking east over former demesne land of the Lord of the Manor. *See Chapters One to Four*

St Leonard's, Thryberg, where a coincidental beam of light led many to believe that a 14-year-old local boy had been chosen by God. *Inset*: Reresby family coat of arms. *See Chapter One*

All Hallows, Harthill, where the Hawksworth brothers joined the mercenary crossbow unit, *Die Wespen* (The Wasps). *See Chapter Seven*

Roche Abbey Great gatehouse ruins. Once a two-storey building where abbot, John Wakefield, allowed the Hawksworth boy to be examined and where a dramatic coincidence of nature convinced him the boy was indeed chosen to be the 'Avenger of Righteous Blood'. *See Chapter Seven*

St Peter's, Conisbrough. In the vestry the boy Edmund caused the lady Isabel to experience an apparent 'Againrising' thus fuelling the growing legend of The Hawk. *See Chapter Eight*

Conisbrough castle dungeon where the condemned Lollard, John Hawksworth, first began to relate the story of his brother, Edmund, who had become a Yorkist legend in 1461. *See Chapter One*

The winding stair at Conisbrough castle once packed with people eager to listen to the previously discouraged stories of the Yorkist hero, who became known as The Thryberg Hawk. *See Chapter Two*

The Lord's Room at Conisbrough castle. *See Chapter Two*

The Lord's Bed Chamber Conisbrough castle where, over a period of one and a half days, the condemned storyteller recounted the amazing tale of his brother to a packed room.

Conisbrough castle, in 1460 the Yorkist firm base for military operations in the north; first for the Duke of York, Christmas week 1460 and three months later for his son King Edward IV who won the kingdom from Henry VI at the Battle of Towton.

Sir Andrew Trollope Lord Sir John Clifford Lord Dacre of the North Earl of Northumberland Earl of Devon Duke of Exeter Duke of Somerset

The seven target shields of Lancaster, the aiming points in the Yorkist crossbow competition shot at Conisbrough castle, Wednesday 25 March 1461. *See Chapter Nine*

Robin Hood's Well at Skellow on the Great North Road near where Lord Dacre's mounted unit was ambushed, Thursday 26 March 1461. *See Chapter Ten*

The grave marker of murdered Benedictine, brother Wilkin, at Monk Bretton Priory, near Barnsley. Warrior monks had a sword carved alongside the usual memorial cross. *See Chapters Three and Seven*

A mysterious lone grave marker at Wentbridge church carries the inscription:

> **Under this stone
> lie the remains of a young
> woman found 1878 while
> making this churchyard
> She may have been
> murdered about
> 1830 – 40
> on whose soul
> God have mercy**

Last resting place of Bridger Blastock, *Ladenschütze* with the mercenary crossbow unit known as *Die Wespen* – (the Wasps)? Killed at Robin Hood's Well skirmish, March 1461. *See Chapter Ten*

Pontefract castle, notorious as a prison and place of execution for nobles. A base for the Lancastrians in 1460, it mysteriously changed allegiance in March 1461 to become a base for Yorkists prior to the Battle of Ferrybridge and Towton. *See Chapter Eleven*

Brotherton church of Edward the Confessor from where Father Bernard observed the fighting for the bridge over the Aire and came face to face with Lancastrian spies. *See Chapter Eleven*

The Battle of Ferrybridge was fought as a delaying action against the Yorkist's crossing the River Aire, Saturday 28th March 1461. The present-day abandoned bridge, built in 1797, replaced the earlier medieval one. *See Chapter Eleven*

St Mary's chapel Lead, situated one mile behind the Yorkist lines on Palm Sunday 1461. It doubtless saw much use at that time. *See Chapter Twelve*

King Edward IV

Eldest son of Richard Duke of York who was slain at the Battle of Wakefield. The nineteen-year-old Edward was hailed king of England by Londoners, who had closed the city's gates against Lancastrian hordes following that faction's victory at the Second Battle of St Albans where Lancastrian king, Henry VI, was recaptured. Edward marched north to Yorkshire in pursuit of the withdrawing Lancastrian host intent on settling the matter of rulership between the cousins. South of Tadcaster supporters of the two Houses clashed on Palm Sunday 1461.

Standard of King Edward IV

Standards representing supporters of the House of York

Duke of Norfolk

Lord Abergavenny

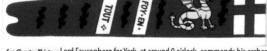

Earl of Essex

Earl of Warwick

Lord Scrope of Bolton

Lord Grey of Ruthyn

Lord Fauconberg

Lord Fitzwalter

See Chapter Thirteen Lord Fauconberg for York, at around 9 o'clock, commands his archers forward in the opening moves of the Battle of Towton.

Painting by Graham Turner www.studio88.co.uk

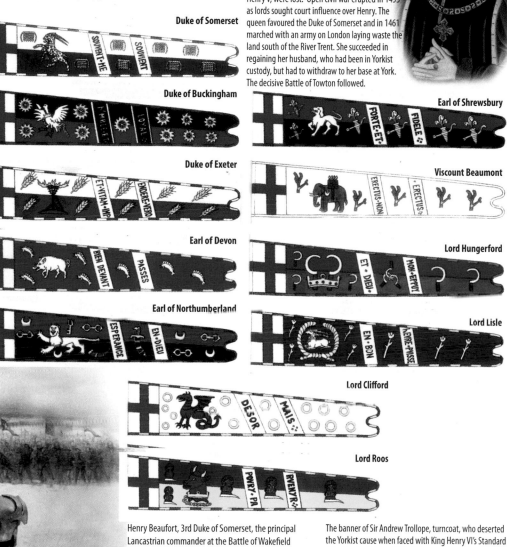

Standard of King Henry VI

Standards representing supporters of the House of Lancaster

Duke of Somerset

Duke of Buckingham

Duke of Exeter

Earl of Devon

Earl of Northumberland

Lord Clifford

Lord Roos

King Henry VI

Weak-minded and devout, given to periods of insanity, Henry was manipulated by his French queen, Margaret of Anjou. He was surrounded by court advisors who lacked competence in managing the country and were enemies of Richard Duke of York. Territories in France won by his father, Henry V, were lost. Open civil war erupted in 1455 as lords sought court influence over Henry. The queen favoured the Duke of Somerset and in 1461 marched with an army on London laying waste the land south of the River Trent. She succeeded in regaining her husband, who had been in Yorkist custody, but had to withdraw to her base at York. The decisive Battle of Towton followed.

Earl of Shrewsbury

Viscount Beaumont

Lord Hungerford

Lord Lisle

Henry Beaufort, 3rd Duke of Somerset, the principal Lancastrian commander at the Battle of Wakefield (December 1460), the Second Battle of St Albans (February 1461), and the Lancastrian defeat at the Battle of Towton March 1461). In the absence of Henry VI at the Battle of Towton Somerset commanded the Lancastrian host. He fled to Scotland after Towton. Pardoned by Edward IV he was finally beheaded after rebelling against the king in May 1464.

The banner of Sir Andrew Trollope, turncoat, who deserted the Yorkist cause when faced with King Henry VI's Standard at Ludlow in October 1459. He became the main strategist for the Lancastrians and planned the defeat of Duke Richard at Wakefield, December 1460 . He was knighted after the 2nd Battle of St Albans 1461. He is credited with choosing the ground on which to meet and fight the Yorkists at Towton on Palm Sunday, March 1461. He was killed during that battle.

5

Lone
Hawthorne
tree

Yorkist Lines

Lancastrin Lines

Looking north towards the Lancastrian positions. The lone hawthorne tree and Ordnance Survey triangulation pillar marks where the right flank of the Yorkist battles were drawn up for the Battle of Towton. *See Chapter Thirteen*

Looking south towards the Yorkist battle lines from behind the Lancastrian positions. Likely at the time of the Battle of Towton Castle Hill Wood was and stretched across the ridge and hence closer to the Yorkist left flank ar from which the Lancastrians launched a surprise attack. *See Chapter Fourteen*

The Old London Road looking towards Tadcaster from Towton village. This section likely appears much as it did 500 years ago. Beyond the wood it narrows to a path leading to the bridge across Cock Beck.

Ralph Vestynden standard-bearer to Edward IV. Following the Yorkist victory he, along with leading captains, received the accolade from his grateful king at a ceremony held in the captured Lancastrian camp.
See Chapters Thirteen and Fourteen
Painting by Graham Turner
www.studio88.co.uk

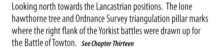

Yorkist Lines | Bloody Meadow | Cock Beck | Castle Hill Wood

Edmund Hawksworth, the boy sniper who commanded *Die Wespen* a mercenary crossbow unit employed by Edward IV at the Battle of Towton. In a few hours the boy, with his brother acting as *Ladenschütze,* had stalled the entire Lancastrian left flank advance. When the Yorkist left began to crumble he reformed his *Fähnlein* of boys and halted the enemy's attack by wounding rather than killing. *See Chapter Fourteen*

The present-day wooden bridge over the Cock Beck. Picturesque now but once the scene of panicking men and boys struggling to escape the battlefield across the broken stone bridge that once stood at this spot. Artist Graham Turner has depicted the slaughter that would have taken place all along the banks of this stream.

The field near Towton Hall and alongside the Old London Road where the Lancastrian baggage train is thought to have been camped. *See Chapter Fourteen*

The rout of the Lancastrian forces at the Battle of Towton by Graham Turner. This scene depicts men being overtaken by Yorkist 'prickers' as they try to escape towards the River Cock down into what would later come to be called, 'Bloody Meadow'. It is generally accepted that over 28,000 men were killed in the fighting over a three-day period, including the Battle of Ferrybridge (Saturday, 28 March 1461), Towton (Palm Sunday) and along the Lancastrian retreat to Tadcaster and York.

See Chapter Fourteen   *Painting by Graham Turner www.studio88.co.uk*

Believed to be the original medieval cross erected over burial pits shortly after the battle. It was likely discarded by the builders of Richard III's chapel. Work on the chapel ceased after the defeat and death of the Plantagenet king at Bosworth in 1485. Later builders used the foundations of the defunct chapel, along with abandoned stone, to construct Towton Hall.

The tomb chest of Ranulph, Lord Dacre of Gilisland at All Saints Church, Saxton. During the Battle of Towton Dacre removed his helmet and bevor to take a drink and was shot in the neck by a boy up a tree. *See Chapter Thirteen*

the wily old clergyman nodded. He then looked at the priest as if to say, 'Was I not telling you just so?'

'I know the rector of Dinnington,' said the abbot. 'We will have questions for my young friend, Sir Richard Nowell, once this matter is settled.'

'My champion the Avenger!' A startled cry came from one of the hooded figures by the altar.

At the sound of that voice John's heart leapt, for it was the beautiful young widow, Lady Isabel del Wardrop. However, the pathetic figure which grovelled at the feet of his brother caused a sickness in his stomach. Deep-sunken eyes peered up from her chalk-white face which was framed by lank, unkempt and unwashed hair.

'Black-faced Clifford took the talisman of good fortune I gave you.' Her voice was weak and pitiful and John could scarce bear to look upon the miserable wreck of that once beautiful child bride.

'My beloved one is buried under that large stone over there,' she wailed, pointing towards a place in front of the altar. 'They have granted my prayer. I am to be laid alongside him before too long.'

Edmund stiffened. 'There is no gain in this,' he said quite loudly and with no hint of a stutter.

'She has only taken a little water in days.' Her young lady-in-waiting spoke out with deep concern.

'Here, see this, my champion.' Lady Isabel made as if to rise, holding out a silken cloth to Edmund. 'For 'tis another more powerful talisman soaked in tears and prayers. See, I am embroidering the arms of Clifford upon it. On the morrow it shall be completed for you to wear. It will safeguard you.' So saying, she grasped Edmund's arms and cried out, 'Return it to me soaked in Clifford's blood.' The wretched girl then fell backwards into the arms of her companion.

'Mercifully it will only be a matter of a few more days now before she is united with her husband in Paradise,' said the priest with authoritative conviction. 'I have recently comforted her with the prospect' He nodded his head.

'Does the church now teach its flock that death is to be regarded as a friend?'

There was a threatening tone in Edmund's whispered voice. His undertones were enhanced in the church nave so that there was no need for John to speak for him.

'If that were so, why did St Paul in his epistle to the Corinthians refer to death as an enemy? If the scripture bears witness to the truth and death is ranked against us, then why are you encouraging our lady to seek it with such heartfelt longing?'

John cast a glance at the face of the Abbot of Roche and was amazed to see his countenance lit up in sheer pleasure and anticipation of what might follow. He was looking forward to the routing of his fellow clergyman and the vindication of his own conclusions regarding Edmund.

'Who are you to be questioning me?' Father William Wynstanley, gasped in amazement. 'Whence did you get this learning? You are a child! Who are you to be commenting on holy writ? Whence came thy ordination?'

Edmund gave no answer and, ignoring him, lifted Lady Isabel and carried her into the vestry where he laid her on a bench. Cradling her head, Edmund took the Communion chalice used in the recent service and put it to her lips. Wynstanley made as if to stop this but was himself prevented by the Abbot. The wine had the desired affect.

Isabel del Wardrop looked intently at Edmund, her head now resting on the lap of her lady companion. Holding both her hands in his, he began speaking to her, as he had to little Eleanor.

'My lady,' he began, 'your husband is asleep awaiting the resurrection and the restoration of an earthwide Eden, which events are to take place at the end of time.' Beginning with this, Edmund began whispering Bible texts to her, along with

178

explanations and reassurances and after some time, declared loudly, stuttering as he did so, 'This place of the dead is not for you, but you should now return at once to the castle and help with the preparations for the coming fight with the House of Lancaster.'

Meekly, Lady Isabel nodded and, turning to look at her companion, she gave a weak smile 'My faithful Maud, can all this be true? Will the graves give up their dead when God's Son calls them?'

'It must be so, my lady, for they are all saying that this boy is a prophet and especially favoured by the Holy Mother and all the saints.'

Edmund concealed his face from them and rolled his eyes in a resigned way. John could see that it mattered little what people thought concerning him, just so long as his fast-growing reputation helped the sickly young widow heed him.

News that Lady Isabel del Wardrop had been brought back from the brink of death by the Thryberg Hawk spread throughout the manor and beyond until it turned into a raising of the dead. It became a part of the legend and was much embellished in the retelling and through the imaginative songs of minstrels. That is until it was repressed.

John and Edmund walked with her supported between them from St Peter's Church, followed by the two clergymen and the lady-in-waiting. The Abbot made no attempt to conceal his delight at the outcome. On the other hand, Father William Wynstanley, embarrassed and increasingly discomforted, remembered that he had urgent matters to attend to and promptly disappeared among the throng of archers gathering in the western aspect of the churchyard to offer them his services.

Upon their arrival within the walls, lady members of the castle household were summoned. Relief and concern was everywhere evident as they entered the Great Hall. The women took Lady Isabel into their care, all the time expressing delight at her returning to them from her morbid vigil that she had been determined would end in her own death.

The Great Hall was filled to capacity with lords, knights, esquires and their attenders. All seemed to be occupied with making themselves as comfortable as possible as they established sleeping quarters on portable camp beds and on the straw-strewn, flagged floor. The Abbot had firmly attached himself to the brothers and the three were offered a place for the night by the kitchen fireplace.

As the grey dawn light crept along the walls of the kitchen, the Lady Isabel, dressed in a long white bedrobe, appeared like a ghost before them. The faithful Maud fluttered about behind her. The abbot and John were awake, but, Edmund slept on. She seemed transformed from the pitiful creature of the night before, with hair washed, combed and falling in gently curling tresses about her shoulders. She appeared beautiful once more, but frail and still but a shadow of her former self. She gazed for some time at the sleeping figure of Edmund before speaking very softly, addressing her words to Father John Wakefield,

'My Lord Abbot, the truth I beg. Does the Avenger speak the words of our faith?'

'He speaks things afresh and is wise beyond his years, my lady. I have witnessed wonderful things concerning him,' he said with great pride.

The deep voice of the Abbot served to awaken Edmund who promptly sat upright at the sight of Lady Isabel, glancing first at John and then the Abbot. Immediately, she dropped to her knees before him.

'Tell me plainly for I hunger for more,' she implored, 'When will I see my darling Richard again? Please tell me once again of the "Again-raising", my lord Avenger.'

Edmund spoke to her directly in whispered voice. To John's surprise, the Abbot also turned his ear to Edmund and leaned forward so as to catch his every word.

'Remember when Jesus went to the vill of Bethany to raise his friend Lazarus from the dead? The man's sister, Martha, told of her belief in the "again-raising" when she said, "I know that he shall rise again in the last day". That faith of Martha's is true and must also be taken into your heart to become your earnest and steadfast belief.'

Edmund stood and helped Lady Isabel to her feet. He seemed to have grown of late and must have stood a couple of inches above her in height. Still holding both her hands, he said, 'When the end of time arrives, then your Richard will stand up, well and alive once more.'

'When will the end of all things be?' Her voice heavy with heartfelt pleading. 'How long must my heart ache for him?'

'It will fall with suddenness on all the earth at a time of wars, hunger, pestilence and great iniquity.'

Edmund answered with a conviction that John found hard to imagine was his own genuinely held belief. Was he play-acting for Isabel del Wardrop's benefit? Or was he beginning to have a faith and confidence in God at last? John determined that he would question him on this at some future time when the opportunity arose. Suddenly Lady Isabel's face beamed with a sudden realisation and she gasped excitedly, 'Then it must be soon, for the very things of which you speak are all about us.'

'"Keep on the watch," Jesus said to his followers, "For you know not the hour."' Edmund answered with authority and utter conviction.

'And now, my lady, we must all break our fast and gain strength for what lies ahead.'

It was about the hour of Terce when they were escorted from the castle by a group of children. As they passed through the barbican a small blonde-haired girl slipped her hand into

John's and announced that she was nearly seven and that her name was Lucy.

In the course of time she would become the Lady Lucy Fitzwilliam and play host to the storyteller of the legend of The Hawk.

Immediately, however, pain and humiliation lay in store for both the Hawksworth boys through the offices of the vindictive *Rottmeister* of the *Fähnlein*, Alvar Fleischer.

Carving of John Wakefield, Abbot of Roche at
St Peter's church Conisbrough.

Chapter Nine

Seven Shields of Lancaster – *Die Schraube des Silbers*

SCREAMING OUT LOUD was the last thing John wished to do, but to his everlasting shame he could do no other, for the pain was searing through his hindquarters as if he were stung by a thousand bees. Forty strokes, less one, had been decreed by Alvar Fleischer. Their misdemeanor? 'Absent at *Appell*'. They had been charged, judged, found guilty and punished by him. 'Province decreed by their betters' served as no mitigation at their short hearing held in St Peter's church. John's protest that they had missed the calling of the roll because their presence was required at the castle was ignored.

The *Fähnlein* had been mustered and, in turn, they were stretched over a barrel and the two jesters, first Daub and then Wattle, had been detailed to lay about them with a broken longbow stave. Edmund had been first to suffer the painful indignity, taking the punishment without blubbering, or giving even the slightest indication of suffering discomfort. The gangling Didi Wattle had whispered to John that he would hold back his blows where he could. However, Fleischer was alert and had cracked Daub about the head with his mace upon detecting his pulling back strokes on Edmund.

Counting each blow was done aloud by the entire *Fähnlein* so that the maximum forty strokes, as outlined in the book of Deuteronomy, were not exceeded, thirty-nine being considered the course of wisdom, otherwise the one administering the beating could himself be punished should he inflict one stroke more than forty.

John's howls brought an end to his suffering at twenty-three strokes exactly. Mater, along with the archer Robin Carle, intervened and an argument ensued between them and the enraged Fleischer. The matter was settled when the fearsome *Hauptmann* Dietz arrived and ruled against his *Unteroffizier*, directing him to some chore or duty away from the church. With their tormentor absent, the boys gathered round and offered many a novel and well-meaning remedy to assuage the burning agony Edmund and John were suffering. All looked upon Edmund with especial awe, he having received the full thirty-nine without so much as a whimper. A goodly number of them had suffered the same or similar punishment at the hands of the *Rottmeister* and had been compelled to cry out during its administering. Fleischer was feared and loathed, by all. Even his loader, his *Ladenshütze*, 'Spotty' Spence, despite his being shown special favour, dreaded and abhorred him.

Willie Daub, the small, cheeky-faced tubby one of the jester duo, could not offer to do enough for Edmund. 'Forgive me, please forgive me, I didn't, I tried,' the distraught youngster stammered. Horrified at what he had done, he struggled to find some form of address. To have used the *Wespen* nickname 'Grunt' would have been unseemly. Then, to the amazement of the entire *Fähnlein*, the youthful jester suddenly dropped to one knee and bowed his head in subjection before Edmund.

'There is no call for this, my friend,' whispered Edmund. 'You did no more than that demanded of you by our betters.' So saying, he raised the hapless Daub to his feet and placed an arm about his shoulders.

'We all need the rod of discipline at times,' Edmund reassured him with a smile. 'For does not St Paul in holy writ tell us, "Chastisement in present time seems not joyous, but is sorrow. But afterward it shall bring rightwiseness most peaceable to men exercised by it"?'

'Then we are still friends?' Daub asked in disbelief and with an amount of caution.

Edmund reassured him in a whisper, 'The best of friends, and all the more so because of the beating.'

The effect upon the company was unmistakable. All, including John, were amazed. Was this boy really the same one who had grown up alongside him, experiencing life together? Much of their suffering shared? John's hopes and dreams, hates, dreads, fears, loves and laughter had been as closely interwoven with Edmund's as a myriad coloured threads in an Arras tapestry. Now his younger brother, with every passing day – nay hour – in that crisis which had descended upon the Manor, was drawing away. It was as if he was taking on a new role and in its adoption was donning the mantle of a total stranger. His fine words and actions manifested behaviour and smacked of chivalry totally inappropriate for their impoverished upbringing. But then John mused increasingly on what their true degree should rightly be. Who really was their kind and gentle mother? Their rearing, it was gradually dawning upon John, had not been usual at all. It served to explain why it was that the Master, William Reresby, had readily assisted in their learning. Nor were they bastards, but legitimate begats, perhaps with noble blood, albeit their mother disowned and disinherited by some mysterious landed family, maybe in the North Riding.

However, of one thing he was quite sure; the beatings they had suffered that morning roundly bonded them to that fellowship of crossboy boys. They had entered into a brotherhood that would hold them in good stead throughout the trials which lay before them. That closeness was becoming increasingly apparent and was seen in the good-natured banter among the boys.

'Don't think I'm going to drop the knee to thee, John Hawksworth, just because I tanned thi backside for thi,' rasped Didi Wattle in an exaggerated Yorkshire accent. 'Nar follow me for some buttock-succour-balm from Mater. Follow after me in this manner!'

Didi waddled off with an exaggerated limp in the direction of Mater's wagon with his rear stuck out and wincing as if it was hurting him. Didi's droll, rolling gait was accompanied, in perfect time, by Willie Daub's blowing of alternate high and low notes on a shawm. The archers, who were gathered about the churchyard, roared with laughter at the antics of the jesters. They were pleased and relieved to be able to contribute to the change of mood following the unpleasantness of the public thrashings.

John and Edmund were provided with a small pot containing a mysterious soothing salve by the much concerned Mater; she was explaining how they were to apply her special concoction when *Die Wespen Mater* was interrupted by an almighty roar from a thousand throats. Chorusing that became further cheers by thousands more. Cheering from men gathered on the castle battlements, spreading to those camped up the hillside until the applause reached the billmen and archers packed into Conisbrough village.

Two of the vanward heralds grabbed trumpets, hastily mounted palfreys and galloped off down to the crossroads and bridge known as Brook Sheen in the valley. Heeling their mounts, they galloped up the Doncaster road to meet foreriders, harbingers of the mighty middleward of Edward IV's host, whose appearance had caused the uproar. Once in position by the road on the steep hillside, the heralds placed themselves where they could be clearly seen by all the massed men of the vanward camped at and around the castle. There followed a truly magnificent spectacle – the thrilling arrival of the main battle force. The view as wonderful as at a Roman theatre.

Out at the front, trotting down the road leading from Doncaster, were the foreprickers, outriders and foreriders, their tasks, for the time being, at an end. Then it was that others began to appear, columns of marching men-at-foot, billmen and archers led by mounted lords, knights, esquires and captains. Identifying great households, manors and townships were distinctive coloured banners, each bearing a cloth badge charge. As each banner, in turn, drew level with the heralds, a fanfare was blown, at which signal the battle standard, carried by the mounted standard bearer for that affinity, was unfurled. That was the signal for liveried retainers and arrayed men for that particular household to chant in unison their unique battle-cries, thus declaring their retaining, such as 'A-Cobham, A-Cobham, A-Cobham!' Upwards of three hundred men roared out that affinity.

Then the trumpet blew again as a red banner bearing the white bear and ragged staff of the house of Richard Neville, Earl of Warwick drew level with the vanward heralds. The battle standard was immediately unfurled, whereupon more than five hundred voices yelled out in unison, 'A-Warwick, A-Warwick, A-Warwick!' Intermingled with the various household contingents were men from the townships and areas of Bristol, Salisbury, Worcester and Gloucester. The towns of Grantham, Peterborough, Stamford, Huntingdon and Coventry were especially well represented in numbers of men under arms; they were on a mission of vengeance. The townships had their own distinct chants, 'Fo-Grantham, Fo-Grantham, Fo-Grantham!' And so the colourful spectacle progressed.

Then a special fanfare ripped out to announce an already unfurled standard. It was the red and blue pennant of Edward IV and the roar which greeted its identifying was prompt and deafening. There was a mighty surge forward as those gathered at Conisbrough craned their necks to catch their first glimpse of the new King of England. Having proved himself in warfare, victorious over Lancaster at the Battle of Mortimer's Cross the previous month, nineteen-year-old Edward was eager to bring his army face to face with Queen Margaret's forces. In his youthful hands he held the destinies of every single man, woman and child gathered on that day to acclaim him.

What a magnificent sight he presented, in shining armour with crested and crowned sallet – truly a leader and king in the fashion of the victor of Agincourt, Henry V. The Almighty had shown His pleasure prior to the battle of Mortimer's Cross by causing the appearance in the sky of three suns – a phenomenon known as a parhelion – which some claimed surely stood for the Holy Trinity. Following that Yorkist victory, Edward used the symbol of the sun in splendour as one of his badges. Would further miraculous displays be experienced in the mighty clash about to take place? Practically every man and woman in the host of the new king fervently prayed for a demonstration of divine approval for what lay ahead, for verily they considered their cause to be just.

It was then that Fleischer appeared and elbowed his way to the front of the crowd of boys, whereupon he squinted at the sovereign's banner waving in the distance. In a pretentious manner, he proceeded to reel off, in heraldic jargon, its description:

'St George in the hoist; azure over murrey a bordure company azure and murrey; a bull sable passant reguardant, crowned about the neck.'

He screwed his eyes up, nodded, then declared with greater authority, 'And, I think I am right, horns and hooves, Or, yes, yes, gold, Or!' He glanced about him to make sure that the others were impressed before adding, 'For a certainty, I can identify Roses en soleil argent!'

Immediately behind the *Rottmeister* the two jesters, Didi Wattle and Willie Daub, were rolling their eyes, pulling faces, and mumming the commander in an outrageous fashion. It was all any of them could do to stop from laughing out aloud. Sensing something was amiss, Fleischer suddenly spun his head and quick as a flash Didi Wattle changed his entire demeanour and countenance. He was now serious, most impressed nodding and shaking his head in disbelief and in suitable admiration he uttered, 'Amazing, *Rottmeister*, bloody amazing.'

The boys were saved from collapsing in laughter by Spotty Spence, who suddenly jabbed an arm towards the military parade descending on Conisbrough, yelling, 'What's that banner, then?' An unpleasant situation was thus averted as all in that smirking band of youngsters pretended to peer across the valley at the advancing column.

Following on the heels of the royal contingent were further households, Lords Hastings, Stanley, Fitzwarin, Herbert, Deveraux, Dudley, Saye and Stourton along with their retainers – knights and esquires. The thump of marching feet and clatter of plate and chain armour and weapons presented a continuous rhythmic roll. Like an unassailable beast, the procession of might resembled a metal serpent from the depths of Hell, weaving and heaving its way across the late winter hillside. The onlookers were thrilled, especially those men and women belonging to the vanward. Then spontaneously, the cry was taken up, 'Hail Edward, Hail Edward, all Hail Edward, King of England, France and Ireland!'

It was still early morning, it being a little past Terce, and for the next three hours men and wagons continued to arrive in steady procession. The common lands stretching towards the vill of Hooton Roberts along the Rotherham road were becoming one enormous encampment. Coupled with this were wagons filling up the roads and tracks from surrounding communities, carrying supplies. Word had been spread that victuals would be paid for at this great muster of the Host of York. Barnsley had shown its allegiance to the present king's father, the Duke of York, at the time of the Battle of Wakefield and had suffered at the hands of Lancaster because of it. Now the burghers of that place, along with monks from Monk Bretton Priory, were arriving to declare and demonstrate their allegiance, bringing along with them cartloads of victuals. The monks were also there to collect the mortal remains of their murdered Benedictine brother, the Yorkist spy Wilkin, for interment at their priory.

King Edward and his commanders met for a counsel of war and gathered within the walls of Conisbrough Castle. The competition for the Silver Bolt had been announced to begin at the period of Sext. The bells of St Peter's would ring to gather all to witness the grand event and to hear an address by the King. In the meantime, the newcomers to the *Wespen* needed to be clear about one or two things concerning the tournament.

Fleischer had demanded to see all eighteen crossbows to be used by the *Fähnlein* in the competition. He then decreed the order in which they were to shoot. Of course, he and Spotty were to go first; Edmund and John were to be the last, with Wattle and Daub ahead of them. Then it was that the *Rottmeister* took himself off to queue at the privies and the boys gathered around.

'We need to be acquainting you two with some unwritten laws of competition,' said Wattle, tapping the side of his nose as he spoke. 'At least of this particular farce about to take place.'

Snowwhite interrupted in his drawling, west country accent, 'Should you two be entertaining any thoughts of winning that silver bolt, best think again.'

'Yes, Fleshy has already claimed it as his,' added Spotty Spence. 'Not that I'll be having a share in its value from the London silversmiths.'

The Welsh boy, 'Mealy' Madoc, nodded his head towards Thomas Moxen, better known as Snowwhite, the white-haired, white-faced lad from Bristol, 'Snowwhite here is as good a shot with a crossbow as you'll find, but he won't be trying to hit the mark.' As he spoke Mealy demonstrated with the finger of his right against the palm of his left. 'He'll drop one vital bolt short. Heed my words.'

'It will be the last one,' announced Snowwhite in a matter-of-fact way, 'so that all of you, including *Hauptmann* Dietz, will know for a certainty that I could have hit the mark had I so wished.' He snorted in disgust. 'At least I'll have that satisfaction.'

'Some miserable satisfaction,' declared Snowwhite's *Ladenschütze*, a gangling youth from the town of Salisbury named 'Poxy' Goite, endowed with more angry facial eruptions than Spotty Spence. 'I expected with Snowwhite as my shooter I'd become rich.'

'Thas more chance of becoming Pope,' said Wattle.

'Suppose the *Rottmeister* misses?' John asked in all innocence. This prompted sniggers from the boys.

'That'll not be easy for him,' explained the jolly-faced Daub. 'He'll be the only one shooting at point-blank! That right, Wattle?'

'Right, Daub! Why do you think he's checked all our crossbows? He was making sure that none of us has mysteriously acquired a bow with a steel lath.'

From the all-round muttering and murmuring it was clear they were not to be given an equal and fair chance of winning that silver bolt, which bauble would have set a pair comfortable for a year or two.

'He'll be the only one using two metal-rigged bows, so outranging the rest of us by a good five yards.' This was said with a deal of bitterness by a freckle-faced, ginger-haired Londoner, called 'Bridger' Blastock. (Bridger, because of having been born and raised in one of the houses on London Bridge). 'He'll make sure we are all having to aim above the line of sighting.'

'And he's going first, so the winning hits will be established at the outset. Woe betide any of us should we try to better it.' Daub's round, usually cheerful face, was no longer lit up, but had taken on a despondent look.

John shrugged his shoulders 'It would seem that he has thought of everything.'

'Everything? Just guess who will be the one setting up the butt,' said Wattle. 'Once he's emptied himself at the privy, he'll be off down to the castle to fix up the range.'

'Nor will he be using any of you to labour at the butt.' There was disgust in Spotty's voice. 'When you march down there you'll be looking over the distance and at the targets and their appearance for the first time.'

The group fell silent as Edmund raised his hand and whispered, 'What of our commander, *Hauptmann* Dietz?'

Snowwhite shook his head 'We have no saviour with the Bavarian mercenary. As long as Fleischer keeps us sharp and in line, metes out discipline and keeps us marching north at a goodly pace, he cares not a fig as to what's fair.'

As predicted, within a short while Fleischer re-appeared, yelled for Spotty Spence and took him off down to the castle. The only available area for the shooting tournament was across a fish-pond and dry moat, which was overlooked by the castle wall and barbican. It was there that the *Rottmeister* set up a line of seven wooden two- to three-inch diameter stakes, four yards apart. The heralds had, on specific orders from the king, painted seven shields, about twelve inches wide, with the charges of certain particularly odious Lancastrian lords and captains. In the forthcoming clash seven marked men had been designated as primary targets.

The Wasps were to make them their main concern. On the occasion of the tournament their distinctive badges were to be the point of aim. There was a rumour that King Edward had other prizes yet to declare in connection with those targeted men.

Already crowds were gathering at the castle to see the competition for the *Boltzen aub Silber* being offered by the crossbow boys' commander, *Hauptmann* Dietz. King Edward had agreed to inspect the special 'marksman' unit, for he was enthusiastic in their employment during the forthcoming mêlée, having witnessed the possibilities at his recent triumph at Mortimer's Cross.

Ordinarily, each pair of boys would have carefully selected twenty-one of the better-made crossbow quarrels from the two kegs (800 bolts in each) carried in Mater's wagon. However, the foregone outcome of the competition rendered that selection meaningless. Only two boys of the entire *Fähnlein* bothered at all with carefully selecting bolts with well-made shafts and neatly-turned fletchings – they were Snowwhite and Edmund. Also Edmund, for some time, had worked on a fast spanning device and John would be the one to try it out. It consisted of a leather strap connected to a chest belt, at the end of which was a hook. To bend the bow and draw back the string John simply bent double, attached the hook and, with his foot in the stirrup, then straightened up, thus using the strength of his upper body to draw the string back to engage the nut. To make sure that the chest belt remained firmly in place, Edmund devised cross-over shoulder belts of canvas for him to wear. Despite the severe beating, with practice John could load eight bolts a minute.

To make sure that they were suitably weary and aching prior to the competition, Fleischer put the *Wespen* through battle drill, forming line, then pyramid and back again. Hence they became familiar with Bavarian commands: *Stillgestanden* – 'attention'; *Aufmarschieren* – 'form up in line'; *Aufstapeln* –

'pile up, pyramid' and the longed for command, *Erleichterung* – 'at your ease'.

With the first pealing of the bells, the boys began to don their padded jacks, mail and calf-length boots. Over their heads they pulled on newly-cleaned surcoats in the distinctive alternate yellow and black material sewn in four-inch horizontal strips. Mater fussed over first one and then another of them; tucking here, pulling there and cutting loose strands with scissors; straightening waist belts and shoulder straps; setting caps at the prescribed angle. As she worked feverishly, her eyes were wet with tears. She was obviously proud of every single one of them and thrived on their adoration of her. Then she came to Edmund and John dressed in the garb of the lowliest common stock. She bit her bottom lip, sighed, made as if to adjust something on John, changed her mind, stood back and folded her arms.

'My Yorkshire boys! What are we to do with you?'

'Hide 'em in t' wagon until after dark, Mater!' called out Daub.

'Stick 'em in a barrel apiece!' yelled Wattle.

'Paint 'em green!' called out another and so the drollery went. John no longer felt discomfort at their humour, for it was obviously well-meant. Mater whispered to her helper, Wee Willie, who hastened away, returning with two *Wespen* caps. At least they were to be set before the king in some form of livery of the famous crossbow boys. John reasoned that perhaps no one would pay them much heed, mingled amidst the smartly liveried other lads.

As the period of Sext slid into that of None the second peal of bells rang out. Fleischer blew signals on his horn and the boys formed up into the two *Rotten*. With John and Edmund in the ranks, there was an equal complement of twenty boys, ten in each *Rotten*. Every boy had a crossbow slung on his back, a quiver containing twenty bolts and either a tabor or a pipe at his belt.

194

'March of the *Wespen*, on my signal!' Fleischer yelled. He held his mace high, then suddenly swung it down, whereupon Snowwhite launched into that drum roll which set John all a-tingle. Then one after another the boys with tabors joined in. Fleischer blew one blast on his horn and the boys in both *Rotten* began to march on the spot. That produced that strange rocking motion; another blast and they were off. At a further signal the boys with the pipes began playing the 'March of the *Wespen*'. In front, mounted on his beautiful black courser, rode *Hauptmann* Jason Dietz, creator of the crossbow unit and veteran of a half-dozen gory wars in Europe, to which his scarred face bore testimony.

The roar of the crowd which greeted their appearance on the castle approaches was both exhilarating and nerve-racking. They were pressed all about and further progress would have been imperilled had it not been for billmen of Warwick, who were easily recognisable in their red tabards bearing the ragged staff badge. They formed lines and made a way through.

Most of the men in the Yorkist host had been paid that morning and were engaged in wagering among themselves on the outcome of the contest. Which one out of the ten *Armbrustschütze* would score the most hits and take the prize? The crowd buzzed with excited chatter as merits were argued among individuals, for there were those well-acquainted with the prowess of individual boys. It seemed that their wagers were falling equally between Snowwhite and Fleischer. However, locals were favouring the Thryberg Hawk and eagerly offered pledges with the unknowing southerners where they could.

An awning had been erected overlooking the range and as they marched before it John could see ladies filing beneath it. His heart jumped when he noted that the Lady Isabel was among them. Lords, knights, captains and churchmen placed themselves in an advantageous position beside the tented covering. The commons, men-at-foot, archers and mounted warriors, crowded around the makeshift crossbow stands. Heralds fussed about, positioning seven men with lances, who were set to indicate the strikes, where they could best be seen. The castle constable, Edmund Fitzwilliam, was to act as arbiter and he proceeded to take his stand alongside the king's herald, Clarenceux king-at-arms, William Hawksloe.

Fleischer brought the *Fähnlein* to a sudden halt, taking Edmund and John completely by surprise. The result was that they stumbled into Snowwhite and Poxy Goite. That provided great amusement for the crowd and John hoped with all his heart that the Lady Isabel had not been looking. But it was not an end to his embarrassment, for Fleischer yelled '*Links-um*' and the entire *Fähnlein* turned to face left leaving Edmund and John, belatedly and clumsily, to follow the manoeuvre. That brought a spontaneous burst of applause and much laughter from the onlookers. It was silenced when Fleischer stormed over and belaboured Edmund and John with his mace. John's hope that they might remain unnoticed was completely dashed; for a certainty, all eyes were upon them. The brothers had many a well-wisher in the crowd, for they appeared very much the underdogs.

The weather was mild on that festival day of The Annunciation of Mary, Wednesday 25th March 1461. It was mid-day; there was a cold blue sky and, more importantly, there was not even the slightest of breezes to concern the ten shooters.

To the blast of trumpets and a rousing cheer, King Edward emerged from the barbican. Over six feet tall, he looked every single inch a king, broad-shouldered and handsome in his ermine-edged doublet, richly embroidered with the quartered blue-and-red coat-of-arms of England; hose of alternate blue and red material served to enhance his powerful legs. A golden crown was set upon fair to mid-brown hair, which was cut short in campaign style. From a golden chain around his neck dangled a jewelled brooch. A calf-length, deep blue cloak edged in ermine hung from his shoulders; his dark leather sword belt was studded with the names of his deceased father and brother in the style: *'Richarius et Edmund'*. In this manner, as closest male blood relative, he was declaring that he had taken on the responsibility for seeking justice for the murders of his father and brother, as outlined in the Old Testament – the God-given right to take life – the role of 'Avenger of Righteous Blood'. The young king was greeted by the gathered leaders, his host, castellan Edmund Fitzwilliam; veteran of the French wars Sir William Lord Fauconberg; Richard Neville, Earl of Warwick and upwards of fifty other lords, knights, esquires and captains.

The king smiled down at the boys from the castle's earthen rampart, raising a gauntlet-clad hand to acknowledge their ranks. Dietz strode to him and first, bending the knee, then, standing upright, he snapped his right hand to his brow in the popular manner of the day. The king acknowledged the salute and turned to address the gathering. Silence descended on the crowd.

'Companions of mine in this greatest of all ventures!'

His opening words rang out loud and clear, aimed not only at the Wasps, but the entire assembly.

'England is want to be swept clean once and for all time of that foul line of usurpers of the crown. Frenchman and Scot have pillaged and raped our fair land under licence from Henry of Lancaster...' he paused and then yelled at the top of his voice, '...for the last time!'

'Hurrah!' was the spontaneous response of the crowd.

'That season has now departed this land. Gone the day when a she-wolf, a foreign queen and her paramours flout our God-given laws and the rights of the common people.'

King Edward warmed to his hearers.

'Lancaster has, in blood, rewritten the statutes governing Christian conflict. It has bid chivalry depart and banished mercy and outlawed benevolence and replaced these with acts most disagreeable and foul.'

'They must repay, life for a life, soul on behalf of soul!' was the involuntary cry from Lady Isabel del Wardrop.

King Edward turned at the interruption, then echoed the distraught child-widow's cry, 'They will repay, my lady! By my father's blood and all that is holy, they will, I vow to you this day – they will surely repay! Blood for blood!'

The roar from the crowd was deafening and continuous and the king had eventually to hold up an arm to quieten the people.

'And now, my faithful brother warriors!' His voice dropped some way as he addressed the *Fähnlein*. 'You are to be employed in a special work, for your stings are especially esteemed by this crown of England. So then, this day, be about your task and God grant favour to the finest eye and stoutest heart among you.'

The king turned to the constable as if to signal the start, but then paused as a thought occurred to him. 'Ah now, tarry but a moment fellow warriors,' he said, turning once again to face the boys. His narrowed eyes scanned their ranks as if seeking out a particular face. He tilted his head to one side, then stroked his chin as if in contemplation.

'Many are saying that there is a presumptuous one among you who is my rival.' He paused to allow the seriousness of what he was about to say take a hold on their hearts, for this nineteen-year-old had the power of life and death.

'There is an earnest party of good folk at this place who are claiming that another Avenger of Righteous Blood has declared himself.'

John heard Edmund groan under his breath as the king paused to let what he had said sink in.

'Is the impudent rascal in your ranks? One set to relieve me of my belt and take on the role of meting out retribution for right royal kinsmen of the House of York?'

An interruption of laughter from a group of Lincolnshire knights and esquires caused the king to turn in surprise. Sir William Skipwyth of South Ormesby, who had served recently in the Duke Richard of York's retinue and had once held office as his steward for Conisbrough, explained the outburst.

'My liege, allow us voice. Do we dare ask?'

Kind Edward discerned the fair mood of his companions and nodded good-naturedly.

'Mayhap, we've happened upon a Plantagenet bastard, Sire?' Sir William bowed.

This was greeted with laughter all round. The young Lincolnshire knight, being some fifteen years Edward's senior, plainly felt no qualms at jesting in such a familiar and forthright manner with the new King of England.

The king laughed along with them 'Best curb thy impertinent head, William, or fain wouldst hold it in thy lap.'

Sir William half-bowed in response to the mock reproof.

The king thought for a moment 'It is said that the Earl of Cambridge, my grandfather, favoured Yorkshire maidens...'

More laughter followed until, about the same time, all began to recall that the king's relative, the Earl of Cambridge, had gone to the block in 1415; which thought reminded one and all that the king's father, Duke Richard of York, three months earlier had been killed and decapitated at Wakefield. With the mood thus changed and the inquiry effectively diverted, King Edward applied himself to the matter at hand.

'Let the tournament for the Silver Bolt begin!'

At a blast on Fleischer's horn, the *Fähnlein* broke ranks and the boys proceeded to gather about five yards behind the first of the seven pegs which marked the shooting stands.

Spotty Spence was employing a 'German winder', or *cranequin*, to span the two steel lath bows that Fleischer was using. It was a manner of spanning which took the longest time, and as a consequence the two youngsters moved at a steady pace between the seven stands. Within ten minutes a crossbow bolt was impaled in all seven shields. However, he had not scored a strike with his first bolt on every target and it had taken a second bolt on two of the shields. Albeit Fleischer was shooting at point-blank; his strikes at fifty yards were still remarkably good shots.

The standard had been set. It would take at least six first-time strikes to outshoot the *Rottmeister* of the *Fähnlein* and take the Silver Bolt. However, the nine remaining boys to shoot knew it had not to be that way, and that Fleischer was set to triumph. At least, as each pair took their turn, they could take comfort from knowing that however shabby a performance they put in, none among their fellow Wasps expected anything different, and that was what really mattered. And so the tournament proceeded with the boys displaying varying degrees of skill, failure and success.

When it came to the turn of Snowwhite and Poxy they all brightened up and those boys who had seated themselves rose to their feet in anticipation. Knowing looks, winks and smiles were exchanged between them and they held their breath as Snowwhite loosed his first bolt. 'Hit' was the constable's call and up went the first lance. Many in the crowd noticed the interest taken by the boys in this particular shooter and, because of this, there was a general buzz.

William, Lord Fauconberg had begun to sense that all was not right with the way the boys were performing. Suspicious and uneasy, he walked over to confer with Jason Dietz.

Meanwhile, Snowwhite had loosed another two bolts and, with Poxy loading as fast he could, using a goat's-foot lever, they were soon at the sixth target. The boys were now cheering the pair on, and many of them stole glances at Fleischer. The *Rottmeister* was staring down the range with unbelieving eyes, mouth slightly agape, his cheeks and back of his neck flushed bright red. He was being out-shot and the Silver Bolt he coveted so much was speedily disappearing from his mind's eye. He had tried to make sure of everything: the bow laths; the tournament ranged to his own bows' point-blank; his going first so that the rest knew what not to beat; even dire threats of reprisal should any entertain foolish ideas of winning. Yet here was one under his charge not merely matching his strikes but out-shooting him.

When the sixth bolt slammed into the sixth target a great cheer went up from the *Fähnlein*. All that was left for Snowwhite to do was to strike the final shield – and he had two bolts to accomplish this – the coveted prize would certainly be his.

As he and Poxy Goite strode to the seventh stand the tension increased. John's arm was suddenly gripped by Bridger Blastock, who called quietly, 'Hit it Snowwhite and to hell with him!' Then the youngster began repeating, softly at first, 'Hit it, hit it, hit it!' This grew louder in volume. All the while the grip on John's arm tightened. Others took up the chant until the entire *Wespen* was chorusing with ever-growing excitement, which in turn was picked up by the crowd.

Without even raising the tiller to his eye, Snowwhite loosed off his first shot at the seventh target shield, the badge of the Duke of Somerset, from the hip. The bolt thudded into the wicker screens which formed the butt. Surely not a deliberate, contrived miss? Likely an accidental discharge.

With tears rolling down his cheeks Poxy handed the other charged bow to his *Armbrustschütze* and, picking up the discharged weapon, he turned and with head bowed walked back to where the rest were waiting to console him.

However, Snowwhite's final bolt could still win the competition and the valuable prize for him and his *Ladenschütze*. Perhaps he was toying with them all, some reasoned. Thousands cramming the castle walls, barbican, castle grounds and hill leading to the village held their breath.

With a look of utter contempt on his face, the sixteen-year-old, Thomas Moxen, known to all as Snowwhite, loosed his final shot from the hip. While the bolt was yet in flight, he spun around to walk away. The crowd looked on in disbelief, which changed to disappointment and then anger, especially among those who had risked a wager on his skill.

Bridger Blastock screamed and burst into tears.

To the accompaniment of boos and hisses, the defiant youth was led away by a sergeant-at-arms to be thrown in the castle dungeon. He would be questioned closely at a later hour, but for the moment the festive mood had to be recaptured. The king knew the boy's family and declared his interest in the forthcoming inquisition. As for Fleischer, he was worried; matters were not going according to how he had envisaged them. What, he agonised, would Snowwhite say under examination by Dietz and Fauconberg? In the meantime he comforted himself with the thought that there were only two pairs left to take part, the idiotic jesters and the swineherders. The bow skills of Snort and Grunt were unknown to him, but were not likely to be up to the mark after the beating they had suffered that morning. As for what Snowwhite might say against him, he could counter that by accusations of rebelliousness. After all, everyone had witnessed his arrogance. He felt better and even applauded with the crowd when the signal horn blew and Wattle and Daub trotted up, one behind the other, to the first marker.

Just seeing the pair together caused merriment for Didi Wattle wouldn't stop growing and had already reached six-feet three inches. His hair was out of control and had been hacked back until it stuck up in random tufts. Some time in the past he had been charged in the back by a war-horse and, as a result, his long neck was out of kilter. Long arms, at the end of which were large hands, scraggy legs and enormous feet completed the picture. He was wearing extra-long pointed shoes, exaggerating and mimicking the popular style of the day.

In complete contrast, Daub was small, stocky but not quite plump, wearing the cheekiest grin imaginable. He instinctively followed his jester partner's lead, enhancing and polishing up Wattle's spontaneous humour at every turn. For their artfully contrived performance, on this occasion, Daub was wearing an oversized tabard stuffed with padding; his head was topped by a large conical hat from which straw-like hair protruded.

When Wattle halted at the first stand Daub, who was following inches behind, collided with him, sending the gangling shooter stumbling and reeling. Wattle snatched off Daub's hat, removed his own cap and began to trounce him about the head. After slamming the conical hat upon his partner's head, he made a show of gaining his composure. They both then peered off down the range as if unable to see the target posts and shields. With hands shading their eyes, they advanced in an exaggerated walk, one step at a time, down towards the upper fish-pond, shrugging their shoulders as they mimed consultation. They suddenly pretended that they had at last seen the targets across the dry moat. They both nodded, shook hands, turned and peered back at the stands. Daub stooped to fasten a boot-strap and Wattle, turning quickly, fell full length over him into the fish-pond. Laughter and loud applause followed these antics as the crowd finally began to warm to the duo's performance.

Wattle chased Daub back up the archery range, shaking his fist. After pretending a reconciliation they began to make ready to shoot. Wattle took up a classic aiming stance and then suddenly began squirming and jerking about, whereupon Daub plunged his hand down the back of Wattle's hose and pulled out an enormous wiggling fish. The crowd went wild.

Attempts to loose a first bolt met with failure as the missile travelled a yard before flopping to the ground. Both jesters peered off down the range, hands to brows, as if the bolt had gone full distance. They congratulated each other and Wattle loped over to the next stand. Daub then spotted the errant bolt, picked it up, examined it, shrugged, then threw it over his shoulder and hopped and skipped to shooting stand two to join Wattle.

After more antics, Didi Wattle pulled off what many considered to be, up to that point, one of the best shots of the day. At the seventh and final stand the two pretended to argue as to who would shoot the final bolt. The crowd became alarmed as the jesters began pulling and tugging the spanned crossbow between them. First one section and then another of the gathering ducked as it appeared that, in the struggle, the bow was being pointed in its direction. What none could see was the wedge firmly securing the trigger, keeping the bow on safety.

When Wattle judged it to be the right moment, unseen, he slipped out the wedge, and loosed the bolt when the bow was pointing upwards. Thousands of pairs of eyes watched the missile soar into the sky and many throats accompanied its passage with a mighty roared-out – 'wooarrr'. At its zenith the errant bolt stalled, turned and began falling. Gathering speed, the deadly missile thudded into a line of temporary privies which had been set up beside the valley road. The crowd gasped and, to the delight of all, the man holding the seventh lance immediately raised it to signal a strike. The two jesters, waving their arms in the air in supposed victory, scampered back, Daub closely behind Wattle, to tumultuous applause. Didi Wattle never would admit, neither then nor later, that he had deliberately caused that bolt to end up where it did. Whereas Willie Daub always maintained that it was a carefully contrived shot brought off by his friend with the sole purpose of entertaining the crowd. The castle retainer who raised his lance to signal a strike, when asked, said that Didi Wattle alerted him to what he might feel he could do should the privies receive a bolt.

'Well, Edmund, what do you intend?' They were to begin their turn any second, once the merriment had subsided, and what Edmund proposed to do was of some concern. A defiant Snowwhite had been marched off to the castle dungeon and John had visions of joining him. The only other course for Edmund, as far as John could see, was to win the competition and hang the consequences. He had every confidence that Edmund could hit every single shield using just one bolt for each if he so choose. However, his aching backside prompted him to consider the utter folly of his brother doing that. Edmund could pretend, put up a fair showing and hope that the lords would fail to note his deception.

With a smile and a wink, Edmund reassured his brother, 'Now, John, pray tell, why would any bowman of merit strive to strike an opponent's shield? Where would be the gain in that, how would he be advantaged?'

'But should you be seen to deliberately miss you will surely go the way of Snowwhite,' John argued.

'Then we must devise a ruse, a compromise, so that every man this day may enjoy satisfaction.'

At that point the horn blew and immediately Edmund's mood changed. Hurriedly he whispered his instructions.

'We will make all haste, John. Call each target position either, "low" "mid" or "high", clear and loud.'

At that, he ran to the first stand carrying his bow and John followed after him at a fast trot with the second weapon. The line of seven poles seemed so far away and the badges on the shields, which were set at varying heights, were barely discernible.

'Hind – white – low!' John called out the green shield of Sir Andrew Trollope, the Calais captain who had turned his coat at Ludlow, thus betraying the Duke of York and causing him to flee the country. Edmund dropped to one knee, raised the crossbow and stroked the tickler all in one continuous, smooth action. The bolt powered into the post full centre above the shield. The steward called a 'miss' and the deep base horn was blown. Edmund dropped the bow and caught the second crossbow his brother tossed to him. He was already running to stand two and John had barely time to follow and yell the target:

'Wyvern – red – mid!', spanning the first bow with the aid of the belt contraption as he called out. Again a bolt hissed through the air and smacked into the post above the shield of Lord John Clifford, the so-named Blackfaced murderer of young King Edward's brother on Wakefield bridge and the beautiful Lady Isabel's husband, Richard del Wardrop. Another 'miss' was called and the bass horn blew. They exchanged crossbows and Edmund sprinted to the third stand. John raced after him. Squinting down the range, John quickly identified the next point of aim.

'Escallop – white on red – high!' The badge of Lord Dacre of the North, a seashell on a field of red. The shield rattled as a crossbow tore into the post above it. It was Dacre's mounted longbow riders who had hung the reeve during the hog-drive last Micklemastide. This time a half-hearted note was blown on the horn to signal a 'miss'.

In an instant Edmund was at the fourth stand and John called over to him as he bent double, hooked the string and straightened, spanning the bow at speed and rattling out as he did so, 'Crescent – white – mid – red, blue shield!'

The bolt splintered the post before falling to the ground. Edmund made a quick decision; he would attempt a second shot. John tossed him the loaded bow and within seconds a bolt was protruding above the shield bearing the badge of the Earl of Northumberland, one of three Lancastrian lords who had taken an oath of vengeance following the deaths of their fathers at the first Battle of St Albans in 1455.

There were gasps from the crowd as, at that point, the soldier indicating for the fourth target, on his own initiative, hesitantly at first, began to raise his lance. He had discerned that the bolts were striking exactly where they were intended.

John's next call, 'White boar – low – red shield!', identified one of the badges of the Earl of Devon and Edmund responded with a bolt that served to splinter the target stake. It must have been rotten for the post sheered clear away under the impact – above the shield. At that, and without any hesitation up went the fifth lance. The steward moved as if to go over to the lances, but a restraining hand was laid upon him by Lord Fauconberg.

'Wheat ear – gold – red and white field – high!'

The pain in John's back was becoming unbearable as he gasped out the description of the target shield for the Duke of Exeter. If fatigue and pain were wracking his brother's frame as it was his own, then it certainly did not show, nor did it affect his aim. Up went the sixth lance indicating a hit.

John stumbled to the seventh stand and sank to his knees, handing the bow to his brother as he did so. There was no breath left in him to call the target. Edmund looked down at him with concern. He smiled and nodded as if commending his exertions. Then, glancing up, he spoke under his breath, 'Yale – white on blue – low!'

Leaning forward in the familiar style of his, Edmund dropped to one knee, raising the bow until the tiller touched his cheek and, without pausing, stroked the tickler releasing the final bolt. The shield bearing the badge of the avowed enemy of York, the Duke of Somerset, quivered as the post bearing it received a crossbow bolt directly above.

Because of the pace set by Edmund, it was all over in a matter of minutes. Never had there been such an exhibition where crossbow shooting had been carried out at such a pace.

All seven lances were now being held at the vertical.

At first there was a buzz from the puzzled crowd and then arguments began breaking out everywhere, as the brothers trotted back to the where the lads awaited them. By this time

John was in agony as constant bending and straightening had stretched tortured flesh and opened the multiple contusions across his buttocks. He could feel the blood trickling down the backs of his legs. Confusion reigned all around: the lords and knights were holding a heated argument among themselves. Fleischer was pointing at the lances and arguing bitterly with the steward.

Jason Dietz was suddenly standing before the brothers, demanding in his rasping, guttural accent that they go with him. He prodded and pushed them to where the king and his lords awaited. Requiring no prompting from Dietz, the Hawksworths dropped to their knees before the king.

'Why did you deliberately miss the shields of Lancaster?'

It was the Earl of Warwick who addressed the words to Edmund in a threatening tone. The Earl was a fine looking man in his early thirties who had decided to remain in harness for the tournament and looked splendid in highly-polished shining armour. He appeared to have assumed authority. Edmund attempted to answer but was overtaken by a fit of stammering and subsided helplessly.

'Speak up, boy! And pay heed as to how you give answer!' The Earl's voice was raised and his annoyance was plainly evident. King Edward raised his hand to stay any further questioning from his companion. In a kinder, but insistent tone the king repeated 'Speak up. Why did you miss the declared targets? With aforethought you chose to miss deliberately, and of that there must be no denial on your part.'

Again Edmund attempted to answer, but once more to no avail as he stuttered and jerked into silence. At that the Earl of Warwick, with growing impatience demanded, 'Who is your father, and what are you named?'

The king, displeased at the interruption, half-turned sharply to rebuke the Earl. 'Were you never in tremble before your betters, Richard Neville, that you lack some affinity for this lad?'

'Who is your father, and what are you named?' The king repeated Warwick's questions. Then hurriedly he added, 'Both of you may arise.'

'I am named John, the first-born of John Hawksworth, who is retained by the house of Clifford of Skipton.' At John's mention of a hated enemy all hands went to sword hilts, as if he was about to assasinate the king at that very moment. John added hastily, 'Our father has neither love nor affection for us, nor we for him, having abandoned us to our own devices these many years.'

This seemed to calm their hearts for the moment and so John continued, 'My brother's name is Edmund, my liege, and as you see he is...'

Before John could make excuses for Edmund's poor speech, the king began repeating the name 'Edmund' over and over again and a great melancholy overcame him. It was Lord Fauconberg who then asked again in a steady deliberate manner, 'Why did your brother deliberately miss the seven target shields of Lancaster?'

'If it pleases you, my lord, my brother says that there can be no gain in striking a shield. The house of York would be best served by striking a point twelve inches above.'

A stunned silence greeted that claim.

It seemed an age before John's words took root with the lords. They began to turn, first one and then another, to peer at the target posts. It was Lord Fauconberg who broke the silence of that group of around thirty incredulous men.

'God's Blood!' he blasphemed.

'I have a dagger with a blade measuring exactly twelve inches,' volunteered a Lincolnshire esquire of Harpswell by the name of John Whichcote, also Sheriff of that county. 'We might determine how close to his declared target our ace crossbow boy has achieved.'

'Be about your measuring, good Sheriff of Lincolnshire!' called out the king. 'We will allow the lad two or three inches of tolerance.' Another voice was suddenly added, calling over to the royal group, 'I wager that the Thryberg Hawk will require no such indulgence, my lords.'

It was the Abbot of Roche, John Wakefield, whose face was beaming with excitement. He was completely confident in Edmund's prowess and could scarcely maintain his composure as he hopped from one leg to the other.

'One foot above – we will allow to the nearest inch – so be it. A measure more or less than that, it shall be deemed a miss!' ruled the king. 'By this we shall discern exactly what prowess we have uncovered this day.'

The seven men with lances were ordered to lower them and await the fresh judgement. The Sheriff of Lincolnshire set off for the target posts. All eyes were upon him as he skirted the fish pond and negotiated the banks of the dry moat. His companions followed him part-way and stationed themselves along the range to relay the results of the measuring. The distance between the top of the shield and the bolt at the first post was carefully measured by the Sheriff. He called to his colleague across the dry moat.

'Trollope: exactly twelve inches.' This was called until it reached the royal party. The king raised a gloved hand and nodded. Up went the first lance.

'Clifford, twelve inches exactly,' was relayed and the second lance was raised. Dacre, Percy, Devon, Exeter and Somerset followed one after another and the measure of one foot was called, followed by the verdict from the king. When the final lance was raised there was thunderous applause from the delighted thousands. Never had they seen the like, for the posts supporting the shields were but two to three inches in diameter and six had a crossbow bolt firmly impaled in the centre. One post securing the badge of the Earl of Devon was severed clean through and snapped off precisely twelve inches above the shield.

Every boy in the *Fähnlein* was jumping about and cheering for all they were worth. Wattle was trotting round with Daub high on his shoulders, blowing the 'March of the Wasps' on a shawm. They all saw it not so much as the winning of a Silver Bolt, but the bettering of their tormentor. As for the locals, it would be many a year before the good people of Conisbrough would have the memory of that day fade. It would be told, retold and sung about for generations to come of how a local boy, a swineherd, out-shot some of the finest crossbow wielders in the kingdom.

Fleischer was beside himself with anger, frustration and disappointment. These feelings were made all the harder for him because of the need to contain and hide them.

As usual, it was not an easy matter to know what Edmund was thinking, although John suspected he was taken by surprise, for by missing the shields he had expected that Fleischer would be deemed the winner. That way, the lives of the boys would be much easier for a while. Now it was not to be. Some further unpleasantness could be expected to come their way in the days ahead.

For the present, however, it was time for deserved and warranted accolades. Silence fell as the King, Edward IV, held high his arm for quiet.

'This day we have witnessed such prowess by the *Wespen* that I fear there will be scarce gainful employment for our fine Burgundian crossbow men and handgunners.'

This was greeted with laughter and cries of 'Verily'.

'All of you have fared so well that it pains me to have to award the Bolt to but two of your number. However, the Hawksworth brothers have won the day by striking, not the defensive devices of our enemies, but rather where their neck would be.'

Again this was received with laughter and some applause.

'Mayhap we have witnessed the birth of a proverb or saying for common parlance on this day of the Annunciation of the Blessed Virgin, in this year of our Lord 1461.'

'And pray explain the saying clear, my liege,' called out Fauconberg, 'so that we all might use it to good advantage!'

Pointing towards the target stakes the king called back, 'Why, getting it in the neck!' my Lord William, 'Getting it in the neck!'

'And there likely will grow from this day yet another adage, my liege!' called back Fauconberg, 'Should any man have been squatting in yonder privy, he surely would have been surprised by "a bolt from the blue". Thus, being caught by surprise is like suffering a bolt from out of the blue.'

Hauptmann Dietz, the scarred mercenary, handed the king a deep blue velvet cloth upon which sparkled the much-coveted solid silver crossbow bolt.

'Step forward Edmund Hawksworth. No doubt we will come to closer acquaintance in the trials which lie before us.'

At that point the Earl of Warwick whispered to the king that the Abbot of Roche wished an immediate audience with him. There followed a short period of intense discussion between the king and the Abbot. John watched this exchange with some trepidation, for, knowing well the abbot's near-veneration of his brother, he could well imagine the matter under debate. Then the king finally turned to them and gave Edmund a long hard look.

'So it is you!' declared the king softly, who then smiled, 'You are the one laying claim to the role of Avenger of Righteous Blood. They are making many assertions concerning you – even that you are "highly favoured".'

Suddenly Lady Isabel surprised the gathering by walking forward and, excusing herself, passed quickly through the lords and knights to kneel before the king. Despite her sombre attire, dressed as she was in a dark grey stomacher and black chemisette, she took away the breath of most men there. Her long fair hair fell in waves around her shoulders and about her head she wore a grieving garland of evergreen berries and leaves.

'Pray grant unto this thy loyal subject a boon my liege.'

Taken aback by her boldness and the compelling beauty, especially those eyes, the king nodded and may have blushed a little.

'This Edmund Hawksworth, the tournament victor, this boy they are calling the Thryberg Hawk, is my true champion and as such he has vowed to slay my husband's murderer, the Black-faced Clifford.'

'And your boon, madam?'

'To be allowed to confer upon The Hawk my favour and amulet, to safeguard him against all the devils of Lancaster.'

The king could only nod and grant his permission, whereupon the Lady Isabel arose, approached Edmund and placed about his neck the silken cloth upon which she had embroided the chequered arms of the Clifford family.

'This will keep you safe,' she whispered 'Return it to me soaked in the blood of Black-hearted Clifford, the butcher of Skipton, and I shall pay unto you the promised forfeit.'

As Lady Isabel stood back, the king suddenly declared in a loud voice so that all around could not fail to hear,

'Edmund Hawksworth, concerning this matter, that is, the heavy responsibility of being the Avenger of Righteous Blood: you have been anointed by Divine hand, blooded in affray, recommended by Mother Church and now confirmed by a lady's favour.'

Unbuckling his belt he removed the sword and dagger, before holding it high for all to see the lettering '*Richarius et Edmund*' that had been worked upon it.

'Therefore for what possible reason could I any longer contend this choosing and withhold the Champion's Girdle? The Avenger's belt, it would appear, is rightfully yours, Edmund Hawksworth of Thryberg.'

An esquire, Thomas Montgomery of Witham, Essex, together with Sir William Hussey of Sleaford, was handed the royal champion's belt and, between them, they placed it about Edmund's waist. They stood back and saluted him.

The king then addressed the *Fähnlein*, which (without orders from Fleischer) had formed up behind the brothers.

'What I announce to you boys, I also say to all men gathered here under arms, and indeed to any who, in future days joins this host gathered against murderous Lancaster with its puppet king.'

The young king raised his powerful voice so that it would carry to the best part of the assembly.

'Lancaster, it would appear, make much sport with the heads of those opposed to their counterfeit reign. Captive Christian lords have had their heads struck from off their shoulders. Henry and his French queen have set new and gory rules. So then let us also be about the game. From this royal purse, one hundred pounds for every head of the Lancastrian lords depicted by yonder target shields!'

This was greeted by a deafening roar. There was now, more than ever, a great eagerness for the coming affray, as a man could become rich at a literal stroke of a blade. There was the usual plundering of a beaten enemy, his camp and baggage train, but here was added the possibility of winning a considerable sum outright.

Edmund indicated that he wished to speak and, with some interest, the party gathered about the king fell silent. After a quick consultation with his brother, John bowed and then addressed them:

'My brother would thank the king for his gift and kind favour. And he would beg this boon...' Edward IV nodded for John to present his request.

'Our brother-at-arms, who has been taken away for inquisition, Thomas Moxen, my brother Edmund requests, as your servant, that he be permitted to return to our ranks without harm.'

Warwick answered before the king could speak.

'This boy has blatantly manifested monstrous insolence before his sovereign and gathered betters. All the assemblage have witnessed this. He must be taught to know his place and receive punishment, for sake of example.'

John bowed and turned to depart as he discerned that there would likely be no change of mood among the mighty-born. However, Edmund was not about to be thwarted. At least the lords would surely know that the words were those of his brother, and that he was not expressing his own sentiments.

'My liege, all are well aware that our Thomas Moxen did a great wrong, but every boy here knows that he meant no insult to you, nor to any other lord, but rather to another of common degree.'

At John's words William, Lord Fauconberg approached the king and spoke a few words in his ear. King Edward nodded and was about to answer when Warwick snapped out, 'In that case we shall extract the rightwiseness of this matter from his own lips, not yours. Lawlessness must be seen to be quashed when it appears or we shall suffer another rebellion like the treasonable rabble from Kent and Sussex who rose up under Jack Cade just ten years past.'

Again, at Edmund's whispered instructions, John addressed the king further 'Your devoted liegemen are about to do battle with a mighty host gathered about the town of York. As you have seen, the one called Snowwhite is one of the finest shots amongst us. Could his punishment await the ending of the matter at hand?'

Before Warwick could interrupt again, the king rebuked him. 'Richard Neville, the last time that I tallied, I noted that I still had a tongue in my head.' He then spoke directly to Edmund.

'Well-spoken Edmund Hawksworth. This Snowwhite will be released to your charge, and unchastised, immediately.'

He sounded like a king, as at nineteen-years he could with full assurance contradict his counsellor, despite Warwick being his senior by some ten years. Edmund and John bowed low before him and Edmund then spoke aloud with very little stuttering. Whilst his words were directed to the king, he had Warwick in mind.

'My liege lord, we are grateful for your mercy and are put in mind of Our Lord and Saviour when he said, "Forgive ye, and it shall be forgiven to you. For by the same measure that ye mete, it shall be meted to you."'

'Nobly, and scholarly said,' exclaimed the king, surprised.

To the amazement of everyone, and the annoyance of Warwick, Edward IV stepped forward and with his right hand he firmly grasped Edmund's right arm below the elbow, causing Edmund's hand, likewise, to grasp the king's arm.

'With such loyal subjects the House of York should wax well in the coming days.'

Later, within the hour, true to the king's word, and to the irritation of Fleischer, Snowwhite joined the *Fähnlein* at St Peter's churchyard. The brothers were persuaded to show Snowwhite the Silver Bolt and he was able to examine it and make appropriate sounds to convey his delight at their winning of it.

'We should have competed for this fair and square, just the two of us,' he said, handing the prize back to Edmund.

'And you would have lost, Snowy!' declared Didi Wattle, smirking from ear to ear.

'The Hawk, that's what they call him in these parts, can hit a spot to within an inch,' said Poxy Goite. 'And at fifty paces!'

There followed an excited welter of chatter as the boys sought to inform Snowwhite of events following his being thrown in the castle dungeon.

'Then you're the better man,' Thomas Moxen said as he gripped and shook Edmund's hand. 'And wear a king's belt.'

'Aye, and don't forget, he wears a lady's favour about his neck.' Daub indicated the checked scarf.

'Did you ever see such a beauty?' wailed Mealy Madoc 'Those eyes! For truly, she made me go all weak at the knees.'

'Not for the likes of you, for a knight right noble is bound to sweep the grieving widow away to the altar,' snapped Bridger Blastock. 'Anyway, she looked plain of face to me and squint-eyed!'

'It's bound to be The Hawk who gains her hand, for he has surely elevated his degree this day,' said Didi Wattle.

The deeply disgruntled *Rottmeister* had things on his mind and took no part in the joyous exchange. Immediately following the tournament, both Dietz and Fauconberg had spoken to him at great length. Snowwhite's rebellious performance was being laid at Fleischer's door. When Dietz had examined the crossbows he had discovered the superior range of the *Rottmeister's* weapons. The mercenary was seething with anger, for he was open to an accusation of complicity in the fixing of a competition in which wagers had been involved.

As the period of Compline became smothered in the gloom of night, the sky over the West Riding became shrouded in overcast as a chilling east wind blew dark storm clouds over Yorkshire. By midnight a freezing chill had gripped the Riding. Many among the over twenty thousand men centred on Conisbrough Castle were awakened frozen to the bone by the dramatic change in the weather and hastened to stoke up their camp fires.

Despite the restless stirrings, it was likely that no one spotted the hooded figure moving stealthily among the sleeping crossbow boys.

Chapter Ten

Skirmish at Robin Hood's Well and Bridger's End

TRUMPETS, HORNS and drums being sounded throughout the Yorkist camp drowned the usual heralds of the dawn, the domestic cockerels, in a militaristic cacophony, as each affinity sought to stir its adherents on that freezing cold March day. A thousand camp fires were coaxed into life and, amidst a growing clatter and rattle, chores were attended to as twenty thousand men prepared to break their fast. It was during that Thursday morn arousing that Edmund discovered the Silver Bolt was missing.

Fleischer had asked to see it, for he wished to show it to some bill men from Canterbury who, he claimed, had approached him for the favour. Their meagre belongings were sought through in a very short time and the Hawksworth boys were left frantically searching about them.

'It's been stolen!" roared *Rottmeister* in an overly loud demonstration of concern. 'We have a thief amongst us!'

He blew the horn signalling the *Fähnlein* to form ranks before placing Spotty Spence in charge and setting off at a trot to alert *Hauptmann* Dietz. It was Snowwhite who made the discovery.

'It's here, wedged under my tabor skin.' It was obvious to everyone that Snowwhite was truly discovering the bolt, and that he had not placed it there.

'Fleshy! The cunning devil! He's after avengement on Snowwhite,' cried Poxy Goite, Snowwhite's loyal *Ladenschütze*. 'Snowy's no robber, for that I'll vouchsafe!'

'No, but we all know who's had an ear clipped for thievery, don't we?' called out Diddy Wattle as he strode through the ranks and took the silver bolt from Snowwhite to hand it back to Edmund.

'Maybe he'd be better balanced if he had the other ear cut to match.' So saying, Willie Daub took the bolt and marched over to where Fleischer's belongings lay upon a tomb chest and rammed the precious item in his pack. His usually cheerful face was fixed in a determined grimace.

'*Stillgestanden!*' yelled Blau Ben Haagan at the top of his voice. Which command brought the *Fähnlein* to attention, as Dietz rode up on his black courser with Fleischer loping alongside.

The mercenary captain was in a foul mood. This inconvenient complication was bound to cause a delay in his unit taking its place at the head of the vanward battle. The Yorkist host could not be held up over the theft of a trophy. However, thievery in the ranks would not be tolerated, nor could dealing with it be left for a later time.

Sensing that something was amiss, a crowd of archers and bill men gathered. This did not please the vintenars and centenars, who could ill afford distraction when the signal to march for Pontefract was less than an hour away. Gallopers, the outriders and foreriders, the eyes, ears and indeed, the nose of the host, had already set out. Hardriders, those charged with the most dangerous task in the army, the infiltrators and spies had, by way of messengers, given a 'clear-terrain' as far as the River Aire. The king was eager to cover that intervening ground before mid-day.

News of the theft having reached the castle, a furious Sir William, Lord Fauconberg galloped up to St Peter's. *Hauptmann* Dietz had begun to address them in his faltering English when Fauconberg interrupted most abruptly and took over the proceedings. The mercenary was Fauconberg's retained 'lance' and the Bavarian's crossbow unit was paid from the Fauconberg purse.

'I am confident that this missing trophy is a childish prank,' began Fauconberg, addressing drawn-up ranks from his saddle. 'Were the lad responsible to admit to his jesting, the matter will be dropped and raised no more.' He waited for some response before trying again. 'The bells will soon be sounding Lauds. Should the prankster declare himself before the church bell rings then we shall tarry hither no longer and no further word on the matter. This oath on my sword, I pledge!'

In the intervening time to the sounding of Lauds, and at a given signal, mounted archers moved ominously closer so as to surround the drawn-up ranks.

'If the thief does not give himself up now, before the bell, upon his discovery he will lose his nose and one ear!'

Before he could utter another word the bell in St Peter's tower clanged for Lauds and an icy dread descended upon them.

'Your chance to redeem is past. Now woe betide anyone caught with the Silver Bolt in his possession.'

Four vintenars from Fauconberg's mounted archers began systematically to search the boys, their baggage and clothing. Fleischer's performance was one to behold, for as the examinations took place he strode to and fro in front of the ranks prodding and poking clothing and packs with his mace. All the time he kept glancing in Snowwhite's direction, awaiting discovery of the trophy. When the bowmen carried on, having searched Snowwhite, Fleischer could no longer contain himself and he charged through the ranks to begin his own search. It was when he snatched the tabors from Snowwhite's belt and began to examine them closely that Fauconberg and Dietz exchanged knowing looks.

Realisation struck as if icy water had been thrown over him – he had given himself away. Wide-eyed, Fleischer began to look into the faces of some of the boys. There was some plot afoot and he was hopelessly compromised. The dawning came too late and in alarm Fleischer spun about to see *Hauptmann* Dietz, dismounted, searching through his side pack and rolled blanket. He pushed through the ranks and, trembling, stood watching in disbelief as his own belongings were gone through. With a chilling clatter the bolt fell on to the lichen-encrusted tomb chest lid. The *Rottmeister's* legs gave out from under him and he collapsed to his knees, shaking his head in disbelief and muttering, pleading and accusing all at the same time, declaring 'The disloyal swine have done for me'.

A savage blow to the head from a bowman knocked the whimpering *Rottmeister* senseless.

Punishment would take place within the castle walls that very hour. The *Fähnlein* was to assemble with crossbows and packs ready to march. Before onlookers, Fleischer would be stripped of his *Wespen* surcoat, then bound and mutilated. At long last the *Fähnlein* would be rid of the cruel bully, or so they all believed. However, they had each arrived at their reckoning without considering the elevated reasoning of the unfathomable Edmund Hawksworth.

Edmund and John were supplied with padded jacks, hose and leather boots; more important, they were presented with newly-made surcoats. Mater had been up most of the night completing the coveted distinctive garb for them. No longer clad in the apparel of swineherders, all at once they became transformed into objects of martial splendour. John felt stirrings of immense pride, coupled with a sense of real belonging, the like of which he had never experienced prior to that day – and rarely since. Whether or not Edmund experienced similar feelings, no one would ever know. In his deportment he carried the black and yellow striped garment, with its oak leaf and acorn badge, with a noble bearing that caused heads to turn. No doubt his appearance was enhanced by the Lady Isabel's favour, the silken chequered scarf, along with the king's bequeathal: the magnificent Champion's Belt, which declared to all that the wearer was the 'Avenger of Blood'.

There were numerous low whistles as the brothers strode from Mater's wagon together and many affected a pretended bow. However, the homage in the case of Edmund appeared to be far from mock servility. In most instances, it seemed genuine enough and truly meant, for it was accompanied by a lowering of the eyes and tightened lips. Perhaps it was the taking of the king's hand, or the royal belt; maybe it was out of respect for Edmund's crossbow skills; or because of the fantastic stories circulating about Edmund's powers which, since the incident in St Peter's, included power to raise the dead. Whether these things or some of the other numerous stories eddying and swirling in the wake of Edmund, it mattered little, but there was no mistaking it, some archers did bow their heads and some even crossed themselves as he and Edmund passed by.

Thousands prepared to move camp from around Conisbrough. Captains rode about issuing orders to centenars, who in turn shouted at vintenars, who then yelled at men under their charge. All seemed to be chaos and disorder but in fact it was highly organised.

The entry of the *Fähnlein* into the castle suffered delay as a steady flow of mounted knights and squires clattered through the barbican two abreast, in what seemed to be a continuous stream of glittering armour. Splitting up, the riders assumed their places at the head of marching columns. A few headed for the ferry and others for the road to Doncaster. In a swirl of colour the mighty vanguard, the forward of King Edward's host, was on the move. Meanwhile, the pace-setters for the march, the *Wespen*, had other matters to attend to before it could take its place at the head of that Yorkist host.

Blau Ben Haagan, acting as *Rottmeister* and wielding the mace of command, marched them into the inner bailey of Conisbrough Castle. Edmund and John were beginning to recognise Bavarian marching commands and able to come to a halt without knocking over Poxy Goite and Snowwhite, marching directly in front of them. On the shouted command, *'Recht um'*, they were able to perform the manoeuvre smartly without embarrassing themselves.

Many knights and squires of the middleward, preparing to set off on the heels of the vanguard and march north at the commencement of the period of Terce, gathered to observe the *Ehrenzeichen*, the stripping of honour and punishment. Jason Dietz had had a pair of sheep-shears especially sharpened and would be overseeing the mutilation himself. Mater hovered by the castle chapel wall with cloths to staunch the bleeding. She cried quietly to herself, for she could envisage what lay ahead. It would be she who would have to make right the damage as best she could to the youngster. Following the disfiguring, Mater, over the weeks would be dressing wounds, keeping putrefaction at bay and administering comfort and words of kindness. Perhaps his days earning a livelihood as a mercenary were at an end. On the other hand, Mater's tears may have been for Robin Carle, the mounted archer, who had just ridden off with the vanguard.

Two castle retainers hurried from the direction of the castle guardhouse dragging a wriggling and sobbing Fleischer between them. No longer in the livery of the *Wespen*, Fleischer was stripped to shirt and hose. A flat plank of wood had been lashed to his back. Ropes pinioned his arms and around his forehead a broad cloth had been tightly bound, securing his head to the plank. The sharpened plank snagged and scraped as it trailed on the compacted ground and cobbles of the inner bailey.

Dietz presented a figure to inspire dread in the stoutest heart, dressed in a black cloak, mail and part plate armour. His badge, and that of the *Wespen*, comprised of oak leaves and acorns and was worn at the left breast. Dietz wore three leaves and two acorns; the boys one oak leaf at their left shoulders and the *Rottmeister* had a two-leafed motif. The Bavarian mercenary would likely have once been handsome before a Turk crossbow bolt had impacted his face, destroying his left eye and boring a hole through his right cheekbone. The fame of his special *Truppen* of keen-eyed crossbow boys was spreading. Edward IV had been quick to see the value of their employment behind the battle mêlée, charged especially, as they were, with bringing down lords and captains. Thus deprived of direction and leadership, the commons would be more likely of a mind to call for quarter. Retained at thirty marks per annum, coupled with the prospect of ransoming prisoners, and with a share of spoils from a defeated enemy's baggage train, the Bavarian could hope to make his fortune 'ere he finally hung up his bow in old age. Mayhap that desirable state could be arrived at before the Plantagenet cousins of the Houses of York and Lancaster ended their sanguinary warring over the crown of England – so he reasoned. The matter at hand must be out of the way quickly. However, Dietz would be expected to address the boys before having the punishment inflicted.

The wooden plank was driven into the hard-packed earth of the inner bailey courtyard until Fleischer's knees were touching the ground. With every blow of the huge mallet the unfortunate youth squealed in pain and horror at the jarring foretaste of what was to come.

'Only infidels steal from *Waffenbruder*!' began the fearsome leader of the *Wespen* in faltering English, before turning and shouting at Edmund and John, '*Hauksvort Jugend, er Kommt!*'

A nudge from Snowwhite indicated that they were to step from the ranks and they hurried to stand before the fearsome *Hauptmann*. John stole a glance at Fleischer and gathered that the poor howling wretch had, by then, lost control of his bowels and bladder.

'*Das Ohr und die Nase er schneidet.*' Shears were thrust into the hand of Edmund and he nodded towards the bound figure at the stake. The Bavarian looked to Blau Ben Haagan, indicating that his commands were to be translated.

'You were victims of Fleischer; he having had you beaten and then stealing from you, the *Hauptmann* would have you carry out the punishment.' As Ben Haagan conveyed this, he glanced nervously, first at Dietz and then Fleischer, 'The right ear and the nose must be cut off.' The dismayed *Ladenschütze* then rasped out in a whisper, 'In the blessed name of the Holy Mother, be as quick about it as you can.'

Edmund took the shears in his left hand and turned smartly to face *Hauptmann* Dietz. In the manner of the day he raised his right hand, with fingers extended, to touch his cap; he paused briefly before snapping his hand to his side. Dietz returned the salute and nodded for Edmund to proceed.

However, the brothers also were to address all hearers gathered on that freezing cold March morning, Edmund had decided. Of course, John would be his spokesman. Quickly, Edmund conveyed his words to his brother's ear.

The tightly-crammed inner bailey appeared as a blurred sea of faces and horses to John. He began to speak out at the very top of his voice, 'My liege, my lords, worthy men at arms and all you supporters of this royal house of York, hear the words of the Thryberg Hawk.' John added these last words to clarify that it was his brother who was really speaking.

'Before the most holy Palm Sunday, we shall be face to face with a foe, whom we're told, is most numerous. Every eye and every hand skilled in the art of weaponry will, on that day, find gainful employment and render a service to his

225

king.' He paused, knowing he was about to disobey the mercenary captain.

'There would be no advantage, at this time, to maim a boy warrior so well skilled in the art of the crossbow.'

There was ne'er a word nor gasp from the crowd – only deathly silence. Edmund quickly added more for John to deliver.

'By right, the bolt was won by Fleischer who struck the declared and intended targets.' Edmund conveyed with some urgency further words 'Therefore, let any spilling of blood at our hand, be the blood of Lancaster.'

Edmund moved quickly to the torture stake and, before he could be prevented, cut through the cloth securing Fleischer's head, followed by the rope around his body. The pathetic figure slumped to the ground and curled itself into a whimpering ball.

What could have happened next, namely Edmund's and John's own seizing, was averted by the intervention of the Abbot of Roche, who stepped from the crowd and, raising his arms in benediction, cried out, 'Blessed are they that are of a clean heart, for they shall see God. Blessed are peaceable men, for they shall be called God's children. Blessed are merciful men, for they shall obtain mercy unto themselves.'

Had there been any one among the lords who would have sought the Hawk's censure, the Abbot's intervention and blessing caused objection to be stillborn.

'Are there any more surprises to come at thy hand?'

Richard Neville, the Earl of Warwick, nudged his fretting, snorting destrier through the crowd and stopped before the brothers, who immediately dropped to one knee.

'I swear, such chivalry have I never seen amongst my equals.' He sounded truly surprised. 'It would seem that you find favour in the eyes of all about you, foremost being the good Abbot of Roche, who never ceases extolling your virtue

226

night or day.' He bid them rise and was about to order their departure when there was a childish cry from the crowd.

Crawling under the legs of men, women and horses, she came at speed, before bursting through the ring of archers and into the presence of the drawn-up *Wespen*. Eleanor the Bastard paused and stood rooted to the spot, realising she had interrupted her betters, and no longer sure how her beloved Edmund Love would greet her. He had so recently been everything to her; gentle and loving as any mother, firm and kind as a father, fun-loving and a companion like a brother – her protector and now a champion of her betters. She froze with fear, terrified of rejection, for the one who stood before her looked so splendid in his livery and harness of war. In favour with the king of all England, lords, knights, clergy, all the mighty-born. Would he now chastise her – or worse – pay her no heed? Would he turn away, slight her, as he went about his most important business?

'Eleanor!' The instant Edmund saw her he called in obvious pleasure and, moving quickly towards her, dropped to his knees and embraced the little mite.

Despite all Edmund had experienced, prominence, prestige and the seemingly ongoing elevation from his degree during those days, John never once noted an instance of swell-headedness in him. John found him irritating and frustrating. And, at those times he swore that if his brother quoted one more passage from holy writ he would scream out aloud. How could one who disparaged the Almighty so much make growing use of the inspired word with such self-assurance? Jealousy would rear up like a jailer to clap John in irons and take him prisoner at all his weakest times. Would his life be spent in Edmund's shadow, forever serving his stuttering tongue? However, at the worst moments for John his brother seemed to sense his inner struggle. Standing with Eleanor in his arms, Edmund turned to John with the kindest smile 'See John, what the north wind has blown into our midst!' So saying, he passed her over, adding, 'Suffer ye that little children come... for of such is the kingdom of heaven.' With that he laughed and kissed Eleanor's cheek.

John groaned inwardly. But, he was gratified to receive a heart-felt embrace from the child and any ill-feeling vanished away.

Dietz was in a hurry to be on the road and, hoisting himself into the saddle, he snapped out orders to Blau Ben Haagan that only the lad from Lübeck could understand *'Herr Falke zum Rang eines Rottmeister befördern!'*

The Bavarian nudged his courser over to join the captain of the Earl of Warwick's mounted archers, whereupon he proceeded to engage the commander in painful English.

Ben Haagan stepped up to Edmund and handed him the mace of office before turning to address the *Fähnlein* and, with a ring of unmistakable pleasure in his voice he called out, 'The Hawk has been promoted to command the Wasps.'

The news was greeted with a spontaneous roar of approval from the boys. Edmund then gave his first order as *Rottmeister.* Turning to Ben Haagan, he commanded him to march the unit from the castle. Next he called out to Snowwhite with only the slightest of stutters, 'If it pleases you Snowy, 'March of the *Wespen!'*

That incredible drumming began, first Snowwhite, followed by one after another of the boys carrying tabors as they sought to emulate the tempo. Then, at a given command, there was the rocking on the spot of the two *Rotten* in flawless time. Haagan blew a loud blast on his command horn and, in perfect step, the entire *Fähnlein* marched forward as one, through the crowds, towards the gatehouse and barbican.

Removing his cloak, Edmund knelt and, covering the sobbing Fleischer with it, gently assisted him to his feet. Mater hurried forward and between them they led the disgraced youth from the castle to the Wasps' baggage cart outside the gate. Fleischer was in a trance that would last the best part of two days, during which time he would assist Mater in catering for the needs of the *Fähnlein*. Meanwhile, the two hackneys harnessed to the unit cart would have to be worked hard in order to catch up with vanward battle, which by that time would have reached the ancient north road to Tadcaster and York.

Mater's support wagon was about an hour behind the last elements of the vanward. A further complication for her was the joining up of two local boys, John Butterbusk and Richard Wyott. The thirteen-year-olds had been thrilled and impressed by the Wasps whilst witnessing their prowess during the crossbow competition and had persuaded their parents to seek permission from the lord of the manor to join the élite unit. There had been little opportunity to test their individual skills and neither of them would be paid a full wage, nor receive a coveted Wasp surcoat or badge until a later date. For the time being they would travel with the support cart.

Dietz had arranged for the *Wespen* to be transported by mounted archers to a point ahead of the vanward battle. There they were to await the arrival of the main body and once more assume position at the point of the marching column. Twenty mounted archers, bearing the badge of the ragged staff of the Earl of Warwick, were lined up one behind the other, each waiting to carry a boy of the *Wespen*. Since Fleischer's demise, Wee Willie, much to his delight, had been assigned as *Ladenschütze* to Spotty Spence.

'*Benedicto salus exeuntibus!*' It was the Abbot of Roche, John Wakefield, blessing them and wishing God speed to all those departing. The brothers had good reason to be thankful to the Abbot, for since that Epiphany Sunday morning the cleric had been their supporter and benefactor.

With Dietz at the head, the twenty horses with their forty riders clattered down the cobbled road to the King's Ferry for the crossing of the Don river. Edmund had suggested to the

Hauptmann that they be taken to a point on the Great North Road known as Robin Hood's Well, near the vill of Skellbrook. This would place them about four to five miles ahead of the advancing vanguard, there to await its arrival

Using the old pack-horse trails criss-crossing the West Riding, the *Wespen* reached Robin Hood's Well by the period of Terce. In normal times that stretch of the Great North Road between the rivers Don and the Aire was, throughout six days of the week, usually busy with carts, oxen, mules and horses plying between Doncaster, Pontefract, Tadcaster and York. But that Thursday, ominously, it appeared deserted.

They bid farewell to Warwick's horsemen, who set off back south to take their place with the middleward, elements of which would already be setting out from Conisbrough.

The majority of the Wasps had never travelled so far north before and a number of the boys were intrigued by the chosen rendezvous, the wayside watering-place associated with the legendary outlaw, Robin of Loxley. The 'well' as such was oddly named for it was more of a deep pond surrounded by a low wall, created where the Skel brook had been blocked. Large flat stones served as a stand for animals being brought down from the road to be watered. Surrounding the stretch of road between Robin Hood's Well and Ferrybridge was dense woodland where for centuries robbers lurked, seeking to relieve travellers and merchants of their valuables. The number of robbers had swelled following the defeat of the English at the Battle of Castillon in 1453, which had signalled the end of the French wars. Unemployed soldiery roamed the land and plundering of English travellers had taken the place of stealing from French peasants.

In more peaceful times manors through which the Great North Road ran were charged with keeping heavy foliage-bearing bushes chopped well back, so as to deny ambush opportunities for the lawless. However, these were years of neglect in such matters as men found other employment, their scythes and pruning shears having been beaten by the smith into implements of war.

As they were to await the vanguard at Robin Hood's Well the boys sought what meagre shelter they could find clustered about the watering place, each one drawing his cloak about or snuggling together to shield against a biting north wind laced with flurries of rain. Two lookouts had been placed up the road to the north and the usual defence chain, 'blindman's hurdle', had been stretched across the road between two trees. Dietz reasoned that enemy riders would be more likely to come upon them from the north. Fortunately, as it turned out, the *Armbrustshütze* each had two spanned bows to hand.

'Best hope is that our two lookouts are as reliable as George-a-Green,' grumbled one of the boys to no one in particular. 'Wouldn't like to be happened upon in this hollow.'

Bridger Blastock, who was wrapped up with Mealy Madoc against the icy cold, called from across the pool, 'Who's this George-a-Green folks in these parts seem to go on about?'

'What? Thou hast never heard of the Wakefield pinder who got the better of Robin Hood and two of his merry band?' called out Willie Daub. So saying, he turned to his jester partner, Didi Wattle, and, taking out a pipe, he played an introduction.

At once the gangly Wattle leapt up and waved his long arms, beckoning the other boys to come closer.

'Gather round, my good and faithful friends, gather round, gather round for I've a worthy tale to tell 'bout a courageous servant who cared for his master's belongings to a fault!'

The weather was forgotten as the band of boys huddled in pairs clustered closer to the two jesters, every face beaming in anticipation.

'Once upon a time, many years ago, in the days of King Richard Coeur-de-Lion, Robin and his merry men roamed these forests of Barnsdale and relieved rich travellers of their purses and wares.' Wattle had captured his audience and was aided by Daub, who began to play a lively tune, by way of an introduction for his friend, who then sang out:

'In Wakefield there lived a jolly pinder,
In Wakefield, in Wakefield, by the name George-a-Green.
'Neither knight nor squire," quoth the pinder,
'Nor baron that is so bold
Dare make a trespass into Wakefield
Ere his pledge goes to the pinfold."

'All this be heard by three witty young men,
T'was Robin Hood, Will Scarlet and John.
For they had aspied that jolly pinder
As he sat there under a thorn.
'Now turn again, turn again," cried the pinder,
'For to a wrong way you are sworn;
For you have forsaken the king's highway
And made a pathway through the corn."

'"Oh that were a shame," said jolly Robin,
The pinder leapt back then thirty good foot
T'was thirty good foot – and one.'

Laughter rang out as Willie Daub trilled an appropriate few bars on the pipe to accompany the scene being conjured up. Then Didi Wattle changed his voice, taking on a dramatic note as he continued with his tale of the legendary George-a-Green. He had found a long bent stick which he flourished like a sword.

'He leaned his back fast 'gainst that thorn
And his foot against a stone,
And there he fought that long summer's day.
That long summer's day did he stand,
Till four broad swords and stout bucklers,
Were firmly stuck fast to the hand.

'"Hold thy hand, hold thy hand," gasped bold Robin
"And my merry men, lest we're floored,
For this is one of the best pinders
That ever I tried with a sword.
'O wilt thou not forsake thy pinder craft
And to the green wood with me go down?
Thou shalt have livery twice in the year
One green, and the other dark brown."'

'Boom-boom!' was the punctuation from two strikes on the large tabor carried by Mealy Maddoc, but banged out by Willie Daub. Didi pressed on to his finalé.

'"If Michaelmas Day was come and gone
And my master had paid me my fee
Then I would set as little by him
As my master does of me.

'This then is the tale of that bold pinder,
The like of which since has n'er been seen
In Wakefield town near Barnsdale,
In Wakefield, George-a-Green.'

Wattle performed a deep bow, accompanied by a long trill blown by Daub to signal the end of the tale. The audience comprising sixteen – two of the boys from *Rotte Gelb* were away keeping watch at the blindman's hurdle – clapped and cheered.

A shriek from Bridger Blastock cut into the gaiety. It served as a warning call; riders were approaching at a pace from the direction of Doncaster. The gay atmosphere melted away, to be replaced by grim alertness as each snatched their spanned weapons and slid a bolt into position.

'That was quick.' The boys naturally assumed that they were outriders of the Yorkist vanward battle.

'It's too soon for our riders, *Herr Hauptmann*!' Edmund called to Dietz

'*Auf Wache sein!*' rasped Dietz, drawing his sword as he spoke.

'Alert – be on your guard!' interpreted Ben Haagan.

Sixteen crossbows were instantly made ready and, moving like wraiths, pairs of boys spread out and crouched along that nettle-shrouded banking.

Twelve riders approached at a canter. They were mounted archers riding with their bows unsheathed and quivers readily to hand. Lances that could be quickly brought to bear for a battle charge stood erect from saddle frogs.

As they drew closer, something about them seemed familiar to John and he was about to whisper to Edmund. They should have been liveried in the white and blue of Fauconberg, for that is what the boys were expecting to see. The wind tugged aside one of the cloaks to reveal chequered red and yellow: further, one lance, they could see, carried a proud banner bearing the scallop badge of Lord Dacre of the north. 'Lancaster!'

The startled black destrier bearing the lead rider whinnied and reared up, its eyes wide in terror. It sensed the presence of hidden human forms close by. Edmund stepped up on to the road in full sight of the riders, his crossbow concealed beneath his cloak.

'Damn you!' yelled the nervous vintenar as his stallion, thoroughly spooked, stamped and reared, threatening to unhorse him.

Edmund flung his cloak back to reveal his distinctive yellow and black tabard.

'God's blood... Wasps!' gasped the shocked rider.

Like a greyhound Edmund sprang into action, whipping up his bow and loosing a bolt in one continuous movement. The vintenar jerked backwards out of the saddle before toppling to the ground instantly dead, a bolt protruding from his neck.

Those in the lead lowered their lances and, spurring their mounts, immediately charged Edmund, who promptly dropped out of sight down the banking towards the stream. That immediate reaction by Dacre's mounted archers would normally have stood them a chance of success in an ambush, but on this occasion they were charging out over sloping ground, past ready and waiting crossbows.

Bolts whizzed through the air and impacted on both horse and man with sickening thuds. Screams and neighs of terror and pain rent the air as riders crashed down the slope and lost their seat to become a downed, writhing tangle of horse and rider. The boys knew that if those seasoned warriors were given time to recover, regroup and form a cohesive fighting unit again, the entire *Fähnlein* would be slaughtered.

Drawing short-length archers' swords – falchions – and daggers, the boys pounced.

The response to John's desperate thrust at the throat of the nearest struggling man was a gushing forth of warm blood, which soaked his outstretched arm.

Gurgling and swinging wildly, the stricken archer sought to land a blow from his war hammer as each heart beat discharged a deep red fountain. Already on his knees, he suddenly slumped forward and lay still.

Waves of nausea flowed over John at the awful thing he had done. So he could also do it – he could kill a man. The question, would he now be damned forever? thudded through his head. His morning's breakfast reappeared on the muddied ground.

Then a blow to the body knocked the wind out of him and he was sent reeling towards the well wall. The clashing and clanging, intermingled with yells and screams, suddenly ceased, to be replaced by moaning and the neighing of a stricken horse. At John's feet lay Bridger Blastock, obviously quite dead, with a pole-axe wound to the head.

Two surviving mounted archers had spurred their mounts and bolted for their lives, seeking to clear the trap. The blindman's hurdle stopped their gallop and the surprised riders catapulted through the air. Before the dazed men could gather their wits, Dietz despatched both with the sword. Two of Lord Dacre's men escaped, fleeing on foot into the heavily-wooded countryside.

It was all over in a few minutes and Dietz nodded his approval. Watchers were posted in case there were more riders in the service of Henry VI and Lancaster on the Great North Road that morning. The dead were stripped of everything useful: items of armour and mail, belts, knives, short swords, maces, food and, most important, valuables such as rings and money purses.

Edmund called John over to one of the dead.

'Do you recall to mind this man?'

That crooked jaw was unmistakable. It was the one they called, 'The Snuffer'. The heartless fiend who had hanged the reeve during the hog-drive last Michaelmastide.

'Scargill has been avenged, John.'

Even knowing that, John could not shake off a feeling of revulsion and deep sadness.

'Innocent blood has been well avenged. There is nothing to regret,' said Edmund

'"Vengeance is mine, I will repay, saith the Lord,"' John replied. 'Who then are we to do these terrible things?'

'But it is you who believes that we are chosen vessels, rightful avengers, that Providence has placed us with the crossbows of York,' said Edmund.

'What of you? Do you believe that?' John asked.

By way of an answer, Edmund gently shook his head.

A nearby hollow in the ground was located and the slain were dragged there and packed in like mackerel in a barrel. The resulting grave was a pitiful affair, the covering of which was barely adequate, but they had neither proper means to dig nor the time or inclination. Bridger was not among the dead consigned to that miserable hole. Bridger Blastock was their only fatality and holy ground would be sought for their comrade to rest in. Those who had received wounds, none serious, were bound up by Wattle and Daub. Mater would do a better job when the support cart caught up.

Within the hour, the leading riders of the vanward battle arrived and could only look around in amazement at what the boys had wrought. The Wasps had taken on a near equal force of the enemy's élite outriders and annihilated it. The news of their victory at Robin Hood's Well would spread like a stubble fire throughout the Yorkist host. They now had ten horses at their disposal. (Because of injuries, two animals had to be killed). Their degree would not allow for them to remain in their keeping, but they would have use of them for the remainder of the journey to Pontefract. With some foreriders escorting them the *Fähnlein,* mounted like knights, rode away from Robin Hood's Well and trotted the four miles to Wentbridge where a hermitage would provide a resting place for Bridger.

The ancient religious retreat, on the north bank of the River Went, was deserted and it was beside that grey stone, crumbling building that the boys dug a two-foot-deep grave. Bridger would wear the Wasp surcoat as a shroud, but the precious padded jack would be removed for re-issue. Mealy Maddoc was carefully withdrawing a stiffening arm from that garment when he let out a yell and jumped back as if bitten by an adder.

'A girl!' he yelled.

How could it be? As they clustered around their deceased comrade there was not a word spoken.

Bridger appeared at peace. Blood from the poleaxe blow to the skull had been wiped away and the lank ginger hair had been tied back from a waxen freckled face; unseeing blue eyes fixed them in a dull, unsighted stare; the mouth was slightly open and pallid lips appeared more gently curved and delicate than John had ever remembered.

Removal of the padded jack had revealed a pair of small, firm breasts.

Bridger Blastock, born in London, raised in a house on London Bridge, who had fought so well at Mortimer's Cross loading crossbows for Mealy Madoc; who had marched, eaten and slept with the *Wespen*, had been a girl all along. A topic for campfire discussion for many a day to come, as all the boys would seek to recall instances and incidents that should have betrayed her secret a score of times.

The padded jack was carefully drawn over her and her surcoat laid over her face. Gently, she was lifted and placed in the grave. They scooped up soil with their bare hands placing it upon their comrade with the greatest of care, as if the weight of the earth would hurt her.

'How could I not know, for we slept together?' sobbed Mealy as he knelt beside the filled-in grave of his *Ladenschütze*. 'By the Blessed Virgin, how could I not know?' he repeated over and over as he rocked backwards and forwards, shaking his head. 'I am nothing but a fool.'

In silence they led him away. Not a word could be found with which to console him.

The Yorkist army began reaching Pontefract according to the timetable ordered by King Edward. The marshy ground, known locally as Bubworth, filled up with thousands of men throughout the day. Over to the west, the mighty fortress of Pomfret Castle dominated the area and stood silent sentinel over the important Aire crossing.

Chapter Eleven

Pontefract Castle and The Battle of Ferrybridge

WAVING OF A PEWTER INCENSE CENSER which emitted billowing clouds of sweet-smelling vapours failed to cloak the reek of putrefaction emanating like marsh gas from beneath the flag stones of the friary church. Following the Yorkist defeat at Wakefield three months earlier, the prominent dead, along with wounded and prisoners, had been carted to Pontefract Castle where they were beheaded the following day. Public decapitation of one prisoner, the Earl of Salisbury, was the main event of that gruesome circus. Following that, heads of the already dead were hacked off and held aloft for the crowds to witness the miserable and inevitable end for 'all traitors who would take up arms against the king'. The trophies were transported to York for presentation, not to gentle King Henry VI, but to his viraginous French wife. These gruesome items served as indisputable evidence to the 'she-wolf' that those who had sought to deny her son the throne of England and hold high the light of another, had been well and truly extinguished. The hereditary right of the seven-year-old Prince of Wales should be questioned no more. So Lancastrian confidence, fuelled by the heady elation of victory, swept through the north. Thence the twelve heads were impaled on pikes and displayed over various York city gates. A crown of twisted rushes and paper was placed on the head of the claimant to the throne, Richard, Duke of York, and displayed over Micklegate Bar. The grisly trophy was turned so as to face inward over the city, so that 'York might overlook York' – the Queen's macabre jest.

Dominicans of the Order of Black Friar Preachers had sought and obtained possession of the more notable bodies of the slain. These they transported for interment beneath the right side of the altar in their friary church of St Richard's, which was situated in the oak woods below the town and castle of Pontefract.

Heralds of the king sought out Edmund and John at the huge military camp forming on Bubworth Heath. They were to repair immediately to St Richard's Friary. They arrived there as light dwindled. It was Thursday eve, the Feast of Saint Ludger, 26th March, 1461. A draughty, wind-swept lane passed between the friars' private church of St Richard's and a large preaching chapel built to serve the masses. The austere edifice loomed above the brothers, obliterating what few stars remained visible in the cloud-clagged sky. A cobbled lane, dividing the friary buildings, led up to town; a layout admirably suited to the function of the Friar Preachers, who served the spiritual needs of the townspeople of Pontefract.

The incumbents, twenty-four torch-carrying, black-robed friars, had proceeded in procession of twos up the lane towards the town to meet King Edward IV, the Earl of Warwick, Sir William, Lord Fauconberg, lords, knights and captains supporting the House of York. The required presence of Edmund at a Requiem Mass was no surprise to John, for the king had accepted in all seriousness his brother's bold claim to be the Avenger of Righteous Blood. The king's conferring upon a commoner the Champion's Belt had caused much dismay among some lords and knights, yet they held their tongues – at least within hearing of the young king.

Following the hour-long Mass, in which incense was liberally burned, and which the boys could only observe as non-communicants, they were ushered forward to join the king, the Earl of Warwick and his uncle, Sir William, Lord Fauconberg. Both the king and Warwick had lost their fathers and younger brothers following the Battle of Wakefield and stood, heads bowed, at the foot of their kinsmen's graves. Sir Richard Jenny, bastard son of the Earl of Salisbury, had arrived from the army bridgehead at nearby Ferrybridge and was permitted to step forward from the silent crowd and join the mourning group. By the light of a hundred flickering candles could be seen, freshly carved in French on five stone flags, the names of the decapitated cadavers lying beneath their feet:

le cueur Richart duc de York
le cueur Edmond Conte de Rotellant
le cueur Richart Neville Conte de Salesbury
le cueur Thomas Neville

The stilled hearts were indeed beneath their feet, awaiting the gathering of noble heads from above the gates of the city of York. Also, on the floor by the wall, was another recently-carved stone bearing the name, 'Thomas de Haryngton'. The unfortunate knight, lord of the manor of the nearby Yorkshire vill of Brierley, had been severely wounded during the battle and it was never known for sure whether he was already dead, insensible or fully conscious when the butcher's block was thrust under his head and the axe brought down. What was beyond doubt, and gossiped about in hushed tones in Pontefract and eventually throughout the Riding, was that the living victims were denied the offices of a priest and benefits of *Viaticum*.

Seven other decapitated bodies of Yorkist knights and captains captured at Wakefield simply disappeared. Likely the corpses found a last resting place in the town midden and gong pit.

As the Hawksworth boys drew near to the mourning group, the king called out to young Edmund, with the slight trace of a tremor in his voice, '"Is thine heart right, as my heart is with thy heart?"'

Edmund knew at once that the question was drawn from the Bible book of Kings and replied loudly and without hesitation, '"It is!"'

His reply rang out, magnified by the vaulted ceiling and echoed through the building. In so answering Edmund borrowed the words of Jehonadab to King Jehu of Israel, who had determined to rid the land of Baal worshippers.

The king continued to quote from holy writ, '"If it be, give me thine hand."'

Sensing the occasion was meant for his brother alone, John hung back as Edmund and the king grasped each the other's right hand. Then Edmund unbuckled the Champion's Belt and handed it back to its former owner, falling to one knee and bowing his head in submission. 'Blood kin should act as Avenger, my liege.' Edmund stammered.

'"Come with me and see my zeal for the Lord!"' called out the king as he buckled on the belt.

Edmund stood up quickly and, stepping back one pace, brought his right arm up smartly to touch his forehead, palm and fingers extended, in salute. At once the entire assembly of lords and knights copied his action. At that instant immense feelings of pride, determination and *camarada* swept over John. His brother was exhalted and surely, by all the saints in Christendom, they would take revenge on behalf of those lying beneath the stones of St Richard's Friary.

Following that stirring affair, they were directed to dine with their betters in the Great Hall at Pomfret Castle, and it was there that they learned of the amazing feats carried out by Sir Geoffrey Goddard's gallopers. Every castellan along the Great North Road from Newark to Pontefract had been persuaded to close their castle gates and draw their bridges against Queen Margaret's marauding hordes. Inexorably, the Lancastrian royal party with its supporters were forced to fall

Pomfret Castle, 1461.

back to its base at York.

Whilst they were enjoying repast at the castle a report arrived from spies ensconced in a vantage point at All Saints' Church, Sherburn in Elmet; they told of a large force massing on high ground south of Tadcaster, and north of a village by the name of Saxton.

'At last, mayhap, that turncoat, Trollope, has selected the ground upon which to position his three battles for the final endeavour,' said Sir William, Lord Fauconberg, stabbing a finger at a large map stretched out among silver plates and tankards on the table. 'He and his "gamekeeper", Somerset, will have chosen to their advantage,' muttered the scarred warrior.

'How lies the land betwixt Sherburn and Tadcaster?' King Edward called out the question, not only of the lords seated at the high table, but of the room in general.

'We know the land well enough,' whispered Edmund loudly.

That comment was heard by Lord Burgh's squire, who made it known that the two *Wespen* present knew the manors

243

and the lie of the land. They were summoned to stand before the top table.

'My liege.' They bowed dutifully, as servants moved about them, removing the remains of the meal. 'From the village of Saxton and Dintingdale the ground slopes up to rolling heath land and scrub, which continues to the edge of some cultivation and a vill by the name of Towton.'

As John described the terrain, Edmund reached forward and indicated to the lords features on the map: a deep valley, in which flowed a stream named the Cock, flanked one side of the ground and marshland the other.

'This field is of Lancaster's careful choosing, so what then their plotting?' said Warwick, moving Edmund's finger from the map with his dagger blade as if it were a discarded morsel. Brusquely, he indicated that they had contributed enough and should return to their places by the buttery screen.

'Time spent gathering all possible intelligence afore an affray is seldom time wasted,' announced the king. 'What is your judgement, young *Rottmeister*?'

There were merely three-and-a-half years of age between the king and John, hence his feelings of affinity with the boys. King Edward obviously resented what he discerned to be unwarranted disparagement of the youths by Warwick.

'Sire, we pretend no knowledge of the art of war,' John spoke out, as Edmund hurriedly whispered to him, 'but should your enemy hold the ground in force between the Ferrybridge–Tadcaster Road and the vale of the Cock, your approach would bound to be made out of a shallow valley; hence, once your battles are deployed you would likely be disadvantaged – should you be pressed back.'

Warwick uttered a forced laugh and, shaking his head, sought to depreciate their involvement. 'Strewth! Oh, if only we had been blessed with such wisdom on the Feast of The Seven Servites at St Albans last month!'

244

'Aye, and had we had some such similar intelligence, mayhap we would have avoided being soundly savaged in flank and bitten mightily in the backside!' snapped the old warrior, Fauconberg.

'We were betrayed, Uncle, beguiled by that treacherous knight, Henry Lovelace, and you know the truth of it!' Warwick blushed bright red as he protested, for he had commanded on that day when Lancaster drove them from their carefully prepared defences and to flight. He had been the butt of rancorous comment from his peers ever since.

'The truth of it?' Fauconberg reached across the table for the vellum map as he spoke 'The truth of it is, 'twas a black day for our cause for we lost the day and that is sufficient. It warrants no "goat for Azazel" neither in the guise of Lovelace, nor laid at the feet of incompetent scouts!'

'That day lost us possession of Henry and his royal banner,' muttered another with bitterness.

Fauconberg, with obvious impatience, beckoned the brothers to step back to the table.

'What substance is there to this claim of yours? How is it that you know the ground?' he demanded, his wrinkled, weathered face screwed up as he sought to focus his tired eyes on Edmund.

'Every Michaelmastide for four years we have collected swine from close by Tadcaster and helped drive them to manors hereabouts,' said John.

'And you say our drawn-up battles will be obliged to approach Lancasters from out of a dale?'

'The dale of Saxton, my lord,' said Edmund.

'I've travelled this road in happier times when bound for Middleham, but cannot bring to mind the fall of the land with any clarity,' mused the king 'Only that the London road cuts a sharp elbow at Towton village.'

'It matters little the ground is of their choosing, for I favour locking horns before Palm Sunday dawns. We will settle

245

accounts with the French she-wolf within hours,' said Warwick. It was announced to the room for effect and he was rewarded by a rousing cheer.

'To bed and prayers, for we begin crossing the Aire in force at cock-crow tomorrow,' announced the king.

'What of Norfolk and the rearward battle?' cautioned Fauconberg. 'For he is under charge to bring ordnance from Conisbrough. His commission of array should have, at best, drawn 5,000 men at arms to your banner. It would be folly to meet Lancaster lacking our rearward.'

'There must be a withholding of fronting Lancaster until Monday and the feast of St Climacus, for on the morrow 'tis the eve of Palm Sunday, which day is for religious observance, and holy preparation, not for the slaughtering of your fellows.'

That remark came from Friar Father Johannes, who had taken it upon himself to oversee the spiritual interests of the lords of York whilst they sojourned at Pomfret Castle. King Edward bit his bottom lip and hurriedly looked down. The impression was that the victor at Mortimer's Cross cared not a jot for the imminent season of the Passion. His closing with the detested and murderous enemy preceded all and every consideration, including that of Holy Mother Church.

'There must be no tarrying at this place longer than the ringing of the hour for Terce on the morrow. The report is that Norfolk is still passing by Doncaster; he must catch up best he can.' The king was in no mood to argue the point and suddenly came to a decision 'Send a galloper with orders for Norfolk not to delay his progress further by dragging cannon from Conisbrough. We want every able-bodied man under his banner here by noon – and moving like a pack of greyhounds to catch our heels.'

Despite being offered shelter of the castle for the night, Edmund asked that they be permitted to return to the *Fähnlein* to ready the unit for the day ahead. That request seemed to greatly please the king, who nodded his agreement. He glanced around at the gathered nobles as if to say, 'I told you so.' However, John detected that their presence and contribution at the counsel of war sat uncomfortably with some among their betters. Whether due to age or degree, John knew not, but concluded that likely it was both.

*   *   *   *

FATHER JOHN BERNARD had just rung for the start of the hour of Compline and, before finally retiring for the night, his curiosity got the better of him. He just had to observe the latest developments down at the Ferrybridge crossing.

The vill of Brotherton, with its church dedicated to Edward the Confessor, was perched on high ground on the northern bank of the Aire and dominated the fetid marshland flanking the river with its historic crossing point. Strategically placed, it was from that vantage point in the church tower that the aging cleric had witnessed the feverish work going on and, like spilled ink on vellum, how the Yorkist advance party had spread among the cluster of houses and up the road towards the ancient Brotherton settlement.

There were still some weak shafts of daylight filtering through the narrow window slots which served to light his way as he laboured up the steep tower steps. Once in the belfry, he shivered all the more. A bitter north wind whistled through the window slots and around the walls, causing the four bells to stir slightly in their creaking wooden frames. In turn, he reverentially touched each of the them, crossing himself as he did so. Each of the bells was dedicated to one of the four Apostles and, having carried out that ritual, he felt secure from any evil which might be lurking on that bitterly cold eve. He was confident in the knowledge that bells ordering the lives of the faithful offered sure protection against the Devil. Thus comforted, he pulled his thick cloak close about him and drew back a slatted window shutter. His gaze followed the straight road thrusting down from the village to the Aire and the activities surrounding the chantry chapel of Our Lady, which was situated on the Brotherton side of the bridge.

The ancient crossing-point had been served in the distant past by a ferry and for the past two hundred and fifty years by a narrow bridge, a little more than the breadth of a cart. Now, in the year of our Lord 1461, the stone bridge not only carried trade over the Aire, but served to mark the limit of deep draught navigation of the river. Supply warehouses handling goods from the port of Hull, along with more than one thriving boat-yard, had grown up around the settlement of Ferrybridge. Warehouses handled all manner of provisions and sales goods serving the honour of Pontefract, the town itself and the mighty, imposing fortress, Pomfret Castle.

At busy times, festivals and markets, a ferry operated to augment the bridge-crossing for wagons and cattle travelling the Great North Road, competing with the bridge warden in extracting a toll from travellers and traders. However, in that unhealthy climate of an increasingly vicious civil war, as England's mighty families, supported by oversized retinues, sought to bring about the extinction of each other, normal trade and commerce was suspended.

Father Bernard mused over the distressing upset of the times: tomorrow, Saturday, should have seen the holding of the traditional large cattle fair at Pontefract, which preceded the Holy day of Palm Sunday, but with the roadways tramped with masses of marching men and lance-wielding riders intent on blood-letting, prudence dictated a halt to such normal affairs. But then, neither an honest trader nor a single one of his beasts could have crossed at Ferrybridge ever since the Feast Day of St Patrick, 17th March last, when the withdrawing Lancastrian rearward burned the ferry and broke the bridge.

During the day he had watched from his vantage point in the belfry as Yorkist engineers had bridged the gap with beams and planks taken from a ship-builder's yard. By that Friday evening, around three hundred men had crossed the Aire and were camped either side of the road leading up to Brotherton. Even now, men trickled across and fretting horses were being persuaded to step on to the makeshift bridge. There was precious little dry ground on the northern bank at that time of the year. Brotherton marsh effectively squeezed all traffic to the confines of the raised roadway. Throughout the day what little dry ground there was available had sprouted tents and a rash of flickering camp fires.

The Yorkist commander's banner, quartered alternate yellow and white, with red chevrons and bars, fluttered over the chantry chapel. The priest should have known which lord, supporting the new contending King of England, had made the chapel of Our Lady his quarters, but the identity of the owner of the banner escaped him for the moment.

The cleric froze; it was as if eyes were boring into the back of his neck. Despite the chill of the approaching late winter night, sweat broke out on his forehead and his mouth went as dry as a tanner's apron. He swung around, not knowing what to expect. At first he could see nothing, then, as his eyes became accustomed to the shadows – there, across the bell frame, between 'St Mark' and 'St Luke', he could make out what appeared to be a tall figure. He peered long and hard but there was no movement from it. Surely a trick of light was playing mischievous sport with his mind? Not daring to avert his eyes nor blink, he took a step forward and tried to mouth a challenge. No words came forth from his parched throat, only a strangled noise, which the priest failed to recognise as his own voice.

He was not mistaken; there, in the belfry, not three yards from him, was a 'presence'. There was an area of shadow, a different shade to its surrounds which, the longer he peered, seemed to take on substance. Could that be a grey countenance – and horror upon dismay – was it grinning at him?

'How many would you reckon?'

Father Bernard spun in direction of the voice, for it was not the object of his terrified attention that had uttered those words. From directly behind 'St John' another figure seemed as if to float up and materialise before him.

'A couple of hundred at least would be my estimate,' answered the other, stepping forward and in so doing giving solid substance to the 'spectre'.

'That's Radcliffe's banner flying over yonder chapel,' muttered the scout, who had been concealed behind the bell.

The trembling priest experienced a sudden wave of relief. These were flesh and blood like him, not evil spirits, and their concern and reason for trespass was not him, but the Yorkist crossing going on below. It was as if he didn't exist as the two archers, scourers for Lancaster, surveyed the busy scene between Brotherton and the broken bridge.

'And that's Salisbury's bastard, Richard Jenny, at the bridgehead point. That's his banner – I'll swear to it.'

The left side of the speaker's face was cleft by a deep, healed scar, an edged weapon wound. The disfigurement rendered the warrior's appearance all the more fearsome.

'You...frightened me near to death,' the priest finally gasped, swallowing hard and slowly backing towards the stairs.

'One more step and we'll see the colour of your bowels!' growled Arnold Reresby.

'Who are you? What do you want?'

'Your silence will do for a start,' snarled the six-foot tall vintenar, John Hawksworth, as he continued to peer out at the scene below.

'They never learn,' said Reresby with a gentle chuckle. 'We caught the dullards like this at Worksop, during Advent!'

'But it won't be Sir Andrew Trollope who gives them a mauling this time. Now it's the turn of the Red Wyvern,' said John Hawksworth, continuing to look out.

Much to Father John Bernard's immense relief, the two mounted bowmen, retainers of Lord Clifford, bundled him down the tower steps and proceeded to bind and gag him. They made it clear that he could spend a night discomforted, locked in the crypt, or die. Either way, he was to be rendered *confuto* until the matter at hand was at an end. At least he would live to tell the tale and surely did so for years to come.

*   *   *   *

The well-being of every member of the *Fähnlein* had to be ascertained by Edmund: their feet in a good state and boots in repair; their clothing sufficiently warm; 'iron-fare' uneaten – its consuming was forbidden until such a time as the order was given. Sufficient spare crossbow war strings carried (usually in the cap); fully-charged quivers, with further barrels of bolts close to hand. Also, Edmund asked how each boy was in spirit, knowing what lay ahead; were they nervous and in need of encouraging? He was applying himself to the office he had been given with his usual conscientious vigour. As a result, his office as *Rottmeister* was respected and his recently elevated degree remained unquestioned by the other boys.

The most important of all his tasks was to ensure that a full complement of crossbow boys was readied. *Hauptmann* Dietz delegated just about everything to his *Rottmeister*, just so long as his captain fielded the maximum number of fit pairs, then he was content. With the loss of Bridger Blastock, a skilled and efficient *Ladenschütze* – despite having been a girl – along with the crushing of Fleischer, a decision had to be made. John suggested that Spotty Spence and Mealy Madoc be paired and that the strength of the *Fähnlein* be cut back to eight bows instead of ten.

'It would be a pity if we were to lose bows on the eve of battles joined,' said Edmund thoughtfully.

Suddenly he made off to where Mater's wagon was drawn up by the roadway, alongside a wooden bridge which spanned a stretch of the bog-strewn wilderness of Bubworth Heath. Mater had fears concerning their former *Rottmeister*. His disgrace and humiliation had devastated him and she feared, given the opportunity, he would do himself harm, or run away. The Bavarian mercenary, Dietz, on the occasions when he visited the wagon, made matters worse by lashing out at the miserable wretch as if he were a kitchen dog. She spoke as she busied herself preparing food for the following day's break-fast. Adding further to her work load, 'Lancer' Lockrill had gone down with measles and was racked with the ague. He was occupying the sickening mattress on the wagon, where he awaited Mater's attention and her apothecary skills. Edmund requested that Mater did not bleed Lancer as, in his opinion, such treatment only seemed to weaken a patient. From where his brother drew such novel ideas completely baffled John. He seemed not to subscribe in the least to the well-proven ancient art of bleeding. He viewed the balancing of the body's four humours with similar disdain to that of religious devotions.

Taking a Wasp surcoat from the wardrobe chest slung under the cart, Edmund approached Alvar Fleischer, who was crouched alone before a spluttering camp fire. Edmund stood in silence before him, waiting for Fleshy to look up. Slowly, the wretched youth acknowledged their presence and raised his small, widely-spaced brown eyes, with an expression for all the world resembling that of a recently beaten animal. Edmund held out his hand and uttered one word, 'Please'.

Ignoring the proffered arm, slowly Fleischer rose to his feet, continuing to glare at the ground all the while as he did so.

'Here, take this.' Edmund held out the surcoat.

Fleshy shook his head, glaring at the ground, his bottom lip quivering and his entire body intermittently shivering in the cold night air.

'Come, would you grant me a boon, Alvar?' whispered Edmund.

At the sound of his Christian name, the cowed youth looked at Edmund for the first time. It had been many a year since anyone had used his given name.

'We are below complement and are in need of your help.' There was a gentleness in his brother's voice that brought visions of their mother to John's mind. Again Edmund held out the coveted yellow and black surcoat to Fleischer.

'Will you please help me?'

Slowly reaching out, Fleischer took the surcoat before sinking to his knees. Burrowing his face in the garment, he dissolved into uncontrolled sobbing, punctuated by muffled pleas for forgiveness.

'Still your heart, my friend, for there is no rancour here. For what gain would there be in that? How would our cause be benefited by ill will?' So saying, Edmund bent and, taking him by the elbow, raised him to his feet.

John preferred to see the thieving, cruel bully in a cringing, broken state. One day his brother would pay for his softness he concluded.

'Would you take your place in *Rotte Gelb*, with one of the new boys, Richard Wyatt of Conisbrough, as your *Ladenschütze*? You will need to drill him in the skill of loading at speed.'

Fleischer nodded slowly, some confidence returning with the assigning of responsibility. Edmund, no doubt, had in mind Fleshy's former conduct when he added, 'You will need to treat Wyatt with kindness, Alvar. The lad joined the Wasps when his blood was up, with shining eyes, enthused with hopes of reward. Now alas, the rigour of life on campaign, and with a bloody affray in the offing, his enthusiasm has worn thin.'

Fleshy nodded, his small, thin lips compressed tightly. He shuffled off to where the two newcomers, Butterbusk and Wyatt were sheltering together.

'You turn your back on him in the affray and he'll do for you,' John warned, hoping Edmund would take heed. 'He has no reason to bear you goodwill, despite your kindnesses.'

Using the youngster, Wee Willie, as *Ladenschütze* to Spotty Spence meant that they could put ten crossbow marksmen, along with their loaders, on to the field of mortal combat. The *Fähnlein* comprising the two *Rotten* would be made up as follows:

Rotte Schwarz: (Troop Black)

Armbrustschütze	*Ladenschütze*
Edmund Hawksworth (**Rottmeister)**	John Hawksworth
Didi Wattle	Willie Daub
Snowwhite Moxen	Poxy Goite
Mealy Madoc	Backsy Butterbusk
Spotty Spence	Wee Willie

Rotte Gelb: (Troop Yellow)

Armbrustschütze	*Ladenschütze*
Blau Ben Haagan	Lancer Lockrill
Alvar Fleischer	Dicky Wyatt
Foxglove	Holy Holy Cantar
Kurt Meyer	Trout Inckershill
Pepper Plasden	Lime Waddesley

There would be no reserve in case of injury and no *Melder* to keep the pairs supplied with bolts. There was still some question as to whether Lancer Lockrill's fever would break in time and thus allow him to take his place.

254

The sound of a tumult emanating from the direction of Ferrybridge had aroused the thousands of men in the Yorkist camp. A glow of burning buildings lit up the east, which light competed with the weak dawn haze that was beginning to lighten a pewter-grey sky. From a vantage point on a hillock, over a ground-hugging mist arising from the dank earth, the boys could see out towards Ferrybridge. There was smoke billowing skyward, mixing with a murky background. It was Saturday, 28th March, the day before Palm Sunday, which heralded the observance of the Holy Passion.

As they watched, three gallopers came racing from the direction of Ferrybridge, heading towards Pomfret Castle, calling out an alarm as they passed through the now thoroughly stirred Yorkist masses. As they thundered by on the wooden causeway-come-bridge spanning a marshy stretch of the heath, they could make out their warning, 'they're upon us'.

Horns blew as centenars sought to form ranks from drowsy billmen and archers. Within a matter of minutes a defensive living wall was formed, over half-a-mile long, clear across Bubwith Heath. A line of steel bills, supported by hastily hammered in wooden stakes, had been fashioned to block direct approach to Pomfret Castle. Frenzied activity centred around the hundreds of baggage carts as carriage horses were hastily harnessed up. Within minutes they were streaming back towards Pontefract and the safety of the huge fortress which dominated the hill town and surrounding countryside.

'There'll be time enough for me to join the exodus,' muttered Mater as she began preparing a breakfast for the *Fähnlein*.

It was by way of a reply to Edmund's urging her to fall back on the town and protection of its walls. Consequently, and with the situation unclear, Edmund ordered *'Aufmarschieren'* and the boys moved into a defensive semi-circle around the wagon.

Within the hour, and scarce their breakfast eaten, the king and his accompanying lords swept down the road from the castle, banners unfurled and amidst a rattle of their armour. Drawing close to their position, the nobles halted and a hurried consultation took place among them. King Edward was to stay behind the drawn-up defence line, while the Earl of Warwick and William, Lord Fauconberg rode to Ferrybridge, about a mile, to investigate the nature and seriousness of the disturbance.

The hillock where they had spent the night became the centre of the Yorkist defence line as the king, along with his standard bearer and others of his fellowship, took their places atop. There they stood high on their stirrups and gazed out across the heath.

Soon Warwick returned at full gallop from Ferrybridge and rode the blowing, sweating hackney up on to the hillock:

'Our crossing force has been wiped out, Fitzwalter and Sir Richard Jenny are either dead or captured. We have lost the far bank and the bridge is contended!'

There was a distinct tone of near panic in his voice as he continued to address King Edward.

'I pray God have mercy on their souls, which at the very beginning of your campaign have lost their lives.'

It must have been in the Earl's mind that the defensive battle line, drawn up across Bubwith Heath, was about to break and run. 'I remit the vengeance and punishment to God, our creator and redeemer.'

Then, as if to take upon himself responsibility for rallying the army, Warwick alighted from his horse and, drawing his sword, plunged it into the chest and heart of his mount. As his horse slumped to the ground, quivering in its death throes, he yelled at the top of his voice, 'Let him fly that will, for surely I will tarry with him that will tarry with me!' So saying, Warwick kissed the hilt of his bloodied sword before holding it aloft to a mighty cheer from those drawn up near enough to observe his theatrics.

The face of King Edward IV matched that of Edmund's. John heard his brother mutter the Latin phrase that was shortly to become his motto: '*cui bono*'. There was no point, no advantage in such drama, and quite obviously the king thought much the same. John noted that the horse so quickly despatched by Warwick was not his favourite pitch-black destrier called Malech, but rather an ordinary hackney he had mounted in haste at the castle.

King Edward spurred his mount off the hillock and began to canter along the front of his battle line, calling out as he did so for steadfastness and resolve.

'At last our enemy has stopped his flight and awaits our pleasure. Should any among us feel faint of heart and have no stomach for this, then let him depart now and there will be no gainsaying him.'

The young king's voice carried loud and clear and some hundreds fleeing from the fighting at Ferrybridge halted. Those new arrivals helped form a living corridor through which the warrior king rode to and fro.

'Once fighting is joined, fleeing will not be countenanced and indeed, a bounty shall be paid to those foreprickers slaying any who would abandon this royal banner in the face of our enemy.'

Apart from a few who had sickened and would stay with the baggage train, no others were seen to withdraw. The king halted opposite the hillock and turned his horse to face his drawn-up army.

'May the Almighty be with every man in this righteous struggle – God be with you!'

At that, the entire army dropped to one knee and, almost as one man, made the sign of the cross. Meanwhile, spread along the battle line, all manner of clergy, from simple friars to richly-garbed priests from 'The Minster of the Marches', All Hallows, Pontefract, gave Benediction.

'Now they are ready to meet their loving Maker,' muttered Edmund in John's ear, in a voice that came as near contempt as he ever mustered. How his brother could maintain such bitterness against God in the face of continual blessing from Him remained a mystery.

Fleeing men belonging to Fitzwalter reported that the Lancastrian force had retired back across the Aire and destroyed the makeshift bridge. A close friend of the king, the nineteen-year-old Earl of Suffolk, John de la Pole, was given charge of the vanward battle. Immediately, to the sound of horns, the young commander brought his drawn sword down, signaling the advance on Ferrybridge.

For the Wasps the journey into battle had taken on an unnerving efficiency. Two boys were assigned a mounted Fauconberg archer. One boy stood balanced each side of the horse on a rope stirrup. There they clung on to the bowman as if their lives depended on it. John suspected that his brother had devised the novelty after discussions with *Hauptmann* Dietz some days earlier. A further two mounted archers carried six pavises.

In no time, it seemed, they were within sight of the broken bridge when Robin Carle, the vintenar carrying them, reined up. All ten horsemen, each with two Wasps clinging on, formed a line abreast. Diddi Wattle, red-faced and much jolted about called across to John, all breathless 'I hope we can flee a fight just as fast as we can join one.'

'There's no money in running away,' John replied. 'Take a look at yonder banner.'

'And the standard over there – look at that standard!' yelled Poxy Goite 'Holy Mother of God, it's the Red Wyvern.'

The whole unit broke into excited chatter as the prospect of the first one hundred pounds bounty lit the boys up.

'Butcher Clifford!' called out Snowwhite 'He's got to be there, that's his standard.'

'The Flower of bloody Craven,' muttered Robin Carle 'It would have to be them. They're as hard as nails.'

The pairs of boys had individually marked their bolts so that there would be no dispute identifying exactly who brought down the marked men of Lancaster, and consequently the winner of the generous prizes to be had.

'We will be fighting against our father,' John blurted out.

'What of it?' said Edmund quietly 'I have picked a quarrel especially for him – it bears our beloved mother's name. She will be avenged, John. I so swear.'

The intense hatred driving Edmund like a demon was as strong as ever. He would avenge their mother's death, of that John had no doubt.

'I see no further banners other than Clifford's!' called out Didi Wattle, whose height when standing in the makeshift stirrup gave him an advantage.

'I swear there cannot be more than five hundred riding with the Craven and yet they are preparing to hold back thousands of us,' said Robin Carle, much impressed.

There were seven arches to the stone bridge spanning the Aire; the centre one was broken. Planking that had been placed to span the gap the previous day, had been tipped into the river. Various movable items, tables, benches and chests, had been taken from the dwellings on the northern side and piled up to form a barricade on that side of the broken bridge.

The chantry chapel of Our Lady was silhouetted against burning buildings which spluttered and crackled in the dawn light. Above it fluttered the banner of Lord John Clifford, St George in the hoist, with a red wyvern on a white background bearing the motto, a single word in French, *Desormais* – 'henceforth'.

On the southern bank, spread around in groups, were slain retainers garbed in the bloodstained colours of Fitzwalter and

Sir Richard Jenny. Maybe as many as fifty, they appeared to have been caught fleeing by Clifford's riders and lanced through. On closer examination, it seemed that those wounded had each received the *coupe de grace* – despatched by a blow to the skull with a pole axe. Seemingly, there was to be no mercy.

The Earl of Suffolk had halted the Yorkist vanward outside of bowshot in order to take in the scene. After consultation with his captains, he called for a search to be made for carts to be used to shield archers, a search that went as far as the nearby village of Knottingley. Meanwhile, Dietz divided the pavises between the two *Rotten* and Edmund was ordered to lead an advance on the bridge. Their task seemed simple enough to John: they were to pick-off the half-dozen defenders manning the barricade. How little he knew of warfare.

Church bells rang for Prime as the entire *Fähnlein* trotted forward and came within longbow range of the bridge. The Flower of Craven watched in silence and ne'er an arrow flew. Edmund blew the horn and halted them. At once the boys formed up behind the pavises for cover and knelt. Edmund gave fresh orders and *Rotte Gelb*, under the command of Blau Ben Haagan, the fifteen-year-old from Lübeck, split off and moved to the right, taking three pavises with them. Once they were in position, they knelt behind their shields awaiting the signal to advance further.

The clatter of a dozen carts being pushed towards the bridge heralded the forward thrust of the main force. At that Edmund blew three blasts on the horn and both *Rotten* moved forward and outward with intent to enfilade the bridge barricade. Still there was no reaction from the force of Lancaster drawn up on the northern bank of the Aire.

A deep groan emanating from Edmund caused John to glance in his direction, thinking he had been struck. His brother nodded to where a figure, in the finest Milanese armour, with brightly coloured feathers sprouting from his battle helm and waving a sword, trotted ahead of the main force. It was the Earl of Warwick, calling for Clifford to meet him in single mortal combat.

'That should do it!' muttered Edmund.

Above the noise of a burning tavern and houses they distinctly heard the command, 'Loose!' Five hundred archers, on a very narrow frontage, released their deadly shafts in unison and the sky, for a moment, darkened. Then they received the full force of arrows tearing and thudding into their pavises. For some of the advancing main force, the carts failed to provide adequate cover against the arrow storm. There were many cries and screams as bodies and limbs were pierced through. Bunched up tightly behind their protective shields, the Wasps' only casualty was a wounding in the foot. Willie Daub just tugged the offending shaft from his boot. The arrow-head had clipped his little toe.

'That's it now, I want to go home!' he said.

'You can go home when you get one in the bum and not before!' said Didi.

Somehow, Wattle and Daub made the whole horror bearable.

Warwick had not survived unscathed from that opening arrow storm. A chink had been found in his armour: a shaft protruded from the join between the poleyn and cuisee (knee and thigh armour) of his left leg. There was an almighty roar from five hundred throats belonging to the Craven, as the Earl began limping out of range. There followed a derisive baa-ing and laughter.

Lying flat and using the two gaps between the three pavises, Snowwhite and Edmund began a steady loosing of crossbow bolts. These were aimed, as ordered by Suffolk, at the archers manning the barricade. Likewise, Blau Ben Haagan followed that lead and began enfilading that position from the right. Immediately, three men at the barricade were seen to flop down. So accurate was the shooting from the Wasps that a man only needed to show his bassinet-protected head but one inch above the low bridge parapet and he would be instantly struck.

Discerning the threat from the crossbow unit, Black-faced Clifford ordered every bow be turned against them. He would annihilate each group in turn. Half his archers would shoot and, as they loaded again, the other half would loose their arrows. That would ensure that over two hundred arrows would arrive on target every five seconds.

Anticipating such a stratagem, Edmund blew retreat for *Rotte Gelb* and ordered three pairs in *Rotte Schwarz* to withdraw out of bowshot.

Didi Wattle, Snowwhite, Edmund and John huddled behind the pavises, which were so impaled with arrows that they resembled hedgehogs. The others were racing for safety when the arrow storm struck; shafts slammed into the wooden shields and thudded into the surrounding ground. Ten more minutes of such ferocity and their cover would be reduced to splintered shards.

Younger and therefore slower than the others, they heard Wee Willie scream out as an arrow furrowed down his thigh. He stumbled and fell, but Willie Daub limped back and hoisted him up. Mealy Madoc also darted back within bow range and, between the two, helped the lad to safety.

'Now it's just the four of us against five hundred of the very best Lancaster can muster,' stuttered Edmund.

'They don't stand a chance!' said Didi, straining as he spanned for Snowwhite. Snowwhite winked at John.

'Didi thinks we have them cornered.'

'They don't seem aware of the tricky situation they're in,' John added with a laugh, though he felt he had but seconds left to live.

'Then let's see if we can bring it home to them,' said Edmund.

'Snowy! Let's clear a way in that solid line of archers. See if we can get them to bunch up,' said Edmund. 'We'll aim for the same group. Over by the ferry landing – see that post, half a man's height?'

Snowwhite squinted between the pavises and the hundreds of arrow shafts standing directly in front. All four ducked instinctively as another flurry of death whizzed in and thudded all around; the metal point of an arrow penetrated one of the shields. The four exchanged worried glances – their defence wall was being shredded.

'Put four bolts into that line, just to your right of that post, I'll do the same to the left. As quick as you can!' Following Edmund's command, the crack of four crossbows followed in quick succession.

'Some have gone down!' yelled Snowwhite, peering between the shields.

Didi and John worked as fast as they could and within a few minutes they had four bows spanned and ready.

'Same again?' asked Snowwhite, and Edmund nodded.

Each time their bolts hit the same portion of the line the Flower of Craven closed ranks and carried on with their disciplined shooting at some captain's order. Then, on their fourth volley, the men began to move away from the killing zone and bunch up.

'Widen that gap, Snowy!'

Every time a man went down to the accurate shooting of Edmund and Snowwhite the gap in the line widened. When a vintenar, who stepped into the twelve-foot breech in the line in order to encourage the men to close up, received two bolts through the head simultaneously, the gap widened further. Consequently, the disciplined and ordered volleying, which had proved so successful, degenerated into individual shooting. This was fortuitous for those moving forward once more to assault the bridge.

King Edward arrived at the head of the middleward and quickly discerned the ludicrous situation, whereby four boys were engaging the enemy whilst the entire Yorkist vanward remained out of bowshot. He urged the protective screen of carts forward. Bowmen of Warwick and Cobham were to assault at once and saturate the northern sector of the bridge and bank with arrows. Under the overwhelming Yorkist arrow storm, billmen were to get themselves onto the bridge and plank across the gap. With the general assault taking place, now under command of the king, Edmund blew for the rest of the Wasps to return and take up their positions and enfilade the barricade once more.

As church bells signalled the hour of Terce there came a pause in the fighting. The Craven still held mastery over the crossing and hundreds lay dead and dying. At one point in the morning the bridge had been forced and Yorkist billmen stood on the far bank. Their success was short-lived, when an unexpected mounted charge drove them into the river.

Suddenly, *Hauptmann* Dietz appeared behind their position and ordered Edmund and John to accompany him to the rear. At a weaver's croft behind the battle line the boys were ushered into the presence of the king and lords Warwick, Fauconberg, Suffolk and Essex, along with a number of knights and captains. Their being there was not approved by some of them, but apparently King Edward had insisted that the brothers be consulted on a matter. Caps in hand, they dropped the knee before their sovereign and awaited the pleasure of their betters.

'Rise, lads!' It was the old scarred warrior, Fauconberg.

'A truly gallant effort by the *Wespen* this day.'

The brothers looked every bit the part of seasoned fighters, for Edmund's forehead was caked in dried blood where an arrow had struck him a glancing blow, and John had a blood-stained rag wrapped around his forearm where an arrow had nicked the skin.

'We are about a ploy to solve this impasse and would value your local intelligence.'

Edmund nodded in agreement, 'Begging your pardon my lords, is it known if the Craven is likely to be reinforced?'

'You are here to answer specific questions put to you, not seek to feed thy boyish curiosity.' Warwick was fuming and in some pain from the arrow wound. He was about to continue with his rebuke when he was interrupted by the king.

'Why do you ask?'

'My liege,' Edmund began, 'should the Lord Clifford not expect support then he will have plans to withdraw once he has discomforted us to his satisfaction. Perhaps, I could suggest, ere long afore his shafts run out.'

Sceptics among the lords, and captains were suitably impressed and John Lord Scrope of Bolton stepped forward. 'To answer your question then, young captain. Our hard riders report that the gathering at Tadcaster continues apace. Neither Somerset, Northumberland, Dacre nor Trollope have a force moving this far south.'

'In that case, mounted archers should haste to Castleford but three miles distant. The Aire may be crossed there and Clifford's right flank turned.' Edmund delivered that without the slightest stumble over words, before asking 'Please forgive me, my lords, what was your question?'

At that, every man but Warwick laughed out loud.

'God's strewth! You've answered our question, and before we were able to speak it.' Fauconberg, stepped forward and clapped his hand on Edmund's shoulder. 'Well, young *Rottmeister*, and what strength should the flanking party be?'

The interruption from Warwick was loud 'Enough, Uncle. Should a boy command this host?'

'Some would say a boy already does command this host, and rules England,' muttered the king. There was a tone of resignation in his voice. He was annoyed at the delay and fuming at the success of his enemy in denying him the bridge.

'Well, Avenger of Blood, your king awaits your answer.' said Fauconberg.

'Considering the number of casualties already suffered by the valiant Craven, a force of one hundred bowmen should prove enough.'

'Then so be it, we will continue our assault within the hour. Our pressing them should hold their attention until Fauconberg's archers should arrive to flank them.' The king was about to end the council of war then and there when Edmund asked to speak.

'Clifford must be aware that he is not to be reinforced.'

'So?' snapped Warwick.

'It is likely that, as we speak, he will be making plans to withdraw.' John could see that every man in that low, dirt-floored dwelling was looking at his brother intently. 'A flanking force may already be too late to catch Clifford,' continued Edmund. 'A fast-moving force of twenty mounted archers, along with the Wasps, could be despatched up the Roman road from Castleford.'

'With a view to what?' asked Warwick in disbelief.

King Edward interrupted 'With a view to ambushing Clifford and the Craven up country!' The king looked at Edmund for confirmation.

Edmund nodded 'As close to the main Lancastrian host as possible – the Flower of Craven should be halted and destroyed.'

At that the king stood up and gave the order, 'Do whatever he tells you. There shall be no gainsaying the *Rottmeister*!'

Edmund spoke in an undertone to one of the lords nearest to him, who then called out, 'He has asked for a bundle of bone-dry faggots, a keg of ale and a flitch of bacon, my liege!'

'Then, in the name of God, get him what he wants!'

Chapter Twelve

Clifford – *Desormais Déjeuner avec le Diable*

COCK CROW ANNOUNCED a cheerful dawn on a delightful June morning and the bells of St Peter's rang out heralding Lauds to the good people and numerous visitors to Conisbrough village. With sore eyes John gazed out of the solar window of the castle at the green hillside and row of crofts where once, forty-eight years ago, a line of makeshift privies had occupied that very same place. The daft face of Didi Wattle floated into his mind. He'd once powered a crossbow bolt high into the sky to fall unerringly among the stalls – out of the blue. How the crowd had roared with laughter when a target strike was indicated by the jolly steward. Where were those jesters now – Wattle and Daub – lads who could dispel despair in a trice, lifting the spirits and transporting onlookers into blissful happiness?

The last John had seen of them was at the surrender of Bamburgh castle in 1464. What he would give to see them just once more performing clumsy somersaults, pretending to argue and fight each other and Willie Daub miraculously producing a plucked goose from his partner's hose. Oh, what he would give to hear Didi Wattle relating stories and songs of Robin Hood with Willie Daub accompanying him on pipe, tabor, bagpipes or whistle – sometimes, it seemed, simultaneously.

The days had sped by since his dreadful inquisition at Lincoln Castle. Now it was St Ethelreda's Day and by sunset he would be in the Kingdom of Heaven with an allotted mansion and seated at the table of the Lord. Somehow that prospect failed to bring him comfort anymore. Would nothing dispel the foreboding? On the morrow, mid-summer's day, it would be the coronation of King Henry VIII and his Queen, Catherine of Aragon. A new sovereign. In his sixty-three years he had seen England ruled by four kings.

Dread of being burnt alive continued to plague his mind, recurring at intervals, welling up and assaulting his composure and stirring his bowels like an industrious buttermaid at her churn. He had witnessed the blackened agony of others. And smelled the cooking of human flesh, which always excited the town's dogs.

Abjuration was an option – he didn't have to burn, and yet others had faced the flames fearlessly. Two years ago he had been at Norwich to witness the burning of one, Thomas Norris, a poor inoffensive man who had trusted his parish priest, voicing his religious questions and doubts, doubts that John had put into his head. His priest had informed on him to the Bishop of Norwich. Then, only last year, there had been that strange event following the burning of a pious woman at Chippen Sudburne. Within minutes following her awful death, a bull had broken loose from a local butchers; it had singled out, charged and gored to death the presiding official of that malevolent assemblage of the Church.

Would some such vengeful agent present itself that day at Doncaster fish market? And following his death, prior to Vespers, would it wreak havoc among his tormentors? Surely the Almighty was showing his disapproval of the bishops? Would the false shepherds never awaken to the truth?

Had his brother Edmund become aware of his plight? Would he come to stay the executioner's torch, arriving at the final minute from France to save him? 'All men that would live faithfully in Christ shall suffer persecution', holy scripture reliably informed him and, further that, '...evil men and deceivers shall increase into worse, erring and sending others into error'.

All around him his faithful audience was stirring as one from slumbering. After food and drink he would complete his tale afore the period of Sext ended and the bells tolled for None. Then would begin that dreadful journey. The stinking gong cart ear-marked for his transportation by the zealous Brother Rollo had mysteriously sustained a broken axle. He suspected that the loyal Tiptoe, whose life had been spared by Edmund at Towton field, had been at work. A more agreeable cart had been requisitioned.

Rumours were circulating that anyone supplying a faggot as a contribution to burn him would receive a written indulgence in the Bishop of Lincoln's own hand. John considered bitterly: no doubt some might be persuaded that a contribution to his agonising death would purchase forgiveness for sins. How could they imagine they were serving the interests of the loving Prince of Peace, when they devised such hideous torment to despatch their brothers in Adam?

Rolls of vellum containing the freshly-scribed account of his brother's early life were rolled neatly on the *tabula plicata*, the product of around eighteen hours of storytelling and writing. Much to John's dismay, he noted that the hurried texts were in three languages: Latin, English and French. Unless it was rendered into one tongue it would likely never serve as a fitting tribute. He harboured some disquiet that those former fabulous tales of The Hawk quickening the dead, rendering himself invisible, conferring with birds and animals and possessing other miraculous powers – and

269

enjoying many fanciful adventures – would prevail, the hitherto suppressed fable being mightily preferred and therefore rivalling tales of Robin Hood and King Arthur. No matter, at least he had served to chronicle his brother's early life as best he could. He had been there to witness his brother's elevation in degree, his transformation from a herder of pigs to a knight, incredibly passing by the office of squire – all achieved in the matter of weeks, from Epiphany Sunday to Palm Sunday 1461.

The time had come for him to relate the first real act of vengeance – a slaying and the striking-off of a head and by so doing winning of the beautiful Lady Isabel's forfeit. Which forfeit was a lover's secret promise to her bridegroom, who was so foully murdered.

*   *   *   *

LIKELY, NEVER BEFORE nor since, had there been such a fiercely determined force gathered at the Castleford crossing of the Aire. On that occasion there were no local worthies gathered to forbid its passage, as there had been last Michaelmastide, when the herders sought to cross the bridge. Little doubt that those very same townsmen were presently gathered shoulder to shoulder at Tadcaster to do battle with the host of the House of York.

Icy rain began falling steadily as the bells at All Saints Church, Castleford, pealed out the beginning of Vespers.

Once across the river, over a hundred mounted bowmen, under the command of Sir Walter Blount, veered off and headed eastwards towards Fairburn with the avowed intent of falling upon Clifford's flank and rear from the direction of Brotherton vill. That was assuming the Yorkist crossing at Ferrybridge was still being contended by the Craven.

Under the captaincy of the 'Redoubtable' Robert Horne and *Hauptmann* Dietz, twenty of Fauconberg's mounted archers, each with a crossbow boy seated behind, headed north at a canter.

Then a solitary rider, thundering hard from the north, was upon them. The monk-like figure in a black cowl answered the challenge, 'Who do you hold with?' with the reply, 'For York!' After a brief consultation with Captain Horne, that self-declared Yorkist hardrider agreed to return to Sherburn-in-Elmet to contact Yorkist spies ensconced in the church tower. A rendezvous was arranged through the Benedictine-robed horseman with the Yorkist agents: it was to be a small church south of Tadcaster, in the vill of Lead.

'Too much trust, I fear,' muttered Edmund to his brother.

They followed after the mysterious hardrider at a gallop, making excellent time along the ancient Roman road from Castleford. Then, with a wave, the black monk disappeared into the gloom of woodland surrounding the vill of Ledston, heading for Sherburn-in-Elmet with the message and tidings of the raiders' intent.

Apart from a few yapping dogs, the cluster of dwellings at Lead village, adjacent to a stream named the Cock, was deserted. About the same time on the morrow, further downstream, the Cock Beck would run red with blood of the slain. The unmistakable glow of camp fires lit the skyline, the Lancastrian main force was encamped less than a mile to the north.

Under the direction of Edmund the raiding force turned eastwards. They had hardly crossed the waters of the Cock and entered dense woodland when upwards of sixty riders bearing the badge of Percy fell upon the place. There followed a scouring of each and every dwelling in Lead. The raiders watched from a distance of a few hundred yards, hardly daring to breathe and with many a hand over a horse's muzzle. They sought no fight with that particular party, for they had other pressing business.

'Our Benedictine was not for York after all,' whispered John to his brother.

Suddenly, a flickering of flames was to be seen from under the eaves of each of the dozen or more clustered dwellings. Within minutes, the whole village, apart from the church dedicated to St Mary, erupted into a roaring, spluttering inferno, torched by Percy's mounted retainers.

'How foolish,' muttered Edmund 'They've impaired their night vision and confused their ears. Our movements are now well masked.'

His words were overheard by *Hauptmann* Dietz and Robert Horne. John noted that the experienced warriors exchanged glances and each nodded in agreement at his brother's observation.

'Who goes there?' You make enough noise to awaken the dead,' came a low voice out of the blackness of the undergrowth. One of the Yorkist spies from Sherburn, Sir Nicholas Gillott had found the raiders. 'You're too trusting – spies, and scourers seeking deserters, are everywhere.'

The sky behind them glowed red as they mounted and rode deep into the cover of the forest. Sir Nicholas led the small force along paths and tracks so as to avoid enemy picquets and outriders. In less time than it takes to relate he brought them to the main thoroughfare to York at a place called Barkston Ash.

Upon reaching the London Road, Horne turned to Edmund 'Where then the ambush, young *Rottmeister*?'

'Within sight of the picquet fires of Lancaster we saw whilst coming to this place – above Dintingdale. Sight of them will present a disarming welcome to the Craven,' said Edmund.

'Ah! crafty fox,' said Horne. 'Then let's move further north along this road to bait a trap, for I perceive you have contrived a wily ruse.'

Sure enough, further north along the highway, where thick woodland thinned, close to a gentle slope and bend in the road, flickering camp fires high on the hillside hove into sight, twinkling in the icy night and stretching along the ridge towards an outcrop of trees known as Castle Wood.

Edmund moved quickly, issuing orders. He sent Wee Willie and Spotty Spence to set up a blindman's hurdle down the road towards Towton vill. It would be drawn into place once the Flower of Craven had entered the 'killing ground'. Using dry kindling, brought along on Edmund's instructions, four camp-fires were lit and within minutes, slices of bacon were sizzling away, filling the cold, damp evening air with the most stomach-stirring, mouth-watering smell imaginable. It was bait which hungry warriors fresh from doing battle, and with a nine-mile gallop behind them, would hardly resist.

An impenetrable bank of blackberry bushes and gorse formed an ideal butt for Edmund's ambush. Years of hunting and trapping animals to supply a meagre table had sharpened his skills, especially during that dreadful winter when they had laboured long and hard to keep their mother alive. Lessons, learned in infancy, driven by necessity and honed by desperation, were being turned against his fellow man in an efficient ands terrible way.

Nine crossbow stands were carefully positioned among the trees, above and overlooking the road, and sited opposite the camp-fires and screen of blackberry bushes. *Hauptmann* Dietz looked to Edmund as if to invite him to indicate a position he should take. Embarrassed at the *Hauptmann's* willing compliance, Edmund nodded towards a spot on the opposite side of the road, which position would enfilade the killing zone. Robin Carle was directed by Edmund to ride off one bow's shot towards Ferrybridge, where he was to signal of any approach by means of a shrieker.

Nineteen longbow riders were spread along the edge of trees behind the *Waspen* and proceeded to take arrows from their quivers, pushing the points into the ground. Their rate of discharging accurately-aimed arrows, fifteen every minute, could mean success or failure. Horses were used by Edmund in his stratagem; they formed a tethered line away from the killing ground. It was planned that Clifford's men should dismount and tether their horses before proceeding into the arena of death so artfully contrived.

When everything was in place, Didi Wattle produced the finishing touch, a neatly-folded banner bearing the Dacre motif. It had been taken by him at the affray at Robin Hood's Well and kept as a trophy. He attached it to a spear and set it among the camp-fires.

The trap was baited: high on the skyline, about half-a-mile away to the north, the disarming sight of friendly picquet campfires of Lancaster; suggesting succour and prospects of shelter, four crackling, roaring fires by the roadside; seducing the senses, the irresistible mouth-watering aroma of sizzling bacon lying heavy in the air; flagons of ale standing just begging to be quaffed completed the deadly ruse, Dacre's banner fluttering in the icy wind implied the comforting proximity of the owners of the meal. Dacre's men were, of course, spirited and friendly rivals – allies, brothers-at-arms with the Flower of Craven.

'Would these battles be elsewhere other than England's fair hills and dales,' the bowman behind John muttered in an undertone to his companion. 'It all seemed far more sporting when France hosted our blood-letting.'

A church bell somewhere sounded Compline, almost drowning the incoming shrieker.

'Here we go,' muttered the bowman. 'Steady you lads,' he called over to the Wasps 'Make every bolt count!'

He had barely finished speaking when the unmistakable sound of a second shrieker was heard above the howling wind, the arrow falling into the woodland across from their ambush position.

'Holy Mary, Mother of God!' gasped another archer 'That means there could be a hundred or more of the buggers!'

Edmund stepped out of concealment and yelled down the line of archers 'Steady! Aim at the man directly in front of you and then at the still-standing man to your right with your second shaft. Wait for my signal.'

Had he not given that order, then the main target, Lord Clifford, might well have ended up resembling a seamstress's pin cushion whilst the rest of the Craven remained unscathed. Edmund returned to his place in front of John and slightly to his right.

'We're ready for them, John,' he muttered over his shoulder. 'This night we may become orphaned – if that is not the truth of it already.'

John reflected on the role he played within the *Fähnlein*, that of a *Ladenschütze*. Being a crossbow loader had not, however, kept him from having to thrust his knife into a man's throat at Robin Hood's Well. Would Edmund slay their father should he be among the riders who, at that very moment, were bearing down on the carefully-laid trap? Indeed, should he come face to face with his sons, would the one who had bestowed life upon them so highly esteem allegiance to the Clifford household that he would seek to slay them? Kinship and accountability had not prevented his abandoning of them on two occasions in the past, the final time breaking their mother's heart and bringing about a great melancholy ending in her death.

Fear gripped John's inward parts as, above the noise of the wind, he became aware of the dull thunder of horses' hoofs.

The Flower of Craven, strung out over the distance of a half-a-bowshot, rode their steaming horses into the trap at a gallop. Near exhaustion of the riders was plainly evident. What was more heartening, their quivers were empty.

They had been involved in action throughout that day, beginning with a pre-dawn surprise attack on Lord Fitzwalter's advance guard. That was followed by a day-long exchange over the Aire with the longbow, keeping an entire

Yorkist army at bay. As light faded they had begun to withdraw from Ferrybridge only to run into forward elements of Fauconberg's mounted archers commanded by Sir Walter Blount. They had fought a running fight, eventually breaking away and galloping nine miles. Dead and wounded retainers clad in the livery of Clifford with its Red Wyvern charge lay scattered around the Ferrybridge crossing, through Brotherton vill and along the Tadcaster Road as far as Sherburn-in-Elmet. The once mighty force of five hundred proud, mounted bowmen had been pared down to less than a hundred. And then, to complete their blood-full day, there lay in wait over thirty covert bows.

Edmund's first bolt thudded into Clifford's bared neck with a revolting thump.

Master of the House of Clifford and captain of the mighty Flower of Craven had dismounted wearily and with obvious stiffness. Swinging aching arms and calling out to his men, he had moved unsteadily towards the inviting fires. His sallet he had already removed during the galloping withdrawal. His black tousled hair, stiffened with sweat, clung to a pale, battle-begrimed face. He reached for a flagon of ale, removing his beevor as he did so. That was when Black-hearted Clifford got it in the neck. That disarming act of his presented Edmund with the opportunity he had reckoned on. The loosing of that bolt was the signal for an arrow storm. With the range at less distance than point-blank the slaughter commenced.

Like a sack of mackerel, the lifeless body of the ruthless favourite of Queen Margaret crumpled to the ground. Immediately, there followed over thirty well-aimed shafts, whizzing and slicing through the icy drizzle, virtually every arrow finding a quarry among the Lancastrian riders.

At first the entrapped bowmen, believing they were victims of a tragic error, filled the air with cries of 'friend', mixed with curses and screams of pain. Another well-aimed volley silenced the desperate appeals and realisation dawned.

Some chose to charge right through the trap. Within seconds, about ten riders and their horses were writhing and squirming about in the road, brought down by the blindman's hurdle.

Like a well-drilled killing machine, *Ladenschütze* faithfully laboured away, yanking on bowstrings – cranking, tugging and operating goat's-foot levers. John Hawksworth, Willie Daub, Poxey Goite, Butterbusk and Wee Willie spanned bows faster than they had ever done in training, loading their individually marked bolts and passing the loaded weapons to their *Armbrustschütze*. Yet there was no hurrying in the aim on the part of Edmund, Snowwhite, Didi Wattle, Mealy Madoc and Spotty Spence and the result was awesome. Over to their right, slightly forward, Blau Ben Haagan, Fleischer, Foxglove, Kurt Meyer and Pepper Plasden were loosing bolts at a steady rate. Also their *Ladenschütze*, Lancer Lockrill, Dicky Wyatt, Holy Holy Cantar, Trouty Inkershill and Lime Waddesley thrust loaded bows into the waiting hands of their partners at death. A man for Lancaster was accounted for almost every shot.

With drawn swords, in panic and desperation, groups of Craven bowmen, many of them wounded, some more than once, formed up and charged the tree line.

Breath was knocked out of John as he was slammed into a tree trunk by a young archer from Skipton.

Since joining the *Wespen* the brothers had each been provided with a short, one-edged arming sword called a falchion. However, when John needed the old, rust-pitted weapon he was pinned down and unable to draw it from its scabbard.

Wild-eyed with terror, Clifford's retainer pressed his blade against John's chest. Then, as a second thought, instead of pushing on the blade, he moved his knife upwards to slit John's throat. That split-second delay by the archer allowed for his helmet to be wrenched aside. Edmund's falchion was

277

brought down with all the desperate fury of a warrior saving his brother. The man's face smacked into John's, breaking his nose. The archer was quite dead, his neck hacked partly through. For the second time in a matter of two days John became soaked in warm Lancastrian blood and, oh, how he loathed the warm, sticky feeling.

There was the sound of clash of steel upon steel and screams of wounded and dying men all around. Suddenly they were face to face with their father. It was as if time halted. All three became frozen to the spot. Helmetless, his deeply scarred face contorted with hatred, shock and fear. Before him, his blood-soaked sons barred his way. Were they to be his nemesis?

Edmund had no spanned crossbow to hand.

Clouds of acrid smoke from the now spluttering campfires suddenly enveloped them, stinging the eyes. Then it was that John Hawksworth, vintenar with the mighty Flower of Craven, looked wildly about him before dashing off into the tethered horse line. Then he was off into the night, heading for Towton.

'Craven coward!' Edmund yelled after him. 'You killed our mother! I have sworn vengeance – a quarrel reserved for you!'

Before the boys could pursue him they were fighting for their lives. Back to back, Edmund and John swung their falchions, parrying a thrust here, blocking a descending mace there. Suddenly it was over, their attackers cut down from behind.

Those who had failed to escape surrendered. Then it was that they paid the price for their brave holding of the Aire crossing. The captured and the wounded were killed with pole-axes and war hammers. John wanted no part of that, nor did Edmund. Weapons, armour, items of clothing – especially boots – purses, finger rings, amulets, chains and every other valuable thing were stripped from the sixty or more bodies. Maybe two dozen – none could ever be sure – had broken out of the ambush. Others coming up behind had scattered into the woodland upon hearing the tumult of battle. The élite of the Lancastrian army, the gallant Flower of Craven had been near wiped out. The bitter and hate-driven commander, Sir John, Lord Clifford was at that moment having his head hacked from his body by Snowwhite. The grisly object was held out towards Edmund.

'Yours, I believe,' Snowwhite called, holding aloft the head by its hair. He also held along with it a distinctive black-painted Hawksworth bolt which had done the work.

'It's a pity he never knew what struck him down,' called out Robert Horne. 'What think you? In death does he appear to wear a stunned look?'

'I'll wager he's looking down from Purgatory or Paradise at this very moment wondering what struck him and contemplating the annihilation of his bowmen,' laughed Sir Nicholas as he wiped his sword on a discarded, heavily-bloodstained surcoat. 'Although I hold that not a man alive knowest what happens at death. No one truly knows.'

'Away with that! More's the like he's gazing on this bloodied stage from the torments of Hell,' muttered Horne.

Sir Nicholas directly addressed the severed head 'Hatred you sowed with alacrity and hatred in abundance you have justly reaped.'

Then, referring to the Clifford family motto, *Desormais*, emblazoned on Clifford's banner which Horne had just had handed to him, Sir Nicholas proclaimed loudly, '*Desormais déjeuner avec le Diable!*'

'Henceforth, dine with the Devil.' A bowman and veteran of the French Wars murmured the translation for the brothers' benefit.

Edmund took the Lady Isabel's embroidered silken favour from around his neck and carefully wiped Clifford's severed head with it.

'This is destined for a city gate at York,' said Edmund 'And this blood-stained favour is for the Lady Isabel. As I vowed, so shall I pay.'

Within the hour King Edward, riding at the head of the vanward, galloped up and dismounted. When shown the head of Clifford, the murderer of his beloved younger brother, the Earl of Rutland, he loudly declared with a burst of emotion-laden satisfaction,

'Edmund Hawksworth, proven Avenger of Righteous Blood. Yet of no royal pedigree and self-declared, approved by Almighty God and anointed by Him on Epiphany Sunday last, has this day begun his work. Praise the name of the Lord, for His will is being done by boys!'

So saying, he bowed his head to Edmund and called his Exchequer and holder of the purse to make the blood payment of one hundred pounds.

William Hastings, who had just ridden up, called over, 'My liege, the lad will surely empty thy coffers afore this matter is set aside.'

Cautious laughter greeted this from the lords and commons alike. Thus blood-lust was relieved. King Edward was quick to reply. 'Then lands and manors of faithful subjects shall surely make up the shortfall in the privy purse. What say you, William?'

That brought a spontaneous chorus all around of a long drawn-out 'ooh', followed by further good-natured laughter. Vanquishing of the much-vaunted Flower of Craven had boosted the spirits of all – especially so, the demise of its master and prominent supporter of King Henry and Queen Margaret. There could be no denying the all-pervading amicable spirit apparent betwixt the Yorkist king and his supporters.

Edmund and John were to stay close to the king, both for that night and the morrow. This did not please Edmund as he had expected to captain the *Wespen* as a unit. Now it seemed that the lords favoured splitting the crossbow boys into their fighting pairs and distributing them so as to do their deadly work behind the entire Yorkist forward battle.

An earthenware pot was located and the terrible trophy placed within. It was then handed to a member of the royal bodyguard for safe keeping and eventual journey to the City of York.

Following the coming final battle, should either Edmund or John survive, they would take the silken scarf and present it to the beautiful Lady Isabel. If Edmund should not survive the morrow, would she pay the lover's forfeit to John, whatever that whispered promise happened to be? John's countenance had hardly been improved by that blow in the face. His nose was much swollen. Hardly a suitable visage for a would-be suitor. John was dreaming again and forlornly so, he feared.

Sir Nicholas was able to provide accurate intelligence as to the position of Henry VI's army camped before the hamlet of Towton. Facing the enemy, but out of sight, a growing encampment was spreading across the gorse and woodland in Dintingdale towards the vill of Saxton. As hundreds of men-of-foot began arriving they were being led off by their captains and centenars to pre-determined postions. All through that freezing night horse-drawn wagons of the baggage train began to turn up. Soon a mass of camp-fires sprang up to roar and flicker defiantly at the few Lancastrian picquet fires on the ridge above and in front of them.

Then the call went out, 'We have kin of the Earl of Warwick and Lord Fauconberg among the slain.'

William, Lord Fauconberg was directed to a heap of dead Skipton men cut down by longbow arrows as they had forlornly banded together for mutual protection and their last stand. A body, as yet not stripped, was dragged forth.

Sir William, Lord Fauconberg shook his head in disgust as, with the aid of a lighted brand, he peered at the fallen man's face 'Another treacherous cousin – John, Lord Neville.'

A low moan came from the grievously wounded man. Immediately the old warrior, drew his sword and administered the *coup de grace*.

'This despicable turncoat, this cur, after seeking and obtaining a Commission of Array from Richard, Duke of York, raised and brought 8,000 men to Wakefield last Christmastide. Then this dispicable fox took the field alongside Lancaster.'

'What then, my Lord Fauconberg?' a bowman called, nodding at the slain man.

'I want nothing of his. Take all he has – but find another earthen pot, for this head shall join that of Clifford's. Both shall provide pickings for the birds on Micklegate Bar.'

The next day was Palm Sunday and it was rumoured that there would be no fighting on such a holy day.

Edmund and John, positioned but yards from the king's tented camp, which had begun to grow in the streets of Saxton village, were well placed to witness the arrival of heralds from the Duke of Somerset. Under a white banner of truce, the Norroy King-at-Arms and an accompanying pursuivant rode up, escorted by Yorkist mounted archers. The group halted at Edward's tent and dismounted, awaiting the Yorkist king's pleasure. When Edward appeared wearing a golden crown the herald gasped at the sight of the regaly-clad young man.

In pompous manner Norroy, William Tyndale – a lettered, scholarly man in his fiftieth decade – with nostrils flared as if the one before him smelled like a midden, announced, 'The present and rightful King of England and France, Henry the Sixth greets his cousin and asks with what intent this host gathers here. If it should be for some treasonous mischief, then your liege lord proposes that the most holy morrow be left unmarked by the effusion of Christian blood.'

'Is there a day that would suit your French mistress, the she-wolf Margaret?'

The once Earl of March, now King Edward of the House of York, with brusque retort was as icy as the March wind then blowing across Yorkshire as he fronted that northern herald.

'The feast of St Climacus is on the Monday,' stuttered the Norroy, discomforted by the tall youth's quiet, calculated insult and confident regal manner.

'By St Climacus Day there will be one rightful king ruling in England. The usurping House of Lancaster is at an end and those houses which would give support and by so doing offend this rightful king, shall suffer attainment.'

'You would defile *Hebdomada Sancta*?' the King-at-Arms asked incredulously. Then the herald added, 'Over yonder hill are gathered to do you battle five peers of the realm, eight lords and a mighty array of knights. The like of such a force gathered to a king's standard has never been counted afore by the heralds in this kingdom.'

'Fear not on our account, good Norroy. Knoweth not thy holy text? Does not King Solomon write, "The race is not to the swift, nor the battle to the strong, for time and chance happeneth to all"?'

The herald, Tyndale, bowed in acknowledgement before countering, 'What then of the advice of our Lord Jesus? "What king will go to do battle against another king, whether he sits not first and bethinks if he may, with ten thousand, go against him with twenty thousand? Else yet while he is afar off, he sends a messenger and sues for peace".'

'We have no messenger sueing for peace while Henry is persuaded to disavow his own sealed promise, gainsaying succession to the throne drawn up by his own Parliament,' snapped Edward, wearying of the exchange with the herald for the North. 'And, Norroy, the hosts are well balanced, for one man taking the field in a righteous cause is worth ten of an army unlawfully assembled against its king.'

'Truly, you are determined to violate tomorrow's most holy day?'

'Palm Sunday we take the field and let the Lord God of Hosts judge on the morrow's holy day betwixt Lancaster and this House of York.'

'I was there, on the Feast of Rufina and Secunda, at Northampton when you dropped the knee to King Henry. Now, like your father, you seek Henry of Lancaster's throne,' said Norroy.

'Henry rules neither in mind, ability, nor by legal right, for his grandfather, Henry of Bollingbroke, usurped the crown from Richard II whom he then had murdered at Pontefract.'

Edward's blood was up and the heralds for the north were to receive a tongue-lashing.

'The barred and bastard line of Beaufort, the so titled Duke of Somerset, rules the kingdom along with the French bitch. They are your masters, William Tyndale, esquire.'

For the first time in the encounter the Norroy was uneasy. Although, by accepted rule the position of herald was deemed neutral, from Edward's manner of utterance, Tyndale clearly felt threatened. He could see no further gain in the exchange and instead asked after a favourite Lancaster captain.

'May I inquire, what of Lord Clifford of Skipton?'

'For your heraldic records: he will never more be joining Henry's battle lines. Henceforth he dines with the Devil.'

Then it was that Lord Fauconberg called over to the group 'And for your record keeping, William Tyndale, you may this night strike from your roll, Baron John, Lord Neville de Raby.'

With a dismissive wave of the hand King Edward turned smartly about and returned to his tent calling back over his shoulder, 'Inform Somerset that places in Hell are reserved for him, Northumberland, other lords, and whosoever else on the morrow is mustered to Lancaster's banner.'

The Norroy instinctively bowed his head and immediately looked as if he had wished that he had not. He and his pursuivant mounted their palfreys and trotted off towards the London Road. They halted for a moment to view the stripped

Ferrybridge to
Towton.

corpses belonging to the mothers of Craven piled by the roadside awaiting burial, before galloping off in the direction of Towton to report to the Duke of Somerset.

Both Edmund and John had witnessed the clipped exchange with the northern herald. There was to be no postponement. The die was cast. Sunday, 29th March, Palm Sunday, 1461, was to be the fateful day when the forces of two kings would take the field and ask the Almighty to decide who should take the throne of England.

The significance of the those days was not lost on the *Wespen* awaiting to greet the first of the baggage carts, that by midnight were arriving at Saxton village.

Chapter Thirteen

PALM SUNDAY FIELD
1461 *Ante Meridiem*

AD THE ALMIGHTY declared in favour of the House of Lancaster? That's how they mused when fifteen thousand and more gathered about Saxton village, bestirred at dawn on that awful Palm Sunday morn. They were greeted by a blinding blanket of falling snow, which whipped and whirled about, driven by a howling northerly. It was beginning to settle on the frost-prepared, hardened ground. They would be fighting for their lives with it stinging their faces blinding their eyes.

Edmund mustered the *Fähnlein* at first light, only to discover that they were missing a boy. Mealy Madoc was absent from the line. Backsy Butterbusk took Edmund and John to where his shooter sat crouched beneath his cloak. The snow covering settled undisturbed on Mealy's motionless form.

'He's been shecking for most o't neet,' chuntered the Conisbrough boy, latest recruit to the ranks of the *Wespen*. 'An' he's been rooring. Either he's got the ague, or he's freetened.'

The rough cant of the Yorkshire boy served to remind John of their upbringing; neither Edmund nor he shared the West Riding guttural dialect. Their mother's parentage had been kept a secret; however, their ever-growing awareness that her birth was not lowly continued to plague John's mind. The conversation overheard between the incumbent at St Peter's and the Abbot of Roche had aroused in him a desire to know their blood-line. What that eavesdropping had done to Edmund anyone who knew him could well imagine. Blood payment from that time on included not only an errant father, but also a mysterious maternal grandfather.

That story would have to be left for another to tell, should anyone harbour enough interest to bring together all loose ends and tie a sufficiently pretty bow.

Instead of beating the boy with the *Rottmeister's* mace as Fleischer would have done, Edmund crouched down with Mealy, as he did so covering them both with his own cloak. Eventually, after many minutes, he stood and raised young Madoc, his arm about his shoulders. He turned to Butterbusk, smiled reassuringly, and gave an order.

'Take him to Mater's wagon and make sure this night's fast is broken – something hot inside him. Tell the Wasps we have a bestowal to make this day.'

The pair shuffled off until swirling flurries of snow swallowed them up. It was already settling to the depth of a dagger blade.

'He's seen barely fifteen summers and yet he's done service within the Calais pale, fought at Mortimer's Cross, taken on Dacre's best at Robin Hood's Well; plus the fighting at Ferrybridge and yesterday's bloody ambush.'

'All too much for poor Mealy? He is to remain with Mater then?' John ventured.

'His tears are for a lost love.'

'Bridger Blastock?' John frowned at the implications, for he felt a tinge of disgust.

'Yes, the girl who fooled him and, indeed, all of us,' said Edmund. 'He keeps saying that she smelled different.'

'I suspected something amiss about Bridger,' John replied.

If Edmund heard him, he chose not to query John's claim to have suspected.

'On campaign she shared his dangers, his food and his body warmth at night. All the time her true identity unbeknown to poor Mealy.'

'The signs were there for all to see,' John muttered, somewhat hurt at being ignored.

Edmund mused aloud 'He is turning over and over in his mind their two years spent together, seeking to recall clues that should have alerted him. Now he misses her as a girl, his once bosom companion, and yet he only ever knew her as a boy. Though he says she had a different smell to the rest.'

John was surprised and irritated at his brother's display of empathy. Edmund was obviously affected by Mealy's confusion. On that strange episode of Bridger Blastock, John took a leaf from his brother's book: *cui bono* – 'no gain' in worrying about it. There was nothing of advantage in continuing to consider the whole strange affair. They had more to concern them on that chilly Sunday morn.

However, John recalled how Bridger had dug her fingers into his arm as Snowwhite thrilled the crowd with his incredible display of crossbow skill. She had squealed like a girl all the while. John had not been as surprised as the rest when her body was being stripped for burial at Wentbridge hermitage. Were there any more girls among the *Wespen*? He thought not.

The huge gathering of carts making up the baggage park was growing by the hour. Before the animals were unhitched, cooks were providing sustenance and support for the two mustering Yorkist battles. For some affinities there would be no hearty breakfasts as their supply wagons still struggled up the clogged and slippery roads, which were becoming more treacherous by the hour. Those unfortunate men would simply delay consuming their ironfare until the order was given to form up into the battles.

Mater's wagon had, with a number of other horse-drawn carts, made good time, she having driven the animals nonstop through the night, following on the hoofs of the raiders' route north along the ancient Roman road from Castleford.

The boys clustered around her, eager to tell of the previous evening's slaughter of Clifford's archers.

'Mater, Mater, we have taken the head off Butcher Clifford!' blustered Wee Willie excitedly, pushing his way to the front as he spoke.

'Have you?' replied Mater in the manner of a mother encouraging a spirited youngster. 'And how is your wound?' Deftly, she changed the subject.

Brought up sharply by her concern, the youngest of the Wasps muttered, 'It hurts sometimes Mater.'

'We had best take a look at it and wax you up afresh.'

Wee Willie was helped on to the cart and Mater pulled down his hose and removed the binding about his thigh. She smelled at the six-inch-long vivid gash and smiled with some relief before washing and redressing it.

'You're healing, Will, and you'll have a limp to be proud of.' Tenderly, she brushed his hair aside. 'At least for a while, but even that will go in a few weeks.'

'Little rascal will make the most of it, Mater, make no mistake,' called out Didi Wattle.

'He's already got Spotty Spence carrying his satchel, quivers and bow,' added Daub, 'And that was before he was wounded!'

This was greeted with titters as a snowball splattered on Wee Willie's head. He detected his full acceptance as a member of the crossbow boys. After all, had he not been wounded in the clash of arms at Ferrybridge – the only one in the *Fähnlein* to receive an injury deep enough to cause concern?

There followed a brisk exchange of snowballs as the Wasps battled among themselves. In no time, others joined in. Mounted retainers and men-of-foot with the house of Wenlock took on the Wasps and were discomforted when some of Fauconberg's mounted archers took the Wasps' side. Soon hundreds of men were hurling white, packed-hard missiles at each other. The ribaldry and jesting served to strengthen the ties, bonding not just the Wasps, but others gathered to their individual banners in the cause of Edward of York.

The jolly battle ceased as quickly as it had begun when centenars blew their horns. Men once more busied themselves, preparing for another fight – one involving cold steel. One that many would not survive before that day ended.

Churches at nearby Lotherton and Lead, along with Saxton, had been kept busy since dawn celebrating Mass for the mighty. Thousands of men-at-foot made content with the many friars who circulated their ranks. Everywhere the penitent were kneeling, off-loading their troubled souls, pouring out misdemeanors in subdued tones to hard-tasked poor-priests. All round about absolution was trotted out in monotonous flow: *'Deinde, ego te absolvo a peccatis tuis in nomine Patris, et Filii, et Spiritus Sancti. Amen.'*

Not a single one of the twenty boys saw fit to confess to a priest. They looked to Edmund, and neither he nor John saw the need. In John's case he reasoned that supporting the new king was the will of God – they were engaged in righteous warfare – and he had done nothing of which to be ashamed. As for Edmund, he neither understood the Almighty, nor did he care to commune with him about anything. If it was true, as the old priest Reresby had declared at the time of their mother's death, 'God needed another angel in Heaven', then the deity was cruel, mean and differed little from the Devil. As for languishing for all eternity in Hell, Edmund would take his chances, for he saw none of its horrors in the teachings of the Christ. 'It's the Devil's world John, and I grasp not one jot of it all,' he said.

A delicious hot-pot had been readied by Mater and with that, along with near-fresh baked bread, the twenty boys partook of a fine breakfast, sheltering snugly under a canvas awning rigged about their baggage wagon.

Sir William, Lord Fauconberg had decided that pairs of boys be positioned across, and behind the entire battle line. There they were to identify and slay the lords of Lancaster. Their mercenary captain, *Hauptmann* Dietz, returned from scouting-out the ground flanking the London Road, the fields chosen by Lancaster for battle. He discussed what he had observed with the two with whom he could hold a conversation, Blau Ben Haagan and Kurt Meyer.

Before the pairs were sent to their assigned positions behind the vanward battle, Edmund did something that served to bolster the spirits of all the boys. He distributed money to each of them from the one hundred pounds bounty paid for the head of Clifford. Everyone of the eighteen boy-warriors received a half noble and promptly lodged it with Mater, along with their other treasures, the rings, lockets, rosaries, purses and coins, trophies each had acquired so far.

'Do you all still have your ironfare uneaten?' Edmund queried as he checked each lad in turn. It was important that all had sustenance for the coming fray, for there would be little opportunity to eat at Mater's wagon once the opposing battles became locked.

Also, there was a distributing of rope hoops to fit over their boots. Mater, as usual, had thought of everything: two circles of thick rope, which passed under the soles and secured about the ankles, enabled the boys to stay upright when all about slipped and slithered in snow and slush.

Around nine o'clock the brothers reached the position assigned by *Hauptmann* Dietz. Edmund and John were on the extreme right flank of the Yorkist battle. Confirming the hour was the remorseless peal of church bells ringing out the beginning of Terce, as if signalling the order for presence at the gates of Hell. Before the boys the now white-blanketed, shrub-covered ground rose steeply out of Dintingdale. It had stopped snowing and the cutting northerly wind had abated.

As John and Edmund hurried up to take their place behind the massed ranks of billmen, the former Sheriff of Devon and Commissioner of Array, John Dinham, mounted on a magnificent chestnut destrier and clad in the finest Milanese armour, addressed the men and youths raised from his shire.

'Upon clearing yonder hill, before your eyes you'll see a pathetic army of northern scum, Scots formed-up in ancient schiltron as at Bannockburn 150 years past; and cowardly Frenchies, the like of which our fathers whipped at Crécy and Agincourt.'

Dinham dismounted and, removing his sallet, revealed a tousle-haired handsome young man in his late twenties. What Edward lacked for support from earls and dukes, he more than gained in knights and able captains. Dinham took his stand on a pile of snow-covered stones and gestured towards Towton with a mailed gauntlet.

'As wicked a rabble as you'll ever clap eyes on, led by a French queen and her paramour Somerset, styled "Duke of". She it was who ordered the plundering of English towns, the ransacking of churches and violating of this country's womenfolk – our liege lord's subjects!' He then roared out a challenge.

'Are you man enough this holy day to set matters to rights, the very day when Christ entered Jerusalem and cleared the Temple?'

'Aye, that we are!' was the response from hundreds of Devonshire men.

At that moment a battle horn sounded the advance.

'Let's cleanse the temple then! Ready your arms! Form stoutly upon your vintenars as you've practised a thousand times. Beware of caltrops spread on yonder hilltop and now forward, gallant scrumpy-heads. To the victor his spoil!'

Unsheathing his sword, he held the glittering blade aloft, crying out 'For God, St George, St Sebastian, Edward IV and the House of York!'

'A-York, A-York!' the mass responded as the banner fellowship surged forward.

A mighty roar greeted their appearance over the crest of the hill followed by what sounded like jeering from densely packed ranks over six hundred yards distant.

'There be thousands of the bastards!' gasped out a tall, heavily-armoured vintenar.

When the men in front of John moved forward and he could glimpse the enemy clearly, his heart sank. A thought instantly sprang to mind: would they spare a boy should the day go badly? He was discomforted by the notion – not a sniping crossbow youth – unless they cut off his hand.

An unbroken line of Lancastrian bills stretched from the London Road and swampy ground in the east, across to the west, as far as his eye could see, for over half-a-mile. It was no sparse line lacking in depth, but three dense battles of heaving, jeering men and boys, seemingly eager to carry out butchery. All along Lancaster's frontage stakes had been driven into the ground, then sharpened forming a defensive barrier which, presumably, they were expecting the attackers to hurl themselves upon. Along that fearsome line brightly-coloured banners and standards were being waved as they sought to intimidate.

John knew for a certainty, at that precise moment, twenty pairs of eyes, would be screwing-up, scanning the jeering line of warriors for specific livery: Trollope, Dacre, Percy of Northumberland, the Earl of Devon, the Dukes of Somerset and Exeter. Should the clearly and individually marked bolts find lodgement in any one of them, then their heads would bring wealth aplenty – maybe sufficient money for a property and livestock. Sanguinary employment could advance any man, or boy, beyond his wildest dreams.

'Do you see there?' said the huge vintenar named Donald Whitmore, pointing towards the lines of Lancaster. 'That group that be galloping behind their centre battle.'

'I think I can see them,' John answered.

'I'll wager they have Henry's royal banner folded up on yonder long pole. You see if I'm not right.'

'What of it? The word is that Henry is absent from the field,' said John.

'It'll not make an iota of difference should they unfurl it!' he continued, 'for it would mean martial law and the king's enemies – us – be placed outside the pale of justice.'

Before them the ground sloped away gradually until a shallow depression cut across the frontage of the two armies. A broken hedgerow consisting of burr elders and hawthorn followed the depression and formed the northern boundary of the meadow the Yorkists were still packing into. That ground, John later learned, was North Acres; in a few weeks' time it would be dotted about with lambing ewes. That was if the northerners hadn't butchered the sheep to fill their bellies. The continuing deepening depression in the ground to the Yorkist left was called Towton Dale, which fell away as it swept westward down to a wide meadow alongside the Cock Beck. Down stream, as the Cock snaked northwards, its eastern bank rose sharply, forming a steep incline along its length for the distance of a mile, until the ground fell away steeply to where the London Road crossed the Cock by way of a small stone bridge. The ancient crossing had been broken and the gap spanned by planking. The same had been done at Tadcaster where the town bridge spanned the Wharfe. Thus the crossings of the river barriers on the approach to the city of York were 'draw-bridged' and controlled by the forces of Henry VI.

'They hold the better position,' Edmund stated, as if he were some battle-hardened captain and veteran from the French wars.

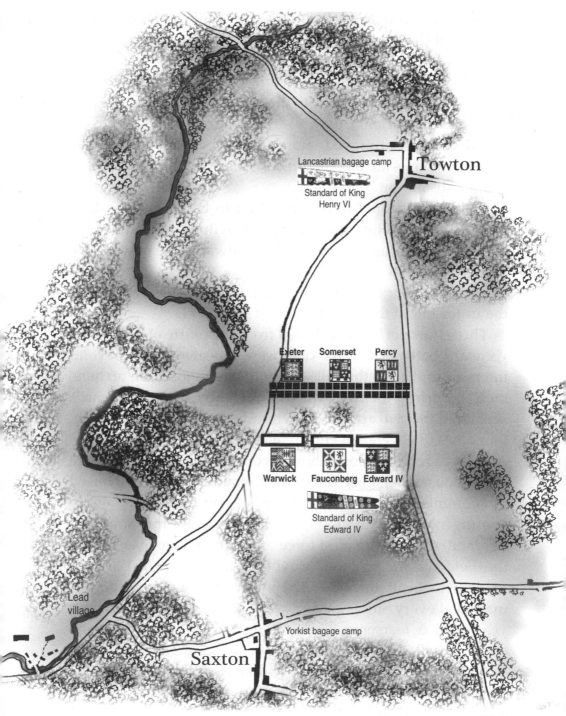

Lancastrian bagage camp

Towton

Standard of King
Henry VI

Exeter   Somerset   Percy

Warwick   Fauconberg   Edward IV

Standard of King
Edward IV

Lead
village

Yorkist bagage camp

Saxton

'Who do you think you are, the mighty John Talbot, scourge of the French?' John muttered. 'What happens now?' He shuddered, whether from cold or fear he wasn't sure. The wind had started up again, this time gusting from the south.

'It's changed! It blows from the south!' Edmund, pulled up the collar of his cloak. 'Now we're advantaged.'

'We're all disapproved, more's the like,' John stammered. 'Shame upon us all, bloodletting on this holy day. I wish I had sought absolution.'

The sky appeared to be struggling to hold aloft the deep grey overcast, weighed down with heavily-burdened clouds, stretching as far as the eye could see towards the city of York and its Minster.

A mighty roar from the Lancastrian battle lines announced the unfurling of the royal banner of Henry VI.

Three trumpet blasts sounded from the centre of the Yorkist vanward battle. The three calls were repeated at five second intervals and then the calls of centenars among the archers' men ordering them forward until three hundred yards separated the two armies. Soon hundreds of Yorkist bowmen, longbows uncovered, were advancing and reforming in front. All was orderly, without a hint of confusion. Before long there were thousands gathered together, retainers and those raised by commissions of array, from every formation, every contingent, every household, mainly from the south of England, until the greatest force of longbow men ever to take the field was in position. Maybe as many as 4,000 archers readied to bend the bow. They were trained from boy to manhood every Sunday, every week of every month and each year until a fearsome force of Englishmen and Welshmen could be called upon by his lord for the king's service. Many had served in the French wars and knew full well the impact they would have on massed enemy ranks.

Suddenly, down came the snow with such density that the opposing line was, mercifully, swallowed up before John's eyes as if it had never existed.

A drum-beat sounded far off to the left, then another louder; still another, nearer this time until a closer-sounding drum caused ranked bowmen immediately in front of the Devonshires to ready an arrow. The cry 'knock!' brought them to position a shaft against the bowstring.

'Draw!' caused every archer to half-turn together, each using his body weight to assist in the pull. Stiffened arms gripped the yew bows, raising the angle so as to achieve maximum range over the distance; hooked fingers drew bowstrings until they touched 4,000 bristly jaws.

Over to the far left, hidden from John's sight by the swirling snow, the first formation released its lethal arrow storm. That was followed in quick, successive flow by other units all along the line until the Devonshire bowmen received the order, 'Loose!'

Time and again the wave action was repeated. They thrilled as clouds of deadly shafts tore upwards to be swallowed from sight in the swirling white clouds. And, hastened by the gusting wind, to find awful lodgement in unseen, metal-covered bodies. 'Knock! Draw! Loose!' seemed to go on for hours, raining hundreds of thousands of shafts down on the massed, invisible ranks of northerners. However, it could have been no more than ten minutes.

John could just discern returning arrows loosed by Lancaster archers failing to make the distance against the head-on wind, the shafts slamming harmlessly into the ground as much as twenty cloth yards short of the Yorkist bowmen.

John could see, over to the left, the blue and white standard of Lord Fauconberg advancing towards the vast field of Lancastrian arrow shafts. Soon thousands of Yorkist archers were following the bold lead and were advancing to gather the arrows of the enemy and send them winging back at their former owners.

About that time the snow abated for some minutes, allowing John to see the results. Once proud ranks of bowmen fronting the forward battle of Lancaster had melted clean away. Some lay quite still on the ground. Some squirmed and writhed in agonies. Others were withdrawing through the packed ranks of billmen, assisting wounded friends and relatives to escape the terrible killing ground.

'Surely, they won't be able to withstand this much longer,' said Edmund, in awe at the terrible spectacle.

Then it was, in the distance and rippling all along their front, the sound of horns and the drums of Lancaster began to beat. Over towards the centre, John could see the standard bearers of Somerset passing through their protective wall of stakes. Likewise, immediately in front, the standard of the Earl of Northumberland began to move towards them.

With a terrible, almighty roar from 30,000 northern throats, massed ranks surged forward and, leaving their defensive position, headed in John's direction. Whereupon Yorkist archers turned and began legging back to the massed ranks of men-of-foot.

'They're coming to us!' yelled Donald Whitmore, the burly Devonshire vintenar from Tiverton. 'Spearhead! Form spearhead!'

At that moment, King Edward's standard fellowship rode up in front of the Devonshires. The king wheeled his snorting battle charger about and yelled, 'No quarter!' With that terrible cry on his lips he and his party began riding off along the entire Yorkist battlefront yelling that chilling order.

Suddenly there was a tremendous banging towards the centre of the Yorkist battle line. Flashes and explosions of handguns signalled the opening fusillade by Edward's Burgundian mercenaries. Soon the air filled with the reek of discharged saltpetre and sulphur. After that first withering volley there was little else heard from them the rest of that day, as the weather dampened their powder, extinguished their fuses and put out their fires. However, for the moment, the frightening, fiery explosions and hail of lead balls smashing and ripping into the advancing ranks stopped the centre company in its tracks.

The left wing of the Lancastrian battle ranged directly in front of John and Edmund kept on coming. 'King Henry! King Henry!' Their roar could be clearly heard as they advanced with the banner of Henry VI ahead of them. Seeing that the advance had been stopped in the centre and carried on against his right flank, Edward IV turned about and galloped back towards the Devonshires, his standard fellowship in hasty pursuit.

'Goodly knights and men-at-arms, do you want me as your king?' cried out Edward, his sword held high. 'Lancaster denies my inheritance! Wouldst help me avenge righteous blood?'

'Aye, we will!' The response was in unison and from every heart.

'To the death, my lord!' yelled John Dinham.

The supporting roar from the massed ranks of Devonshire men was deafening. At that, King Edward dismounted and took his place at the head of the front ranks with men of his standard fellowship each side of him.

Three blasts on a horn and John looked on fascinated as the long straight line reformed into scores of spearhead formations. Heavily-armoured vintenars wielding mauls, battle hammers, maces, morning stars and other such preferred weapons, each in command of nineteen men, took up point-of-spear positions. The wedge-shaped formations appeared as if by magic, with five men either side bearing bills. Immediately behind the vintenar were his two lieutenants, who would take over a spell at the point in case of needed rest or injury. A further six billmen, three either side, likewise stood ready to relieve and take the place of those on the outer edge. The final position in the spearhead was usually taken by 'The Gleaner' youngest, or in some cases, the least able; he would supply drink, bind wounds, find replacement weapons for the others.

It was on those fearsome spearpoint formations that the men from Wetherby, York, Newcastle and Carlisle were about to hurl themselves.

The initial clash was loud and soon the screams of injured men fell upon John's ears. The brothers were stunned, helpless and frozen to the spot. Ferrybridge had not prepared them for this horror, nor had the clash with Lord Dacre's mounted bowmen at Robin Hood's Well. John's part in the previous day's annihilation of Clifford's exhausted and beguiled Flower of Craven seemed as a minor scuffle. It was John and Edmund's introduction to Hell on earth.

Soon men with awful injuries emerged out of the falling snow, staggering past clutching at bleeding stumps where fingers and arms had been cut off. One had lost an eye, another an ear and one youngster had his left cheek sliced clean away to reveal his teeth. At least they were out of it and were being helped towards Saxton and the baggage park. What kind of a life could they look forward to?

Then John heard a mighty cheer as the northerners broke off the fight and fell back towards their line of defensive stakes. The kingly presence of the mighty Edward, wielding his sword all about him, had served to first slow, then stop the advance. Although Henry Percy, Earl of Northumberland and his brother, Sir Richard Percy, had advanced King Henry VI's standard alongside their own, the Lancastrian king was at his prayers in the town of York, twelve miles distant. The presence of one of the contenders for the throne on Palm Sunday field, and the absence of his rival, made a perceivable difference in the opening moves of that terrible contest.

There followed a further arrow storm when Yorkist archers moved forward once more through the battles to unleash their deadly hail. That apparently prompted the Lancastrian centre, under the standard of Henry Holland, Duke of Exeter, to advance. At once King Edward mounted up and galloped off to rally the line in that sector.

'Come, John, for I fear we are woefully unemployed,' Edmund suddenly decided.

True, there was, for the time being at least, a dearth of targets for their particular skills in the position they had been assigned. True, they had clearly identified the standard of Northumberland during the repulsed attack, but had no opportunity to locate a £100 target in all the confusion and falling snow.

They were able to move swiftly in the trampled slush as they made their way to the rear and the centre of the line. Then withdrawing bowmen came pushing through the battle; they were Sir John Wenlock's men. 'Lancastrian right and centre battles are advancing!' yelled a wide-eyed archer from Birmingham as he pushed past. Then they distinctly heard an almighty crash as both sides met head on. Horns blew and drumming began over to our right, in front of the Dinham's Devonshires.

'Northumberlanders are attacking again!' John gasped.

'Let's get back!' John shouted and they raced back the way they'd come.

'There is no gain in this, we can't see a thing!' shouted Edmund above the hideous racket of screams and clashes of metal on metal as men chopped, stabbed and hacked away at each other.

It seemed to John as if they were in no position to add to the mayhem and were running about like headless chickens trying to find meaningful employment.

'We are in need of a platform!' As Edmund shouted this, he pointed to a tree close to, and just behind the mêlée.

'Come on!' he yelled as he began to run forward.

Catching him up, John took hold of his arm and shook his head and begged, 'You jest!' He had to dissuade him, for it was far too near the butchering for his liking.

'Come on, John, lest our line gives way!'

All about the tree the snow was no longer white but a horrible twelve-inch deep, porridge-like dark red to dark brown slush. Bodies from the northerners' first attack of the morning were piled about everywhere. In front of the tree, the rear of the Devonshire spearhead formations stretched either side for about thirty yards. On the left, fighting shoulder to shoulder with them, were men from Kent under the captaincy and banner of Walter Blount.

The Yorkist line at this sector looked woefully thin and the men from Cumberland stabbing and hacking at it were in some impressive array – up to ten men deep. Sheer weight of numbers would surely prevail the longer the bloody exertion persisted. John felt heartily sick and he had an overwhelming urge to run. As they stood undecided – Edmund looking at how he might climb the tree and John looking back intending flight – the burly vintenar from Tiverton was assisted from the spearhead by the gleaner. A spiked and edged weapon had been shoved clean through his beevor and into his neck.

'French metal... like parchment... serves me right for pillaging it,' the poor giant of a man gurgled at them before slumping with his back to the tree trunk.

Attempts by the gleaner to stop the warm spurts of life-blood were proving fruitless.

'I must get back!' The gleaner said.

Edmund waved him off and, cutting a piece from a padded jack from a nearby fallen northerner, sought to staunch the bleeding. There was a gaping gash that sliced the neck artery and bared the vintenar's windpipe.

'Come, lads... drop some of their captains for us,' he urged as he slid into a sitting position. 'I'm done for, but you can use me as a ladder.'

With his remaining strength, he pushed himself up, crouched over and shoved out his leg as a step. Swiftly, Edmund handed John his crossbow and, using the human ladder presented, was soon pulling himself up on to the first branch. In minutes they were engaged in a deadly routine. Edmund, well positioned to see over the heaving mêlée and able to identify worthwhile targets, was releasing well-aimed bolts. Below him, John was spanning for all he was worth, handing the bow up and catching the discharged weapon. All the while the vintenar, wedged against the tree, served as a bleeding ladder. At some point his life-blood finally ebbed away, but the Tiverton giant remained frozen to the trunk, still serving the cause of his Yorkist masters in death.

When distant church bells rang the onset of None, Edmund had accounted for no less than eight lords and captains commanding Northumberland and Cumberland contingents. Two of the strikes were against declared targets, Henry Percy, Earl of Northumberland and Ranulph, Lord Dacre. Northumberland's brother, Sir Richard Percy, had also been been felled. Mortally wounded, the two Percy brothers were carried off to the vill of Towton by their retainers.

Lord Dacre of Gilisland was killed outright. He had mounted his charger in order to obtain a better view of the fighting and, upon removing his beevor in order to take a drink, a bolt had slammed into his neck. A remarkable strike, even for the Thryberg Hawk.

'They've broken through – we're undone!' came the chilling cry. Sure enough, Lancastrian cavalry had appeared out of nowhere and swept through the Staffordshires, causing a collapse on the left flank. That news sped through the entire length of the Yorkist battle lines, causing thousands of hearts to sink.

Chapter Fourteen

PALM SUNDAY FIELD
1461 *Post Meridiem*

CLEARLY, THE ARTFUL, cunning and masterful planning of erstwhile Calais captain Sir Andrew Trollope had succeeded once again in catching the Yorkist commanders napping. Somehow, the veteran of the French wars and notorious turncoat in the conflict between the two great houses, had managed to conceal 250 mounted spearmen, under the captaincy of his brother, David Trollope, in a wood which aligned with the left flank of the Yorkist battle line. With foresight and tactical genius Trollope, who had carefully selected the ground, forced his enemy to take up a position which would allow for his carefully-crafted ambush. At a time when Yorkists were tiring, weary and hungry through hours of fighting, he sprang his trap. Fresh fighting men sallied forth from concealment at the same moment that he committed his reserve under command of Henry Holland, Duke of Exeter. Within minutes, that assailed sector of the Yorkist battle line wavered and began to crumble.

There seemed to be no immediate danger of the formation ranged before John and Edmund joining in the fresh Lancastrian assault. To the contrary, the northerners massed under the Percy banner had become noticeably less aggressive and more defensive. Far more significantly, they were beginning to give up ground and some contingents from Hartlepool and Sunderland were back behind their defensive stakes.

Despite frantic urgings by an irate Duke of Somerset for the Northumberlanders to join the present attack, they failed to respond. Likely the sight of the royal standard fellowship riding off to the rear at the very time the Percy brothers were fatally wounded by crossbow bolts served to still their aggressive spirit. Remaining captains had become aware that a skilled marksman, operating undetected from behind the falling snow screen, was picking off prominent leaders with monotonous and alarming regularity. Until such a time as the sniper was located and killed, the captains of array and centenars would keep their heads down, distance themselves from their banners and subdue and limit their rallying cries.

The Lancastrian left had, for a time at least, become inhibited and was committed to fighting a holding action.

'We must eat, John, ere we give out,' said Edmund dropping from the tree.

For a few seconds they stood looking at the terrible and somehow magnificent sight, the vintenar from Tiverton who had bled to death. His lifeblood had formed a hideous glue that had frozen and bonded him to the tree. They had used his body as if it were a ladder – true, he had bidden them – but, it seemed a callous thing to have done, even unwittingly.

The sudden appearance of the Devonshire captain, John Dinham, gasping from his exertions in the slush, shook them from their reflections.

'Wasps – they're calling for Wasps!' he shouted as he slithered towards them, using his blood-caked poleaxe as support. His fine armour had taken a beating down his left side and would present a skilled armourer with hours of painstaking work to return it to its former glory. He placed an arm on each of their shoulders.

'May the Blessed Virgin herself shower favours upon you both, for never have I seen the like – just look at 'em,' he said, nodding towards the Northumberlanders and men from

Cumberland who could be seen clearly, as the downfall had abated for a time.

They turned to follow his gaze.

'You've stopped the blackguards. Just look at 'em! Their entire line, see, see, there isn't a vintenar who dares draw attention to himself for fear of a bolt in the neck.'

There was no denying it, a perceivable difference had come about; a definite abatement of aggressive noises coming from their packed ranks.

'I'll warrant you'll see the colour of gold for this work. By all the saints, I vouchsafe it!'

He turned them both about. 'But now see, Fauconberg is rallying the Wasps. There be more work for you two, for we are broken through on our left.'

As they were hurried to the rear, Devonshire 'scrumpyheads' began cheering and calling out to them, 'propa' bo!' and 'well done Wasps'; many chorused a buzzing sound which was taken up until the entire middleward was buzzing. News was fast spreading of Edmund's part in first stalling, then halting, the northerners' entire left wing advance.

All along the Yorkist rear line mounted bowmen were galloping through the snow picking up crossbow boys. Reining their snorting mounts about, they skidded, slid and, in flurries of slush and snow, they spurred and raced for the crumbling Yorkist left flank, their boy passengers clinging on.

The cause seemed lost for York when John and Edmund arrived above Towton Dale. David Trollope's cavalry had charged from ambush into the Earl of Warwick's men-of-foot. At the same time, his brother, Sir Andrew Trollope, at the head of hordes of Welshmen numbering upwards of 2,000, had slammed full tilt into the Warwickshires. Thus, assailed on two fronts, many sporting the badge of the ragged staff broke and fled down the fields towards the blackened and burnt crofts of Lead village.

Simultaneously, the Lancastrian commander of their rearward battle, the Duke of Exeter sounded the advance. With Lord Rivers at their head, 1,000 previously uncommitted men of Somerset's last reserve surged forward in the centre to exploit the disarray in the Yorkist battlelines.

Richard, Earl of Warwick yelled at Edmund, 'Into the line and stop this or we're undone!'

Wide-eyed and clearly on the edge of panic, he jabbed a gauntlet towards the struggling mass of men of the Yorkist reserve from Grantham and Peterborough, who had been flung into the battle line to fill the gaps left by the fleeing and fallen and prevent a total rout.

When all the Wasps had arrived they began looking from Fauconberg to Edmund, waiting for a command. Serving to further confuse them, *Hauptmann* Dietz had not turned up. Were they to charge headlong into the mêlée and try, somehow, to hit a worthwhile target? Fauconberg, veteran of a score of critical situations, yelled, 'Bring down their leaders. Ten marks for every centenar!'

However, Edmund had already decided what was needed. Ignoring his betters, he took mastery, *'Stillgestanden! Aufmarschieren!* Fall back – defence position – *Schnell!'*

Edmund called the orders with confidence and authority, indicating a piece of slightly raised ground behind them. Dutifully and as if at training, sixteen boys doubled back to the hillock and assumed positions; eight *Armbrustschütze* kneeling in the first line; behind each shooter stood his *Ladenschütze.*

Two boys had failed to arrive, the *Rottmeister* of *Rotte Gelb*, Blau Ben Haagan and his loader, Lancer Lockrill. Both, it turned out, had been caught in a shower of arrows loosed by Harlech archers, which shafts had carried the distance. They would die of their wounds before nightfall.

Facing the *Wespen*, Edmund called out his orders above the din of screaming and shouting from the hellish, heaving mass of men struggling, slashing and stabbing twenty yards behind him.

'Aim low – legs, shin, thigh, groin!'

Dutifully, and in unison, the Wasps chanted Edmund's command: 'Shin, thigh, groin.'

To Fauconberg, Edmund yelled, 'My lord, prepare to pull the towners back.'

At the instant that he judged the entire *Fähnlein* to be ready he called out, 'Pull back now!'

The warrior hesitated – after all, the Wasp's captain was but a boy whose voice had barely broken. The old scar-faced veteran took in their readied position on the hillock with narrowed eye; then he nodded, grinned and shook his head, mouthing an oath as he did so 'God's Blood! The cunning little grunt!'

Fauconberg knew what was about to happen and, grabbing a crossbow from a Warwickshire lad, he ran over and took his place beside John to begin the support work of a lowly *Ladenschütze*.

Three short blasts on a bugle, repeated at two second intervals, was all that was needed for the near-exhausted towners to disengage. Men and boys from Grantham, Stamford, Peterborough and Huntingdon suddenly broke off contact with the levies ranged against them. Turning about, the towners dashed for the rear, dragging their injured with them as best they could. Once they had passed either side of the drawn up *Wespen*, Edmund gave the order for the opening shoot.

'Loose! Stand fast, Wasps... and – loose!'

With lethal monotony, *Ladenschütze* spanned and passed loaded bows to their shooters, who in turn let fly at the packed ranks of men-at-arms from Dewsbury, Wakefield, Castleford and Pontefract. At first the effect was not discerned as the wounded were being pulled to the rear by their fellows. Then, it was as if their entire line suddenly dissolved towards the ground and changed into an awful writhing, thrashing, screaming mayhem. Crippled and in agony, the Yorkshires squirming about in that blood-stained slush were immediately transformed into a living barrier that no warrior, no matter how determined, could pass. Those who tried were themselves brought down and became part of the living obstacle of sixty or more wounded, screaming men.

With the desired effect achieved in that particular sector, Edmund called a halt and barked an order: '*Rechte Flanke* – realign.' The *Fähnlein* moved with drilled cool precision so as to target 'spears' rallied to the banner of Swansea. '*Schiessen!*' Edmund called, and the wounding continued.

To their surprise and relief, about that time, Mater, leading two rounceys laden with pavaises, crossbow bolts and food, appeared out of the whiteness. The boys' spirits soared, for they were greatly heartened at the sight of her. They had no sooner placed the pavaises across the front of their position when arrows began hissing through the air, thudding into the shield wall. Lancaster captains had decreed the Wasps a priority target that must be eliminated without delay. Thanks to Mater, her boys now had their protective shields.

'Three hinds passant!' called out Didi, pointing over the dropped, writhing warriors at a green banner being advanced beside an especially well-harnessed knight of Lancaster. 'Trollope!'

Immediately, Edmund responded to the sighting, '*Aufstapeln!*' he yelled.

As rehearsed so many times the boys clustered about Didi Wattle to form a pyramid. In an instant, he became the foundation support of a human platform as the boys surrounded him forming a triangle – three boys a-side – linking arms. Two boys on each side climbed on the shoulders of the others.

'Heads together!' Yelled Edmund at the topmost boys.

Wee Willie began placing the pavaise as protection to the human tower.

'Snowwhite!' called Edmund. 'Wouldst like to expand thy purse by £100?'

'Yea, verily, *Rottmeister!*' Snowwhite answered, grinning from ear to ear at the thought of it.

'Trollope to the Devil then!' called Edmund, taking Snowwhite's place in the pyramid.

In the blink of an eye, Snowwhite was upon on the boys' shoulders and resting his bow on the platorm of heads. John, along with William, Lord Fauconberg, prepared to act as his loaders. Their services were not required, for Henry's mighty captain and artful planner, the pride of Lancaster, was killed outright by Thomas Moxen's first bolt. In a trice the pyramid broke up and the boys resumed their former positions. They were greatly relieved, for a pyramid was not a formation to hold for long in an affray.

With their captain brought down and the Wasps halting forward progress, the right flank of Lancaster became enfeebled and dispirited. Following the failure of that flanking attack, the centre battle of the Lancastrian advance also stalled. It was all in tatters. The crafted battle ploy, for a coordinated frontal assault all along the line, coinciding with that surprise flank attack, was to have driven the Yorkists backwards and down into Dintingdale breaking them.

With his battle front holding, King Edward and his fellowship raced on foot through the now heavily falling snow towards the Wasps' position.

'Right grandly you have stopped them, William!' he called. He was still full of spirit and energy after hours of fighting and his armour gave evidence of his full involvement. There were dents, gouges, creases and puncture holes everywhere. Also dried and drying bloodstains in splashes and streaks from his shoulders to his feet. He removed his crested sallet and handed it to his armour bearer, whereupon he was passed a flagon of wine by his standard bearer, Ralph Vestynden, the contents of which he drained at once.

'They threw everything at us, yet we are holding,' called out Warwick as he detached himself from the affray where men were still hacking away with bills, axes and mauls, some thirty yards distant.

The Wasp defensive block was continuing to keep up a steady rain of bolts, causing the Lancaster men to fall back and put some distance between them so as to try and lessen the effectiveness of the shooting.

Fauconberg jabbed a mailed gauntlet in the Wasps' direction.

'That's why our line mended and finally held! Look at them, Edward, bloody bairns, little more than linen soilers – blasted children!'

'I see no children on this field, William, I see the Avenger of Blood and his warriors. For just as King David of Israel had his Mighty Men, here attired in yellow and black, I have mine!' There was great pride in his voice. As he spoke he raised his arm to salute.

Simultaneously, every kneeling boy responded by rising to his feet, turning and together with the already-standing loaders, they raised their right arms, bent at the elbow, and touched their foreheads.

'The little beggars!' laughed Fauconberg, shaking his head and obviously swilling with admiration. 'I love every last one of 'em!'

The sight brought no small amusement to the king's fellowship and other gathered captains, providing a welcome distraction from the horrible maiming and butchery going on all around.

Suddenly, a cry arose, which became an almighty roar and swept through the Yorkist lines. 'A-Norfolk A-Norfolk A-Norfolk' was on the lips of thousands of weary men-at-arms, signalling at long last the arrival of the Yorkist rearward battle.

Within minutes two foreprickers, directed to the king's standard, rode up escorting a knight, a hard rider, who had been liaising between the two Yorkist battles and the Duke of Norfolk's rearward formation.

Sir William Hussey of Sleaford knelt before the king.

'John Mowbray, Duke of Norfolk sends his greetings, my liege, praying that this day goes well and begs to be informed where to deploy.'

'And how fares Norfolk, for we hear he's sorely pained?'

'He's led the rearward to this place, but I fear another must take command, for he is smitten with a grave mal-humour and flux,' said Sir William.

'No matter, for the sight of your face could bring no less glad tidings than that of Gabriel himself, good William,' said the king.

A breathless Earl of Warwick, struggling to remain upright as he approached, interrupted,

'Best bring Norfolk up to reinforce this, our vanward battle, for we are greatly thinned and desperately cut about.'

Disregarding his lieutenant's suggestion, the king inquired as to the numbers in array to the banner of Norfolk. When King Edward learned that 5,000 were at that moment forming up in Dingtingdale he declared to all around him his wishes and issued his battle directive.

'The Lord has granted that this day be ours. Hence, let there be a hurrying to end this matter, forthwith.'

John's heart soared, for this was the voice of a true and magnificent warrior King of England, cast in the likeness of Edward III and Henry V. So contrasted and so unlike the gentleness of the oft moonstruck Henry VI, who had lost to England so vast a dominion in France.

King Edward IV called out loudly for all to hear, sweeping an arm in the Wasps' direction,

'Behold! these Wasps provide the stoutest hinge!'

'Then, it's Norfolk to the latch!'

'Let us kick open this rotted door, afore the light fails on this Palm Sunday Field!'

His words were greeted by a roar as hundreds roundabout gathered their hearts for a final effort.

The forty-six-year-old John Mowbray, Duke of Norfolk was sick through hosting a tumour, yet he had raised a small army in the cause of the House of York and had led it to Towton Field. He had months left to live. It was King Edward who, knowing of the duke's plight, took command of the rearward battle.

The lines of struggling opposed armies had, during the morning and early afternoon, been gradually swinging until Lancaster no longer had its left flank resting against the marshland across the London Road. Instead it had become aligned with the highway. The road to Towton vill and the Lancastrian baggage park camped there was wide open for capture However, the king resisted the temptation to march on to the village, which would have threatened the Lancastrian flank and line of withdrawal. The sight of the enemy's carts and the spoil to be gained could have proved too much for the men arrayed under the white lion of Mowbray. The prospects of plunder would have served as an overwhelming distraction.

King Edward formed up his fresh troops into fighting formation and, with drums beating the advance, led them behind his standard on to the bloody field. At their arrival, John Dinham sounded the retreat for his tired Devonshires. As they disengaged, many crossed themselves in relief at being spared, for a while at least.

With a mighty roar, men from Bishop's Lynn, Downham Market, Thetford, Swaffenham, East Dereham and Norwich slammed full tilt into the northerners. Within less than an hour, the now desperate Northumberlanders were pushed back and the Cumberlanders found themselves with an open flank. In a trice, Edward, upon seeing the opportunity, committed his small reserve, thrusting arrayed men from the manors of Hellesdon, Drayton and Caister through the gap.

Panic spread like ripples in a mill pond.

Small groups at first – survivors from fighting wedges which had lost their vintenars and hence their cohesion – began running. Some knights and retainers stood their ground, but all such desperately defending units were quickly isolated, environed and hacked down by the fresh warriors.

From the instant that Yorkist forces had crested the hill earlier that morning, captains of Lancaster had with confidence and assurance cried havoc, so confident were they in their superior numbers and their masterful war plan. They could expect nothing less from their victorious enemy. There was to be no mercy shown on Palm Sunday Field. A simple matter of flee or die applied. Bills by men-at-arms and indeed, every other manner of weapon, were being cast away. Furthermore, to assist easy escape through the foot-deep snow, drifted in places to waist-height, items of armour were being discarded in every direction. Once proud banners were flung aside and trampled on by their former bearers as they fled the field.

Lords' squires were bringing forward mounts to spirit away their masters from the dreadful catastrophe that was unfolding on a massive scale. London Road, which twisted and turned northward in the direction of Tadcaster and York, soon become clogged with fleeing riders. Instant death awaited any who were overtaken. It came in the form of a blow to the head or a stab in the back.

Because the array of battles had swung until the lines were no longer from west to east, but had finally ended in battle formations running from north to south. So the direction of flight was towards the deep valley of the Cock and a single narrow bridge.

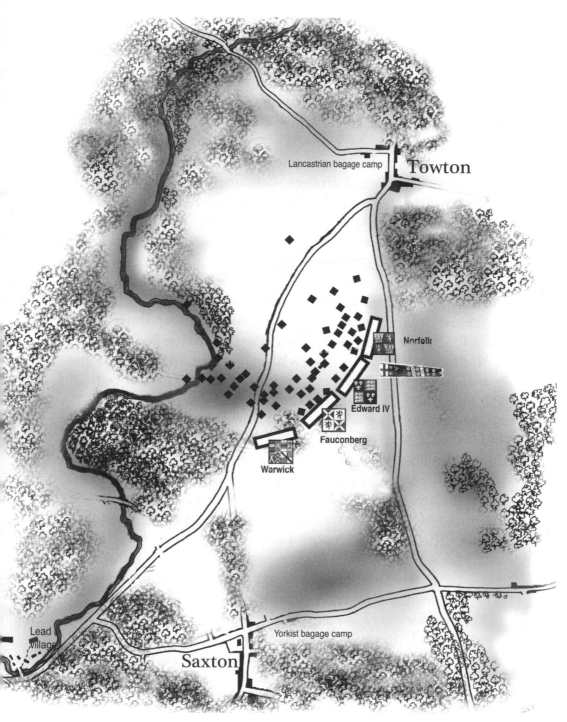

Lancastrian bagage camp

Towton

Norfolk

Edward IV

Fauconberg

Warwick

Lead Village

Yorkist bagage camp

Saxton

'Look, they turn the back! See how they run!' cried Didi, clapping Daub on the back.

Holy Holy Cantor, a *Ladenschütze* in *Rotte Gelb*, dropped to his knees, crying, 'We have survived, have we not? The day is ours and we're still upright and unarmed – thanks be to God.' The youngster from Canterbury sobbed uncontrollably.

From the baggage camp ranged about Saxton Church horses were being hastened forward for Yorkist lords, knights and captains. Mounted archers were arming themselves with lances. Foreprickers and other cavalry were arriving on the field, their mounts slithering and neighing. Fauconberg and *Hauptmann* Dietz rode up to where the Wasps stood gaping at the incredible rout unfolding before them.

Mounted on a stout-legged destrier which reared and fretted, eager for the off, the old soldier, Fauconberg, waving a vicious-looking mace, called out, 'We're for the chase, boys – to the victor his spoil – if you'll take my advice you'll hasten to their baggage camp!' He wheeled about and spurred his horse, calling back over his shoulder, 'Rich pickings to be had. You've earned it. Let none deprive you!'

Thousands of men were casting off their liveried surcoats and tabards and running into the deep vale of the Cock, taking the only route of escape from Towton Dale. The beck was swollen by the day's heavy and almost constant precipitation until its former banks could no longer be identified with certainty. The wide water-flow swilled and surged through the snow-blanketed valley, forming a formidable barrier to the fleeing men of Lancaster. Hundreds could be seen up to their waists as they fought against the icy flow and struggled to reach the other side.

When they were overtaken by mounted pursuers, they were hacked down from behind. There was little mercy shown on that most holy-tide. Church bells sounding Vespers could be heard; the fight had gone on all day. The outcome had been far too close-run for leniency or mercy to stay the victors' rancour. Throughout that Sunday the northerners had taken a heavy toll on family and friend. Also, Lancaster's hordes had, in the weeks leading up to the frightful day, plundered and killed south of the Trent. There had been a spoiling of Yorkist properties in the county. At their instigation, on their initiative, supporters of Henry VI had ruthlessly started the all-too-familiar practice of beheading vanquished lords. The tables had been well and truly turned.

However, a demonstration of outstanding mercy was shown that day which served to add to the ever-growing legend of The Hawk.

'Save us, in the name of the Blessed Virgin, save us!'

The plea came from a wide-eyed billman from Dewsbury, who had been shot through the thigh by a crossbow bolt. Unable to run, he dragged himself towards the Wasps, his hands trying to contain and hold back spurts of blood. Assisting him was a young lad, who had suffered a hip wound. Both gasped in pain at every step. They were obviously closely-related kin.

'We'll finish 'em!' called out a Warwickshire man, stomping through the snow in their direction, swinging a vicious-looking war hammer.

'In the name of the Lord Jesus, I beg you, no!' the man screamed, grabbing the boy and shielding him with his own body.

Edmund strode forward, positioning himself between the intended victims and their would-be executioner. 'Quarrel wounds are our brand mark,' he said threateningly. 'The Wasps lay claim on all who bear them, for they are our spoils of war.'

The ragged-staff vintenar stopped in his tracks, his countenance displaying a sequence of emotions beginning with anger, then bewilderment, followed by nervousness and ending in servility. Lowering his eyes, he backed away and clumsily half-bowed in embarrassment. Then, shaking his head as if he hadn't the faintest idea why he felt discomforted, he hurried off to join the men of his spearhead, who were busy delivering the *coup de grâce* to the wounded and filling bags with items of value.

Stripping off his black and yellow striped surcoat, Edmund attached it to the lance which had formerly flown the Lancastrian banner of Trollope. Didi Wattle had retrieved Trollope's flag – green field charged with three hinds – to present to Snowwhite.

Holding the makeshift banner aloft, Edmund began shouting, 'Quarter, with the Wasps!' And soon all the boys were chorusing the cry.

Then it began. First those who had fallen wounded to the crossbows hobbled as best they could, where they gathered for safety all about. Then others began an awful race of life and death, dodging and weaving between the slashing and stabbing of executioners intent upon finishing them off. Fathers, sons, uncles, nephews, brothers, neighbours and friends clutched each other. Weaponless, they warded off blows and began running – running for the banner which meant mercy and life.

Soon there were upwards of three hundred souls pressing in upon the Wasps on every side. All eyes of the terrified captives were fixed on the pole and surcoat fluttering from it, for all the world as if a single glance aside would result in instant death. As Moses holding aloft the copper serpent in the wilderness meant salvation for all those sore-afflicted who looked towards it, likewise it was with Edmund's banner on Towton field.

'We must take them from this slaughterhouse to our baggage camp,' Edmund called to John.

Then Mater was with them and, linking arms with Edmund, the two led the Wasps in the direction of Saxton vill in ragged column. Wasps were spaced either side of the prisoners to act as their protectors.

After feeding and binding of wounds, Edmund advised the shaking and shocked crowd that first they rest, sleep if they could, then on the morrow make for Castleford via the Roman road. He further advised that they remain together until they crossed the Aire before dispersing to their homes.

'Who are you, please?' one of the prisoners, a blanket maker from Heckmondwike, asked, his chin quivering, in cold, pain or from fear.

Before any could answer, another prisoner cut in – a voice that John recognised. It was Ralph Reresby, their former master. 'They are from our manor, at Thryberg. At least, the two Hawksworth brothers are.'

His tone of voice had lost the biting edge since John had last heard it at Thryberg Hall over two months ago on St Paula's Day. His recent brush with death may have been responsible for the softening. Though John wondered then, if they would ever return to herd pigs at Reresby Manor. Their services would be required by the new king for some time to come. Would they continue to follow the Bavarian mercenary, Jason Dietz? Then there were riches in head bounty that had surely amassed; a tidy sum already. Certainly the heads of Clifford and Dacre were in the bag. Percy of Northumberland had been brought low, wounded and, should he have succumbed or been captured, they could rightfully claim a portion on his head. It had annoyed John when Edmund handed the chance to claim Trollope's head to Snowwhite – given him it on a plate. Would they ever be rich with such foolish and reckless generosity?

Then there was the mystery of their mother's family, likely some supporters of Lancaster in the north. There might surely be wealth to be had there, for the brothers were not bastards. Their mother may have been disinherited, but what about grandchildren? Once the family knew who they were, they could hammer on a northern gate. Although, John remembered Edmund's fierce hatred of any he considered to be a contributor to the death of their mother.

So he wondered and dreamed about their future until the bells for Compline brought him to his senses.

'Hawksworths!' The call came from a red-nosed herald who nudged his palfrey through the packed ranks surrounding Mater's wagon. 'Hawksworths of Thryberg!' The pursuivant was leading a horse intended for their use. They had been summoned to attend the royal quarters of Edward IV situated among the captured baggage train and former Lancastrian camp at Towton vill. They would reach the encampment by way of the London Road.

Along the way to the village there were terrible sights of carnage. Corpses bearing fearsome wounds and stripped of clothing were being dragged to where piles were being created. Once there, they were thrown, like so many pigs' carcasses post Michaelmastide, on to the pile until each horrible heap mounted up to the height of a horse's bridle. The odd dismembered limb was flung, without regard, atop the obscene heap. Blood spread about from the base of those awful piles, mixing with the brown slush. About the heaps there was the repugnant smell of faeces, emitting from ruptured entrails where some unfortunates had suffered disembowelling. The whole mess resembled what any glimpse into Hell would disclose.

The Duke of Somerset's spacious tent had several compartments. It was tucked behind a small hill where the London Road made an abrupt turn towards Tadcaster. The baggage camp was being prepared for the victors' advancements, elevations, rewards and honours. Edmund and John sheltered in the lee of the royal tent and were in a position to hear the goings-on of their betters, so flushed with victory and high spirits.

'There's no sign of Somerset, Exeter, Wiltshire or Devon among the slain – oh how they run!' laughed the Earl of

Warwick, striding in and throwing down his gauntlets on the camp table.

'While ever anyone of that brood of peers draws breath there remains a threat to the throne, and ourselves,' said Fauconberg.

'Of the commons there are plenty about, but there can be little doubt, the lords are over the Wharf at Tadcaster by now and riding hard for York,' said Warwick.

'There's still light left this day and they may still be overtaken, for Norfolk's riders are in hot pursuit,' Edward said as he emerged from the inner compartment of the voluminous tent. 'Should they evade our spears tonight, then the morrow awaits them.'

The king had divested himself of the harness of war and looked relaxed in royal surcoat and fur-lined, full-length robe, on his head a golden crown.

'There are those who wish to pledge to you their allegiance, my lord.' The King-at-Arms for south of the Trent, William Hawkslowe, bowed low as he spoke.

'I'm sure they do, faithful Clarenceux,' said the king, seating himself in a grand, high-backed chair embroidered with the Beaufort arms. 'And I'll wager a king's ransom that among them is your counterpart for the north.'

'The wager would be easily won, my liege.'

'Then bid him in, for we have an unfinished communion.'

It was only the previous night that Edmund and John had witnessed the exchange between the herald for the north and King Edward. It was with some interest, at least on John's part, that they prepared to eavesdrop and observe the meeting. Lanterns were being lit as the Norroy King-at-Arms entered the tent and stood before the king, bowing stiffly as he did so.

'In view of yesterday's exchange, William Tyndale, methinks a more obeisant attitude appropriate.' Immediately, the herald dropped to his knees, for there could be no mistaking the veiled threat in Edward's voice.

'At the outset of this holy day we implored the Almighty to rule between Lancaster and York. What has been His answer, Norroy?'

'My liege lord, there can be no denying, God has granted York the victory. And I beg mercy for my exchange with you last evening past.'

'You were truculent and offensive, Tyndale.'

'If it please, my lord king, I was under charge and hence compulsion to Henry and so ordered with delivering certain messages.'

'You executed your duties with relish. But no matter, you have much work to do counting and recording dead nobles and knights, for there must be many vacant titles in my kingdom this night. Castles, houses and manors have vacancy and will require new owners. When I next see your face, you will be the bearer of a completed list.' So saying, the king dismissed the herald and his assistant pursuivant with a wave, for there was a pleasant task for Edward to perform and he was eager to be about it.

It was time for the advancement of faithful subjects and, as darkness descended, hundreds packed around the king's tent. Glowing hot braziers provided warmth and light to the scene. It had stopped snowing. The grand high-backed chair of Lancastrian Henry Beaufort, 3rd Duke of Somerset, had pride of place on slightly raised ground, above it a hastily erected canopy. Each side stood armoured men of the king's fellowship, their shining armour cleaned of the day's gore and polished. The standard of Edward IV fluttered stiffly in the gentle westerly blowing across the now silent battlefield. To receive those about to be honoured, a bearskin had been placed before the makeshift throne.

Rousing cheers were deafening as Edward IV stepped from the tent and men clapped their hands in sheer joy. Relief, too, for the day had begun for each of them harbouring horrors both well-known and unimaginable. Yet they were alive and much richer, for earthenware pots of coinage had been discovered in the paymaster's wagon. And what further prospects? The future held promise of much more to come under the new warrior king.

When the king drew his sword, silence fell. He turned to his herald for south of the Trent, William Hawkslowe, who stepped forward bearing a scroll from which he announced, 'For fidelity, and good faith, for saving the life of his royal person numerous times this day, step forward... Ralph Vestynden esquire.'

There was a gasp of surprise in some quarters, especially from behind the throne, for Vestynden was Edward's standard bearer and not immediately thought of when there were so many captains of array gathered. His grateful king held out an arm and indicated the bearskin.

'Come, Ralph, why so shocked? For thou didst ward off many a blow aimed at my handsome poll.'

The mood of the gathering was judged aright by the king, for there was much good-natured laughter, especially as the tall Londoner slipped in the slush as he rounded the chair and stumbled, on all fours on to the bearskin.

'I was about to invite you to kneel, Ralph, but in eager haste thou hast arrived already knelt.'

All were delighted and applauded. Tapping the flat of his blade on Vestynden's shoulders, the king declared, 'For services to this royal person, Ralph Vestynden esquire, I dub thee knight of this realm. Arise, Sir Ralph!'

Next the name of one of Edward's retainers – and friend – William Hastings; then Devonshire captain, John Dinham, and so the advancing in degree of forty and more men proceeded for the next half hour. Until finally, the king called for Edmund to step up, sheathing his sword as he did so.

'There would have been another knight, had I been allowed my way.' He placed his hands on Edmund's shoulders, turning him around to face the crowd. 'No man of you has fought harder than this boy. No vintenar, nay, no captain, hath placed those under his charge so effectively. He and his brother loader,' acknowledgement was made in John's direction, 'singlehandedly dispirited Northumberland and in so doing secured our right flank.'

The king waved for John to join Edmund, 'When our left flank faltered and was about to crumble because of a sneak attack, who did we turn to that we might stop the rot?'

He stood between the brothers, his hands about their shoulders, '"*Wespen*! Throw in the Wasps!" was the cry from my captains. Yet, I am advised by my elders, we cannot advance boys into knights. What I can do, is put them on the way to knighthood by securing for them both the office of squire.'

There followed much cheering and applauding, accompanied by the crowd making a buzzing noise.

*   *   *   *

WHEN ALL ABOUT lay down that night to sleep – a deep exhausted sleep – a murderous band crept through the snow towards the king's tent.

John and Edmund had been allowed a space beside a brazier close by and, in his usual way, Edmund had built up snow walls into a snug shelter. Using the bearskin as flooring, the brothers were soon snugly wrapped for the night.

About the hour of Matins a heavy fellow stepped on John's foot, then cursed under his breath as he stumbled away and was engulfed in the blackness. The brazier coals glowed low and gave little light, explaining how the soldier had failed to see where the boys lay. John was about to say something, when Edmund placed a hand against his brother's chin and made a low shushing sound. Another figure passed over them and crouched beside the king's tent – then another. How many were there? John and Edmund appeared to be in the middle of an assault force of assassins about to launch an attack any second.

At the instant a knife pushed through the canvas of the king's tent and began making a slit so as to allow entry, Edmund yelled at the top of his voice, 'Alarm!' At the same moment, he swung his falchion in a sweep at the nearest figure. A loud scream told them that it had struck flesh. A blow from a pole-axe cracked against the heavy brazier with such force that glowing coal and logs shot and danced across the encampment. The wielder of the weapon had missed John and was about to have another go when Edmund barged into him. He must have been off-balance for he fell forward with his arm extended to prevent his fall. Using both hands, John brought his falchion down on the back of his neck with all the strength he could summon. The assassin's head dropped to his chest and he slumped to the ground, his body jerking in spasms.

Edmund had placed himself at the entrance to the king's tent and was swinging a pole-axe from side to side, denying three or four men entry. It would only be a matter of seconds before he would be overwhelmed. John launched himself at them from behind, hacking at the backs of their legs. One went down squealing, his tendons severed. As they turned to meet John's attack, Edmund lunged at the nearest to him. The pole-axe spike found a vital spot and the Lancastrian crumpled without a sound.

By then the encampment was wide awake and the brothers were no longer outnumbered and alone. With the attackers environed and being hacked down, the boys turned and ran into the king's tent.

In the compartment containing the cot, King Edward was kneeling helpless before a shadowy assailant.

With arm raised about to bring down a battleaxe, stood their father, John Hawksworth. Wide-eyed, stalled in the act of regicide, he glared at his sons for a moment, his deep scarred cheek seeming to quarter his face.

'John and Edmund, what a pother, what an ado. Now boys, begone.' His voice became low and urgent, 'This is no place for whelps of mine. Begone!'

Edmund leapt forward and plunged his dagger under the would-be assassin's rib-cage.

Craven vintenar, John Hawksworth had failed to adjudge the inveterate hatred which, like a demon, drove Edmund to destroy him. Too many days, far too many nights, the brothers had worked until exhausted to keep their dear, beautiful mother alive. Spoon feeding, attending her infirmity; watching, ever keeping vigil, helpless to reverse her enfeeblement until on that terrible winter's night her life finally drained away and she breathed her last, cradled in Edmund's arms. That howl of despair, frustration and hatred John would never forget. Edmund had stood at the door of the croft, overlooking the piggery, and screamed at the stars, 'I hate you! I swear on my mother's blood – there will be an avenging!'

Vintenar John Hawksworth would never have understood, not in a millennium, to what depths his desertion had scarred his sons. Their mother had defied her parents for his love and, as a consequence, lost everything. He had repaid her by abandonment and sought adventure and to make his fortune as a retainer with the Cliffords of Skipton. Not a single penny did he send to his family, thus ensuring its dire penury.

Surprise and hurt, carved on alabaster, was how he appeared to John as his father, white-faced clutched at the bollock dagger protruding from his chest. 'Why... how' he gurgled, his eyes rolling up until only the whites showed.

A wave of revulsion swept over John. He should have felt pleased but there was no satisfaction only sadness. '*Cui bono.*'

John said aloud. 'Pray where is the gain in this?' Ignoring John's belated protest his brother heartlessly continued:

'Our mother's parents! Who are they? Quickly, for you are finished.' Cold, callous questioning, considering what he had just done. Their father couldn't or wouldn't answer and slid to the floor where he passed away with a rattling sound.

'He's stabbed his own father to save the king.' The Earl of Warwick sounded incredulous.

'It's the first time today I felt sorely afraid,' said the king bewildered. 'I was as helpless as a lamb before the slaughterer, our cause lost forever.'

The tent became full of lords and knights, none of them in harness, yet many with bloodied weapons after dealing with the forty and more assassins hell-bent on murdering the new king and victor of Palm Sunday Field.

King Edward picked up his sword-belt and, unsheathing the blade, he commanded Edmund kneel. And before there could be uttered a word of protest, he said to those gathered,

'I will not be gainsayed again. Here kneeling before you, lords and knights, is the true Avenger of Blood.'

Addressing Edmund the king announced, 'I care not for thy tender years, nor for thy low degree.

'Thou hast never served as squire? Bah! it matters not a jot!

'Never has there been a master so well-served as I,

'Nor monarch found such loyalty among all his subjects.'

Placing the flat of his blade on Edmund's shoulder, he proceeded with the accolade,

'By Divine anointing and confirmed by valiant deeds –

'Thou truly are the Avenger of Righteous Blood.

'Before this gathering of lords and these witnesses here gathered, I dub thee...

'Paramount knight in all England,

'Arise, Sir Edmund Hawksworth of Thryberg!'

Epilogue

The Heretic Shall Burn on St Ethelreda's Day

DONCASTER DITCH was reached by the mile-long procession led by a single cart as church bells sounded the onset of None. The despondent and sullen procession from Conisbrough had come to a halt. Swinging across from his horse and onto the cart the serjeant-at-mace muttered regrets as he secured manacles about John's wrists. There was a gentleness in his actions not usually reserved for the condemned. Ahead, across the bridge leading to St Sepulchre Gate, townspeople were gathered waiting to throw faggots onto the cart, lured by promises of Divine favour from conscientious priests.

John, at that moment, became aware that his remaining life on earth could no longer be counted in hours, but in minutes. For him time was pouring away relentlessly, like fine sand in the glass and that dreadful realisation served to heighten his awareness to each sight, sound and smell. Stench from the ditch, which served as a depository for the town's chamber pots, offal and every other kind of filth, was particularly pungent and made more keen by the warm June day. Excited chatter from a crowd of children which had poured across the bridge to enjoy the spectacle, was silenced. The mites received short shrift from the ill-tempered crowd. Each side of the dusty road larks were busy trilling their songs as they soared and descended over the green fields of growing corn. For the first time in his life John noted that the song they sang in the ascent differed to the one in the descent. Grinding of millstones and creaking and rattling of sails, wafted down from a nearby windmill perched on the only hillock on the otherwise flat approaches to town. Flocks of startled carrion noisily took to the wing, disturbed in their scavenging by the children who, thwarted in their intent to harry the condemned man, instead, flung stones at the birds.

A gust from a brisk summer breeze tugged at John's coat before deftly removing his cap, sending it bowling into the crowd.

'Who was your family in the north? Were your grandparents truly of high degree?' asked the finely clad minstrel. 'Did The Thryberg Hawk exact his revenge upon them?' The minstrel, mounted on a dun-coloured courser, had ridden behind the cart from Conisbrough. With the cart stopped he was alongside eagerly awaiting the reply.

John was brought from his daydreaming with a jolt 'Our grandparents were the de Plumptons of Spofforth.'

'Then the blood of the gentry was in your veins?'

'Sir William de Plumpton was among the Lancastrian battles on Palm Sunday Field, but he escaped the rout,' said John. 'However, his son, our uncle, was killed.'

'And did Edmund forgive them for your mother's disowning?'

'Edmund had yet to learn the beauty of Christian forgiveness. He faced them in the summer of 1461, on St Margaret's Day, and sought mortal combat. Another uncle, Robert, championed for his father and was slain by Edmund.'

'What of the bride's forfeit?' the minstrel asked.

The procession was on the move again and the narrow bridge did not allow for the minstrel to remain alongside. Then they entered Doncaster's streets.

En route along Baxter Gate to the designated place of execution faggots were tossed on to the cart by those who had accepted the bribe offered by the church. There were promises of indulgences to commit sins for forty days for those who contributed to the execution of the heretic, excommunicated by Pope Julius II. Yet there was something missing from the occasion – the baying of the crowd. There were no insults, no jeering as the procession proceeded along Baxter Gate. It had become widely known that the condemned prisoner was the elder brother of the Plantagenet hero Sir Edmund Hawksworth. They would rather that he lived to tell more of the tale.

'What of the bride's forfeit?' The minstrel, once again had managed to regain his position beside the cart. 'Was that secret paid to your brother?'

'The Lady Isabel became my wife following the Battle of Hexham,' John said.

'But the forfeit?' The ministrel persisted.

'That surely is a private matter. But, anyway, my brother could not countenance its payment to himself when my Lady was so mentally tortured.'

Objections by the Guild of Bakers had failed to prevent the heretic, John Hawksworth, being carted past their members' shops. Along St George's Gate the silent column paraded slowly amid a crowd of mute onlookers; on past St George's Church and Moot Hall into Fisher Gate where a halt was called to remove carts and benches which had been flung across the street to form a barrier. Clergy from St George's worked in a near frenzy to clear the way.

'Where is your brother, Sir Edmund, now? You never did tell us.' It was Brother Naulty, the Conisbrough chaplain, who asked the question, reaching up from the pressing throng and handing John back his cap as he did so. 'Wear your cap and keep your dignity.'

'My thanks good friend. Edmund is in France, at least he was,' said John.

A Woodcock's feather had been attached to his cap. The sight of it lifted John's heart, for among the crowd a kind soul had decided he would die wearing a symbol of victory.

'Did Edmund continue to command the Wasps?' Called the minstrel.

'Until after the fighting at Berwick, where they suffered mightily,' replied John. 'Following which, Edmund and I found ourselves on opposing sides at Barnet, when the kingmaker was slain.'

'Surely he must know of your plight today,' called Tiptoe from where he was busily tripping clergymen up and throwing items they were removing back into the road.

'It would make no odds to him now, he also became a Wycliffite. Following the Battle of Tewksbury he renounced revenge seeking and embraced the role of a peacemaker.'

'But verily he would do all he could to save you?' said Tiptoe.

'Not so, for both of us, Edmund and I, believe with all our hearts in forgiveness and in yielding to the wrath. Both our lives were wasted in doing the Devil's work these many years. God has permitted my dying this day, and I accept no saviour other than Our Lord.'

Suddenly they were on the move again. Brother Rollo had grabbed the reins of the horse and, beating the animal with a stick, began pulling it through the barricade.

John's heart sank as he clapped eyes on the stake awaiting him down by the river – an upright timber wedged tight in an old 32-gallon ale barrel. Choice of position for the execution, close to the convergence of the Cheswold with the Don, would ease clean-up afterwards. His charred remains would simply be swept into the river. His legs began to shake uncontrollably and, in a cold sweat, he sought to recall words of comfort. Words of St Paul, the first pistle to the Corinthians, he remembered, for there had been previous occasions of late when those words had eased his torment.

'God is faithful, he will not allow you to suffer beyond your strength,' John muttered aloud. 'He will help you to bear it.'

He closed his eyes and began to pray that he would die with dignity, without outcry.

'Halt!' The weary old carriage horse stopped immediately, stubbornly resisting all the tugging and pulling by the priests. 'Get him down at once!' The town bailiff was pushing through the crowd. 'A pardon. There's a king's pardon!'

With growing excitement, the cry 'king's pardon' was taken up by the crowd. The outstretched arms of his two guards offering to help him down brought tears to John's eyes. Then there was Jack Naulty by his side shaking his hand and clapping him on the back. Tiptoe and old Tom Philip, who had faithfully accompanied the cart the three miles on foot, were attempting to hoist John on their shoulders. With good-natured laughter the serjeant-at-mace and his companion nudged the struggling older men aside and lifted John high on their own shoulders. An altogether different crowd turned about and made its way back along Fisher Gate towards the Moot Hall.

Blocking the way was the priest, Father Rollo, and the vicar of St George's, along with other priests who served the church chantries. The determind clerics had raced through the back streets and now barred the road.

'Stop this madness! The prisoner was found guilty by a bishop's court. Thus there can be no pardon but from His Holiness the Pope himself,' yelled Rollo at the crowd.

'You are challenging a pardon by Henry VIII? This matter should be judged aright,' called back Jack Naulty.

With as many of the crowd who could gain access, John, still in manacles, was taken up into the nearby Moot Hall. The rest of the crowd packed into the undercroft and on to the stairs.

Oddly, a slight woman in her fifties took it upon herself to preside over the impromptu hearing. From head to foot she was dressed in black and held a purse-banner bearing a cartouche with the arms of Sir Marmaduke Constable, High

Sheriff of Yorkshire. She ordered the clergymen to be seated on a bench along one side of the hall and indicated that John should stand to her right along with his guards. In a powerful voice, unexpected because of her age and diminutive size, she announced to the gathering, 'You must all be aware that the present king's father, Henry VII, granted pardons. You would also have come to know that his son has carried on this merciful tradition and on the event of his coronation, likewise grants pardon to any supplicant.'

Father Rollo was on his feet. 'By what authority do you interfere in ecclesiastical matters?' His face flushed with embarrassment and annoyance.

'Since when did Mother Church assume execution of the condemned as her prerogative?' she cut back coolly. 'The ecclesia hand over to secular authority to do to death the miscreant. This matter is no longer within the Church's jurisdiction.'

'His offence was against the Church and it was an ecclesiastical court that found him guilty,' said Rollo.

'That is not in question here. We possess a king's pardon.' So saying, she handed the letter to Jack Naulty. 'If you please, good Brother, read it aloud.'

In a clear voice the Conisbrough cleric began to read:

'For John Hawksworth – Dispatch of pardon

'The King, greetings to all his subjects and faithful to whom Henry VII granted favour. May you know that from our special grace we have pardoned, remitted and released and by the present royal pardon, remit and release entirely to John Hawksworth, bachelor, otherwise called Jonathan, or by any other name whatever any riots, murders, treasons, felonies, insurrections, confederacies, conspiracies and all other offences whatsoever committed or perpetrated by John Hawksworth himself before the twenty-fifth day of April last, passed against the pledge of his allegiance.

Henry VIII, at Westminster the nineteenth day of May, 1509.'

Father Naulty held the document high allowing others to examine it.

'You carry the badge of the High Sheriff of Yorkshire, but on whose authority?' asked Father Rollo, who was beginning to realise that the burning might not take place after all.

'On the authority of the Lord Lieutenant of this County,' said the lady in black. 'Your betters, those holding high office in this land who are in London for the coronation on the morrow.'

Rollo stepped forward and gestured to read the pardon.

'Where is your warrant for this prisoner's execution?' she asked.

'He burnt it 'Rollo pointed at a spot in the crowd where Tiptoe was standing, arms folded, with eyes turned heavenward.

'You have no written authority to present before us that would stand as evidence and counter this pardon?'

'I need time to return to Lincoln for another warrant,' said Rollo.

'Enough! This pardon is dependent on the subject's sworn compliance,' she said. 'Do you, John Hawksworth, before all here gathered as witnesses, do you pledge your allegiance to your king?'

John knelt before the lady and placed his right hand on the High Sheriff's badge, 'Verily, I swear before all my solemn oath to be a faithful subject of King Henry VIII and all his issue.'

'Our business is completed. There is nothing more to be said,' announced the lady in black.

A mighty cheer rang out and it was taken up by the crowds in the street. The brother of the Thryberg Hawk would not burn on St Ethelreda's Day.

The defeated clergy were borne away by the press of the crowd leaving the Moot Hall chamber, down the steps and into the street, protesting as they went. When last seen Father Rollo was fleeing into St George's Church, calling 'sanctuary' with a yelling mob in pursuit.

334

The serjeant-at-mace removed the manacles and another handed John his precious English language Bible and the writings of Wycliffe.

'To whom do I owe my life?' said John bowing before the mysterious woman in black.

'Do you still not know me?' She reached out and took the hand of the serjeant-at-mace. Holding out her other hand to John, she said, 'Make me a bell, John love. O, do make me a bell.'

'Could it be... little Eleanor?' gasped John in disbelief, as smiling she curtsied low before him. 'Is it really you, Eleanor?'

'...the Bastard,' she confirmed, with a twinkle in her eye.

Appendices

THE WARS OF THE ROSES

EDWARD III (1327–77) sired five sons who reached manhood. The eldest, Edward, the 'Black Prince', died in 1376 months before his father. Edward III's grandson, Richard II ascended to the throne at the age of ten. The youngster's rule became tyranical and he was overthrown by his half-cousin, offspring of Edward III's third son, John of Gaunt. The reigns of Henry IV (1399–1413) and Henry V (1413–1422) followed. Henry V died suddenly at the age of thirty-five in 1422, apparently from dysentery. With the accession of Henry VI in 1422, problems began.

At the time of his succession, Henry VI was a nine-month-old baby. Henry's infancy and subsequent insanity were factors in the enmity which developed, with representatives of the Houses of Lancaster and York eventually competing for the crown of England.

The two main contenders for influence with Henry and his queen, Margaret of Anjou, were Richard Duke of York, and Edmund Beaufort, Duke of Somerset. Somerset's military disasters in France left him open to criticism from the party led by the Duke of York. By the summer of 1450 the bulk of the English possessions in northern France were back in French hands and there were further losses in the south of France. The loss of Castillon in 1453 ended the Hundred Years War.

That year Henry suffered his first bout of insanity and the Duke of York became Lord Protector. The Duke of Somerset was imprisoned in the Tower of London and his life may well have been saved only by the king's seeming recovery in late 1454. When Henry became aware of the intrigues around him, York was dismissed and Somerset returned to favour.

In 1455, the Duke of York initiated armed conflict against Henry's favoured court advisers and at the First Battle of St Albans Somerset was killed. Henry, who took no part in the

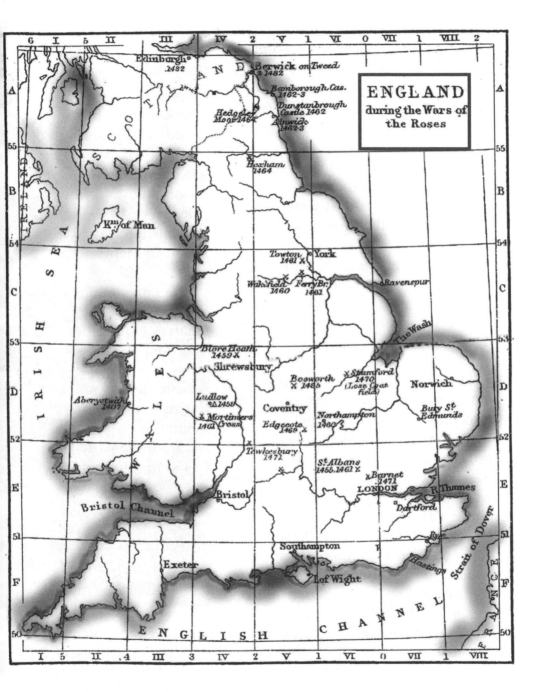

fighting, was captured, enabling York to become Lord Protector once more – only to be dismissed by Queen Margaret a year later. An uneasy peace prevailed until 1459, when warfare broke out once more, resulting in a Yorkist victory at Blore Heath to be followed by an ignominious rout for them at Ludford Bridge.

In July 1460, a Yorkist victory at the Battle of Northampton saw King Henry captured by them again. Despite having a successor in Prince Edward, Henry was forced to agree by Parliament that the Duke of York would succeed him. At last it seemed that the dynasty of the House of York was secured.

However, Queen Margaret and Lancastrian nobles gathered their forces in the north of England, and when the Duke of York moved north to protect his properties, he was killed at the Battle of Wakefield, Christmas week 1460. Triumphant, a Lancastrian horde advanced south and defeated Warwick at the Second Battle of St Albans. Again the House of Lancaster seemed to be winning the struggle for control of England when its forces recaptured King Henry. However, the

worthies of London had closed the city gates and subsequently Queen Margaret had to withdraw to Yorkshire and the city of York. The eldest son of the slain Duke of York, Edward, Earl of March, was proclaimed King Edward IV. He gathered the Yorkist

Rout of the Lancastrians at Towton; the struggle in the Cock Beck.

armies and marched north to confront the Lancastrians. He won a crushing victory at the Battle of Towton on Palm Sunday 1461.

After minor Lancastrian revolts were suppressed in 1464 Henry, who had been in hiding in Scotland and the North, was

341

captured once again. The young King Edward IV fell out with his chief supporter and advisor, the Earl of Warwick (known as the 'Kingmaker'). Edward had secretly married and in so doing alienated many friends and family members by favouring the upstart family of his new queen, Elizabeth Woodville. Warwick plotted first to supplant the king with Edward's younger brother George, Duke of Clarence.

Warwick and Clarence went on to exploit a disagreement between a member of the king's household, Sir Thomas Burgh, and one of Warwick's relations, Lord Welles. When Edward intervened on Sir Thomas' behalf, Welles' son, Sir Robert, raised an armed force, intending to join up with Warwick, who had been given permission to raise an army in the king's name. The conjunction did not take place, and on 12 March 1470 Edward defeated Sir Robert near Stamford at the Battle of Losecoat Field, so called because the rebels discarded their livery as they fled – it was found to be Clarence's. Warwick and Clarence were denounced as traitors and fled the country.

After failing in his attempt to replace Edward with Clarence, Warwick changed sides and threw his lot in with the House of Lancaster, turning to his former enemy Margaret of Anjou. He proposed a marriage between his daughter Anne and Margaret's son Prince Edward. Margaret agreed to join forces with Warwick. With men and supplies readily donated by Louis XI of France, Warwick returned to England, landing on the south coast on 13 September 1470.

A ruse drew King Edward off to the north. Challenged at Pontefract by Lord Montagu who had changed sides, he panicked, fleeing through Lincolnshire to Bishop's Lynn (present-day King's Lynn) from whence, in company with his brother Richard (Duke of Gloucester) and Lord Hastings, he sailed for the Low Countries, the dominions of Charles the Bold. His wife and mother-in-law were left to seek the sanctuary of Westminster Abbey. Edward had been overthrown without a fight and Henry VI was back on the throne for a second reign

MAJOR BATTLES OF
THE WARS OF THE ROSES

1455 First St. Albans *(22 May 1455)* Yorkist victory

1459 Blore Heath *(23 Sep 1459)* Yorkist victory

1459 Ludford Bridge *(12 Oct 1459)* Lancastrian victory

1460 Northampton *(10 Jul 1460)* Yorkist victory

1460 Wakefield *(30 Dec 1460)* Lancastrian victory

1461 Mortimor's Cross *(2 Feb 1461)* Yorkist victory

1461 Second St. Albans *(17 Feb 1461)* Lancastrian victory

1461 Ferrybridge *(28 Mar 1461)* Yorkist victory

1461 Towton *(29 Mar 1461)* Yorkist victory

1464 Hedgeley Moor *(25 Apr 1464)* Yorkist victory

1464 Hexham *(15 May 1464)* Yorkist victory

1469 Edgecote Moor *(26 Jul 1469)* Lancastrian victory

1470 Losecote Field *(12 Mar 1470)* Yorkist victory

1471 Barnet *(14 Apr 1471)* Yorkist victory

1471 Tewkesbury *(4 May 1471)* Yorkist victory

1485 Bosworth *(22 Aug 1485)*   Victor: **Henry Tudor**

1487 Stoke *(16 Jun 1487)*   Victor: King Henry VII (Tudor)

referred to as his 'Readeption'. It was to be short lived. Warwick and the supporters of Lancaster never became a strong, unified party; the common enemy had been vanquished in a bloodless engagement and former common grievances were easily revived once Henry was back on the throne.

In March 1471 Edward returned with a vengeance, landing at Ravenspur on the Humber. He claimed to be seeking merely the duchy of York, which was his right, and those who opposed his arrival were taken-in by this. He passed on to Nottingham and Leicester where he had a following and his ranks grew. Warwick withdrew to Coventry to await Clarence who was on the move with a sizable army. However, Clarence, faced by his brother, changed sides and joined him. Together they marched on London and arrested Henry VI.

Warwick with his supporters, his brother Montagu, Earl of Oxford and the Earl of Exeter confronted Edward in Hertfordshire near Barnet and were defeated. Warwick and his brother Montagu died in the fighting and Exeter was captured. So ended the activities of the so-called 'Kingmaker'. His alliance with the House of Lancaster was unappreciated by them and disparaged. Edward's other opponents were over in the west of the country and were gathering force.

The Duke of Somerset and the Duke of Devon rendezvoused with Queen Margaret and her son Edward, Prince of Wales, and played a cat-and-mouse game with Edward's army. At length the Lancastrians arrived at the crossing of the River Severn by a ford near Tewkesbury. Instead of crossing the river they decided to fight.

The Lancastrians were defeated and the principal leaders fled to take sanctuary in Tewkesbury Abbey. Queen Margaret was captured; her son Edward, Prince of Wales, killed. Somerset, Lords Wenlock and other leaders were executed. One Lancastrian leader named Tudor fled abroad.

All throughout the country it was realised that it had been a decisive battle. Henry VI, who was held prisoner in the Tower of

London was murdered immediately following the battle. The gentle, pious religious-minded monarch could no longer be used as a rallying point by those favouring Lancaster. Once hardened Lancastrians now made their peace with Edward IV.

A period of comparative calm followed, until King Edward died suddenly in 1483.

His surviving brother, Richard of Gloucester, made his move to prevent the unpopular Woodville family of Edward's widow from participating in government during the minority of Edward's son, Edward V. At a meeting at the Tower of London in June 1483 Richard stopped the proceedings, denounced a faithful supporter of the princes, William, Lord Hastings, and had his head chopped off immediately. He declared his nephews illegitimate using the suspect legitimacy of Edward IV's marriage to Elizabeth Woodville as pretext. The two boys never left the Tower and simply vanished.

The brief reign of Richard III ended when Henry Tudor, a distant relative of the Lancastrian kings who had inherited their claim, overcame and defeated him at Bosworth in 1485. Henry Tudor was crowned Henry VII, and married Elizabeth of York, daughter of Edward IV, to unite and reconcile the two houses. By this time the red and the white heraldic roses had come to the fore as devices for Lancaster and York and Henry Tudor adopted a composite badge.

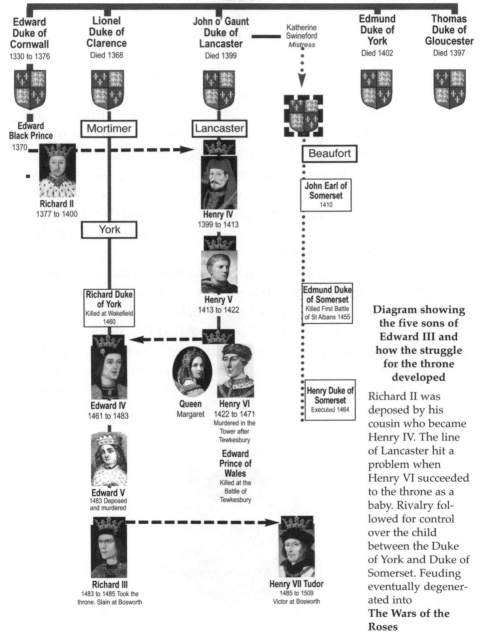

EDWARD III
1327 to 1377

Edward Duke of Cornwall	Lionel Duke of Clarence	John o' Gaunt Duke of Lancaster	Katherine Swineford *Mistress*	Edmund Duke of York	Thomas Duke of Gloucester
1330 to 1376	Died 1368	Died 1399		Died 1402	Died 1397

Edward Black Prince
1370

Mortimer

Lancaster

Beaufort

Richard II
1377 to 1400

John Earl of Somerset
1410

York

Henry IV
1399 to 1413

Henry V
1413 to 1422

Richard Duke of York
Killed at Wakefield 1460

Edmund Duke of Somerset
Killed First Battle of St Albans 1455

Edward IV
1461 to 1483

Queen Margaret

Henry VI
1422 to 1471
Murdered in the Tower after Tewkesbury

Henry Duke of Somerset
Executed 1464

Edward V
1483 Deposed and murdered

Edward Prince of Wales
Killed at the Battle of Tewkesbury

Richard III
1483 to 1485 Took the throne. Slain at Bosworth

Henry VII Tudor
1485 to 1509
Victor at Bosworth

Diagram showing the five sons of Edward III and how the struggle for the throne developed

Richard II was deposed by his cousin who became Henry IV. The line of Lancaster hit a problem when Henry VI succeeded to the throne as a baby. Rivalry followed for control over the child between the Duke of York and Duke of Somerset. Feuding eventually degenerated into **The Wars of the Roses**

346

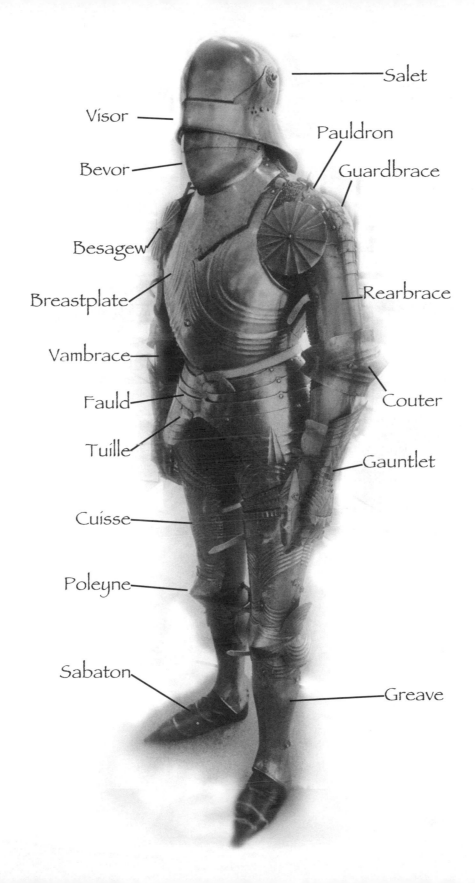

Salet

Visor

Bevor

Pauldron

Guardbrace

Besagew

Breastplate

Rearbrace

Vambrace

Fauld

Couter

Tuille

Gauntlet

Cuisse

Poleyne

Sabaton

Greave

A selection of English bills, lance and axe.

An early type of hand-held firearm. Edward IV favoured employing guns in his army and there is evidence of their use at Towton.

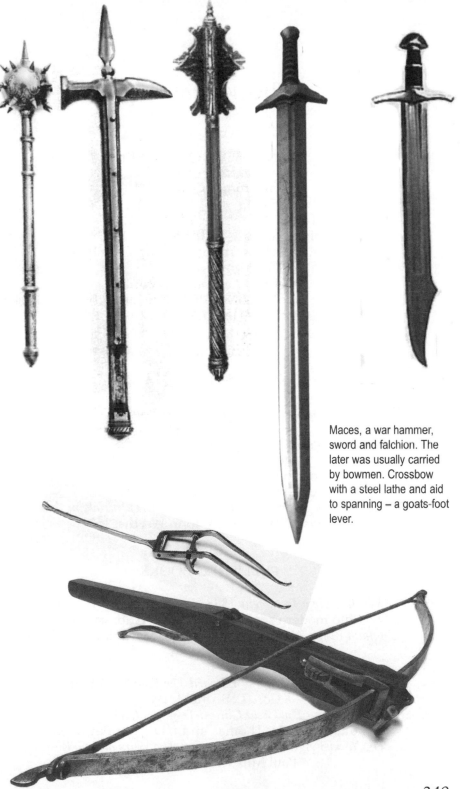

Maces, a war hammer, sword and falchion. The later was usually carried by bowmen. Crossbow with a steel lathe and aid to spanning – a goats-foot lever.

BIBLIOGRAPHY

ORIGINAL SOURCE MATERIAL

Conisbrough Court Rolls:
November 1459 to April 1460 DD YAR/C/1/40
October 1460 to September 1461 DD YAR/C/1/41
September 1461 to May 1462 DD YAR/C/1/42
(Doncaster Archives) Translated by Celia Parker

Duchy of Lancaster Records:
DL 37/30/80 (National Archives PRO) Translated by Celia Parker
DL 29/560/8899 (National Archives PRO)
Translated by Celia Parker

SECONDARY SOURCE MATERIAL

BARNSLEY CHRONICLE 1903 *History of Barnsley and District* series
by Eli Hoyle
The Pastons – a Family in the Wars of the Roses,
Edited by Richard Barber, 1981
Lincoln diocese documents 1450-1544
Edited with notes by Andrew Clark
*Collectanea Topographica, College of Arms (L1) Burials in the Black
Friars of Pontefract* by John Wrythe, 1504

PUBLISHED BOOKS

The Wycliffe New Testament 1388 Transcribed by W. R. Cooper
(into modern spelling) The British Library 2002
England in the Age of Wycliffe, George Macaulay Trevelyan,
1943 edition

The Life and Reign of Edward The Fourth, Volume I
Cora L. Scofield, 1967
The Great Chronicle of London,
Edited by A. H. Thomas and I. D. Thornley, 1983
The Yorkist Age Daily Life During The Wars of the Roses,
Paul Murray Kendall, 2001

Medieval South Yorkshire, David Hey, 2003
The English Manor c.1200 – c.1500, Mark Bailey, 2002
Making a Living in the Middle Ages, the People of Britain,
Christopher Dyer, 2002
Church and People 1450 – 1660, Clair Cross, 1983

Duke Richard of York 1411–1460, P. A. Johnson, 1991
Edward IV, Charles Ross, 1975
The Reign of Henry VI, Ralph A. Griffiths, 1981
Lancastrians, Yorkists and Henry VII, S. B. Chrimes, 1966
Warwick the Kingmaker & The Wars of the Roses,
Paul Murray Kendall, 1972
Kings in the North The House of Percy in British History,
Alexandra Rose, 2002
North-Eastern England During the Wars of the Roses,
A. J, Pollard, 1990

Wars of the Roses, J. R. Lander, 2000
Wars of the Roses Peace & Conflict in 15th Century England,
John Gillingham, 2001
Wars of the Roses, Robin Neillands, 1999
The Wars of the Roses, Hubert Cole, 1973
Wars of the Roses and the Lives of
Five Men and Women in the Fifteenth Century,
Desmond Seward, 2002
The Later Plantagenets, V. H. H. Green, 1970
Lancaster and York, The Wars of the Roses Alison Weir, 1998

The Battle of Towton, A.W. Boardman, 2001
Towton 1461 England's Bloodiest Battle, Christopher Gravett, 2003
From Wakefield to Towton, Philip A Haigh, 2002
Bosworth 1485 Psychology of a Battle, Michael K. Jones, 2002

The Bowmen of England Donald Featherstone 2003
English Longbowman 1330–1515 Clive Barlet, 1995
A Guide to the Crossbow, W. F. Paterson, 1990
European Crossbows: A Survey by Josef Alm,
Translated by Bartlett Wells

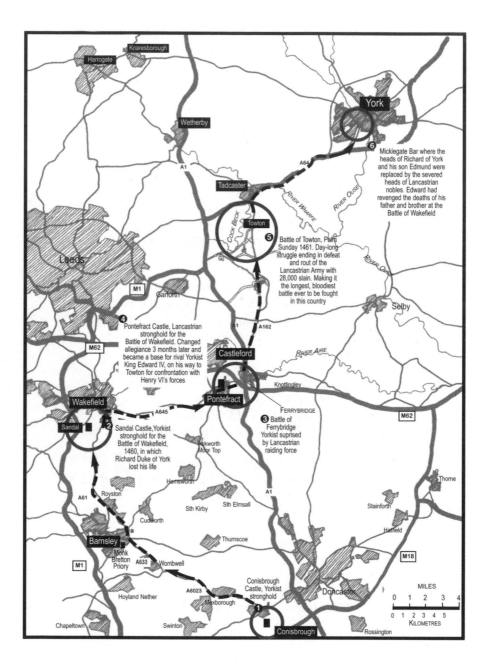

Mickegate Bar where the heads of Richard of York and his son Edmund were replaced by the severed heads of Lancastrian nobles. Edward had revenged the deaths of his father and brother at the Battle of Wakefield

Battle of Towton, Palm Sunday 1461. Day-long struggle ending in defeat and rout of the Lancastrian Army with 28,000 slain. Making it the longest, bloodiest battle ever to be fought in this country

Pontefract Castle, Lancastrian stronghold for the Battle of Wakefield. Changed allegiance 3 months later and became a base for rival Yorkist King Edward IV, on his way to Towton for confrontation with Henry VI's forces

Sandal Castle, Yorkist stronghold for the Battle of Wakefield, 1460, in which Richard Duke of York lost his life

Battle of Ferrybridge Yorkist suprised by Lancastrian raiding force

Conisbrough Castle, Yorkist stronghold

MILES

KILOMETRES

HISTORY TRAIL covering events from Christmas 1460 to Palm Sunday 1461 during The Wars of the Roses.